LEAVE NO TRACE

Also by Sara Driscoll

No Man's Land

Storm Rising

Before It's Too Late

Lone Wolf

LEAVE NO TRACE

SARA DRISCOLL

KENSINGTON
PUBLISHING CORP.

www.kensingtonbooks.com

KENSINGTON BOOKS are published by

Kensington Publishing Corp.
119 West 40th Street
New York, NY 10018

All Kensington titles, imprints and distributed lines are available at special quantity discounts for bulk purchases for sales promotion, premiums, fund-raising, educational or institutional use.

Special book excerpts or customized printings can also be created to fit specific needs. For details, write or phone the office of the Kensington Special Sales Manager: Kensington Publishing Corp., 119 West 40th Street, New York, NY, 10018. Attn. Special Sales Department. Phone: 1-800-221-2647.

Library of Congress Card Catalogue Number: 2020944005

The K logo is a trademark of Kensington Publishing Corp.

ISBN-13: 978-1-4967-2249-2
ISBN-10: 1-4967-2249-3
First Kensington Hardcover Edition: January 2021

ISBN-13: 978-1-4967-2250-8 (ebook)
ISBN-10: 1-4967-2250-7 (ebook)

10 9 8 7 6 5 4 3 2 1

Printed in the United States of America

LEAVE NO TRACE

CHAPTER 1

Flying Head: An undead monster of Iroquois tribal legend portrayed as a huge, disembodied head that flies through the air pursuing humans to devour.

Monday, April 8, 11:10 AM
Georgia State Route 515
Blue Ridge, Georgia

"Take the next exit." Meg Jennings pointed to the sign on the shoulder indicating the turn for Old US 76 ahead before scanning her map app. "This says we're about ten minutes out."

She twisted around to peer through the mesh divider separating the canine compartment in the rear of the SUV from the driver and passenger. Two sets of eyes blinked back at her—Hawk, her black Labrador, and Lacey, Brian Foster's German Shepherd. The dogs were lying side by side in companionable ease, both wearing their navy and yellow FBI K-9 work vests.

"They okay back there?" Brian asked, glancing toward the compartment.

"Keep your eyes on the road. They're doing fine, but they won't be if you look away the moment a deer runs into our path. And neither will we." Meg playfully jabbed her left elbow lightly against his upper arm. "Crazy male driver."

Brian tossed her a mock glare. "You see those dogs?"

"Better than you can."

"Those dogs are the picture of relaxation. They know they're in capable hands and don't have a care in the world." He risked another sideways look at Meg. "Which is more than I can say for you. Why are you so tense?"

"Your driving's enough to make anyone tense."

"You're a riot." He shook his head in feigned disgust, then pushed back the dark hair that fell over his forehead. "You were tense before we got in the car. Actually, it's been since we got off the plane and you turned on your phone. You've had this whole ride to spill your proverbial guts to me. And yet you haven't." He curled his fingers several times in a give-it-to-me gesture. "Go."

"What if I'm feeling apprehensive about this case?"

Brian's bark of laughter earned him a slit-eyed glare from Meg. "Try again," he said. "It's me. You know you're going to tell me sooner or later, anyway, so why not now? You'll feel better. . . ." He singsonged the last.

"What are you, my shrink?"

"You don't need a shrink when you have me. Now, spill it, girlfriend. Before we have to get in the zone on this case." He shot a glance at the map on her phone, crawling forward with their progress. "In ten minutes."

Meg sighed and rolled her eyes. "Not going to let this go, are you?"

"I'm like a dog with a bone. Just ask Ryan. He can't ever keep a secret from me." Brian took the turn onto Old US 76. "Save yourself the trouble and tell me."

"Fine." Meg slumped down in her seat and stared out the window as the forest flanking them on both sides for the last hour and a half gave way to cabin rentals on one side and a car dealership on the other. "Todd texted me."

When the silence dragged on for more than five seconds, Brian tapped her knee twice. "And . . . ? Getting a text from lover boy should be a good thing, not bad. Or are you fighting?"

"We are *not* fighting. Well . . . not exactly."

"Now we're getting to it. What are you not exactly fighting about?"

"Remember when I told you Todd wants us to move in together?"

"Of course."

"Well, he keeps trying to find places."

"This is good."

"Unless none of them suit."

"None of them? Not a single one?" Incredulity rang in Brian's tone.

"We have specific needs. Todd needs it to be close to downtown so it's convenient to the firehouse. I need a backyard for Hawk. We need it to be local to a green space for exercise and training. I'd like to still be close to Cara." She paused for a moment. "And I need to be able to afford it. Turn right here on Industrial."

"Yes, ma'am." He took the turn, the SUV angling higher as they wound up the hill. "The money could be the hardest part with those requirements. Although the other points don't make it easy, either, not in DC. As far as staying close to your sister, that's kind of going to depend on her, isn't it?"

"Yes. And the fact that my moving out means she's now forced to be in the housing market is also weighing on me. She'll have to carry the whole cost of a house on her own. That was the original point of us buying a house together—individually we couldn't afford anything much, but together we could manage something nice in Arlington. It's not downtown DC, but it works for us."

"You're dragging your feet because you're feeling guilty

about leaving Cara behind. Why isn't she shacking up with McCord? Surely the *Washington Post*'s crack investigative reporter must be pulling in a decent salary."

"Because he hasn't asked her."

"You do realize it's not 1950, right? She can ask *him*."

"She almost did, but she doesn't want to rush their relationship because of finances. She's afraid he might see it as angling for his paycheck versus him if she asked him now."

"McCord would get it. He's a pretty down-to-earth guy. I mean, not as down to earth as Todd, but firefighters are a breed unto themselves." He flashed her a saucy grin, his green eyes laughing as he wiggled his eyebrows. "Thank God for that."

Despite her grim mood, she chuckled. "Only you would say that."

"Any gay man or straight woman with eyes in their head would say that. Now that I've lightened your mood, continue."

"Todd texted he's found yet another place he'd like me to look at."

"How many would this make?"

Meg's shrug accompanied a vague hand gesture. "I don't know. Twelve? Fourteen?"

Brian winced. "If he thinks you're stalling, I can see his point. And that's definitely what it looks like. He asked you to move in together last November. You're pushing five months now."

"I'm trying to find the right place. And yes, before you point it out again, because I know you will, I *am* feeling guilty about leaving Cara behind."

"You're not leaving her behind. She's a thirty-year-old woman; she can live on her own. She had to know your living situation wouldn't last forever. But fess up, you're also feeling guilty about Hawk. He loves living with Saki and Blink. You're worried about him getting lonely on his own."

Meg thought back to that morning before the call came in—Hawk, curled up on the dog bed in a pile with Saki, Cara's mini blue-nose pit bull, and Blink, her retired brindle racing greyhound. "Yeah, I am. We could always get another dog for Hawk. But then I'd be leaving that dog alone every day when Hawk and I went to work, and that's not fair, either. Take this right." Knowing they were getting close, Meg gathered her long black hair into a twist, wound it into a loose bun, and pulled a hair elastic off her wrist to secure it. "Then the next right after it onto Snake Nation Road."

Brian's lip curl paired with a shudder nearly made her laugh again.

"Seriously? Snake Nation? Maybe Lauren and Scott would be better suited to this case," Brian said, referring to the other two members of the FBI's Human Scent Evidence Team, along with their dogs, Rocco and Theo. "It's not too late to give them a call."

"No such luck. It's all you and me."

"Is that really what it's called? You're not trying to distract me from your tale of housing woes with snakes?"

Meg scanned the surrounding forest, a mix of evergreen and deciduous trees that hinted at their altitude in the Blue Ridge Mountains. "It's springtime and we're headed up into the wilderness at the peak of Rocky Mountain. I'm not sure snakes are going to be our biggest threat here. I think a bigger risk will be all the moms out there with their babies. Bears, bobcats, coyotes, foxes. We're going to have to steer clear of those, especially now."

"You're not making me feel any better. So, did you answer Todd's text?"

"Not yet. I'm running out of excuses to say no, aren't I?"

"You are. You told Todd your concerns?"

"Yeah. And he's trying to take it all into account."

"You may have set the bar too high. It sounds like Todd's been more than patient, but he won't wait forever." He gave her forearm a comforting squeeze. "Seriously, you know I give you a hard time because I can and because it's fun, but don't blow this one. He's a good man, and you're lucky to have him. To have each other. Make it work. Find a way to compromise and meet him halfway. You won't regret it."

"Is that how you and Ryan do it?"

"Hell, no. It's my way or the highway, babe." He laughed, belying his own words. "Of course we do. It's not always comfortable, even after five years of marriage. But in the end, we're better for it."

"Okay, okay. I hear you. Thanks, Dr. Foster."

"Anytime. I want my best girl living her best life. And on that note, bring on the snakes and the black bears."

"That is *not* living my best life."

"You're telling me. Are we getting close?"

"Your next left is Grandeur Drive. That's where we're headed. We're looking for number 2301." Meg leaned forward to peer out the windshield. Stands of trees flew by as they drove higher into the hills, only broken periodically by a driveway on either side. Then, the forest abruptly opened up on their right side to a long stretch of grass, leading back toward a sprawling ranch-style house. "That's it there."

Brian whistled as his eyes locked on the line of cars in the driveway. "I thought we'd have a few officers, but I didn't think there would be this many." All levity was gone from his tone.

A quick scan told Meg they had all levels of law enforcement in attendance: A white cruiser from the Blue Ridge Police Department. A white and gold Fannin County Sheriff's Department SUV. A bright blue cruiser with the insignia of the Georgia State Patrol. And a single black SUV that Meg would bet her next paycheck was the FBI agent they were to meet for the case.

When the murder victim was a cop, it was all hands on deck. No matter the day-to-day interagency squabbles, when one of their own was lost, law enforcement wrapped a thin blue line around the case and held firm.

Now Meg, Brian, Hawk, and Lacey would close that circle.

They were silent as they pulled into the driveway behind the black SUV. Getting out of their vehicle, they circled around to the back hatch to retrieve their go bags—the knapsacks they wore on every search that contained everything they or the dogs might need for safety, first aid, hydration, or sustenance to fuel their efforts. Meg ensured her Glock 19 was safely secured in the holster on her right hip and then clipped her can of bear deterrent on her left.

"You realize that wearing this stuff is like daring Mother Nature to send us a bear," Brian said, putting on his own holster of bear spray.

"No, not wearing the stuff is like daring Mother Nature to send us a bear. Bringing it along probably guarantees we won't see one."

"Suits me."

They let the dogs out, snapped on their leashes, and started up the thin strip of driveway not occupied by police cars, the dogs heeling easily at their knees.

As they approached the house, Meg realized what looked like a long, rambling bungalow was actually a two-story dwelling built into the side of the hill with the entire lower level hidden from the front of the house. As they topped the rise, they saw a cluster of men and one woman gathered at the end of the driveway.

The only person not in uniform turned at their approach. A man with light bronze skin, dark hair and eyes, and wearing a navy-blue suit that instantly pegged him as a federal agent broke away from the crowd, holding out his hand. "Special Agent Sam Torres, out of Atlanta. You must be Beaumont's team," he said, referring to Special Agent-in-Charge Craig Beaumont, who ran the FBI's Human Scent Evidence Team as part of the Forensic Canine Unit out of the J. Edgar Hoover Building in DC.

"We are. I'm Meg Jennings and this is Brian Foster." Meg held out her hand to Torres and he shook it with a firm grip before repeating the action with Brian. "These are our search-and-rescue dogs, Hawk and Lacey. Can you bring us up to speed so we can get started before the trail gets any colder?"

Torres started introductions around the group. Meg studied the officers, quickly intuiting how close-knit law enforcement must be in this rural area. Each and every one of them displayed some reaction to the death—from fury to devastation to determination. Clearly, Noah Hubbert had been a valued member of this community, and his death touched them all.

Craig had given them the bare bones of the case before they left DC—Hubbert, a sergeant in Troop B of the Georgia State Patrol, had been shot and killed that morning outside his home as he was about to leave for his shift at Post 27 in Blue Ridge. What made the killing unusual was that the murder weapon wasn't a bullet, but an arrow. By the time his wife realized his car was still in the driveway and her husband was dead, the shooter was long gone.

Despite the regional law enforcement presence, because the case concerned the death of a state police officer and because of LEOKA—the federal Law Enforcement Officers Killed and Assaulted program—the case had been bumped up to the FBI field office in Atlanta.

Craig had been brought into the picture shortly after the

case had landed on Torres's desk because when Torres had learned about the case, he had immediately connected it with a similar death just ten days earlier. One death in the state at the hands of a bowhunter during turkey-hunting season was an accident. Two deaths in ten days started to look like anything but. Being familiar with the varied terrain of the Blue Ridge Mountains and knowing how a good hunter could disappear into the forest, Torres contacted Craig at the Forensic Canine Unit to see if they could send out a dog team or two to track the killer.

Hours later, Meg and Brian were on-site and ready to start.

"This is Officer Howard," Torres said. "She responded to the nine-one-one call from Sergeant Hubbert's wife."

A slender brunette with her hair tied back in a severe knot under her peaked cap nodded in response. She stood beside an older man whose collar insignia marked him as the Blue Ridge Police Chief. "I responded to the call at oh-seven-fifty this morning. When I arrived here at the house, I found Sergeant Hubbert down the hill lying in the grass." She pointed down the slope to a grassy area cordoned off with police tape. The crimson stain drenching the grass was unmistakable. "Sergeant Hubbert was already deceased. At first glance the entry wound looked like it was from a rifle, but Mrs. Hubbert said she didn't hear a shot. That's when I realized it was an arrow strike. But I couldn't find the arrow until I put together that he was hit when he was about to get in his car up here on the driveway. The arrow passed clean through his body, and he fell and rolled downhill."

"So where is the—" Brian cut himself off as he turned to look behind, only to spot the arrow embedded in a tree. "Holy . . ." His voice trailed off as he studied the arrow. "That thing must be close to three feet long. And it passed through him?"

Brian's tone radiated the horror Meg felt.

"Yes. Depending on the draw weight, the amount of force behind an arrow, especially one with that kind of arrowhead, is significant," said Fannin County Sheriff Don Maxwell. "It would also leave a hole several inches wide behind because it's a mechanical, expandable arrowhead."

"Meaning . . ." Brian prompted.

"When the arrow is shot, the blades of an expanding broadhead are folded back so the arrow is aerodynamic. But when it hits the target, the mechanical blades snap out, slicing through anything in the way. Remember an arrow spins when it flies, so it would be like getting hit by a three-inch high-speed drill. It would simply carve a tunnel through soft tissue."

Brian shuddered and exchanged a disgusted look with Meg.

"He didn't live long afterward," Maxwell finished.

"I guess not," Meg murmured. She cleared her throat to raise her voice. "So, what you're telling us is caution is warranted and we're dealing with a very dangerous suspect."

"Without a doubt."

"Hawk, come." Meg strode to the tree and studied the arrow. The narrow black shaft was embedded in the tree at a slight downward angle. Four colored plastic fletches circled the base of the arrow. The arrowhead was barely visible in the tree trunk, but as she leaned in, Meg could just see the expandable blades Maxwell described. She straightened and turned back to the men. "Neither of us are hunters. Can someone tell us what we're looking at? It may give us some insight into the suspect."

Maxwell looked over at a stout man in a powder-blue uniform shirt, gray trousers, captain's bars on his shoulders, and wearing the flat-brimmed hat of state patrol. "Wilcox, you know more about this than the rest of us."

"Yup, been bowhunting for over thirty years." Captain Wilcox moved to stand on the other side of the arrow from Meg.

Meg stared pointedly at Brian and gave a head jerk. *Get over here.*

He grimaced, but called Lacey over to stand with him beside Meg.

"This here's a custom-made carbon fiber arrow," Wilcox began.

"You can tell just by looking at it?" Meg asked.

"Sure. I can tell you, these components are top of the line. And most arrows, certainly all the commercial ones, have only three fletchings. This one has four."

"That gives the shooter an advantage?"

"Makes the arrow quieter. And with four vanes, you can make each one lower profile, which minimizes wind drift. Gives the arrow extra stability."

"Like if you're making an extra-long shot and want to ensure the accuracy?" Brian asked. "And you don't want your target to hear the arrow coming."

Wilcox nodded. "That's right. Granted, at three hundred feet per second on an average seventy-pound draw, even if you hear it coming, you won't actually have time to get out of the way."

"So we're looking at someone who's making their own arrows. How common is that?"

"Not unusual for serious hunters. But most don't put this much money into it. As I said, these are top-of-the-line components. Not from around here; none of our shops carry anything this fancy. These were ordered by someone and shipped in."

"Could the materials be traced?"

"Something to look at, but a lot of serious hunters and archers across the country make their own arrows. We'll most likely find the materials were mass-produced and are nearly impossible to trace."

Meg turned and followed the path the arrow must have flown over the hollow behind the house and over the rise as it climbed up the mountain. "Can you estimate where the shot came from?"

"Based on the direction of the arrow, I'd put the shooter"—Wilcox extended an arm and pointed toward a small, open space inside the forest line—"right about there." He squinted at the spot, glanced at the arrow, and then returned his gaze to the tree line. "That must be about a hundred yards, maybe a little more." He swiveled back to face Meg and Brian. "We're talking about an expert shot. You're going to need to be extremely careful. If you get close, this is someone who could take you out. Or your dogs. And there's no way they'd survive a shot like that."

Meg dropped her hand down to rest on Hawk's sun-warmed head and tried to tamp down on the wave of fear that rose at his warning. She'd already lost one canine partner during a suspect chase. She wasn't sure she'd survive it a second time. She took a deep breath to settle suddenly raw nerves.

Brian was still standing with his hands on his hips, staring at the break in the trees as if he'd missed the warning altogether. "Wouldn't the shooter be visible over there?" he asked. "I mean, if the shooter can see the victim, then wouldn't the victim be able to see the shooter?"

"Probably not," Wilcox replied. "Most serious hunters go out in camo so they blend in and can't be spotted. What works for deer and bears also works for people."

"And that's legal?"

"For bowhunting."

"Good to know. So how armed do you think this guy is? He'll be carrying a quiver with a dozen arrows? Two dozen?" Brian stopped dead when the officers around him chuckled or rolled their eyes. "What?"

"Definitely a city boy. As I said, this person is an expert shot," Wilcox said. "An expert shooter can go out with only one arrow and have a successful day hunting. This isn't like carrying ammunition. You're not looking for someone who has an unlimited supply of arrows. They won't need that. They might be carrying three or four at most. When you can aim like that, you don't need many."

"No?" Brian glanced sideways at Meg, and she could read the caution in his eyes.

"No, a single, well-placed shot is all this guy will need. So be aware—if you get within three hundred feet of him, that will be all he needs to take you out permanently."

CHAPTER 2

Track Rock Gap: Located five miles east of Blairsville in Union County, the Cherokee called it *Datsu-nalas-gun-yi,* meaning "where there are tracks."

Monday, April 8, 11:47 AM
Rocky Mountain
Blue Ridge, Georgia

Meg and Brian stood in the small clearing they'd glimpsed from across the hollow. The term "clearing" was generous—it was really just a gap in the leaf canopy caused by a fallen tree. The majority of the tree was gone, but part of the toppled trunk still remained.

Before they'd left the driveway, Hawk and Lacey had investigated the arrow, still buried in the tree, in an attempt to catch the shooter's scent. Now, on command, the dogs cast around for that same odor, circling the stump, noses to the ground, scenting the dirt and the gnarled, twisted mass of exposed roots.

Meg studied the ground. The area around them was lush with new spring growth, but the earth was firm under a thick layer of last autumn's leaves, and there was no trace of boot or shoeprints.

"I don't see any obvious sign that anyone's been here. If the shot came from this location, he had to stand right here, but the leaves don't seem disturbed." Meg studied the foliage over their heads. "I guess he could have shot from the branches, but that would be even harder. At least from ground level, there's a clear line of sight to the driveway. Going up into the trees would put the leaves and branches in the way."

"Maybe our archer is a ghost. But an impressive ghost. That's quite a shot." Brian stood, leash in hand, uphill from the stump as Lacey scented the ground at his feet. But his gaze wasn't on his dog; it was fixed out across the open space to the driveway a hundred yards away. Through the gap in the trees, they could see the group of law enforcement officers as a cluster of light blue, navy, taupe, and black uniforms as they broke up, some of them heading to their vehicles to continue the investigation. "How high up are we?"

"Somewhere between two and three thousand feet."

"He had to strike at Hubbert from this distance, over that wide-open space, taking into account the winds you get at this altitude, and he still precisely hit his target. This archer has serious skills."

"That's what Captain Wilcox said."

"But suddenly I can see his point."

"This is someone who has trained extensively to be able to make that shot. If the conditions were right, I could have done five times that distance with a sniper rifle during my academy training days."

"Impressive. They must have been unhappy when you decided K-9 patrol was what you wanted."

"They weren't thrilled. But my point is, you may be born with an innate talent, with a good eye and absolutely steady hands, but only training and practice gives that elite level of skill. If it's a young person, it would be someone who's been bowhunting since he was a child and has been practicing for years." She paused, considering another angle. "If one more person goes down, we can bring this to Rutherford." Meg referred to Supervisory Special Agent Rutherford of the FBI's Behavioral Analysis Unit. Rutherford had assisted the team on several recent cases, but for an official request, the BAU needed three victims to start building a profile of the killer. "Rutherford would be able to tell us more about this person's psyche, but from pure practicalities, I suspect this is someone in their late twenties or thirties. Old enough to have developed this kind of skill set, but young enough to manage a mountainous climb to get here and then get away."

"Makes sense to me. We're definitely looking at someone in excellent physical sh—" He cut off as Lacey let out a small whine, her posture snapping from relaxed ease to attention. "She has the scent. Good girl, Lacey. Find."

"Hawk, you too." Meg brought Hawk over to where Lacey caught the scent, and his head came up immediately, his tail held high and waving. "They both have it. Here we go. Hawk, find."

Together, the dogs pushed into the bushes, heading straight uphill. Meg and Brian followed close behind, but both used long leashes, giving the dogs freedom to settle into their search patterns. There was no physical trail for them to follow; they simply pushed through the underbrush and trotted around and through stands of oak, hickory, and white pine.

"They have the scent," Meg called to Brian, "but I still don't see a physical track they're following. How does someone move through the forest without leaving a footprint or breaking a tree branch?"

"Maybe that's just a different kind of training," he called back. "Or he really is a ghost."

Meg rolled her eyes and turned her attention once more to her dog.

The path led them behind and around a half-dozen houses, spread out over the side of the mountain and across a single winding driveway. Occasionally the sound of a car told them they were near a road, but their path stayed in the thick forest up the steeply angled slope.

"Would have been easier if he'd taken the road," Brian said between heavy breaths.

Meg was beginning to feel the burn of exertion in her legs from climbing the mountain slope and in her lungs from both the exercise and the slightly lower oxygen level. "Would have been easier physically," she agreed, "but would have greatly increased his risk factor. He had to come into civilization to make the shot. He needs to get back out without being seen. Once word gets out, people in the area will be thinking about who they saw this morning on the way to work. The shooter would be an idiot to take that kind of chance."

"Agreed. Also, this is a bowhunter. Patience has to be a huge part of the sport. Taking a little extra time to escape doesn't sound like it would be an issue for that kind of personality. And if Wilcox is right and he's in camouflage, he'd be instantly noticed as out of place walking along the road."

They continued up the hill. The forest was thicker here and sunlight only barely pierced the heavy canopy, instead filtering through the bright-green spring leaves as a soft glow. The undergrowth was sparser, and the dogs easily picked their way across ground strewn with soggy brown leaves, branches, and twigs, and over and around moss- and lichen-covered rocks.

Meg studied the dogs. They were about ten feet apart climbing in parallel up the hill. Instead of climbing in a straight line, both dogs employed a zigzag pattern, weaving from side to side. This was the dogs' way of following the scent cone left by a suspect as he walked along a trail, shedding skin cells. As air currents picked up the cells, they spread them out in an ever-widening cone of scent that narrowed the closer the dogs got to their target.

Lacey and Hawk were used to working together and easily fell into a mirror image pattern with both dogs slanting out to the outer edge of the scent cone, before angling in. If they were working solo, they'd have continued on that track until they lost the scent on the other side of the cone before curving back in again. But when they worked in tandem, they each took an outer edge of the cone and worked into common territory before expanding the search outward again. The significant width of the pattern supported the fact the trail was several hours old.

Meg suspected the shooter was simply too far ahead and would have gone to ground long before they lost the trail.

They left the inhabited area, moving higher up Rocky Mountain. More pines dotted the increasingly rocky landscape as deciduous trees thinned out, and the wind swirled through the forest with more ferocity and a bite of cold.

A sound reached Meg's ears and her steps slowed as she concentrated on it, her heart sinking. "I hear water," she called.

"Yeah, me too. Maybe the track will run alongside it."

"We are *never* that lucky."

"Nope. All part of living our best lives."

She tossed him a smile. He was right. She wouldn't trade this life for a million dollars.

The sound of running water grew closer and the dogs' patterns became wider.

"I have a bad feeling about this." Meg stepped onto a craggy, moss-covered rock to give herself extra height as she peered through the trees. "I can't see anything so far, but their pattern is opening up. Like there's an open space ahead of us allowing the incoming wind to disturb the scent trail."

"And there's definitely at least a small creek in front of us," Brian yelled back. "Unless we get really lucky, we're going to get wet."

Meg glanced down at her laced hiking boots. Expensive and custom fitted for comfort in what could sometimes be hours-long hikes through challenging landscapes, they were waterproof, but no boot could keep the wet out when the water level was higher than the top of the laces. And at this altitude, mountain runoffs could be brutally cold. Which meant freezing feet through the rest of the search, chafing, and cold and miserable dogs. Hawk and Lacey would be game to ford whatever water hazards they came across, but they would need to be dried off and kept from becoming chilled. Luckily, Rocky Mountain wasn't too high—just over 3,000 feet at the peak—so any creek or river running downhill at this altitude was unlikely to be too wide or deep. Still, only a few feet would do the damage.

The sound of running water grew louder as they broke from the trees to find a creek, easily fifteen feet across, with swiftly moving water so deep the rocky creek bed was completely submerged. Hawk and Lacey trotted over to the bank and stopped dead.

"It looks like he went through here," Brian said. Leaning out, he scanned up and down the creek. "I don't see a better crossing. The water level looks pretty high all along this section."

"This whole area has had a very rainy spring. The runoff is essentially drainage from all those storm systems passing through, practically one on top of the other. Before we get soaked, let's make sure he didn't follow the stream bed. Hawk, come." She directed him along the creek, following the slope downhill, but knew instantly this was the wrong direction simply from Hawk's lack of physical alertness. She went another ten feet, then stopped and turned around.

Brian had gone the other way, taking Lacey upstream, but Lacey was similarly not signaling a scent trail. Brian turned around, shrugged, and came downhill to meet Meg at the stream where both dogs sat, their signal that the scent ended in that location.

"Did you see a better place to ford the stream uphill?" Meg asked. "Downhill, it's even worse than here."

"It looks about the same uphill." Brian bent and submerged his fingertips in the fast-flowing water, quickly yanking them out and giving them a hard flick. "Yikes. Okay, we're going to want to go through this fast. It's maybe fifty-five degrees."

"Air temp is about sixty, so that's not a surprise. It's been a cool spring up and down the eastern seaboard." Meg eyed the water. "No exposed rocks to use to stay out of the water, so we're going to have to trudge through." Bending, she unclipped Hawk's leash, coiled it, and stuffed it into the side pocket of her FBI jacket. Then she unbuckled his FBI vest and slipped it off, rolling it up and tucking it into a side pocket of her backpack. "They're going to be cold enough, better to keep their vests dry."

Brian squatted down and unbuckled Lacey's vest. "Might also help them warm up faster to get it back on at the far bank."

Meg stepped around Hawk so he was on her upstream side. If, God forbid, he lost his footing, she needed to be able to block him from being carried downstream. "Ready?"

Brian was similarly standing downstream of Lacey as he tucked away her vest. "As I'll ever be. Come on, Lacey girl. This will be . . . refreshing."

"That's one way to put it. Hawk, come."

Together, they stepped into the freezing water. The cold immediately shot through the material of her boot and Meg gritted her teeth, bracing herself for the oncoming soaking. But Hawk and Lacey gamely picked their way through the icy depths of the stream, carefully placing their feet before proceeding. They instinctively knew a full dunking would be dangerous.

Brian muttered a curse under his breath, but plowed forward, one hand splayed toward Lacey in case she ran into trouble. "Careful," he wheezed, as if holding his breath, "some of these rocks are slippery."

"They're all slippery. And some of them are pretty big. Don't trip. Either of us gets a full soaking, we may not be able to finish the search."

"Screw that. No wimpy little creek is going to take us out." But Brian slowed slightly, taking a little more care with his footing as they reached the midway point and the water came nearly to their knees.

Meg eyed the far bank. *Nearly there, thank God.* Hawk was holding his head high, but the water was up to his chest, and she knew how water this cold could steal your breath and turn your muscles into lead, making coordinated movements nearly impossible.

Another few steps and the ground under their boots rose higher and the current buffeting them eased. With a sigh of relief, she stepped onto dry land, quickly moving away from her dog as Hawk shook violently, trying to rid himself of the freezing water. Brian, stuck in between the two dogs, yelped as he was pelted from both sides with icy water.

"Honestly, if I wanted to wake up that quickly, I'd rather have several shots of espresso," Brian said through gritted teeth. "IV delivered right into my vein. Damn, that was cold."

"I could go for a coffee," Meg said. "Though I might be more tempted to pour it over my head than drink it. How can getting your feet that cold make the rest of you freeze as well?"

"I don't know, but I'm tempted to join you in the coffee shower. First thing after this search is done."

Meg shrugged off her backpack, then quickly rooted through it for a towel. She held it up for Brian. "You need one, too, or did you pack one?"

"Packed one. You never know what these cross-country searches will bring."

They quickly toweled down the dogs, buckled them into their vests, and attached the leashes.

Meg stamped her feet, wrinkling her nose in distaste as water oozed around her socks. "How wet are your feet?"

"I think I have DC's Southwest Duck Pond in there."

"Same. Watch for blisters. You know how much easier it is for them to develop with wet feet. We'll need to stop and deal with them ASAP. Okay, Hawk, find." She was pleased to see how fast the dogs picked up the scent, easily falling back into their pattern and even increasing their pace. "Our shooter apparently cut straight through and kept going. Didn't try to disguise the trail at all."

"For someone who moves through the forest like a

ghost, clearly he thought his only pursuers would be human, not canine."

Meg pointed an index finger at Brian. "Very good point. Which means if we don't catch him today and he strikes again, it's going to be tougher next time because he'll be keeping the dogs in mind and will be purposely trying to lose them. Blue Ridge only has a population of about twelve hundred. There's no way someone isn't going to comment on our presence, and then word will spread like wildfire. If the shooter is local, he's going to find out and will take precautions accordingly." She glanced down at her boots and grimaced. "Which means more water hazards because we all know that's the best way for the dogs to lose the scent."

"Let's nail him today then, and we won't have to worry about that."

The ground inclined steeply, and within a few minutes they clambered over a line of boulders—with much less grace than their dogs, who leapt from surface to surface—to find themselves on level ground.

"Hey, we made it." Brian's breath came hard from the exertion. "This looks like the top ridge. Now we'll be able to make some serious gains in time. Lacey, find."

Lacey and Hawk immediately headed southwest, following a path only they could see, weaving through trees and between boulders. Meg let the leash play out, giving Hawk his head and letting him set the pace. He trotted ahead, his undulations only slight on the narrow ridge, but his head was high and his tail waved proudly. He didn't care if his feet were cold, he was in his element, doing his favorite job, with the woman he loved above all else. She thought about her wet, chilled feet and realized she could take a lesson from him.

The dogs leapt over a tree, fallen across their path, and Brian and Meg hopped over behind them to find the long track of a footpath curving away from them, having climbed the side of the mountain to their right.

Beside the path, a sturdy wooden post with an arrow pointing southwest decreed both the direction of Stanley Gap Trail and Fall Branch Falls, located 2.9 miles away, while a second arrow indicated the Benton MacKaye Trail broke away to the northwest. However, Meg didn't have long to look as the dogs headed directly down the Stanley Gap Trail.

"Out of the forest and back on a trail," Meg commented. "Probably felt he was far enough away from the site of the shooting to risk the trail and pick up time on an established track."

"Wonder if anyone saw him?"

"Depends on how long he stayed on a public trail. On a weekday morning, he might have been spotted, though our chances would have been better if this was the weekend. Less people hiking on a workday."

The dogs increased their pace, and Meg and Brian broke into a jog to stay with them, following the trail silently for a while up a gently inclined slope. When they reached the apex of the trail, at a spot where three ridges met at the peak of Rocky Mountain, Meg called for Hawk to stop.

"Let's water the dogs. They've been on the go for almost an hour now. It looks like we're going to be onto the descent after this and it may not be easy to stop."

Conscious of their exposure at the peak and Wilcox's warning about the archer's skill, Meg and Brian knelt down on the rocky ground so they would be both less visible and smaller targets if the killer was still in the area. Neither truly believed he was nearby, but caution was deeply ingrained in their search protocols and most times was simply an automatic response.

They pulled collapsible bowls and water bottles from their packs, and the dogs settled in for a long drink. They then grabbed water bottles for themselves and slaked their own thirst. As Meg took a moment to rest, she scanned the vista spread out before them. To the north, behind several smaller rises, the town of Blue Ridge spread out as a pale smear of buildings and roads. To the northeast, the blue-green waters of Blue Ridge Lake sprawled, its central body spreading out in small bays and inlets like grasping fingers reaching for the hills above. To the west, the dark line of GA-515 ran north toward Blue Ridge and stretched off to the south to disappear into the hills. Due south, a range of smaller peaks rose into the blue sky. And all around was the bright new green of spring as trees burst out in leaf and fields of wild grasses found life again.

Meg looked down to find Hawk had finished his drink. She downed the rest of her water bottle and then packed everything away. "Ready?" she asked Brian.

"When you are."

"Onward ho, then. Hawk, find."

The short rest refreshed them and they picked up their pace, jogging steadily along a path winding downward through the trees. Soon, though, the path narrowed, the slope on either side steepening as if they were running a ridge pole.

Meg's heart pounded, more than simply from the exercise. She'd hated heights ever since she was six years old, when she'd defied her grandparents' safety rules and walked out on the widow's walk at their cottage in Nantucket. The centuries-old wood railing had collapsed, tumbling her over the edge to dangle over a fatal drop until her grandfather hauled her up to safety. From that moment, heights were a terror for Meg, one that often plagued her on searches, depending on the location. She never let it stop her, but it gave her some extremely bad moments.

This was one of those moments.

Meg looked down the slope and then glanced sideways at Brian, now too close beside her on the path. If one of them slipped, or bumped the other, it would be game over. "Let me go first."

Brian's gaze flicked from her to the drop on her side of the path and back again. "You bet. Lacey, slow."

Meg jogged past Lacey and then they were off at full speed again. She couldn't help furtively glancing to either side. Hawk, lower to the ground and on four feet, continued to trot at an easy pace, following the scent. Clearly, heights didn't bother him.

But when Hawk stopped dead in the middle of the path, Meg skidded to a halt behind him, quickly scanning the area but finding it unremarkable. She tried to pick up any trace of sound of an oncoming threat, but she couldn't hear anything over the shrill whistle of the wind. "Hawk, what is it, boy?"

The only reason he would stop the search like that was because he could sense danger. Could smell it.

The angle of the descent on either side of the path and the rough terrain made it difficult for Meg to see down to the ground; what was visible was simply the upper branches of trees. She glanced behind her to find Lacey standing frozen and alert, her nose constantly scenting the air and her ears perked forward.

Something's coming, but from where? Should we move forward or back to avoid it?

Impossible to tell when you couldn't see danger coming.

Two black bear cubs suddenly clambered out of the trees and over the ridge, directly onto the path about forty feet in front of them.

Meg's mouth went desert dry. *Where there are babies, there's always—*

A massive adult bear lumbered into view behind the cubs. She took one look at the dogs and humans threatening her young, reared up on her back legs, and let out a furious, throaty roar.

CHAPTER 3

Stoneclad: A giant, evil witch of Cherokee mythology called *Nûñ'yunu'wï*, which translates to "dressed in stone." Stoneclads protect the forests, ridge lines, and creatures of the forest.

Monday, April 8, 1:12 PM
Rocky Mountain
Blue Ridge, Georgia

"Talon, back!" Meg's voice was low, the command in it unmistakable. The tone was unnecessary—if anything had been trained into Hawk, it was the use of his "don't mess with me" name. When she called him "Talon," instantaneous obedience was required. Lives could depend on it.

In this case, they did.

Hawk carefully backed toward Meg and she dropped his leash, giving him the freedom to move and not tying him to her if she commanded him to retreat as the bear charged.

Behind her, she heard Brian calling for "Athena" to move back with him.

She had two weapons, the bear spray and the Glock in a worst-case scenario, but for all its power, the Glock was actually the less preferable weapon. Yes, it could kill, but that would require a precise shot at a quick-moving target; if she only injured the bear, it might become more enraged. Temporarily blinding the animal in a wide cloud of pepper spray was safer for all of them, including the bear.

Without taking her eyes off the six-foot terror in front of her, Meg blindly reached for the holster at her hip with her left hand. She flipped it open and thumbed off the safety clip as she pulled the spray can from the holster. She kept the can in her left hand and extended it outward, pulling her Glock with her right hand, just in case. She might not be able to aim as well with a spray in her non-dominant hand, but it likely wouldn't matter because of the wide delivery system. More than that, with a wind this strong, she wasn't sure how much of the spray would reach the bear and how much would fly back onto her. But if the bear charged, she'd have no choice but to try.

They were in serious trouble. A black bear was bad enough, but one with cubs made for a potentially fatal situation. She and Brian knew the drill: Don't approach the bear. Don't make eye contact with it. Be non-confrontational at a distance, but make as much noise as you could up close. Make yourself as large as possible. Move away slowly, but never turn your back on the bear. Carry bear deterrent in case the bear charges.

She was beyond thankful for the training and temperament of the dogs. Deadly calm, they stayed quiet, waiting for their next command, which should help keep the bear non-confrontational. A vicious, defensive dog would only bring out the bear's aggression.

In front of her, the bear made a blowing noise and clacked her teeth, warning them away from her young. *We're going, we just need to not fall down the mountain slope while we're doing it. It's death by bear vs. death by heights.*

They needed to back away from this bear and then let her and the cubs continue on their way. Hopefully in their original direction, across the path on the far side, and not along it in front of them, because they still had a suspect to track and they couldn't do it if the path was blocked by bears. For them, it was this path or nothing as they followed the suspect's exact trail.

However, she understood the bear's motivation. She only wanted to protect her young, and until the threat was neutralized, she wouldn't move away. She couldn't know they intended no harm to her babies.

"Keep coming," Brian said quietly. "*Carefully.* A wrong step will take you over the edge."

"Roger that," Meg said. "Talon, back." Hawk passed Meg as she stayed in place; then she took a step back herself. "She's not taking her eyes off us. I think we better move on to plan B. Time to get loud to scare her off." Brian and Meg started to yell, and Meg caught a flash of Brian's arms in the air, waving wildly, trying to frighten the bear. But Meg kept the Glock at the ready and the repellent aimed directly at the bear. If it moved, she needed to already be in position.

They inched away, going as fast as they dared, constantly cautious of sliding off the path, but it wasn't fast enough for the bear, who dropped onto all fours and swatted the ground, growling again. Behind her the two cubs stared at the group of dogs and humans and stayed close to their mother.

Moving backward on the narrow ridge path was tricky while Meg kept her eyes fixed on the bear, who continued to paw the ground, leaving deep gouges in the hard-trodden earth from her massive claws. Meg gained a foot of distance, then two, but as the bear's dark eyes locked on her, she knew instinctively they were out of time. They simply couldn't move fast enough.

Meg half turned to yell clearly over the noise. "Talon, Athena, down. Peekaboo! Brian, cover your eyes!"

The words were barely out of her mouth when the bear sprang, charging at them, moving in ground-eating strides. Meg pulled the trigger on the bear spray as Brian went silent behind her. A stream of yellow burst from the can, shooting toward the bear. The wind immediately diffused the spray, tossing it into the air as a diaphanous cloud, so Meg continued to pull the trigger as the bear charged closer and closer. She couldn't shut her eyes, but watched the oncoming bear through slitted lids, fighting to keep her aim true.

The edge of the cloud blew into her eyes, and she nearly screamed at the searing pain. She closed one eye, squinting the other, desperately trying to see through the tears welling in reaction to the assault. She heard the bear cry out, halting in her tracks, coughing and choking, shaking her head, before turning and running in the opposite direction. The cubs fell into step behind her, and the three of them ran down the hill to the west of the ridge.

Meg waited for a full count of three, listening to their crashing slowly fading away. Then she dropped to her knees, letting go of the pepper spray and fumbling her weapon blindly into its holster. She pressed her fists to her eyes and crouched into a ball, rocking back and forth, a low, keening wail breaking from her.

"Meg! Meg! Hawk, out of the way." Brian was beside her, his body pressed to her side, his hand on her back, and his voice in her ear. "God, did you get it in your eyes?"

All Meg could do was moan.

"We need to wash it out." He tugged on the strap of her backpack. "Slide off your pack. I need your supplies."

Meg shrugged off her backpack, and then Brian's warmth left, only to be replaced with a silky glide of fur and the cool wetness of a dog nose.

Meg nearly reached out for Hawk, but pulled back, terrified of getting some of the oily spray on him. "It's okay, boy. It's okay." Her voice was hoarse even to her own ears. "God Almighty, Brian. Help me."

"I'm here. Hawk, buddy, shove over." Hawk disappeared and Brian was back. "I need you to turn your face to the side. I'll run the water over your eyes one at a time to wash some of it into the dirt."

"Is she gone?"

"Yes, and the dogs will tell us if she comes back, but she won't. You saved us."

"The dogs are okay? You're okay?"

"We're fine. The peekaboo trick worked like a charm for the dogs. I got a bit of spray on my cheeks, but that's nothing. Just a little sting. My eyes are perfectly fine. You took the full brunt."

"It's not good," she ground out.

His hand gently lifted her face and tilted it the way he wanted. "Now open your eyes." When she tried and ended up blinking furiously, he said, "Sorry, I'm going to have to hold your eye open. I know this is going to sting like hell." As gently as he could, but with enough strength to force her compliance, he held open her left eye and poured the contents of an entire water bottle over it. She groaned and reflexively tried to pull away, but he followed her and kept flooding her eye. He tossed the first bottle, then loosened the top of the second with his teeth and unscrewed it. "When we get into town, we'll get some baby shampoo and wash your eyes out properly, but this will have to do for now." He turned her face the other way and then washed out her other eye. The third bottle rinsed the spray from her forehead and cheeks; then he splashed more over her hands and rubbed her palm over his pant leg to scrub off any sticky residue. Then he repeated the entire process.

When the bottles were empty, he sat back and tipped her face up toward him. "Open your eyes."

Meg forced her eyes open. Blinking, she found Brian's wavering form in front of her. Blinking a few more times, her vision steadied and his concerned face came into focus.

"How's my girl?" he asked.

"Living her best life," Meg croaked on a half smile.

Brian let out a small laugh and kissed the top of her head. "That's my girl. Kicking ass and taking names." His expression turned serious. "You going to be able to manage to get off this hill?"

Meg shifted away from him, braced her hands in the damp earth at her knees, and pushed to her feet. She wobbled slightly, but then got her balance. "To hell with off this hill. We have a search to finish."

"You sure you can manage?"

"Better than Sergeant Hubbert did. We can do this for him. Where's my pack?"

Brian helped her into it and she shrugged it into place. He packed away the empty bottles, then picked up the discarded canister from the ground, slid the safety clip into place, and put it into her holster. "God forbid, you might need it again. But it will only be to back me up. I'm leading for the rest of this hike."

"No arguments here." She grasped his forearm. "Thanks. I'm not sure what I'd have done without you."

"You'd have managed, like you always do. I just made it a little easier for you. Thank God bear repellent is only two percent strength. It's nowhere near as bad as the twenty percent pepper spray law enforcement uses."

"No kidding. Hopefully, I'll be better in a few hours and recovered by tomorrow. That other stuff must be like burning in the flames of hell. That wasn't all our water, was it?"

"No, I left us a couple each for drinking and for watering the dogs."

"Good." She bent and picked up Hawk's leash from the dirt. "Hawk, ready?"

He looked up at her alertly and thumped his tail a few times.

"Okay, we're ready."

Brian sidled past her carefully on the narrow path, Lacey trotting behind him to get in front of Meg and Hawk.

"Lacey, find."

"Hawk, find."

The dogs took off at an easy lope down the southward path, Meg and Brian behind. For the first few minutes, Brian kept checking to make sure she was okay. Each time, she gave him a thumbs-up and he turned back to the trail ahead.

They had a job to do. No matter what, the search would continue.

CHAPTER 4

Dancing Ghosts: In Cherokee legend, the Appalachian Mountains were once covered by a great flood. When the floodwaters receded, the ridges were lined with great piles of bone, where the ghosts of the drowned danced at night.

Monday, April 8, 2:20 PM
Blue Ridge Police Department
Blue Ridge, Georgia

Meg, Brian, and the dogs were directed to a small conference room on the first floor of the Blue Ridge Police Department. Once Blue Ridge's city hall, the old stone, two-story building was a historic landmark and one of the oldest structures in town. But for all the external charm and craftsmanship, inside the building was straight-up generic cop.

Torres sat at the table, a laptop opened in front of him, several files at his elbow, and a paper coffee cup in his hand. He looked up at the sound of footsteps and then froze, staring at Meg standing in the doorway. His gaze shifted to Brian behind her, the dogs at their feet, and then back to Meg. "What happened to you?"

"Bear spray. We ran into a mother and her two cubs."

Meg had checked out the damage in the sun visor mirror of the Blue Ridge cop who had picked them up at the end of the search—with puffy lids and patchy redness spread across her cheeks and forehead, she was not a pretty sight. On top of that, while her eyes were much better, they still burned slightly and she suspected it would be another hour or two before that went away, and at least a day before the puffiness and redness went down.

"Are you all right?"

"Getting there."

Torres braced his hands against the edge of the table as if ready to stand. "What do you need? Medical supplies?"

Meg shook her head and waved him down. "At this point, just time. We stopped and bought some no tears baby shampoo. All the oil that can be flushed off, has been. As for the rest, I should be better tomorrow."

"Then at least come in and take a load off." Torres motioned to the empty chairs around the table. "I heard the search was unsuccessful."

"We never had a chance." Brian pulled out a chair and fell into it. "Lacey girl, come and lay down. That's it. Good girl." He leaned over and rubbed at her fur as she settled beside him with a canine sigh of relief. "The shooter was hours ahead of us. And had a vehicle waiting. He was probably long gone before we even landed in Atlanta." He craned his neck to look back at Meg, who still leaned against the doorjamb. "Sit down. That's an order."

"You can't order me around," Meg said, but pulled out the chair next to him and sat.

"Thank you."

"You're welcome."

Torres looked from Brian to Meg, shaking his head. "How long have you two worked together?"

"Three years," they said in unison, then looked at each other and grinned.

"I could have sworn it was longer. You're like an old married couple."

"Thanks . . . I think," said Brian. "So where are we on the case? Did you make any headway while we didn't?"

"Actually, yes."

"Really?" Meg leaned forward in her chair. "In what way?"

"I've tied the victims together. At first I couldn't find any connection beyond the method of death, including the handmade arrows, so I thought they had to be random hits by a common predator. Until I stumbled on what may be the key. But let me back up. What do you know about the first victim?"

"Nothing. SAC Beaumont didn't have any of the details when he scrambled us."

"Then let's start at the beginning. The first victim was Tim Reynolds, Chairman of the Fannin County Board of Commissioners. He was out bowhunting and was hit with an arrow and killed. It looked like a tragic accident. He was wearing camo and he blended into the surroundings. Everyone assumed another hunter saw movement and shot his arrow, only to find out he'd killed someone by mistake and fled in horror."

"Until the second death," Brian said.

"Once Sergeant Hubbert was killed in the same fashion, with the same type of arrow—"

"In his own driveway," Brian interjected.

"In his own driveway," Torres continued, "and not out in the woods, then things became clearer. But the connection between the two men wasn't evident. They're separated by twenty years in age, they didn't come from the same town, go to the same schools, have any social connections, or cross paths in their jobs. Until I found out Noah Hubbert was the son of Ethan Hubbert, the CEO of Atkins Power."

"I don't recognize the father's name," said Meg, "but I've heard of the company. Isn't that a huge, multistate corporation?"

"It is. And as part of that huge, multistate corporation, Atkins Power has been working with the Fannin County Board of Commissioners on the Copperhill Dam."

"Never heard of it," Brian said.

"That's because it's not built yet, but there's a local argument that it's needed to manage rising water levels and flooding as the climate changes. Copperhill, Tennessee, and McCaysville, Georgia, are twin cities, but in reality, they're a single community on the Toccoa River that's split down the middle by the Georgia/Tennessee state line."

"Rather than the river itself?" Meg asked.

"Correct. The river is not the dividing line. But it cuts through both towns. And in the past four years, those towns have experienced both a five-hundred-year flood and a one-thousand-year flood."

Brian whistled.

"The dam is just in the planning stages, but it's ruffled a lot of feathers." Torres took a sip of his coffee. "By the way, help yourself." He pointed at the coffeemaker set up on a side table against the wall.

Meg started to push her chair back and Brian laid a hand on her arm. They exchanged a silent look, Meg nodded, and Brian rose to make their coffee.

"People don't want to see the dam built?" Brian asked. "Even after all that flooding? I assume the dam will help control the river level?"

"It will. And the citizens of Copperhill and McCaysville are one hundred percent in support of the project. However, there's a number of people who are against it. What do you know about reservoir dams?"

"Probably just the basics," Meg said. "The dam blocks

the river, letting water through at a controlled pace, and a reservoir fills behind it."

"That's part of it. Power generation is the other part. The deeper the reservoir, the farther the water has to fall, the more kinetic energy it carries, the more power can be generated when the water is directed into a turbine and generator. For all the dams in this area, and there are a number of them, it's still not enough for the power needs of Georgia and Tennessee."

"Especially as the world and the economy are moving away from coal-fired power plants and fossil fuels and are looking for dependable renewable energy sources." Meg accepted a coffee from Brian. "Thanks."

"You're welcome." Brian sat down again. "So flood control and power generation. It all sounds good so far. Clearly, there must be a catch."

"The catch is the reservoir. As I said, the deeper the reservoir, the better flood control, and the better the power generation. But that land has to come from somewhere. In this case, it's going to come from the Toccoa River valley that runs from Blue Ridge, Georgia, nearly all the way to McCaysville and Copperhill."

"That area has to be occupied."

"It is. Farms, businesses, houses. Everyone would have to abandon their property and then the valley would be flooded. The people who live in the valley, some of whom have lived there for over a hundred years, are fighting tooth and nail to keep their land. There's a suspect list right there. But that's not all. The Eastern Band of Cherokee Indians have also made a claim on the land. It was their land up to the 1830s, until the American government took it away from them, and they want it back."

"What are the chances of that happening?" Meg asked.

"Recently, the EBCI has reclaimed some of its hereditary land in Tennessee, on the border of North Carolina. They've been successful once, so they want to try again, which adds them to the suspect list. But then on the other side of the argument, we have all the people who support the project. Beginning with the Tennessee Valley Authority, the group in charge of all the rivers and dams, power generation, and the economic development within the Tennessee Valley, in an area that goes from Kentucky all the way to Virginia and North Carolina, down to Georgia, and west through Alabama and Mississippi. Then there's Atkins Power, Roswell Engineering—the construction company that has already bid for and won the dam project, which will be worth billions in federal, state, and county funding—local residents, and business owners. And that just scratches the surface. I have my work cut out for me in compiling a suspect pool and then narrowing it down."

"The method of death seems to be a good way to narrow down the list," Meg said. She took another sip of coffee and set down the cup. "Not everyone is going to know how to shoot a bow. And even fewer will have any kind of skill with it. And then we're looking for someone with an elite level of that skill."

"And don't forget the outdoor skills," Brian said. "It's pretty clear I'm not a country boy, but I couldn't see the path the dogs were following. Not a boot print, not a broken branch, not anything to disturb the surroundings. This isn't some business magnate who blows in from LA for the weekend and does a little shooting. This is someone who lives the outdoor life."

"I'll second that. I couldn't see a path, either," Meg said. "One question, though. We saw the arrow, but do we know what kind of weapon shot it? I'm not a country girl"—she cocked an eyebrow at Brian—"but even I know there's more than one kind of bow."

"I'm not a hunter myself, but Wilcox told me it's either a recurve or a compound bow. They can both use the same kind of arrow. But he also said that because of how the seasons go in Georgia and the surrounding states, there's a lot of bowhunting overall, especially right now. Finding someone who owns a recurve or compound bow is not going to be a sign of guilt."

"Unless you disapprove of hunting for sport," Brian muttered.

"The way these things are tricked out these days with scopes and laser sights, I'm not sure there's any sport in it at all," Torres said. "Taking what Wilcox said into account, the bowhunting angle will limit the suspect pool, but maybe not nearly as much as we'd like. That's my mission in the next few days. You both are heading to DC?"

"Yes," Meg said. "Unless you think we're going to be needed, SAC Beaumont wants us back and available for other deployments. We're headed to Atlanta and we'll catch the next flight out."

The question was—would they need to return and, if so, how soon?

CHAPTER 5

Thunderer: A storm spirit who lives in the sky and commands thunder and lightning.

Monday, April 8, 5:55 PM
Ronald Reagan Airport
Washington, DC

Meg made sure Hawk was well back from the door and then closed him into his travel compartment. Lugging her bags around to the rear of the SUV, she popped the hatch, loaded their gear, and slammed the door shut. Her steps dragging slightly, she circled around to the driver's door. Getting in, she glanced at Hawk to see him comfortably settling in to take a nap on the ride home, and let out a long breath as she sagged back against the seat. She was still tired from the strenuous search, smarting from the pepper spray, and discouraged by the whole day. If the kills were ten or more days apart, there was no sense in staying there waiting for the next shoe to drop, but not being on-site essentially made the searches useless.

How do you catch someone who is clearly an elite hunter and who knew how to hide his tracks when he had a three or four hour head start on you? It seemed futile. Sure, the dogs could follow an hours-old trail, but the chances of catching up were nearly nil in that kind of environment where there were dozens of hazards and multiple places to lose the scent. And if the person they were trailing knew he wasn't being immediately followed, he could take all the time in the world to disappear.

She wanted to talk to Craig about how this case was being handled. Yes, it had been bumped to the federal level because of the death of a state law enforcement officer, but maybe the FBI should be relying on local K-9 assistance. Surely the Georgia Bureau of Investigation had tracking dogs. Maybe that would be a better support system for Torres. It would certainly be faster.

Meg studied her face in the rearview mirror. The angry red splotches smeared across her cheeks and forehead had faded only slightly, and her eyes were bloodshot, the lids red and puffy. She groaned. That explained all the odd looks she got on the trip home. She'd hoped it would have faded more by now.

Instead of running home, she wanted to go to the Forensic Canine Unit in the J. Edgar Hoover Building to talk to Craig. He wasn't expecting her until tomorrow, but she knew he wouldn't have gone home yet and she wanted to run things by him while they were still fresh in her mind. And who knew when the next assignment would come along to distract her? Maybe as soon as tomorrow morning, so it was better to talk to him today.

She pulled her phone out of her pocket to check for messages. Webb was on shift now, but she'd texted him they were on their way back before they left Atlanta. So far, there was no response.

"Probably a busy shift," she muttered. "Maybe out on a call."

Which gave her an idea. She opened the glove box and pulled out the handheld radio Webb had given her months before so she could track him when he was at work. It was set to DC Fire and Emergency Medical Services main frequencies, but he'd marked the tactical frequencies they used on it as well. Sometimes during longer incidents, she'd tune in and follow the action, occasionally hearing his voice on the main channel.

She'd been a cop with the Richmond PD before she joined the FBI. She knew the risks of first responder work, be it law enforcement or firefighting. But Webb had given her a window into his world and a way to reassure herself during dangerous fires that he was okay.

He's a good man, and you're lucky to have him. Brian's words rang in her head. He was right, and the radio in her hand was an example of Webb finding ways to meet her halfway. It was time for her to do the same.

She laid the radio on the passenger seat. Then she started the SUV and maneuvered her way out of the parking garage to merge onto the George Washington Parkway. Reaching over, she turned on the radio.

She could tell right away the house was out on a call—a structure fire in the Washington City neighborhood, and within a few minutes she heard Webb's voice.

"Engine 2 at scene, switching to tac."

He'd explained their use of radio frequencies to her. They used a main channel, one amplified by a repeater to reach dispatch anywhere in the city. But they also used two tactical or "tac" channels on scene for active communications while attacking the fire. That channel could be received only at short distances—under two miles—but Meg had been able to tune into the tac channel from the Hoover building because of the proximity to Engine Company 2's firehouse and many of their calls. So, she'd be able to follow along once she got into DC proper.

She took the exit to I-395 over the Charles R. Fenwick Bridge, the Potomac streaking by through her window as she listened to the details of the fire reported to dispatch by the incident commander. It was going to be a tricky one—the fire was on the upper floors of a hoarder's house, so maneuvering through the flaming debris would be difficult. Not to mention the fire was spreading fast. It would be an offensive attack with crews taking lines into the house long enough to search for occupants. The incident commander clearly had his doubts they'd be able to do anything else after but pull back and fight the fire defensively, trying to protect the surrounding structures. The fire was already too involved by the time they arrived, and there were simply too many flammable items inside to feed the inferno.

Meg took the 12th Street exit on her way to the Hoover Building and switched over to the first tactical channel. And went from the single cool voice of the commander to a flurry of communication from the teams actively fighting the fire. It sounded like a nightmare scenario: Heavy smoke. High heat. The floor-to-ceiling contents making navigating each floor nearly impossible. Hoses catching on piles of junk. Firefighters having to climb over hoarded debris to proceed through the house. Air levels in SCBA tanks dropping with increasing speed due to the work required simply to move through the space.

"Engine 2. We've made access to the second floor. Engine 2 will scout ahead of the hose line." It was Webb's voice, calmly leading a team of two other firefighters through the second floor, moving ahead of them to scout the route through mountains of books, clothing, boxes, and furniture.

It was only as she approached East Street NW that Meg realized she was so focused on the hoarder fire that she had driven through the National Mall on autopilot without seeing it. She signaled her turn quickly and took the corner faster than she would have liked to the blast of a horn behind her and the scrape of Hawk's nails as he slid sideways in his compartment.

"Sorry, buddy." She glanced back, but Hawk simply stared at her, unperturbed. "You're a champ. And I need to pay better attention."

"Mayday, Mayday, Mayday!"

Meg started, jerking the steering wheel, and then had to swiftly compensate before she hit the curb.

Mayday. The call given only in the life-and-death crisis of a firefighter.

But she barely had time to contemplate what might be happening before details came at her fast.

"Engine 2 to Command. Ceiling collapse. Lieutenant Webb was underneath. Two of us on a hose line. He's ahead of us and we can't see him or raise him. Second floor. Bravo Charlie corner."

Meg's heart rate spiked in panic and she didn't think. She just hit the accelerator. Washington City was only blocks away from her current location. She could be there in minutes. Part of her knew there was no reason to be there and many reasons to stay away. They would already be mounting a rescue operation, one she couldn't assist in. One she could get in the way of. She and her dog were going to turn up at an active fire with an ongoing crisis to do . . . what?

She knew there was no reason to be there. But God help anyone who was going to try to stop her.

Todd. When he'd given her the radio, he'd done it so she could be assured of his well-being. He never would have thought it might give her a window into experiencing his death in real time.

She recognized the high-pitched, repetitive whooping in

the background behind the voice of the Engine 2 firefighter as Webb's personal alert safety system. It was
rigged to sound the alarm after thirty seconds of inactivity.
The longer the firefighter remained motionless, the louder
it got. From what was coming over the radio, Webb had
been down for far too long.

He had to be unconscious under all that rubble.

The incident commander was back on the radio, his
voice calm despite the urgency of the situation. "Command copies your Mayday, Engine 2. Lieutenant Webb
has had a structural collapse on the second floor and is
separated from his crew. We are sending in the RIC. Command to Rescue 1."

"Rescue 1." It was a different voice, the leader of the
RIC—the Rapid Intervention Crew, the team that stood by
the entrance of an active fire, ready to go in to perform a
rescue at a moment's notice.

"We have Lieutenant Webb on the second floor, Bravo
Charlie corner. He is separated from his crew and we have
a structural collapse."

"Rescue 1 to Command. We have deployed."

Meg drove faster, weaving through heavy rush-hour
traffic, running a yellow light so close she knew it had
turned red a fraction of a second after she entered the intersection.

She knew she couldn't help, but she needed to be there.

The radio on the seat beside her continued to tell the
tale of the rescue in progress. The incident commander
had all the other units in the building switch to tac 2, leaving tac 1 open for the rescue. He informed dispatch they
had an incident and requested a second alarm and an additional ambulance. The RIC was making their way to
Webb's location. The men with Webb were trying to clear
debris to get to him, but the amount of debris that had

poured down from the third floor had essentially buried Webb and blocked their way.

Meg tore up 2nd Street NW, knowing she could cut over into Washington City from there. While she recognized the street name, she hadn't caught the house number, but knew that wouldn't be important. With a man down, the incident commander had added an alarm to the fire, and additional teams were incoming. If she couldn't spot the incident from the units already there, she'd follow the responding vehicles.

As she drove, she fought to bring her shallow, rapid breathing under control. Now was not the time for panic; she needed to stay calm. Webb would want her to stay calm.

"Engine 2 to Command. We're both down to one red light. Coming out."

Dread pooled in Meg's gut. One red light meant the two men in Webb's team were nearly out of air and had to leave Webb before they ran out completely or became incapacitated.

What did that mean for him? Was he trapped under flaming debris, burning to death? Or buried, with his air supply dwindling and slowly suffocating?

"Command to Engine 2. Message received. Come out. Rescue 1 is on the way."

Meg had no trouble finding the place. It was a three-story brownstone on New York Avenue NW, just past 1st Street NW, surrounded by engines, a ladder truck, and the chief's vehicle. Not wanting to block incoming responders, she found an open parking spot on the opposite side of the street well away from the scene and jumped out as soon as she yanked the key from the ignition. She grabbed a leash from the back, opened the door for Hawk to leap out, snapped the leash on his FBI work vest, and then they were sprinting across the street, weaving through traffic bottled up around the fire, Hawk easily keeping pace with her frantic strides.

The incident was organized chaos, as so many crises are. The ladder truck was pulled up to the curb, the ladder extended and a man on top ready to open his hose once crews pulled out of the house. Fat lines of hose snaked into and around the house from the engine pumping water into them. A RIC stood at the front door, a second team poised to go in when the first team needed to be spelled off for heat or diminishing air reserves.

She could only pray Webb's air would hold while they tried to get to him. Surely if he was unmoving and unconscious, he'd use less.

Hang on, Todd.

Please.

A firefighter staggered out the door and stumbled down the steps, unsnapping his chin strap to rip off his helmet and then his mask, gulping in lungfuls of fresh air. His commander pointed him toward the open rear doors of an ambulance parked across from the ladder truck, and the firefighter turned and walked toward it. Meg spotted the blond hair at the same time as he changed direction, revealing the name at the bottom of his DCFEMS turnout coat—SMAILL.

Chuck Smaill, the firefighter who'd helped with a case during the previous fall. The urbexer who'd taken them into the sites of so many body dumps. A good firefighter and a man who'd become a friend and, for a brief while, an integral part of their team.

Chuck would be able to tell her what was going on.

"Hawk, come."

They redirected toward the ambulance. Smaill was sitting on the back bumper, a paramedic at his side, holding an oxygen mask over his nose and mouth. An empty water bottle sat on the bumper beside him and a second half-empty one was in his hand. His eyes went wide when he recognized the woman and dog running toward him.

"Todd. I heard on the radio. The Mayday." Meg knew she was babbling and stopped to drag in a panting breath. For someone who was used to working in a crisis situation, her calm center had completely disintegrated at the thought of the man she loved dying inside an inferno one hundred feet away.

"Meg." Smaill reached for her hand, caught it, and squeezed tight. He started to drop the oxygen mask and the paramedic slapped it back into place. Smaill tossed the paramedic a sour look and turned to Meg. She saw the question in his gaze when he looked at her face more closely, saw him discard it in the face of the current crisis. "How did you know?"

"Todd gave me a handheld radio so I could tune into incidents while he was on shift. I just flew in from a case in Georgia. When I didn't get a text back from him, I turned on the radio as I drove in from Reagan. I was only a mile away when I heard the Mayday, and I headed right here. Have they found him?"

Smaill shook his head. "They're still making their way up. It's a God-awful mess in there. So much crap. And it's making an already challenging situation almost impossible." As if realizing what he'd said, he quickly added, "The fire, I mean, not the rescue. We're going to lose the house, but we'll get Webb out first." He held on tighter to her hand and met her eyes. "This RIC team is the best. They'll find him, and they'll get him out."

"But if he runs out of air first—"

"They'll find him." Smaill ruthlessly cut her off, and Meg wondered who he was trying to convince. "They'll get him out." He dropped the mask and glared at the paramedic who moved to put it back in place. "I'm good." He stood, keeping a tight grip of Meg's hand. "Come with me. And keep Hawk close."

They quickly crossed the street, heading for the battalion chief's SUV and incident command. The rear hatch was thrown open and a white board inside held a list of every man on-site and his current location. The chief glanced at them as they approached, his gaze flicking from Meg's face, to the FBI logo emblazoned on her navy-blue windbreaker, to Hawk in his FBI work vest. Recognition dawned in his eyes—they'd only met briefly once, but Chief Koenig knew all about Webb's work with the Human Scent Evidence Team.

Koenig gave her a brief nod, barked, "Keep that dog out of the way," and turned back to his radio. His attention was drawn to the ladder truck and an engine pulling up to the house signaling the arrival of more men. "Smaill, stay with her."

"Yes, Chief." Smaill gave Meg's hand a tug and dragged her away a few paces. "We'll stay here. We can see and hear everything from here."

Meg nodded. "Hawk, sit."

So they waited. Waited as two firefighters careened through the open doorway, ripping off their masks and nearly falling down the stairs before being helped down by fellow firefighters. As the RIC inside on the second floor reported dangerous levels of heat, smoke, and flame; that they had low visibility; and their way was mostly blocked by debris. As they found a way over the debris. As they finally found Webb.

"Rescue 1 to Command. We have Lieutenant Webb. Standby."

"Command to Rescue 1. Message received."

Sensing the tension, Hawk whined fretfully and Meg let go of Smaill's hand to sink down and kneel beside her dog, throwing an arm over his back as they waited for word on Webb's condition. Smaill's hand came down on her shoulder to bolster her, his fear wordlessly communicated in the strength of his grip.

A fellow firefighter would know exactly how bleak the situation was. The knowledge that Smaill feared for Webb's life was absolutely terrifying.

"They've got him, that's good. They'll get the debris off him and the first thing they'll do is check his air." As dead air continued on tac 1, Smaill explained what was happening inside, as much to give himself something to do as to make sure she understood the process, Meg suspected. "They're carrying a spare SCBA, the RIC pack, and they'll do a mask swap and get him onto a new tank."

"How will they get him out?"

"They'll use a McGuire sled. It's basically a cloth rectangle with six built-in handles made out of this incredibly rugged military-grade fabric that doesn't tear. They'll load him on the sled and either drag or carry him out of there." He cut off any further explanation as the radio sounded again.

"Rescue 1 to Command. We are packaging Lieutenant Webb. He's unconscious. RIC mask is in place. He has two thousand pounds of air. Coming out."

"Command to Rescue 1. Message received."

Meg surged to her feet. "What does that mean? He's okay?"

Smaill grimly shook his head. "We can't evaluate in those conditions or even take the time to try. The best we can do is make sure he's got air and get him the hell out of there." He motioned to the paramedics wheeling a gurney up the front walk. "As soon as he's out, they'll evaluate him. Then we'll know where we stand."

"But he's been in there a long time, hasn't he?"

Smaill paused for too long and she had her answer before he responded. "It's been a while, yeah."

She closed her eyes, fighting the rising fear, and wrapped her fingers around the glass pendant she wore.

She'd been lucky enough to never experience the death of a family member. Her grandparents were still alive, as were her very vital parents, living in Virginia, running their animal rescue. Fellow Richmond PD officers had gone down in the line of duty while she was on the force, but none of them had been close to her personally.

Without a doubt, her most crushing loss had been the death of her Richmond PD K-9, Deuce, who was shot and killed while they were tracking and apprehending a suspect. The German shepherd had bled out in her arms, and she thought she'd lost a part of herself forever. She had, but when she'd left the force and escaped to her parents' rescue to grieve, she'd helped nurse an extremely sick, abandoned black Lab puppy back from the brink of death.

That sick puppy was now the very healthy search-and-rescue dog at her side. He'd survived, and she'd survived with him. The part of herself she'd lost with Deuce's death would never be replaced, but a new part had grown stronger as her connection to Hawk intensified. Now all she had left of Deuce were memories and the soft gray swirl of his ashes entwined with the electric blue and black glass in the memory pendant she wore when not out on active searches.

But to lose Webb. She would never be able to hide at her parents' rescue to lick her wounds following that loss. She wouldn't be able to hide away anywhere from that kind of grief.

"There they are!" Smaill's shout ripped her from her thoughts as four firefighters in DCFEMS beige jogged down the front steps carrying a still figure on the McGuire sled. He reached around her and yanked the leash from her hand. "I've got Hawk. Go!"

She didn't think twice about it, knowing Hawk knew Smaill well and trusted him. She jumped to her feet and sprinted across the grass, winding around firefighters and leaping over hoses, reaching the gurney just as they deposited Webb on it. His slack face was sheet white, and blood ran in trails from under his helmet and down over his left cheek. She wanted to reach out and touch him, but he was completely protected by his turnout gear, gloves, boots, and mask. And she knew she'd be in the way. She had to let the medical team work if there was any hope of his survival.

One of the paramedics unsnapped his chin strap, slipped off his helmet, and pulled off his air mask, replacing it with an oxygen mask, while the second paramedic unzipped his turnout coat and started tallying vital signs.

"Good breath sounds on both sides. Pulse ox is eighty-five. Heart rate is sixty."

He's alive.

Meg hung back, her gaze fixed on his face, not daring to get in their way. One of the paramedics looked at her, then down at her FBI insignia, and up again in confusion. But said nothing.

"Pupils are reactive. He's stable. Let's move him."

They strapped him down to the gurney and ran with it to the ambulance, Meg right behind them.

"Where are you taking him?"

They loaded the gurney into the ambulance, one of the paramedics climbing in after him. The other paramedic slammed the doors. "MedStar."

Meg turned and sprinted back to Smaill.

He held out the leash for her. "How is he?"

"Vitals look stable, but he's still out. They're taking him to MedStar."

"Go. We'll come when we can. Tell him we're with him."

"Tell him yourself when you come." She reached up on tiptoe and kissed him on the cheek, giving his arm a squeeze. "Thank you."

"He's ours, so you're ours, too. Now go see to our guy."

They ran.

CHAPTER 6

Crisis Management: The process by which a group deals with a disruptive or unexpected event.

Monday, April 8, 7:24 PM
MedStar Washington Hospital Center
Washington, DC

For the second time that day, Meg was grateful she and Hawk were both wearing FBI outerwear, though when she'd come flying into the ER, she already had her FBI badge in hand, willing to use whatever leverage was needed to get in to see Webb. It had gotten Hawk through the door under the disapproving gaze of the charge nurse and the two of them into the waiting room, where she had alternatively sat fretting or paced while Hawk sat patiently beside her chair.

That had been a full hour ago and there had been no update in the interim.

She was going out of her mind.

"Meg Jennings?"

Meg sat bolt upright in her hard, plastic chair in the waiting room. "Yes?"

The twentysomething nurse gave her a sunny smile. "Come with me, please."

Meg shot out of her chair and tightened up on Hawk's leash. "Hawk, heel," she said quietly, and then followed the nurse.

They pushed through a set of double doors and into a long corridor of treatment and exam rooms. Webb's room was nearly at the end of the hall.

The nurse pulled open the glass door and then pulled aside the curtain covering the entrance. "Go ahead. The doctor will be in to check on him shortly."

"Thank you." She slipped through the curtained doorway.

Webb lay in the bed beyond, dressed in a hospital gown and covered with a blanket, an IV in his right hand and his left arm in a sling. A narrow white bandage ran along the edge of his short-cut dark hair over his left eye. His face was still pale, but his brown eyes were open, clear, and fixed on her, a sheepish smile curving one corner of his lips. "Hey." But then his brows drew together as he stared at her, clearly confused by her appearance.

She froze for a second in the doorway, just staring at him, alive and breathing, and then she moved. Sitting down gingerly on the side of the bed, she cupped his face in her hands, leaned down, and kissed him, long and slow. When she finally pulled away, she touched her forehead to his, closed her eyes, and simply breathed him in. After a moment, she sat up and let out a shaky breath. "You know, you haven't done good things for my rep as a rock-solid FBI handler today."

He stroked a loose strand of hair behind her ear with his free hand. "No?"

Her laugh had a sharp edge to it. "Not even kind of. I'm normally a very calm person. Apparently today, standing outside that house, waiting for them to find you while you slowly ran out of air, we found the red line of that calm."

His gaze went sharp. "You were there? *At the scene?*"

"Yes."

"I thought someone had called you and you'd come straight here." His expression softened as he searched her face, reading new meaning into the lines of stress and exhaustion that had to be etched around her eyes and mouth. "How did you know about the call? I didn't know you were back in town."

"I guess you never got my message that I was coming back. Brian and I flew into DC late this afternoon. When I couldn't get in contact, I turned on your radio as I drove to the Hoover Building. I heard the Mayday come in." He grimaced, but she kept going. "And then I drove right to the incident because I needed to know you were safe."

He gripped her hand. "I'm so sorry. When I gave you that radio, it was to reassure you when I was out on a call. I never meant for you to listen in on something like this as it happened."

"There's nothing to apologize for. You and I, we know what we got into with each other. Neither of us have the easiest of jobs. Today was your turn to scare the life out of me instead of the other way around, which is how it usually goes." Her voice dropped and took on a husky edge. "Chuck and I both thought we'd lost you for a few minutes there." She met his eyes. "I don't want to experience those minutes again. It was like Deuce all over, only much, *much* worse."

He wrapped his hand around the back of her neck and tugged her down to him for a kiss that held an unspoken promise. A few moments later, Meg jerked away when a cold, wet nose poked between them. She pulled away laughing, the tender moment broken by seventy pounds of black Lab.

"Apparently I wasn't the only one who was worried." She patted the edge of the bed. "Hawk, stand."

Hawk stood up on his rear legs, his front feet braced on the edge of the bed as he leaned in to lick at Webb's face.

Webb laughed and rubbed the Labrador's neck. "Good boy, Hawk. Good boy."

"Okay, Hawk, down," Meg said.

The dog obediently dropped down to the floor and then went to lie down against the wall, as if reassured that all was well now and he could rest.

Webb reached toward Meg's cheek, hesitating a fraction of an inch away from her skin, then shifted slightly and touched her temple, well clear of the irritation. "What happened to your face?"

Meg let out an exhausted chuckle. "It feels like this happened weeks ago, not six hours ago. There I was thinking 'poor me,' and then a house fell on you."

"It looks painful. And your eyes . . ."

"Pepper spray. Brian, Hawk, Lacey, and I had a moment today with a mama black bear and her two cubs."

"You know you're supposed to spray the bear, right? Not yourself?" The quirk at the corner of his mouth told her he was trying to lighten the mood.

"Yeah, I tried for that. You use a can of bear deterrent on the top of a mountain in a stiff forty-mile-per-hour breeze and see how much blows back at you." When he winced, she continued. "Luckily more hit the bear than me and she and the cubs took off." She raised two fingers and pressed them gently to her raw cheek. "It's getting better. I could barely touch it four hours ago. Should be gone by morning. And the swelling around my eyes is coming down. They probably look worse than they feel at this point. Brian did a good job of flushing as much of it out of my eyes as he could right afterward. We kept going, but we never had a chance of catching the suspect."

"And then you came back to town, hurt, irritated, and discouraged, only to land in the middle of my crisis. God, Meg, I'm sorry."

"It's not your fault. I'm just having a pity party for one,

which is absolutely ridiculous and probably has more to do with being tired and hungry and my stinging eyes than anything else. We've had this case for less than a day."

"You've barely started."

"Right. But if these deaths continue, we can't do the searches from DC. We need to be there. We're losing too much time not being on-site." She shook her head. "Why am I telling you this while you're lying in a hospital bed hooked up to an IV?"

"Because it frustrates you. Like me, you don't like to lose. And when you start at the back of the pack, how do you make it to the front by the end of the race?"

"That's it exactly."

"Brian and the dogs are okay?"

"Yes. We taught them a trick for that kind of situation because we do a lot of wilderness searches and running into a bear is always a risk." Sitting up straighter, she looked down at her dog. "Hawk, peekaboo."

The dog immediately rolled to his side and hooked one paw and wrist over his closed eyes, partially covering his face.

"Good boy." She twisted back toward Webb. "I gave them that command just before I sprayed the bear. Had enough time to tell Brian to cover his eyes. But I was in front and had the can of spray out and had to look where I was shooting."

"Until you couldn't see."

"Until I couldn't see," she confirmed. "But enough about me. None of that compares to what you went through today." She leaned in to brush her fingertips lightly over the very edge of the bandage on his forehead. "I couldn't miss the blood when they brought you out. Did you need stitches?"

"Just a couple. The padding on the headband in my helmet is a little worn so when all that weight landed on it, it cut into my skin. It's nothing."

"It was enough that you needed stitches. It bled quite a bit."

"That's a head injury for you."

"Sounds like you need a new headband."

"I'm going to need a whole new helmet after that. It saved my skull from cracking like an egg, but it's lost all integrity after a hit carrying that kind of force."

"What's with the sling? We were concerned you bashed your head in. We didn't think there were any other injuries when the ceiling collapsed."

Webb's brows drew together as his eyes went flinty. "That goddamned house."

"It sounded bad."

"Unbelievably bad. Whoever lived there kept every last item that ever came into their hands. And every one of them was flammable. It was a nightmare. Was I the only casualty? The docs said no one else came in from that fire, but . . ."

"No one else was hurt."

His whole body relaxed in relief. "Good. My guys were probably fifteen feet behind me, wrestling with the line around all the junk. In some ways, that junk saved them. I had about a half second of warning the ceiling was going, and just managed to get my left arm over my head before it all came down on me."

"It all came down is about right. It wasn't just the ceiling; it was everything the owner had hoarded and stored on the top floor. It's why it took so long to dig you out. As I understand it, you came perilously close to running out of air." She ran her fingers lightly over his left arm. "So you wrenched your shoulder to protect your head? Not that it worked perfectly. You were out cold from what I hear. You know what that sounds like? That sounds like a concussion." She narrowed her eyes at him.

"You would know." He winked at her. "Sure gave me a hell of a headache, though."

"You had a ceiling and likely hundreds of pounds of debris fall on you. What did you expect? What's the damage on the shoulder?"

"Strained rotator cuff. They did an MRI to confirm it wasn't a tear, and it's not, thank God. This is bad enough."

"How? It sounds like you got off lightly, considering how it could have gone down."

"I'm not disagreeing there. But this is going to put me on the disabled list for three or four weeks. It's not a terrible injury, but in a position where perfect fitness and brute strength might be the only thing to save your own or your buddy's life, I can't return to active duty until I check out. So it's going to be a few weeks of rest, ice, exercises, and physical therapy before I get the all clear to go back on shift."

"Which will drive you crazy by the end of it, but I'll take it. When I think of what might have happened . . . well, I'll take you being grouchy, bored, and irritable, because I'll have *you*. Which reminds me . . ."

When she paused, Webb gave her a little push. "Of?"

"That text you sent. About the new place. When you're cleared to be up and about, let's go see it. I don't want to waste any more time. We'll make it work."

He just gave a slight shake of his head.

"What? Isn't that what you want?"

"Of course it's what I want, but not at the extent of 'making it work.' This is going to be our place, so I don't want either of us to settle. We need to both love it. And—"

He cut off at a knock on the door.

The same nurse stood in the doorway. "Lieutenant Webb, are you up to visitors?"

Webb glanced at Meg, who nodded. "Sure."

"Uh . . . A lot of visitors?"

Webb grinned. "Definitely."

The nurse turned and waved to someone down the hallway. In the next moment, the doorway was filled with firefighters, Smaill leading the charge, a look of such relief on his face it warmed Meg's heart. These men and women, the hardworking members of Engine Company 2, had been as terrified as she that they'd lost their brother-in-arms.

Meg gave Webb's arm a squeeze and rose from the mattress to stand at the head of the bed, Hawk at her side. But he caught her hand, holding it, keeping her close, marking them as a unit to the members of his company. One by one, the firefighters trooped in to see him, to laugh and poke fun, using humor as always to manage the daily risk and stress of their working lives. But each of them also made a point of including her in their conversations. Because she was one of them now.

Smaill was the last to leave, having drawn up chairs for both himself and Meg.

"When are they letting you out of this hellhole?" Smaill asked.

"This isn't a hellhole. That house this afternoon, *that* was the hellhole," Webb replied. "And hopefully soon."

"Then you're headed home?"

Meg held up an index finger an inch from Webb's lips before he could form an answer. "No, he is not."

Webb quirked an eyebrow. "I'm not?"

"No, you're coming back with me to my place. Where we can make sure you don't overdo it."

"We?"

"Cara and I. She's pretty good at concussion watch now."

"She had enough practice with you." Meg sent Webb a dirty look, making him laugh, and then he squeezed his eyes shut, pressing the fingers of his free hand to his temple. "Don't do that."

"Don't be stubborn."

"Deal. At least for now."

Smaill laughed. "You two are a pair."

"What gave it away?" Webb asked dryly. "The tendency toward matching concussions?"

"That's definitely part of it." He stood and gripped Webb's forearm. "I have to get going, but I'll check in on you tomorrow. You take it easy. That's an order." As the inferior officer, Smaill's words carried no official weight but the weight of friendship.

"Yes, sir."

Smaill grinned and slipped out with a final wave.

Meg leaned forward and took Webb's hand, being careful not to foul his IV line.

He frowned down at it. "I don't need it anymore. I should pop it out."

"Don't you dare." Meg covered the needle with her hand. "Paramedics make terrible patients."

"That's firefighter/paramedic to you. And yeah, we do. We know too much and question every decision made by everyone else."

"Let's get one thing straight. We're doing this by the book. The doctor says rest, you rest. He says exercise, you exercise."

"Yes, sir, General, sir."

"You're funny." She shook her head at him, but then her expression sobered. "I'm not willing to take any chances. Maybe next week, or next month. But not today. I've hit my limit for today."

"Then we do it by the book." He held out his right hand, pinkie finger extended.

Meg eyed it. "What are you? Twelve?"

"This is a very serious thing. Pinkie swear with me."

She laughed and linked pinkies with him. Then he rolled her hand over and pulled it up to kiss the back before holding her fingers against his cheek.

Another crisis averted.

They'd be all right.

CHAPTER 7

New Echota & the Trail of Tears: On December 29, 1835, US government officials and about 500 Cherokee Indians claiming to represent their 16,000-member tribe, met at New Echota, Georgia, and signed a treaty that led to the forced removal of Cherokee from their southeastern homelands to Indian Territory west of the Mississippi River. Although the majority of Cherokee opposed the treaty negotiated by Cherokee leader Major Ridge, and Principal Chief John Ross wrote a letter to Congress protesting it, the US Senate ratified the document in March 1836 by one vote. In 1838–1839, the US government forcibly removed the Cherokee from their lands in North Carolina, driving them on the infamous Trail of Tears to the Indian Territory of present-day Oklahoma. A small number of Cherokee successfully resisted removal, however, by claiming North Carolina citizenship and by maintaining the right to remain on lands they owned. These people and their descendants were recognized in 1868 by the federal government as the Eastern Band of Cherokee Indians. In retaliation, Major Ridge, his son John, and Elias Boudinot were executed by other Cherokee in 1839 for violating the Cherokee Blood Law.

Monday, April 8, 9:41 PM
Jennings residence
Arlington, Virginia

"Hawk, in you go. That's a good boy." Meg held open the front door, letting Hawk precede her before turning to Webb. "Let me give you a hand."

"Going up one step? I think I can manage."

"You can't fool me. You're not as steady as you're trying to make it look." Ignoring his directive, she wrapped an arm around his waist as he stepped into the house, and swallowed a comment when his free hand shot out to steady himself on the wall.

"I seem to recall you running around a warship graveyard and a Civil War historical site while you were concussed." Webb's tone was surly.

"That was two days later, not hours after I got my bell rung."

"That's also because her sister's life was in danger, and nothing and no one was going to hold her back." Meg's sister, Cara, a near carbon copy of Meg's own black Irish fair skin, ice-blue eyes, and straight, dark hair, came out of the kitchen, trailed by tall, blond Clay McCord. McCord's bouncy golden retriever, Cody, and Cara's mini blue-nose pit bull, Saki, followed behind. Cara stopped dead when she saw her sister, her welcoming smile melting away as her eyes went wide.

"We knew about him, but what happened to you?" McCord blurted, his blue eyes locked on her bloodshot, puffy eyes and reddened cheeks.

"I had a one-on-one with a mama bear that wasn't completely successful." Meg pinned McCord with a flat stare as she gave a head jerk toward Webb. "Don't stand there gawking. Give me a hand."

"I can still walk," Webb protested.

"Suck it up, man." McCord stepped around Cody, who clearly thought Webb was the most interesting scent to enter the house in a long time. "Cody, shift it. You're in the way. Go wait over there with Saki. Maybe you can learn some manners from her example." He shooed Meg out of the way, then pulled Webb's right arm over his shoulders to steady him. "When the lady says march, just shut up and ask which direction." He gave Webb a sideways glance. "You look like hell."

"I feel like hell," Webb muttered.

"We heard that," Cara said. She laid a gentle hand on the wrist protruding from his sling and took a long moment to search his expression for any sign of pain. "When Meg was running around Maryland with a concussion, she had you and your medical experience with her in case anything went wrong. You don't have that. You're stuck with us."

"I'll take that any day." Webb's attention was caught by Blink, Cara's brindle greyhound, the shyest of the dogs, as he peered around the corner at them. "Hey, Blink, it's me." He wiggled his fingers at the dog. "Come here and say hello."

Blink immediately retreated, disappearing from view, the sound of his nails tapping on the kitchen floor growing quieter as he fled.

"Just when I thought I was actually making progress with him."

"Don't be offended. He might have taken one look at my face and run for the hills," Meg said. "Or maybe it's because you don't have a piece of bacon in your hand." She watched the men shuffle down the hallway. "McCord, take him down to my bedroom. He needs to rest."

Webb stopped dead, forcing McCord to follow suit. "I am not going to bed. I'm not five. I'm also not tired."

"Not to mention you were resting all that time you were unconscious," McCord quipped.

"Not helping," Webb growled in an undertone.

His eyes sparkling with humor, McCord turned his gaze up to the ceiling and mimed whistling a tune.

"Fine," Meg conceded. "But I want you horizontal. What about the couch?"

"That'll do."

"Come on," McCord coaxed, pulling Webb forward. "Let's get you settled. I was about to grab a beer. Want one?"

"No," Meg and Cara said in unison.

"Apparently not," Webb said. "Which is a crying shame because I could really use one right now." He turned imploring eyes on Cara. "If I can't have beer, can I at least get some coffee?"

"Absolutely." Cara waited until he smiled his thanks, and then said, "Decaf. No caffeine while you're recovering. It can interfere with your sleep patterns."

Webb's smile fell away. "This is seriously no fun."

"You're not supposed to have fun." Meg led the way into the living room, Hawk and Saki at her heels. "You're on medical leave."

As he went by, Cara poked McCord in the biceps. "And you can have coffee, too. It's not fair for you to have a beer when Todd can't."

McCord and Webb exchanged dour glances. "You nailed it," said McCord. "This is seriously no fun."

A few minutes later, Webb was carefully settled on the couch, a pillow under his head and his injured shoulder supported by the rear cushions. Saki, a trained therapy dog, lay on the floor by his head, as if instinctively sensing his injury, while Hawk and Blink piled on the dog bed by the sliding door next to the deck, and Cody settled in nearby to gnaw on his favorite rubber bone. Meg bent over Webb, adjusting his pillow and asking for the second time if he'd like a blanket. He caught her hand and tugged her down to sit on the hassock at his hip.

"Don't do that. You'll hurt yourself."

"There's nothing wrong with that arm." Webb waited until she met his eyes. "It's okay. I'm here, and I'm not going anywhere. Just sit with me."

Meg slumped, bracing her elbows on her knees. "I'm turning into my mother, fussing over you like you're an invalid."

"Worse things could happen. Eda Jennings is a fine woman." He squeezed her hand. "And you're not totally wrong about the invalid bit. But even for this hellish day, you're on edge. You know I'm going to be okay, so it has to be work. Tell me about what happened in Georgia."

"You were in Georgia?" McCord fell into Meg's comfortable, ratty old recliner, a piece of furniture she couldn't bear to part with, no matter its ugliness. "You and Hawk were on assignment?"

"Possibly the beginning of a serial murder case."

"I take it you haven't caught the killer?"

"Not even kind of." She looked up as Cara carried a tray of mugs, cream, and sugar over to the coffee table. "Do you need a hand?"

"Nope. Coffee is still brewing and I'll bring out the pot when it's ready." She laid the tray down and sat down in the armchair. "You went bolting out of here this morning. You were headed to the airport?"

"Yes." She frowned as her memory suddenly recalled her last trip from the airport. "Damn. When I left the airport on the way back, I was going to stop at the Hoover Building to talk to Craig. It's too late to talk to him now. I'll have to do that first thing tomorrow." She took a breath to center her overtired brain. "Okay, let me start from the beginning." She fixed McCord with a pointed stare but didn't say anything.

McCord rolled his eyes. "What does a guy have to do to get a break on a story around here?"

Meg continued to stare at him silently.

"Okay, okay, all of this is off the record and if there's a story in it, I'm under a gag order until I get the green light."

"Thank you."

"You know, we do this every time. How about we make a pact that if it's your case, until you tell me otherwise, it's confidential. But then you don't go giving the story to anyone else, capiche?"

"That's not always in my control. The Press Office might object to my making a blanket statement on that." When McCord continued to stare at her, she rolled her eyes at the ceiling as if asking for strength. "Fine, I capiche. As long as they also clear it."

"Good enough for me. Proceed."

Meg started at the beginning, taking them through Craig's phone call telling them about the death of the Georgia State Patrol officer, to the teams' arrival in Georgia, the arrow, the bow, the search, the bear, the unsuccessful conclusion of the trail, and finally meeting with Torres. By the time she finished, they were all halfway through their first cup of coffee.

"That's a pretty wide field of potential suspects to start with," McCord said.

"Considering the scope of the project," Cara said, "that's not a surprise. Imagine having family land for more than a hundred years, making your livelihood off that land, and then being told unceremoniously you have to give it up. They may not even be fairly paid for it. Do you know those kinds of details?"

"Not so far, but hopefully Agent Torres is looking into it."

McCord's mug hit the coffee table with a light thump as he levered himself out of the recliner.

Meg watched him with suspicious eyes. "Where are you going?"

"Where do you think?" McCord disappeared out of the living room and returned about twenty seconds later with his laptop bag in hand. He sat down, pulled out his laptop, and booted up.

"You know, sometimes I think you hang out so much because you're looking for a new story."

"That might have been true at the beginning until your sister worked her wiles on me." He winked at Cara, who sat back in her chair with her coffee mug, looking smug. "But now it's a happy side gig." He met Meg's gaze. "For both of us, and you know it."

"Yeah, yeah, I do."

"So it's not just about my listening and then not passing on the information. You actually want my help." It was a statement, not a question.

Meg sighed. "Of course I do. How would we manage without you?" At his quiet chortle, she shook her head at him. "Don't let it go to your head or you'll be impossible to work with."

"Would I do that?"

Cara snorted, then hid her smile behind her mug.

"Okay, maybe I would do that." McCord opened a blank document, pushed his wire-rimmed glasses up his nose, and started making notes.

"The trick, as always, is convincing each new agent in charge of the case that you're trustworthy and reliable. You know a lot of them don't have good relationships with investigative reporters. They think you're searching for a way to make them look bad or to leak confidential information that could lose them their suspect or their whole case." Meg threw up a hand in McCord's direction before he could argue. "I know that's not you; I'm just telling you what many agents experience from *other* reporters. Keep everything on the down-low until I have a chance to run this by Torres."

"Can do. Now let's run the list of involved parties again. In favor of the project we have the TVA—the Tennessee Valley Authority—Atkins Power, Roswell Engineering, the towns of Copperhill and McCaysville and all their residents, Fannin County, the state of Georgia, and the US government. Against the project we have current valley residents, local businesses, and the Eastern Band of Cherokee Indians. Where is the town of Blue Ridge on the project?"

"That's a good question, but one I can't answer."

McCord stopped typing and sat back to study his monitor. "When you think of all the individuals involved, this could be a pretty big suspect pool."

"With a lot of high emotion," Webb said.

Meg looked down to where Webb lay propped into a half-sitting position against the pillow, a mug of coffee cradled in his right hand. His color was starting to return and his eyes seemed sharper. "You look better. How's the head?"

"Headache is starting to back off a bit. Part of that is probably getting out of the glare of the ER. More of it is being here with you guys. Either way, I think I can rub a few brain cells together now. That was harder a few hours ago."

"I bet. By high emotion, do you mean the landowners?"

"Yeah, but also the Cherokee. They got screwed and they're trying to get some of their own back. And that's going to be *tough*. Not only because of the current political climate, but simply because of past history and bad blood."

"How much do you know about the land lotteries?" McCord asked.

"Some. Probably a little less right now because my brains are scrambled. But I know it predated and was a part of the Trail of Tears."

"My high school history is pretty foggy and I think this is going to be important, so that's not good." Meg scooted forward on the hassock to pour herself another cup of coffee. "McCord, you're the history buff—"

"Try walking encyclopedia," Webb interjected.

"That too. I bet you can bring us up to speed on it?"

"I can. I know the basics, but it's not my area of expertise. I'll want to dig in deeper and make sure what I know is correct if that history could be a basis for a killing motive, and it sounds like it could be. Give me time to do some research. But in very rough terms off the top of my head, in the early nineteenth century there was a system in Georgia to give away parcels of land to qualifying applicants of European descent. The problem was, as far as the Native Americans occupying the territory were concerned, it wasn't the US government's to give away. That led to forced relocations and the deaths of more than ten thousand Native Americans. It was a horror show."

"I seem to remember they all got sent west of the Mississippi because the government at the time never thought they'd need to expand west of the river," Webb said.

"And look how well that turned out. It delayed additional conflict, but certainly didn't end it." McCord met Meg's eyes. "You realize you may be looking at both sides of those lotteries in this case? Not only the Cherokee who gave up or were forced off their land, but the descendants of the settlers who won those parcels and may be the current landowners."

"Some people would call that karma," Cara said. "With the government's help, they forced Native Americans off the land they'd likely lived on for centuries. And now nearly two centuries later, the government is forcing *them* off that same land."

"Or the TVA is," McCord supplied, "but while it's not strictly a government body, it essentially fulfills that role as a federally owned corporation. So, yeah, karma."

"I'm pretty sure they wouldn't see it that way." Meg thoughtfully took a sip of coffee. "The question is—would they be willing to kill to keep their land?"

"Some of them, absolutely," Webb said.

"We're going to need detailed lists of who holds land in the valley, both residential and business. Then we need to know who wants to lay claim to that land. Then, out of those, we need to find out who the hunters are. Past that we need to find out who has the skills to kill like that. Then you need to start collecting alibis." McCord looked up from his screen. "This case more than most, it's going to be a process of narrowing down the list. That's assuming we're starting with a full list. What if we're missing someone? Or several someones?"

"What if it's not someone who wants the project terminated, but only delayed?" Cara asked. "What if it has to do with time lines and expired contracts for construction? It doesn't have to be just someone who feels the land is threatened. It could be someone who is threatened by the project in its current form."

McCord was already adding to his list. "That's a solid point. We need to make sure we include all possibilities right from the start." He lifted his hands from the keyboard and turned to Meg. "I know where I'm going with this. What about you?"

"We're on hold for now. Until the next call comes in. But the truth of the matter is, we're too far away to be useful. We're hours behind before we even find the starting line. If this continues, I think we need to be there on-site.

That would allow us to follow in near real time. That's what I wanted to talk to Craig about earlier today." She hid a yawn behind her hand.

Webb rubbed a hand up and down her back. "You sound exhausted."

"It's been a hell of a day, no doubt about it. I think I'm ready to turn in. And I'm taking you with me, tired or not." Meg put their coffee mugs down on the tray.

"I think I could sleep now." Webb slowly pushed himself into a sitting position. He gave himself a few seconds for his head to acclimatize before he swung his feet to the floor. Standing, Meg offered him her hand. He grasped it and she steadied him as he pushed to his feet. "Thanks."

"You have everything you need, McCord?"

"For now, yes. Let me do some research and I'll get in touch in a couple of days."

"Hopefully we'll have more time than that," Meg said. "But if the killer gets wind of the fact that local law enforcement is tying the deaths together, we may not have long to wait." She met McCord's eyes. "I'd prefer it's not another death pushing this case forward. Let's try to beat him."

CHAPTER 8

Old Copper Road: Built in 1853 to link the copper mines in the Copper Basin of Polk County, Tennessee, and Fannin County, Georgia, to the railroad terminus in Cleveland, Tennessee. The twelve miles of the road that winds through the Ocoee Gorge is known as the Ocoee National Forest Scenic Byway.

Wednesday, April 10, 11:03 AM
Forensic Canine Unit, J. Edgar Hoover Building
Washington, DC

"Meg!"

Meg looked up from her desk and swiveled her office chair around, carefully placing her feet around Hawk, who was sprawled on the floor next to her. Through the glass wall of his office, Meg could see Craig Beaumont on his feet behind his desk, a phone to his ear, his dark head bent.

"What's going on?" Lauren Wycliffe asked. The tall, stylish blonde sat at her desk writing the report from her latest outing with Rocco, her black and white border collie, who was currently snoring beside Lacey under Brian's desk. Brian had just drawn the short straw and stepped out to get them all coffee.

"I'm not sure." Meg stood and stepped over Hawk, who raised his head. "I'm going to go find out. Hawk, stay." She quickly wove between desks to Craig's office. She paused in the doorway with one hand on the jamb.

Craig bent over his desk, the phone pressed to his ear and a pen in his right hand as he quickly made notes. "Chattanooga, got it. I'll get them on that flight. Thanks." He hung up and straightened. "There's been another death in Georgia."

"Is someone closer going to handle it?" Meg asked the question, but considering what she'd heard before Craig hung up, she already knew the answer.

"No. That was Torres. He wants you. Says he understands your concerns about the delay, but there aren't resources available to him."

"But—"

"I know, what about the GBI? He says they can't do it. Maybe they don't have dogs trained and ready to go. Either way, it's you and Brian. Brian!"

"He stepped out for coffee, but he'll be back any second. I'll brief him as we go. What do we know?"

"A little more this time." Craig unbuttoned his suit jacket, sat down in his chair, and picked up a notepad covered with almost illegible scratchings. Hieroglyphics, as Brian once coined Craig's writing. "The victim's name is Gord White, and he's with a construction company. He was at a Tennessee dam to oversee repairs when he was shot with an arrow and killed."

"Same type of arrow?"

"Torres says yes. So you're on your way to Turtletown, Tennessee. I'm going to get you on the flight to Chattanooga that leaves from Reagan in"—he checked his watch—"just over an hour. Grab your stuff and get out there. I'll text you the details."

"Got it. We're off."

Meg strode to her desk. "Hawk, come. Time to go."

"Craig's sending you out?" Lauren asked.

"Yes, Tennessee this time. Same case, though." Meg bent and pulled her go bag from under the desk and double-checked the firearm at her hip. She reached for her phone. "I'm going to text Brian to get back here ASAP, but if he doesn't get the message—" She broke off as Brian came through the door with a cardboard tray of takeout coffees. "You're back. We need to go."

Brian stopped dead. "Why?" His voice was full of suspicion.

"For exactly the reason you're thinking. There's been another killing."

"Damn it. And we're going to be hours behind again." He handed Lauren her coffee and then grabbed his go bag. "Lacey, come." He extended the tray to Meg. "You can drink your coffee in the car." Once she'd taken her cup, he grabbed his and tossed the tray onto his desk.

"Good luck," Lauren called as they jogged out of the office.

We're going to need it.

Wednesday, April 10, 1:32 PM
Ocoee Dam #2
Turtletown, Tennessee

Torres pulled his SUV into a parking spot next to several Polk County Sheriff's Office vehicles. "This is it. We're supposed to meet the sheriff and he'll take us to the kill site, which is on private land. You'll go on from there. It doesn't sound like we'll be back here in the short term, so bring everything you need for the search."

"Sounds good." Meg turned in the passenger seat to where Brian sat in the back with the two dogs. "You ready?"

"Let's do it."

They got out of the SUV, gathered their packs, and leashed the dogs; then Torres led them down the parking lot. To their right, US-74 curved along the river bank, wedged in between the waterway and the surrounding Appalachian Mountains. A sheer rock face slanted steeply down to the road, the site of a previous significant rock slide, while a pine forest rose above it on a ridge towering 400 feet over the road. To their left, the Ocoee River pooled peacefully behind a 450-foot-long timber and rock dam, with only a small amount of water snaking down the rocky riverbed thirty feet below the top of the dam on the upstream side. A narrow wood and cable suspension bridge hung over the dam, stretching from bank to bank and leading to a cluster of buildings on the far side.

Brian glanced sideways at Meg as the dogs trotted beside them. "You know it's inevitable we're going to go over that bridge."

Meg studied the narrow bridge with resignation. "Of course we are. Because I'm doomed."

"For this case, you seem to be. You're in the Appalachians. Chances of every search being at ground level is pretty much zero."

"Chances of *any* search being at ground level seems to be pretty much zero."

They moved from the parking lot to a wooden boardwalk leading to the bridge labeled with a large white on blue sign marking it as property of the TVA.

"Hello!"

As a group, they turned to see a man getting out of a Polk County Sheriff's SUV. Tall, lean, gray haired, and in a brown uniform complete with sheriff's badge, he covered the ground to them quickly. "You must be the FBI team. Sheriff Burt Hastings." He held out his hand, and Torres stepped forward to shake it.

"Special Agent Sam Torres. These are FBI handlers Meg

Jennings and Brian Foster and their dogs, Hawk and Lacey."

They shook hands. Meg noticed his gaze quickly dart over her face—she was looking better, but some splotches remained—before dropping down to study the dogs with interest.

"Those are fine-looking animals."

"Thank you," Meg said. "They're also great trackers." She turned to study the dam. "Where was the victim killed?"

"Over there, on the far side of the river." Hastings pointed to several short buildings across the dam.

"The body has been removed, I assume?" Torres asked.

"Yes."

"You left the arrow for the dogs to use for scent?"

Meg knew Hastings's answer simply from his wince. "Pretty much no. There was no way. And I don't think you would have gotten much scent from it."

"You'd be surprised," Meg said. "Why was there no way?"

"Because the shot pinned the victim to the wall of the tram house. Hit with enough force to take him right off his feet and left him dangling there, dead. I doubt he even struggled. From the placement of the arrow, it went through or between his ribs, through his heart, and out the other side before embedding in the wall. He died instantly. To recover the victim, it was either lift the body up and off the arrow, or cut the arrow off right behind the arrowhead, leaving the shaft inside the body, and transport them together. The county coroner wanted it done the second way to preserve the body for autopsy."

Torres grimaced for a second and then controlled his expression into neutral lines. "The coroner will be doing the autopsy? Is he qualified?"

Hastings's laugh had a cynical edge to it. "Hell, no. He's an elected official. He's a construction foreman in his real job but moonlights as the coroner. Most importantly, since it's a federal case, he can order an autopsy by the medical examiner in Chattanooga when there's a suspicious death, which he did. And considering the placement of the arrow, he thought he'd better leave it in the victim." He nodded toward a white panel van in the parking lot. "My crime scene guys are still here waiting to collect everything that's left once you've checked it out and done whatever it is you do to get the dogs started. Just in case there's anything that might be useful for you."

"Thanks," said Meg. "We understand the victim, Mr. White, was here to oversee some repairs to the dam."

"Not the dam. The flume."

"A flume? Like at an amusement park?" asked Brian.

"Only in the strictest sense of the word if you consider a flume a man-made channel to carry water. In this case, that's all it carries. You never heard of the Ocoee Flume?"

Brian shrugged his apology. "We're from DC?"

"That could do it. If you live in this area, you practically live and breathe facts about the flume because it's our most important local landmark. I guess you didn't watch the 1996 Olympics? The white-water kayaking was done upstream from here on our Class III and IV rapids. The flume is a national historic landmark and it got some PR at the time."

"I guess we missed that part of it. Is it going to be important?"

"Might be."

"It's also owned by the TVA?" Meg asked.

"Yup."

Brian exchanged a glance with Meg. "Then you better give us some background on it."

"Sure. It was completed in 1912 and is an eleven-foot-high, fourteen-foot-wide wooden channel that runs five miles from Ocoee Dam #2 to Ocoee Powerhouse #2."

Brian stared unblinkingly. "Why would you run water five miles to the powerhouse? Wouldn't it be easier to have it closer? That's a long distance to move water."

"It is, but you need to be able to drop the water from a height to get energy for power generation, and this dam is only thirty feet high. That'll generate nothin'. Five miles downstream, it drops two hundred and fifty feet to the powerhouse. Come this way."

He led them along the boardwalk and past the gated and screened entrance for the suspension bridge to the walkway on the far side. They stood at the apex of the dam with a calm, level body of water on the upstream side. On the downstream side, the concrete overtopping of the dam dropped in jagged steps down thirty feet to the shallow riverbed below. At the far end of the dam, a gush of water flowed into the river, the remaining river water held back by the dam.

"That's the flume over there." Hastings pointed across to the far bank. "That wooden structure."

Meg tipped her hand over her eyes to shade them from the sun. Just above where river water spewed in a white froth, a wooden structure branched off from the top of the dam to run along the side of the mountain rising above the south side of the river. Long, horizontally stacked planks formed a solid wall running parallel to the river, held in place every five or six feet by vertical staves. A wooden railing topped the structure.

"You said it's made of wood. How does it keep from leaking?" Meg asked.

"Precisely fitted tongue and groove pine that was assembled wet because that's the state where it's waterproof. It's a marvel of engineering and carries over eight hundred million gallons of water per day."

"There's a number that's hard to wrap your head around. White was on-site because of some repairs?" Brian asked.

"He wasn't doing them himself, but was coming to check out some concerns about leaks."

"I thought it didn't leak."

"Normally it doesn't, but you see the location? The flume is built into a rocky shelf carved out of the slate hillside. Any system built around a mountain, be it roads, bridges, or flumes, has to deal with the risk of rock slides. They happen a lot around here." He turned and looked up at the sheer rock wall behind them. "We have to do a lot of road clearing." His gaze slid back to the flume. "When a rock slide hits a wooden structure like the flume, it can do catastrophic damage. In 2014, the flume got knocked out for about eight months. A previous rock slide did considerably more damage and left the whole area highly unstable. It took years to get the flume and power generation going again."

His hands resting on the railing, Torres studied the structure across the water. "That's a long time to be without power generation. Is that one of the reasons for the new dam project?"

Hastings nodded. "So they say. They have no intention of closing down the flume—when it functions, it creates a significant amount of energy for the TVA—but they need a contingency plan for when it fails, which seems to be every few years lately."

"White was somewhere on the flume when he was killed?" Brian asked.

"No, he never made it that far. The repair site is about a mile downstream. He was over there"—he pointed at a squat white building on the far side—"getting ready to get into the tram that runs up and down the flume. One shot was all it took."

Torres stepped away from the railing. "Can you take us across? I'd like the dogs to get started ASAP."

"You bet. Follow me. The bridge is single file, though you might be able to manage the dogs beside you." Hastings led them to the gate for the bridge, pulled a key out of his pocket, unlocked the gate, and opened it wide. "Go on through. I'll follow behind and lock the gate after us."

Torres stepped through first. "Is anyone on the far side?"

"I left one officer to watch the site, but pulled everyone else out. Once you mentioned dogs, I wasn't sure if having guys on-site would contaminate the scene or confuse the scent, so after we removed the body, I thought it best to pull all but one out."

Meg went through the gate, Hawk heeling at her knee. "Thanks, that's helpful."

She and Brian stopped at the edge of the bridge. The narrow suspension bridge stretched all the way across the dam, hanging roughly twenty feet in the air. Heavy metal cables were anchored in the rocky hills on either side of the river, supporting the host of smaller cables that braced the wooden floor of the bridge. Three horizontal cables ran parallel to the decking all the way to waist height, supplying a hand rail and providing safety in case of a slip on the bridge.

Meg scanned the bridge, taking in the width. "There's no way to go two abreast. I'm going to take Hawk off lead."

"Ditto." Brian bent and unsnapped Lacey's leash.

"Agent, why don't you go first," Hastings said from behind as he relocked the gate. "I'll bring up the rear. Just be warned ahead of time, especially with this much foot traffic, the bridge really bounces. But it's solid. It won't give way."

"Terrific," Meg muttered.

"It's not that high," Brian murmured. "You'll be fine."

"I'm going even if I'm not fine. I'll go after Torres, send the dogs after me, then you come after them."

"Go get 'em, Tiger."

Meg gave him a pointed look, then stepped out onto the bridge about ten feet behind Torres. "Hawk, come." She turned to make sure Hawk followed her out onto the bridge and then faced forward, gripping the twisted metal top cables alternately in each fist as she moved forward. The first few paces were stable, the wood steady under her hiking boots, but once she got about fifteen feet out, the motion started. What began as a gentle wave soon turned into an elastic bounce from not just her own footsteps, but the group as a whole.

It made her stomach pitch and she almost felt like she was floating, taking each step with the bridge decking ending up at a different height than she anticipated when she put her foot down. She glanced to her right, looking out over the dam to the rock-strewn riverbed several stories below.

Undulating bridge aside, they made good time over to the far side of the river, and Meg stepped off the bridge onto a small concrete pad with an audible sigh of relief. She knelt down to snap Hawk's leash on and stayed there for a few seconds longer than needed as she got her legs under her again. Then she stood and studied her surroundings.

They were beside the small control house situated right over the flume gate, where a small amount of water was allowed through the dam to spill out over the nearly dry riverbed. Ahead of them, a slightly larger structure sat at the head of the flume.

"Where was he killed?" Torres asked.

"Here." Hastings led the way across a short steel bridge over the spillway and onto a larger platform behind the second building. A set of stairs carried them down a level

to the space under the building where a single sheriff's officer stood keeping watch over the site. The platform
under their boots was constructed of wooden planks built
around a set of railway tracks that entered the space,
dead-ending just in front of a large, bright yellow buffer
stop. A yellow tram, with likely enough room for at least a
half-dozen people, sat at the end of the track.

Meg looked down at Hawk. He stood ramrod still, his
body a straight, alert line from nose to tail, pointing to the
corner of the building past the tram.

He can smell the death scene.

"Hawk, find," she said quietly. She let him lead her to
the site of the murder just inside the concrete pilings.

Blood had streamed down the wall to pool in an ob-
scenely large puddle. The arrowhead was lodged into the
wall, with only a very short section of shaft protruding before abruptly terminating.

"Definitely a heart shot." Brian's voice sounded behind
her. "It looks like he bled out onto the floor."

"Not totally, but that's likely about half his blood volume." Meg studied the little that was visible of the arrowhead. "We won't be able to get the dogs close enough to
try to scent it without them wading through the blood.
And the rest of the arrow is gone. As if being hours late
wasn't already a big enough disadvantage."

"Hey, buck up. Our dogs have skills. Don't under-
estimate them."

"You're right. We just need to get them started and
they'll be fine." She took a step back, studied the arrowhead, and then turned 180 degrees to follow the straight
path it must have flown.

The tracks spread out in front of them, running along
the river bank for several hundred feet before banking to
the left. A steep slope, heavily treed in the bright green of
new spring growth, rose hundreds of feet above them. Her

gaze tracked up toward the peak, down again, and then back to the arrow. She stepped toward it, lining her index finger up with the shaft, but not touching it.

Her finger ran parallel to the floor.

She spun around. "The shot came from this level. The shooter wasn't in the hills, he was . . . on the tracks?"

"On top of the flume," Hastings stated. "That's how I read it, too."

"Ballsy," Torres said. "The shot that killed Hubbert was through the trees and over a gully. We assumed the shooter was wearing camouflage, because no one saw him. One of the responding officers was Georgia State Patrol Captain Wilcox. He seems to know a thing or two about bowhunting, and he was impressed with the skill of the shooter. Said it came in from about a hundred yards away. If we assume about the same distance here . . ." He stared down the wooden structure of the flume.

"That's almost all the way to the bend in the track," Hastings said. "That's a hell of a shot if that's true."

"We'll take the dogs out there and we'll find out for sure if that's where the shot originated from. If so, we'll track from there. We'll call you from wherever we end up."

"Signals can be touch and go around here," Hastings said. "You might not get through with your cell phone."

Brian patted the pack on his back. "We have our satellite phones. We'll get through one way or the other."

"Good."

"Ready?" Brian waited for Meg's nod. "Let's go, then. If it's just a matter of running along the top of the flume, this won't be that hard."

"Hang on a second." Hastings made a grab for Brian's arm as he moved to step out into the sunshine. "This isn't going to be as easy as you think."

"No?" Brian studied the track. "It looks straightforward. Is the structure not secure?"

"It's secure, but there's less of it than you think. Follow me."

Hastings stepped out into the light and strode down the wooden planks between the tracks. The first twenty or thirty feet was about twenty-five feet wide, likely to allow for the loading of people and materials into rail vehicles. But after that, the platform narrowed down to only fourteen feet across, resting directly on top of the flume. More terrifyingly, shortly after that, the platform simply disappeared to reveal the churning waters of the flume below.

The bottom dropped out of Meg's stomach as she stared down in horror. The top of the flume was open to the elements, only crossed every five or six feet by beams attached to the external support staves. The railing ran along the length of the flume, and beside it ran paired 1" × 5" boards nailed to the cross beams, the only way to traverse the rushing water of the flume beneath.

She instinctively pulled back on Hawk's leash with clammy hands, her gut instinct to protect her dog. He resisted for only a moment, his head already in the search, which meant forging ahead.

How were they going to manage running along the top of a five-mile flume when they each had only ten inches of path to balance on? And there was no way she could tie herself to Hawk, or vice versa. One misstep, one wobble, one second of faulty balance and you'd be in the raging water. You could try to hold on to a cross beam, but it's doubtful anyone would last for long against that kind of current. And if you let go and were floating down the flume, you wouldn't be able to keep your head above water without risking a crushing, fatal blow against a cross beam. Yet to stay in the water meant death by drowning in the strong, sucking current, for human or dog. The water had to be ice-cold, but on the bright side, hypothermia wouldn't be a concern. You wouldn't live long enough to freeze to death.

Meg met Brian's gaze and saw the same foreboding in his eyes.

"To follow the suspect this way means a pretty risky run over wet, slippery boards. Can you follow alongside on the slope?" Hastings asked.

"We have to follow the direct trail the dogs pick up. If that's along the flume, then that's where we need to go. If he shot from the hills beside the flume, then we have a mountain search." Meg studied the water where it flowed from under the wooden platform. "And there's only one way to find out." She stepped back a few paces. "Hawk, come." She knelt down and unsnapped his leash. Then, reaching under him, she unbuckled his work vest and pulled it off. She held out the vest to Torres.

Stepping forward, he took it. "What's this?"

"I don't want to carry the extra weight of the vest for what could be a long search, so I need you to hold on to this for me. If there's any chance that Hawk gets into the water, I don't want the bulk of the vest weighing him down. It's likely a fatal dunking, but on the off chance he can stay afloat, I need him as buoyant as possible." She stood and faced Brian. "Maybe it's a good idea to throw the net wide at the beginning. If you and Lacey find a way to get onto the peak over there"—she pointed at the rising hills to her left—"we could cover both—"

"No."

Meg froze at the cutting tone in Brian's voice. "What do you mean no?"

"I'm not sure how to make it clearer. No, we aren't going to cover the safer route. No, the hill isn't where the shooter shot from; we both could see that from the angle of the arrow. No, you're not going to tell me Hawk is a water dog, so if he goes in, he'll do better than Lacey.

Just . . . no." He crossed his arms over his chest and Meg could see there would be no shifting him.

She sighed. She knew he was right, that they'd do better as a team, but her gut instinct was always to protect, even if the other person didn't want it. And Brian was not about to take the easy way out. "You take the right side then, and I'll take the left."

"Damn straight." Brian quickly removed Lacey's vest, handing it to Torres as well. "We'll call you when we have news. But, like the last time, this could take a while."

Torres nodded and clutched both vests against his suit jacket. "Good luck."

"Stay safe," Hastings called.

"We will." Meg seated her pack more firmly on her shoulders, checked her dog—Hawk stood alert, clearly waiting to start—and took a deep breath. "Ready?"

Brian stood poised beside Lacey and gave her a nod. "Ready."

She bent and lay a hand on Hawk's sun-warmed back. "Hawk, find."

Her heart in her throat, she watched her dog step out onto the narrow boards over the rushing water.

CHAPTER 9

Ocoee: Built by the Eastern Tennessee Power Company starting in 1910, the Ocoee powerhouses, dams, and flume comprise an ambitious hydroelectric project constructed entirely in a twelve-mile stretch of the narrow Ocoee River Gorge. Besides being a national historic site, it was also the site of white-water events for the 1996 Atlanta Olympics.

Wednesday, April 10, 1:57 PM
Ocoee Flume
Turtletown, Tennessee

Head high, Hawk stepped confidently onto the boards. Rather than head-down tracking, he was using a head-up scenting technique, searching for a scent before he put his head down to follow it.

Meg guessed they had to cover at least another fifty or sixty yards before they'd come near the spot where the shooter stood to make his kill. If they went much farther than that, they'd have to rethink the shot and find a way off the flume, or retreat and start again from the beginning.

But Meg's gut told her they were on the right track.

Meg followed about two feet behind her dog, miming a

runway model, carefully placing her boots along the center seam between the two wooden planks to give herself as
much room between her feet and the precarious drop into
the flume waters as possible. She walked with both arms
extended, as if treading a balance beam, keeping her left
hand hovering over the railing at her side. She didn't want
to run her fingers over it—that would lead to multiple
splinters—but she needed to be able to grip the wood for
support in case of a stumble or false step. A quick glance
at Brian confirmed he did the same, and the dogs carefully
watched their steps. Both dogs wanted to push the pace,
but their handlers ordered them to keep the pace slow. It
was all about safety before speed during this search.

It was just before the flume curved to the left to disappear from view that Meg caught Lacey's change in attitude. Her tail shot up and her head dropped toward the
pooling scent. Turning her attention to her own dog, Meg
waited to see if he caught it as well.

Hawk's steps slowed and his nose dropped toward the
planks. *Got it.*

"Hawk, stop. Brian."

"Yup, they have it. Lacey, stop."

As one, they both turned to look down the rail line. In
the distance, the tram house was a straight line from their
current position.

"He shot from here," Brian stated. He looked over his
shoulder, down toward the curve. "And then escaped via
the flume. Lacey's on the outside edge, so she caught the
scent drifting around the corner first. It took Hawk a few
more feet to enter the scent cone."

"That's how I read it, too. We need to let Torres know.
If he's on this track, he may follow it to the end. Torres
and Hastings need to get men out to the other end of the
flume and any middle access points between." She pulled
her satellite phone out of her pack and speed-dialed Torres.

"Sam Torres."

"It's Meg." She looked down the track to where Torres still stood with Hastings. Raising one hand over her head, she waved and he waved back. "We have the trail."

"Excellent."

"Can you find out from Hastings how many locations along the flume can be driven to?" She listened as Torres asked her question, and heard Hastings's indistinct response before Torres's voice came back on the line. "He says two. This end and the powerhouse at the far end. If anything is needed in between those two points, they bring it in by rail over the flume."

"Okay. Can you ask Hastings to get some men out to the far end? I don't know if the shooter's going to stay on the flume for the entire distance, but if he does, we need men there to apprehend him just in case he's still out here. I don't know how long it will take to run the entire flume, but it can't be done quickly without risking your life, so we may still have a chance."

"I agree, we at least have to try. We'll make sure it gets done from this end. You just worry about the search from yours."

"Will do. Thanks." She ended the call, tucked the phone in her bag, and seated it squarely over both shoulders. "Now we can really get started." Grasping the railing, she squatted down behind her dog, balancing on the balls of her feet. "That's it, boy, have you got the scent? Good. Now find him, Hawk. Find." She pushed to her feet as Hawk moved forward, his pace faster. Swallowing her rising discomfort with the search, Meg glanced down at the eddies and froth shooting under the cross beams. Was it moving faster here, or was that her imagination?

She forced her gaze up to her dog, watching his sure steps, and took a little fortitude from him. Head up and eyes bright, he loved the hunt and was damned good at it.

The flume curved around the bend, following the bank of the river. The water became rougher at the curve as the direction changed and splashes rose out of the flume to soak the planks under their boots. They slowed, picking their way with more care until the waters calmed slightly.

Meg glanced at Brian, whose eyes were cast down at his feet and at his dog. "Years ago, when we were first considering search-and-rescue as a career, seriously, *what were we thinking?*"

"Some days, honestly I don't know." He tossed her an eye roll and then went back to watching his dog and his feet.

As they moved along the flume, they learned how to manage it. They learned that every half mile or so, the platform extended from side to side for about eight or ten feet, allowing them a respite from the high-stress balancing act and giving them a place to safely catch their breath and water the dogs. They learned that straightaways were safest and driest, with the water flowing swiftly but relatively calmly, and that the curves in the track held hidden dangers. Those sections caused the deepest eddies and highest splashes as the water navigated turns that followed the natural landscape, soaking the walkways for large sections. Terrifyingly for Meg, they learned that deep gullies ran down from the peak, causing the flume builders to have to build bridges across them. As the landscape around them dropped, those bridges were suspended higher and higher, and Meg's fear of falling into the flume waters was compounded by the fear of going over the railing and dying hundreds of feet below.

Normally, if Meg and Brian were out for a morning jog together with the dogs—as they often did because staying in shape was a necessity in their job and misery loved company—they'd jog a comfortable mile in about ten minutes, aiming for five miles in total. But here, balanced on the top of the flume, they were at best managing only half that speed in a careful, power walk. But after nearly an hour, while the dogs still firmly had the scent, the high tension of the search was beginning to wear on all of them.

"How you doing?" Brian asked, still breathing a little more heavily than usual as he poured water into a collapsible bowl for Lacey where she stood beside Hawk in the middle of the platform.

"I was doing better when we weren't this high up." Meg gratefully dropped her go bag on the planks and dug out water for both herself and Hawk.

"Well, you know what they said about power generation. It needs height." He looked out over the railing on his side and down, down to the river below. "We must be up about two hundred feet at this point."

"If two hundred and fifty feet is the highest point, then we must be about three-quarters of the way there." She drank half a bottle of water, then backhanded the moisture from her lips. "Dogs are saying we're still on track, though. I can't believe this guy went all this way on foot. There have been a couple of places where he could have bailed into the trees, but he didn't."

"I bet it's because of the terrain around the flume. Look at the progress we're making even on this difficult and dangerous track. We can keep up an even pace on a flat surface—"

"As long as we don't fall in," Meg interjected.

"Good point. But to cover the same distance at ground level would take a hell of a lot longer. And distance seems to be the operative term. This one doesn't pick killing grounds with an easy escape route."

"Possibly because he thinks he'd be more easily tracked if he keeps a getaway car nearby. With a long trek, there are more ways to lose pursuers."

"Unless you do it on a closed track like this." Shading

his eyes, Brian peered up the rail line. "He took a real risk coming here. What if we'd been right behind him? We might have actually seen him and called in backup to either meet him at the far end or get onto the flume at that end and bookend him."

"Maybe he heard K-9 assistance is coming from out of town and he didn't feel the need to rush? Or maybe he never heard we were following him on Stanley Gap Trail? Maybe he's cocky as hell and thinks he's smarter than us and the dogs. It's impossible to say." Meg packed away the water bottles and Hawk's bowl. "Ready?"

"Ready."

They separated again at the edge of the platform to continue tracking. Meg felt more confident now and she suspected Brian felt the same. Both were more secure on the narrow path, and they followed the dogs at their pace instead of trying to slow them down for safety's sake. They were narrowing in on the scent, and the dogs' natural instinct was to run faster as they closed in on the target.

The next corner was the sharpest turn so far as the flume abruptly banked left. Water crashed into the far side, arcing over the crossbeams and boards in drenching splashes.

"Hawk, slow. This is getting slick. Slow." Meg grabbed the railing as her boot slipped fractionally, dimly registering the green tinge highlighting the planks as if some type of algae coated the boards with slime. She clutched at the wood, keeping herself upright, and was about to tell Hawk to stop so they could ensure they crossed safely, when out of the corner of her eye she saw Brian start to go over backward, his arms windmilling madly.

"Brian!"

His feet went out from under him and he hit the planks on his back, the bulk of his backpack rolling him sideways toward the open water.

One hand still clamped to the railing, Meg stretched out as if she could reach him across the ten feet separating them, but all she could do was watch with her heart in her throat as Brian desperately threw himself toward the railing post. His hands scrabbled, then clamped on, but the movement swung his body out, and the current grabbed at his boots with greedy hands, clawing him into its depths. His legs were pulled in right up to mid-thigh, and only his desperate grip on the post kept him from being sucked under completely.

"Brian, hold on! Athena, pull!"

The German shepherd immediately sank her teeth into the shoulder of Brian's jacket, bracing and pulling with all her might.

Save him.

Meg looked around frantically for a way to the other side of the flume, but there was no way she could traverse a cross beam without falling in herself, and she was no good to him dead. She looked back, then ahead, quickly calculating distances. The platform ahead was closer.

"Talon, down! Stay!"

Hawk instantly went down to the boards, his head sunk between his front paws.

No other way.

Meg took a step back and then leaped, pushing off the slick boards, her hand extended, fingers reaching for the far railing as she launched herself over her dog to reach the planks on his far side. She landed, slid, recovered with the help of the railing, and then was running, one hand on the rough wood, no longer caring about splinters. It took almost twenty precious seconds to reach the platform, where she shrugged out of her pack, dropping it on the wooden boards between the rail tracks because she couldn't risk being overbalanced by its weight, and then ran as fast as she could up the planking on Brian's side.

Ahead, Lacey was desperately trying to hold on to Brian, but he was slipping from her grasp. Meg was only about twenty feet away, but it was almost as if everything moved in slow motion as Brian pulled out of Lacey's grip and then lost his battle against the current, his fingers ripping from the post with a scream.

"*NO!*"

With one final desperate attempt to save himself, Brian twisted as he was sucked into the flume and lunged forward, not aiming for the crossbeam, but for the metal rail track on his side, jamming his forearm under it to wedge himself into the corner of the track and the crossbeam, buying himself several crucial seconds.

"Brian, hang on! Athena, move!"

Lacey got out of the way, giving Meg space, as if instinctively knowing Brian was out of reach to her, but maybe the human could still save him.

Meg quickly summed up the situation. Brian was submerged in the flume up to mid-chest, but his arms and shoulders were still out and his head was above water. His jacket, punctured by Lacey's teeth, was in reach, but so was his go bag, the sturdy black handle rising from the top of the bag behind his neck. The go bag that Brian always buckled over his chest to give the heavy pack stability during long searches, so there was no way for her to yank it out of the water without bringing Brian with it.

There was hope.

Meg skidded to a halt, sat down on the planks, and wrapped her legs around the adjacent railing post for leverage and to anchor herself. She wrapped both hands around the handle of Brian's bag and pulled with all her might. "Try to . . . help me if . . . you can," she ground into his ear through clenched teeth. "Only way to . . . get you . . . out."

"Trying." Brian's voice was a low thread of exhaustion

over the roar of the water. He had to be drained from fighting the frantic pull of the frigid water.

But he had to keep trying. Meg refused to consider any other outcome. She put her back into it, her biceps screaming at the effort, drawing Brian closer, fighting the current, using her lower body as leverage, and keeping her legs wrapped about the pole to keep him from taking her with him to a watery death.

One inch.

Hold and gasp in a breath.

Pull.

Two inches.

Hold. Another breath.

Four.

Again.

A sound that started as a groan and morphed into a scream was ripped from her chest as she screwed her eyes shut and pulled with everything she had. She felt Brian fumble for the far side of the planks, heard his own strained cry, and then his weight crushed down over her, pinning her to the boards, his cheek against hers and one arm wrapped around her head, pressing it to his shoulder.

For long seconds, all she was conscious of was the pounding of her heart, the sawing of their breaths, and the iciness of the water seeping from his clothing into hers where their legs intertwined.

Brian finally shifted his weight to rise up on one elbow over her. His face was ashen, his green eyes wide, and his lips parted as he panted, trying to get his breath back, but the corner of his mouth quirked into a smile that was a pale echo of his usual humor. "You know, if I was into women, this could be embarrassing." But his eyes went serious as he looked at the frothing waters. "I thought it was game over for a few seconds there."

Meg reached up to squeeze his shoulder. "Me too. I wasn't going to accept that."

"No, you weren't." He dropped a kiss on her forehead. "Thanks, pal. Not quite sure how to pay you back for that."

"No payment required. How many times have you saved my ass? The house collapse in Virginia Beach comes to mind, just to start. But if you're done manhandling me"—she gave him a playful, but gentle shove—"how about you get off me?"

It took a few seconds of careful maneuvering to ensure that neither of them ended up in the water, but then they were both on their feet.

Looking across the chasm, Meg took in Hawk, still lying on the boards as commanded, and gave him the hand gesture to follow along with them. "Hawk, up. Let's go."

Keeping her eyes on her dog and one hand gripping the railing periodically, they made their way to the platform and Meg's bag. Once on the wider area of safety, Brian sank down to his knees, his hands braced on the planks on either side of them, his head bowed, and just breathed.

Meg rubbed her palm over his shoulder. "You okay?"

Brian tipped his head back to squint at her. "Yeah, just taking a minute. My legs need to warm up a bit. They're clumsy from the cold."

"Clumsy is the last thing we need up here." Meg knelt down beside him, unsnapped the clasp of his bag over his chest, and slid it off. Digging through it, she found one of his energy bars, unwrapped it, and handed it to him. "Eat this, and take a few minutes. The shooter is so far ahead of us that a few more minutes won't make a difference. Cold, weak legs will be a hazard, and we're not doing that again." Meg dove back into the bag, found Lacey's high-energy treats, and gave her a handful, then did the same for Hawk out of her own bag. She grabbed an energy bar and peered down the flume as she ate. "We must only have another mile or so to go. If he went all the way to the power station and was through before Hastings could get men there, it's going to be a whole lot easier for him to lose us."

"Yeah. There's going to be traffic going in and out of the power station, and that means roads. He could have left a car in the power station parking lot. If so, he'll be long gone by now and there won't be anything to track."

Meg drummed her fingers on the platform in frustration. "Flying back and forth isn't working. It puts us behind and we're taking risks because we're trying to fast-track the searches. Craig and I are going to have a talk when we're done with this search. I mentioned it to him before, but it's time to bring it up again." She took another bite of her bar.

Brian jammed his wrapper in his bag and pushed off the platform to stand, marching in place for a few steps as if testing new legs. "Okay, I'm warmer now and don't feel so stiff." As Meg stood, he met her eyes, his glinting with a stubborn determination. "Let's go get this son of a bitch."

CHAPTER 10

Jistu: Trickster Rabbit is the central character of many Southeastern Indian tribal legends.

Wednesday, April 10, 2:15 PM
Ocoee Flume
Turtletown, Tennessee

Meg had a few moments of terror when they hit their highest bridge yet.

They'd passed over several sections where the flume builders had supported the structure over the span of a valley, and the rock wall on Meg's side dropped away. She gritted her teeth and pushed on through those sections, but they'd been blessedly short.

This one was not.

The flume rose high in the air on spindly-looking metal legs, although logically she knew they supported several tons of wood and water, and the weight of two handlers and two dogs wouldn't add any significant strain. But she'd found security knowing the rock face was on her left side, even as the water raged to her right. Now there was death to the left with a 250-foot drop, as well as death to the right. She knew Brian had been contending with that scenario for a while, but Brian didn't mind heights.

Meg hated heights, as her knotted stomach and flop sweat attested.

"Brian, I need to slow down a little." She kept her eyes fixed on her feet and her grip white-knuckled on the railing. Her heart rate was back up where it was when she was trying to pry Brian out of the water, and she was fighting to keep from hyperventilating.

"That's okay," he called back. "Take your time. Keep your eyes on the boards."

"Trust me, I'm not looking anywhere else."

When the rock finally closed in on her left side, Meg relaxed somewhat. *Now it's just the death trap of the flume.*

They went about fifteen feet farther when Hawk's pace slowed and he whined.

Meg's head snapped up to stare first at Hawk, then over to Lacey. Lacey's head was up, scenting the air. Trying to find the trail?

"They've lost it," she called to Brian. "Hawk, stop." As her dog froze in place in front of her, she looked around. "The scent has been uninterrupted so far, but now it's gone?" Clamping both hands on the railing, she turned to look behind them. There was only one possibility. "He went over the side?"

Brian peered down over the railing on his side. "Not this way, he didn't. Not unless he was suicidal. There's nowhere to go on this side. Your side?"

"Let me look. Hawk, sit. Stay." Reversing direction, she walked back along the flume, carefully studying the rock wall beside her until she found a section that came close to the flume in a sequence of rocky steps. The rocky outcrop led backward, toward the crevasse they'd just crossed, and from there, out of sight. "We're going to have to bring the dogs to confirm, but I think he went over the railing here and climbed down."

"He must have known that as soon as the body was discovered, the authorities would be out looking for him. And, just like we requested, officers would be sent to the power station end of the flume. He must have had another way down in mind right from the start."

"We need to make sure. Let's take the dogs to the next platform, turn them around, and bring them both back on this side. See if they confirm the theory."

It took them a few minutes to cover the distance, re-arrange themselves, and get back, Hawk followed by Meg, then Lacey followed by Brian. The handlers could tell the minute the dogs walked into the scent cone and, with a grim nod of acknowledgment, leaned over to look at the rocky getaway.

"There is no way in hell to get the dogs down this slope," Brian stated. "It's going to be a climb even for us. It may be a waste of time, but I'll follow him."

"You? On your own?"

Brian's look was pointed. "That's a damned steep slope, a lot of it rocky, going down a few hundred feet. How are you going to feel about that?"

Meg's shoulders slumped "Crappy."

"And we both can't go or we're abandoning the dogs. Can you manage them both?"

"Of course. Lacey will listen to me, and they'll work to-gether like the pros they are."

"Then you take both dogs and continue on to the power house. It's maybe another half mile or so. Then when you're back on terra firma, call my sat phone. If I have a hand free, I'll answer. If I don't, I'll call you as soon as I can."

"I don't like the idea of you dealing with that climb alone. What if you fall? Accidents happen."

"They do. If I don't appear from under that big-ass bridge, you'll know the path I was taking and will send help up to retrieve my broken body."

"Brian . . ." The word was a growl.

"Kidding, babe. We've only got the two choices. We either both head for the powerhouse, or we split up here. There's a very good chance that without the dogs following his scent, I won't have a hope in hell of tracking him, but I have to try. Chasing him down put me in the goddamn drink. And nearly in the morgue."

Meg recognized that Brian wanted a little of his own back and respected him for it. "Okay. But be careful. You kill yourself down there, you're going to answer to me."

He flashed a grin at her nonsensical statement. "I'll keep that in mind, although you may have to get in line behind Ryan." He pulled Lacey's leash out of his bag and passed it to Meg. "You'll need this later, but I'll hold on to my pack. You won't be able to manage two packs, and you've still got the rest of the flume to navigate. *You* be careful. What you're doing isn't without risk, either."

"I know."

"How are you going to manage the two dogs?"

"We'll stay on the same side. I'll send Hawk through first, then Lacey, then me. We'll go slowly and carefully. We're not following any specific trail now and can opt for the safest route. Off you go."

"Yes, boss." Brian carefully climbed over the railing and then stepped off the outside wall of the flume onto the rocky ledge.

"See any boot prints? Any sign he went through here?" Meg asked.

"Nothing. Too rocky. Okay, here I go."

Meg waited for several minutes as Brian negotiated the rocky outcrops and trunks of stubborn trees that somehow managed to take root in the minimal soil. With a final wave, he disappeared, dropping below her sight line.

She faced the dogs. "Okay, team. It's just us. Back to the next platform so you can turn around, then it's forward ho to the powerhouse."

It was another twenty minutes before she got to a maintenance platform, complete with outbuildings on the hill to her right, and she and the dogs could step off the flume. Several Polk County Sheriff's vehicles were parked nearby, and she could see more down below at the power station. Farther along the hill, the flume navigated its final path before its contents were split between two massive blue-green pipes that ran straight downhill into the power house and from there back into the Ocoee River.

She called Brian, who didn't pick up but called three minutes later. He was down at river level and there was no sign of the suspect.

"How did he get away?" Meg asked. "There's no bridge across the river until here at the powerhouse."

"No, but there are a couple of places where the river was narrow enough and shallow enough to ford."

"You think? Even after the spring rains?"

"It looks like most of that water is diverted into the flume. If anyone ever uses this area for white-water rafting, they could only do it by opening the spillway and putting power generation on hold. Right now, there are some definite shallow areas. Shallow being relative. It's maybe mid-thigh. And since I'm already wet, I'm going to go through myself."

"Cross and then stay where you are. I'll get one of the deputies to pick you up; then we'll meet with Torres."

"I'll be here. Just look for the wet, muddy hitchhiker standing by the side of the road."

One quick phone conversation later, one of the sheriff's deputies loaded Meg and the dogs into his SUV and they were driving down the hill to the bridge leading to US-74 and Brian.

Meg sat back in the passenger seat as the river came closer, her mind racing.

It was time to call Craig.

They needed a new plan of attack.

CHAPTER 11

Unicoi: Comes from the Cherokee word ᎤᏁᎦ meaning "white," and refers to the low-lying clouds and fog that often drape the Southern Appalachians in the early morning or on humid days. The   Turnpike was part of the infamous Trail of Tears, where over 3,000 Cherokee people were forced to march from   Butler near Murphy, North Carolina across the mountains to Fort Cass at Charleston, Tennessee.

Thursday, April 11, 11:31 AM
Lake View Cabins
Blue Ridge, Georgia

"**D**id I hear a door slam?" Brian called from the balcony overlooking the great room.

Seated on the couch, Meg tipped her head up to find him above. "I sure hope so. The only thing we're expecting is the FedEx truck, and it better be that. I'm past needing a change of clothes. These could practically stand on their own."

"Luckily mine got a quick rinse yesterday." With a roll of his eyes, Brian disappeared.

Yesterday, Meg had convinced Craig they needed to stay on-site in Georgia. Whatever the killer's motive, Meg was convinced he wasn't finished, and they were consistently losing the suspect because there was simply too much time between the crime and their arrival on scene. After two fruitless attempts, Craig was now in agreement that the only way the searches were going to work was if they could start as soon as the crime was discovered. Then they might have a hope of tracking the suspect while he was still on the move. Torres was working the case from standard investigatory angles, but the suspect pool was so large, he wasn't making significant headway. As a result, they needed to rely more on the searches, which meant those searches needed to be optimized.

Lying on the couch beside her, Hawk raised his head, ears perked and at attention; he'd clearly heard something, too. Then he was up and off the couch, running for the front door to meet Lacey on her way down the stairs in front of Brian.

"If this is our clothes, I'm calling dibs on the shower," Meg said. "I want a shower, then clean clothes. Then I can deal with the rest of the day."

"There are enough bathrooms in this place, there's no need to call dibs. We can both shower at the same time and I don't think it will make a dent in the hot water." Brian stepped off the stairs to join her in the front hallway as three sharp raps sounded at the front door.

With help of a recommendation from the Blue Ridge Police Chief, Craig had booked them into a large, shared cabin in the mountains for a song. The ski season in nearby North Carolina and Tennessee was over for the winter, and the summer water and climbing season had yet to begin, so rental prices were rock bottom. This way they could stay together instead of booking individual rooms. Also, the cabin had the added advantage of having the outdoor space the dogs required between searches for exercising and the constant training reinforcement needed to keep their skills razor-sharp. Meg was thrilled with the accommodations and had spent ten minutes walking around the cabin, finally stopping on the wide porch to take in the breathtaking mountain and lake views.

If she only had fresh clothes, the place would be perfect. Meg opened the front door of the cabin with Brian at her heels. "Good morning. Are we ever—" Her greeting for the FedEx driver died on her lips.

Clay McCord stood on the doorstep, flanked by suitcases, with Todd Webb behind him, a duffel bag in his good hand and another suitcase at his feet. His left arm was out of the sling, and the previous white gauze bandage on his forehead was replaced by one with a more subtle flesh tone.

Meg blinked twice to ensure she wasn't seeing things. "What are you two doing here?"

"Well, hello to you, too." McCord grinned, picked up a bag in each hand, and walked right in, leaving Webb behind.

"Hey." Webb stepped forward, the lower step putting them eye-to-eye as he gave her a warm smile. "I wasn't sure you'd want us strolling in on you like this on a case. If you're mad, say so, and we'll scram."

"I'm not mad. Just totally surprised. And good luck getting McCord to scram when he has his teeth into a story." Meg laid a hand on Webb's chest and leaned in for a kiss. She pulled away, searching his face, looking for any sign of strain, pain, or exhaustion. She ran her thumb over the lower edge of his bandage. "How are you feeling?"

"I was feeling cooped up before McCord decided we both needed an adventure. Otherwise, I'm okay. Granted, when the shirt comes off, I look like an Arizona sunset, but that'll fade. Give me a hand with your bag? I carried it this far but don't want to push it." He pointed at the suitcase still sitting on the step. "Cara packed that one for you."

Meg stepped past him and picked up the suitcase, needing to give it a solid jerk to lift it. "My God, this is heavy. What did Cara pack?"

"That's why I didn't want to push it. And pretty much everything but the kitchen sink from the conversation she and McCord had last night. She wanted to make sure you and Hawk had everything you needed, especially when you weren't sure how long you'd be here. We had to pay extra for the bag because it was overweight."

"I get that. Go on in."

She let him precede her into the foyer and then closed the door behind them. They found McCord had already gone through to the back porch and stood, hands on the railing, taking in the breathtaking view. They put down their bags beside the couch and followed him outside.

He turned his head as they came out. "This is amazing. How does Beaumont justify spending this much money on your accommodations to the brass?"

"Apparently he doesn't have to. This is low season, and they're willing to have anyone stay for minimal payment to keep the place occupied."

"We'd be happy to occupy it with you if there's room." McCord turned back to the view. "I'd enjoy working with this view."

"I figured that's why you were here."

" 'If the mountain will not come to Muhammad, then Muhammad must go to the mountain.' Once Cara told me you were going to be staying in Georgia to be in place for the next hit, I knew I needed to come down. And Sykes is one hundred percent behind it. When Cara told me she and Ryan were supposed to be packing and shipping clothes and supplies for you, I offered to fly down with it. And since Webb was at loose ends—"

"Getting stir-crazy from cabin fever, you mean," Webb muttered.

"I brought him with me. He can do all his resting and icing and exercises from here as easily as in DC. Cara was happy to take Cody for me while I was gone, so we hopped on a plane this morning and here we are. I'm a simple man; I'll sleep on the couch if need be."

"There are three bedrooms, so you can have the last one," Brian called. He had his suitcase open on the couch and was searching through the contents. He pulled out a small, square green tin and held it up. "I totally forgot to put the Bag Balm for Lacey's paws on the packing list. Leave it to Ryan to know exactly what I need. The man is a miracle." He tossed the tin in the suitcase, flipped the lid closed, and walked through the open French doors to join them on the veranda.

Meg gave Webb's good arm a tug, pulling him toward a pair of wide Adirondack chairs. "Come and sit down. You look tired. But at least the sling is gone."

"Everything is better, but traveling took a little more out of me than I anticipated. Just proof that I still have a way to go." He stroked his fingertips down her arm. "Worth it to see you, though. And McCord is right. It would be nicer to recuperate looking out over mountains and a lake."

"As long as you don't push it." She looked over at Brian. "We only laid in supplies for the two of us."

"That's easily fixed. McCord, vittles run?"

"You're on."

"Don't you want to get settled first?" Meg asked.

"Show me my room and then we'll do a vittles run." McCord rubbed his belly. "Lunchtime is fast approaching, and the breakfast I had at six this morning is a faint memory."

"Grab your bag then, and I'll show you to your room." Brian took one step through the doors and then leaned back out again. "Meg, can I leave Lacey with you? The grocery store might not appreciate her the way I do."

Meg chuckled. "No, probably not. And of course."

After Brian and McCord left, Meg opened her suitcase, unpacked Hawk's things—Cara had included everything from food to favorite toys—and then took Webb and the bags to her room to get settled.

"It looks like you got the master bedroom," Webb commented, noting the private balcony and the huge bathroom with a whirlpool tub that could easily fit two. "How did you swing that? Did you and Brian have to arm wrestle?"

"Apparently all I had to do was save his life." Meg opened one of the wide glass doors to step out onto the small balcony that held two comfortable chairs with a small table between them. "I told him we could flip a coin. He insisted. I gave up fighting him. I do think he got the short end of the stick, though. He saved my life and he got a fraction of a bottle of red wine." She threw her arms wide, encompassing the view. "I save his and get this. Granted, I'm on a case, so I won't get much of it, but still."

Webb came up behind her, wrapping his right arm around her stomach to snug her against him as he rested his chin on her shoulder. "Don't worry, I'll enjoy it for you when you're out working like a dog and I'm here relaxing with my feet up."

She could hear the teasing smile in his voice and gave him a gentle elbow to the gut in retribution. He gave an exaggerated grunt of pain and she laughed. "I'm glad you came. I might not have seen you for weeks otherwise. Who knows how long this case will take?" She turned in the circle of his arm and wound hers around his neck. "I admit I felt guilty about leaving you like that, two days after thinking I was going to lose you. Especially since you decided to go back to your apartment. Cara would have taken care of you, you know."

"I know. But it would have been weird without you there. And, really, by that point I didn't need watching anymore. I don't need anyone to crack the whip to keep me on schedule with my exercises and rehab. No one wants me back in my turnout gear more than me. Being useless is frustrating."

"You're a firefighter and a paramedic; helping is part of your personality. Being forced to sit on the sidelines is uncomfortable."

"It really is. A vacation is one thing. If I was needed, I could spring into action at any moment. Right now, I can't. But I also can't rush it or I could extend being on the DL."

Meg ran one careful hand over his shoulder. "When was the last time you iced it?"

"I'm past icing it. Now I'm at the point where heat helps to loosen the muscles because they're tightening up. I treated it this morning because it's pretty tight first thing, but could use another treatment after the flight."

"Time for another round, then. Go out and sit on the porch while you treat it. I want to grab a fast shower before I get into clean clothes; then I'll be right down."

When Brian and McCord returned, their arms overflowing with bags of food, they found Meg and Webb on the back porch, enjoying the view while Webb used a heated shoulder wrap.

Bracing her hands on the wide arms of the Adirondack chair, Meg levered herself up to stand. "Stay here," she said to Webb, "and get a few more minutes in. I'll give them a hand and then we'll get organized on lunch." She stepped into the house and followed the men into the kitchen, where they dumped the bags on the counter. She stared openmouthed at the sheer volume of food. "Just how long do you think we're going to be here?"

"I have no idea," McCord said, "but we're going to eat well while we are."

"I also picked us up some extra supplies for our packs," Brian said, pointing at one of the bags.

"Good thinking." Meg peeked into the bag and nodded her approval. "Let's get this put away and then have lunch. If we can find a place for it all, that is."

"We got stuff for sandwiches." McCord pulled out several loaves of crusty bread and bags of fresh-cut deli meat. "And while we're eating, I can bring you up to speed on my historical research. Now that I'm here, I'm going to start diving into the players."

Fifteen minutes later, the group gathered around the patio table on the porch, their plates loaded with fat sandwiches. McCord's laptop sat open beside his place setting, a long, text-filled document on-screen.

McCord waggled his beer at Webb. "Brian says he can't have one while he's on duty. You sure you don't want one?"

"Oh, I want one." Webb saluted McCord with his glass of ginger ale before taking a sip. "But I better lay off it for a couple of weeks while I'm recovering from the concussion. Nothing is getting in the way of my getting back on duty."

"Can't blame you for that. I'll have to enjoy it for you, then. Okay, ready to catch up?"

"We are," Meg said. "You said historical research. Of the area?"

"Of the area, though really it was of a much bigger area than this geographically, but I think you're going to see that what happened nearly two hundred years ago is maybe setting the stage for some of what is happening today."

"The Trail of Tears?" Webb asked.

"Or, as one of the Choctaw chiefs more accurately dubbed it, 'the trail of tears and death.' That got softened into the Trail of Tears, probably by whites to make themselves feel better." McCord stopped to take a long draw from his beer bottle.

Webb studied McCord over his glass. "You sound pissed."

"Hard not to be. I don't know . . . maybe it's modern moral sensitivities. Maybe it's knowing how we royally screwed over the Native Americans, but the more I got into this, the more disgusted and angrier I got. Take the political wrapping off and it's nothing short of an ethnic cleansing of indigenous people." Another swig of beer and his bottle thumped down on the table. "Okay, let's all get on the same page.

"Up until the Revolutionary War, populated settlements of Europeans and their descendants were pretty much concentrated along the East Coast. But after the war, and with the establishment of the United States as a country, Americans started moving west. Cities were filling up, and the population was increasing at a substantial rate, going from 2.5 million people in 1776, to 5.3 million in 1800, to nearly 13 million in 1830. All those people had to go somewhere, so they went west, right into the lands occupied by the five eastern tribes—the Cherokee, Creek, Choctaw, Chickasaw, and Seminole. The existing structure of the tribes—thousands of chiefs with no common voice—played against them in dealing with the US government because there was no centralized leadership. The US government could bargain for what they wanted, or just take it. The tribes eventually came to the conclusion that they had no choice but to assimilate into the Colonial way of life to preserve their lands. They were forced to live in both worlds, and part of that was learning to speak English. That's why you will also hear them described as the 'Five Civilized Tribes.' "

"It sounds like they did what they had to do to survive,"

Brian said. "They were outmaneuvered and outnumbered. It was a peaceful way to compromise."

"Some saw it that way; some saw it as a betrayal of their ways and traditions. That's going to be a common theme in this story. Compromise and betrayal and how what some saw as one, many saw as the other. All five tribes were affected, but for simplicity's sake let's stick with the Cherokee since they were involved specifically in Georgia and are relevant to this particular area. They had their own written language, their own constitution, even their own newspaper, the *Cherokee Phoenix*, first published in February 1828. The Cherokee read the writing on the wall and did everything they could to preserve their way of life and their lands. When they wrote their constitution in"—McCord turned to his laptop and scrolled down his notes—"1827, they clearly dictated they were a sovereign nation and, as such, would not cede any of their land to the US government. In return, Georgia's state legislature passed 'harassment laws,' decreeing what the Cherokee could and could not do on their own land. The Cherokee objected to the power grab, but Georgia had a militia to back up their laws, and did so, to the detriment and death of the Cherokee."

Webb swallowed a bite of his sandwich. "Sounds like they were trying to make life so hard for the Cherokee, they'd leave."

"That's absolutely what they were trying to do. When that didn't work, they moved onto the land lotteries. Georgia sent in surveyors to map Native American land, and then the government of Georgia seized it and divvied it up into parcels. White male settlers could register for a chance to win a plot of land in the lottery, only paying fees that covered running the lottery itself. Essentially the land was free. As you can imagine, it was popular, especially for people who had nothing. In 1832, 85,000 people registered for about 18,000 parcels of land."

"They were raffling off land that didn't belong to them," Meg stated.

"That's right. But think about the geography. We all know the end of this story, that they moved the Native Americans out. Then what happened to their lands?"

Brian snapped his fingers and then pointed at McCord. "Cotton. It was all about the cotton trade."

"That was most of it. There was also a small but significant gold rush in Lumpkin County, just south of here, but it was cotton that affected the entire state. The cotton trade was already lucrative, but it became an economic juggernaut with those additional lands and eventually evolved into the world's biggest economy, especially when combined with the slave trade. When you think about it, the Trail of Tears and the history behind it were responsible for what might have been the largest forced migration the world has ever seen—Native Americans to the west and African slaves to North America. It's clear that white Americans would, and did, kill to possess that land. And Andrew Jackson, who wanted every East Coast Native American gone beyond the Mississippi, was happy to oblige that desire for land with the Indian Removal Act in 1830. John Ross, Principal Chief of Cherokee Nation, however, had other ideas."

"John Ross?" Brian pushed away his empty plate and sat back in his chair. "That name seems so . . ."

"British?" McCord supplied. "It sure does. Ross was one-eighth Cherokee, the son of a Scottish father and a one-quarter Cherokee mother. He became a wealthy landowner, cultivating tobacco with slave labor, and a respected lawyer who worked for years in DC. He even founded the city of Chattanooga. But that didn't matter to the settlers. The Native Americans weren't white; that was all that mattered. So John Ross took Georgia to court. All the way to the Supreme Court, in fact. And won."

Webb whistled. "That must not have gone over well."

"It really didn't. More importantly, the judgment invalidated the Indian Removal Act passed by Jackson. But Jackson didn't care and ignored the ruling. After all, he had an army standing behind him to do whatever he wanted. That's when some Cherokee in the Treaty Party, including the influential Ridge family with Major and John Ridge, decided the only way to ensure the Cherokee Nation would survive was to sign the treaty, turn over their lands, and head for the land promised to them in Oklahoma by the US government. That was the Treaty of New Echota, signed in 1835. In it, they traded all Cherokee land east of the Mississippi for five million dollars."

"And the Cherokee agreed with them in signing the treaty?" Meg shook her head in disbelief. "They were giving up everything they'd known."

"They *didn't* all agree. Many Cherokee felt the Ridges had betrayed them. A petition was created and the majority of Cherokee signed it, but Congress never acknowledged it. They just went right ahead with removal. They gave the Cherokee two years to vacate their lands, but many of them refused to leave. Those who didn't were removed after the two years at gunpoint and were held in concentration camps with deplorable conditions, sometimes for months. The first Cherokee to make the trek were dispatched in the middle of the summer heat during a drought. So many died during the march they didn't send the next group until the fall. But that meant the later groups walked through what turned out to be one of the worst winters on record. It was a nightmare. Sixteen thousand Cherokee left to be relocated. At least four thousand of them died en route."

For a moment there was only silence as everyone absorbed those numbers.

"A trail of tears and death, indeed," Brian said quietly.

"That number also doesn't account for any deaths that happened after they arrived, even if it was from the strain of the journey or disease caught on the way. And their arrival wasn't a peaceful one, either. The US government promised them land west of the Mississippi. But once they got there, many of them found there were western tribes occupying that land. The US government had granted them lands it didn't own."

Meg braced her elbows on the table and knit her fingers together, watching McCord pensively over them. "The displaced Native Americans must have had a bone-deep hatred of the US government and the settlers."

"Not only for the government and the settlers, but also for the Treaty Party members responsible for New Echota. The party members paid for that treaty with their lives."

"You mean literally paid?" Webb asked.

"Literally. John Ridge was pulled from his bed in the middle of the night and beaten to death. His father, Major, was ambushed riding home the same day and shot. They were killed by people seeking vengeance for the deaths of their loved ones and for violating Cherokee Blood Law. But now let's get into how the Trail of Tears has impacted modern times. In the 1830s, when the Cherokee were forcibly removed from their land, approximately eight hundred Cherokee remained behind."

"I don't get it," Brian said. "They let some of them stay?"

"Not on purpose. For instance, one of the leaders objected and hid out in the mountains in a cave with his family, avoiding removal. Slowly, word spread among the remaining Cherokee, and those who also wanted to stay joined the growing band of resisters. They stayed in the mountains, living off the land. Finally, the leader made an agreement with the US Army pursuing them—his life for the safety of his whole group. He was executed, but the rest of the group survived by giving up their tribal affiliation and becoming American citizens. Today's Eastern Band of Cherokee Indians are descendants of those resisters. They've been relegated to a small parcel of land called the Qualla Boundary in North Carolina."

"And now they want their land back," Meg stated.

"Can you blame them?"

"Absolutely not. But I don't have a personal stake in this. For those who do, those landowners whose descendants possibly occupy that land, they're not going to look at it the same way. As far as they're concerned, that land is theirs."

"Especially when my research shows a lot of the land raffled off in the lotteries is still owned by the original families."

"Which means they'll be bonded to that land." Meg sat back in her chair and gazed out over the hills as they slid down to the deep blue waters of Blue Ridge Lake. "That would make for a powerful motive to kill."

"The same could be said for the Eastern Band of Cherokee," Webb said. "The ones who moved west lost their land but kept their identity. The ones who stayed in the east lost both their land and their identity, at least initially." He swiveled to McCord. "Do they own Qualla Boundary, or is it reservation land?"

"It's not a reservation. They bought the land and the federal government holds it in trust for them. They're a sovereign nation with their own government, laws, courts, schools, and police force, even including one of the few SWAT teams in western North Carolina that works in conjunction with other local law enforcement bodies when they require assistance."

"And they have an eye to taking back what's theirs."

"They've already had some success at it, too. They recently acquired seventy-six acres of historic Cherokee land in Tennessee that holds a number of Cherokee memorials. And now they're looking at Georgia."

"Except the TVA is getting in their way," Brian said. "You have to wonder what one of the EBCI might do to stop the dam project."

"And what retribution they would consider fair game in the name of Cherokee Nation when it comes to the past." Webb met Meg's eyes. "Considering the toll of the Trail of Tears, you have to know at least some of them would consider a life for a life entirely justified."

A handful of lives to make up for four thousand?

If that was who was responsible, Meg had to wonder how many lives would satisfy that kind of killer.

CHAPTER 12

Coevolution: Social, psychological, and cultural changes that occur in individuals and groups as different cultures learn to coexist.

Thursday, April 11, 4:26 PM
Lake View Cabins
Blue Ridge, Georgia

"Hey, Meg! Torres is here," Brian called from his room. Situated on the east side of the cabin, his room had windows facing three directions, one overlooking the driveway.

Meg glanced at the time on her fitness tracker. "If he needed us, he could have called and we'd have gone into town. He didn't need to come all the way out here." She grabbed a fleece jacket from the end of the bed and shrugged into it. "You okay?"

Webb cracked one eye open from where he lay on the bed. "Absolutely. Go on. I'll stay quiet and out of sight so he doesn't know I'm here."

"You're not the one I'm worried about. I haven't even run McCord past Torres yet. I'd like to introduce him to the idea of McCord before introducing him to the man himself."

"Don't worry, McCord won't endanger a story. He'll stay out of sight until you give him the green light."

"You're probably right, but I think I'll go remind him, anyway."

When Meg passed by McCord's room, she found him seated at a compact desk, working at his laptop. She simply put a finger to her lips. He gave her a salute in acknowledgment and she headed downstairs. She just reached the landing when she heard Brian greeting Torres at the front door. She came down the stairs to find Torres carrying a briefcase and surrounded by dogs. "Hawk, Lacey, let Agent Torres get in the door."

Torres paused in the middle of petting Lacey. "Not to worry. I love dogs. And call me Sam. We may be on the case for a while; no need to stand on ceremony."

"Sounds good to me. We weren't expecting you. We could have come down to Blue Ridge if you needed us."

"I was on my way home for the day, so I thought I'd swing by and touch base."

"You're more than welcome. Come on in. Can I get you anything to drink? Coffee is on, or there's soda or juice."

"Coffee sounds good. I take it with cream, if you have it." Torres followed Meg and Brian into the great room and from there into the kitchen. "Great place."

"We can thank our SAC for that." Meg pulled three mugs down from a cupboard. "Do you live nearby?"

"Just north of Atlanta, in Marietta. It's only about an hour and a quarter from here. But you're making me regret living so close or else I could be put up in a place like this." He ran a hand down Lacey's back where she stood beside him. "Not that I don't want to see my own boys."

"You have dogs?" Meg asked.

"Two Bernese mountain dogs. I love them, but, my God, can they shed."

Meg laughed as she poured the coffee. "Ah, there's a story we're both familiar with. At home every day we vacuum up at least one new dog." She fixed Torres's coffee and handed him the mug, then fixed her own and Brian's. "Why don't we take this into the great room. I'd suggest the porch, but at this time of day it's starting to get a little cool out there."

They settled on the couch and in chairs. Torres opened his briefcase and pulled out a file folder. "I wanted to show you the suspect list I've been working on so you have an idea of what we're up against." He pulled out a pad of paper and dropped it on the coffee table between them. Two columns of names ran from the top of the page to the bottom. Only a few were struck out.

"Whoa," Brian breathed. "That's the list we're starting with?"

"Not quite." Torres flipped over the top sheet to reveal another single-column half-page of names, and then a third sheet with a shorter list. "That's the rest. That I have so far. By no means is this a closed list."

"That's already a lot."

"I'm hoping it will be an advantage to have you here in town to start searches right away. But in the meantime, it's good old-fashioned, shoe-leather detective work." He flipped the pad back to page one and tapped it with his index finger. "And a lot of it."

"Speaking of a lot of detective work, can I make a recommmendation?"

Torres pulled his gaze from the list of names. "Sure."

"I have a contact who could help in this case. He's a whiz with research and one hundred percent trustworthy. And . . . what?" Taking her cue from Torres, who was staring at her with narrowed, calculating eyes, she ground to a halt.

"When I heard you and Foster were coming to do the searches, I looked you both up so I had a feel for who I'd be dealing with. Then I went deeper into agency scuttle-butt and touched base with a buddy who works out of the Hoover Building. Foster, you have a great record and have a fantastic rep. But you"—he turned to Meg—"you have the rep of someone who bends the rules occasionally when it suits her. You've ignored directives and brought in peo-ple who had no right being on a case. And one of those people is a reporter. Is that your great contact?"

Meg didn't look away, making it clear she wasn't em-barrassed by her record. She always stayed firmly inside the law, but she had no regrets about doing what needed to be done to get a case solved successfully and to bring justice to the victims. "Yes, his name is Clay McCord. He's with the *Washington Post.*"

"Why would I be stupid enough to bring a reporter into my case? I know reporters—they can't be trusted not to twist their knowledge to fit an agenda, which they all have. Or not to blow that story wide open, making us look bad and giving suspects the opportunity to rabbit, but also giving them a headline breaking news story."

Meg sat back and took a second to bring her mug to her lips and take a slow sip as her mind whirled, trying to de-cide the best way to handle the discussion. "It sounds to me like you've been personally burned." She kept her tone mild.

"By a reporter? Hell, yes." He put his cup down and a little coffee sloshed over the rim to run down the side of the mug in rivulets. But Torres never noticed. "At the *At-lanta Journal-Constitution.* She had an agenda and used her podium at the paper to shill it."

"What was her agenda?"

"That dirty spics like me have no right going after established good ol' boy politicians, even if they're on the take." Torres's voice cracked like a whip. "It's an opinion a lot of people have in Georgia. They think all Latinos are involved in the local drug trade and are lazy leeches on top of that. I don't need to be called incompetent in twenty-point font by the biggest paper in the state. And I definitely don't need it in a national paper like the *Washington Post*. I don't care about my greater reputation as long as my colleagues know I'm solid, but she nearly cost me my case and nearly lost justice for a victim and his family, which was all I could do for them at that point. It wasn't like I could bring him back. If we hadn't gotten him justice, an already devastated family would have been even more lost." Looking away, Torres raised a palm toward Meg and then sucked in a breath before slowly blowing it out. He dropped his hand limply in his lap and turned to face her. "I'm sorry, snapping at you was uncalled for."

"It's okay. It sounds like you have a history there that goes deeper than one reporter."

"Yeah, it does. In this neck of the woods, if you have a name like Torres and you look Hispanic, assumptions are made before you even open your mouth."

"Does your ethnic background interfere in your cases?" Brian asked.

"It can. Not so much in Atlanta, and that's where the majority of my work is done. But out here, out in the country, there's definitely a difference in attitude. It can make things . . . challenging." He picked up his coffee and took a long sip.

"Do your superiors know?"

"If they read the *Journal-Constitution* they do. But they never hear a word of it from me."

"McCord wouldn't do that to you," Brian said. Torres's

head jerked toward him, but Brian's expression remained relaxed. "I know McCord personally, though not as well as Meg. I've worked with him on multiple cases. He has the nose of a bloodhound and the work ethic of a shepherd." He dropped his hand into Lacey's fur where she lay at his feet and massaged his fingers through it. Lacey let out a deep sigh of contentment. Brian looked up to meet Torres's gaze head-on. "He's saved lives."

"He saved victims. He saved my sister." Meg paused, letting those words sink in. "But more than that, he's a good man and a damned good investigator. He'd be a good addition to the team, would share whatever he knew, and would sit on any and all information until you released him to publish it. And if you had concerns, I bet he'd let you see the article before he submitted it, so you'd feel secure it would do no damage. But I can tell you now, it wouldn't. McCord's only agenda is to tell the story as it happened. He doesn't lie, or embroider. He just reports truthfully. Being inside the story gives him a Technicolor view of the case, so he doesn't need to blow it up. I can also provide FBI references for you—SAC Craig Beaumont, SSA Rutherford from the BAU, and Special Agent Kate Moore. What I can tell you is if McCord doesn't write it, someone else who wants a clickbait headline will. And it's quite possible that person won't be as honest as McCord. Something to think about." Meg sat back on the couch, cradling her mug. "Back to the case . . . who's on this list and who have you talked to?"

"It might be better to say who isn't on this list." Torres picked up the pad of paper and scanned it. "I've tried to break the list into groups, and I've outlined the affected people on this map." He pulled a document out of the folder and then spread it out to lie flat on the table, revealing a large satellite image. Relevant data points were marked on the map. The town of Blue Ridge was a small break in the green patchwork of the hills and valleys west of Blue Ridge Lake. McCaysville and Copperhill were at the top of the map. In between, the Toccoa River meandered through the green valley. Dotted around the valley, Torres had marked cabin rentals and lodges, river-rafting facilities, churches, restaurants, and various businesses, including a tanning salon, a marine repair shop, and a storage facility. "What's not added here is the land the Cherokee are contesting. It centers around the river, so it's essentially included. But so far, they don't have possession of any of the land. They're just arguing for it."

"Are you going to go up to North Carolina to talk to their principal chief?"

"That's definitely on the agenda."

"How far away are they?"

"About two hours."

"So it's not inconceivable one of them could be the killer."

"Not based on geography, no. And I have a parallel line of investigation going as well." He flipped over the first two pages to a much shorter list. "These are the known, skilled bowhunters in the area that I've compiled so far. Not just bowhunters, but elite bowhunters, so it's a slightly shorter list. Granted, there are going to be people with this skill that may not be as well-known. If I was preparing to use my skills to murder someone and it wasn't common knowledge, I'd keep it that way. So, this list is a work in progress."

"Any commonalities between those two lists?"

"Actually, quite a few." At Meg's raised eyebrows, he continued. "You're city folk, so you may not understand how rural people live, but hunting for many of them is a way of life. Depending on where you're hunting in the area, you can't use firearms at certain times of the year.

Like now, for instance, in North Carolina. It's turkey season, so bowhunt all you like, but no firearms are allowed."

"I take it that's not a new law?"

"No, these are the rules the locals have lived with for a long time and they've learned to adapt to them. If guns aren't allowed and bows are, then they learned how to use the bow, especially this close to the state line because lots of people cross state lines to hunt. So it's going to be a big pool."

"We're here with time on our hands. We've both got our laptops now and have time to meet the townsfolk and can still be available for a search at a moment's notice. Let us help with these suspect lists."

"I admit I'm hitting a wall with some of the townsfolk. Some of that is the badge, so you may have the same problem, but some of that is me. I'm really feeling the pressure to winnow these lists as quickly as possible, so help would be appreciated. Before he strikes again."

"I hear you." Meg rose and pulled her cell phone from her pocket. "I'm going to grab photos of your list. We can start looking into some of these names." She took pictures of each page, then the map, checked to make sure her pictures were clear, and slid the papers toward him.

"Thanks. And there's one other thing I wanted to let you know about. After three deaths, there's been some local concern about safety, so the mayor of Blue Ridge is going to hold a town hall on Sunday."

"In town?"

"No, there's no place in town big enough to hold the expected crowd and the potential media circus this could attract. It's going to be at a local vineyard with banquet facilities. She wanted to do it tomorrow, but there's a wedding there, so it's going to be Sunday at seven. I'd like you both to come if it's possible."

"Wouldn't miss it. You're hoping the suspect will attend," Brian stated.

"I would bet three months' salary on him being there. Getting lost in a big crowd of people, watching the chaos and hysteria. Any serial offender would find it satisfying."

"And hard to resist," Meg said. "Part of them would want to stay away, not risk being seen. But a larger part would want to bask in the panicked glow of his efforts. Yeah, he'll be there. And so will we. Text us the details, time and place."

"Will do." Torres packed all the paperwork into his bag and stood. "I'll talk to you tomorrow, then."

Brian and Meg followed him to the door, said their good-byes, and then Brian took the dogs outside.

Meg met McCord on the landing as he was coming down. "I tried. I'm not sure if I made any headway, but I tried."

"I know, I heard every word. Thanks."

"Eavesdropping, McCord?"

"Didn't have to. Cathedral ceilings and an open balcony to the second floor did all the work for me. I never left my room." He cast thoughtful eyes at the ceiling. "I may have made notes. I may have made quite a lot of notes."

"I'd have been shocked if you didn't. I took some photos of his initial lists of names. Do you want to see it?"

"Nope."

"Really?"

"Sure. Up to now, you've been forced into working with me because a bomber was using me as his conduit. Or you talked Beaumont into using me. Or Beaumont talked another agent into using me. This time you hit a wall. I need to show your Agent Torres I'm not only trustworthy, but can be useful to him."

"And you're going to do it without his lists?"

"Absolutely. I'm not dragging you into the middle of this so he knew you gave me the info. I need to find something on my own. Something invaluable. Something he can't find because the locals won't talk to him. If you present him with that kind of information, maybe he'll realize you were right about my agenda." He grinned at Meg. "I'm going to knock his socks off. This case isn't going to have a chance."

CHAPTER 13

Plott Hound: A scent hound with a brindle or black coat and long, drooping ears, developed specifically for hunting big game (bear and boar) in western North Carolina. This large coonhound—the state dog of North Carolina—is one of only four breeds of American origin.

Friday, April 12, 3:21 PM
Blue Ridge Police Department
Blue Ridge, Georgia

"Hey, it's me." McCord's voice came down the line. "Where are you?"

"In Blue Ridge. Brian and I just parked and we're heading in to see Torres at the police department."

"I want to come with you."

"I'm not sure that's a good idea." Meg shot a warning glance at Brian as they crossed the parking lot behind the police station. She mouthed *McCord* in response to his questioning look.

"Trust me, it is a good idea. I'm onto something."

Meg stopped walking, and Brian and the dogs immediately followed suit. "Onto what?"

"Now that would be telling, wouldn't it? I think I have information Torres doesn't."

"We've all been investigating. Not sitting at the computer but walking the streets. Torres has, too. I know we have new info. He must as well."

"But did he go to Suches?"

"To where?"

"Suches. Suches, Georgia. It's about a half hour away. I'm coming in now and I'll be there in about fifteen minutes. Wait for me. But if he hasn't been there, and hasn't spent time talking to Beverley, who is a peach, by the way, then he may not have what I have. And he needs it, whether he likes reporters or not. Wait for me."

"Fine. The police station is at 301 Church Street. We're in the parking lot behind the building. I'll stall Torres and we'll meet you here." She hung up.

"We're waiting on McCord?" Brian asked.

"Apparently he has something Torres needs. It sounds like he's been sweet-talking some gal who gave him some good leads."

Brian laughed. "Yeah, that doesn't surprise me. In he strolls, tall, blond, and blue-eyed, and opens up a charm offensive. McCord's a smart guy, but he doesn't mind leaning on his looks when it gets him what he's digging for." He pulled out his phone, checked the time. "Instead of being ten minutes early, we're going to be ten minutes late. You better tell Torres."

"I'll text him, that way we won't have to make excuses."

"Until you walk in the door with McCord."

"Then I'll have no excuses. And Torres is not going to be pleased."

"I would think not. You worried about that? Makes you look like you're blatantly going against his wishes."

"Me? The handler with the rep of bending the rules to suit her and the case?" Meg rolled her eyes. "No, I'm not worried. McCord does the work and has the results to show it. It's just a matter of convincing Torres of that. We'll give him the chance to hear what McCord has to say and then let him make the call. McCord better have something solid, though, or he'll be finished after a stunt like this."

Fifteen minutes later, McCord pulled into the parking lot in his rental SUV. He got out, grabbed his laptop bag, and then jogged across the lot to the grassy hill, where they waited for him in the sun. "Thanks for waiting. I came as fast as I could."

Meg shaded her eyes with her hand as she looked up at him from where she sat with her legs stretched out in front of her. "This better be good, McCord."

"I think it is. I think it will complement the information he's gathering. How did you guys do?"

"Not bad, but we got a definite vibe from residents and government workers."

"What kind of vibe?"

"The 'federal law enforcement isn't welcome here' kind of vibe. I think the dogs helped because most people love dogs, but it gave me some insight into what Torres is dealing with." She held out her hand to him and he grabbed it, hauling her to her feet. She looked down at Brian, who lay in the sun, his eyes closed, his hands behind his head. "Brian." She nudged him with her boot. "Wake up."

"I'm not asleep; I'm just enjoying the warmth." His eyes opened, then squeezed shut in the brightness. He sat up and then pushed to stand before bending to pat his dog. "Sorry, Lacey, you too. Up." The German shepherd bounced to her feet.

Meg watched McCord as he scanned the area around them. They stood on an invisible border where local businesses merged seamlessly with the adjacent residential area as the town climbed the hillside. Down below, the main street ran from east to west, with glimpses of the classic, flat-fronted, two-story buildings that graced so many small-town American main thoroughfares. At the far end, the tall white spire of a church broke from the tree line to pierce the cloud-scattered blue sky. To their left, the old field-stone police station was backed by a row of white Blue Ridge Police Department cruisers. Up the hill, a mix of smaller, older homes was scattered between larger, modern dwellings, all set deep into trees and shrubbery revitalized with spring.

"Pretty town," McCord commented. "Classic Americana. Like it's out of a Rockwell painting."

"Especially on a sunny day like this. Hawk, up," Meg commanded. "Let's go. I made our excuses to Sam, but I don't want to stall him longer than necessary." She jabbed an index finger at McCord. "You stay quiet until I say so. This is already going to be touch and go as far as bringing you in."

"Got it. I'll leave my introduction in your capable hands."

Meg walked away, muttering to herself about reporters.

They circled the old stone building to Church Street and climbed the steps to the main door. Meg flashed her badge at the officer at the front desk, informed him they were to meet Special Agent Torres, and the officer waved them through. They found Torres in the same conference room, seated at the table, surrounded by files and piles of documents.

Meg waved Brian through and then paused in the doorway, McCord out of sight around the corner of the jamb. "Hi, Sam."

Torres looked up. There were dark smudges under his eyes and the furrows in his forehead spoke of frustration. "Thanks for coming in. Not that I have much to share with you at this point." He slapped his palm down on papers surrounding him and shook his head, his lips a compressed line. "Hitting a lot of walls."

"That's where we're hoping to help. We've had some luck today, but I can maybe go one better." She reached behind her, grabbed McCord's arm, and drew him into the doorway beside her. "This is Clay McCord."

Torres's eyes went to slits. "We discussed this already."

McCord took a step into the room, so Meg stood behind him. "This isn't Meg's fault. I insisted. I've been following the case, because I follow all of Meg and Brian's cases. They do good and interesting work, and because I know the personalities and the dogs in the unit, I can write about the case like no one else. Frankly, it shines a positive light on the unit and the FBI as a whole." His voice went flat. "In this day and age where certain law enforcement agencies are getting an unfairly bad rap from the leaders of the country, I'm happy to counter that. In this case, because I've been following along, I took it upon myself to do a little research."

"So you can write a headline-grabbing story? Sorry, not interested."

"I'd be lying if I said I wasn't going to write a story. The relevant issue for you is when, and it's not now."

"Won't that make your editor angry?"

"Sykes? Not a chance. He doesn't expect me to file stories daily. He knows that would actually backfire. Great investigative stories take time. More than that, they take discretion. Someday there's going to be a Pulitzer on my shelf and it's not going to be from a racy exposé. It's going to be from a thoughtful, well-researched piece. I have information I think you'll find useful. I'd like to offer it to you."

"With what string attached?"

"I'm not sure I'd call it a string. I'd like to write this

case, but only when it's wrapped and you have a suspect in custody. Up to then, the story isn't complete."

"And if it takes weeks or months?"

"I've had stories take longer. Would you like to hear my information?"

Torres's gaze shifted from McCord to Meg.

"I wouldn't have brought him if he couldn't be trusted and wouldn't be an asset. I've learned over a number of cases that having McCord on board is never a bad thing. He has contacts we don't. He can talk to people who won't talk to us. And he won't say a word until we clear him. You won't be sorry."

"And if you are, you can cut me out at any time and I still won't write the article until the case is closed. It just won't be nearly the story it could have been. So it's in my best interest to play by the rules."

Indecision played out over Torres's face as his gaze darted from McCord to Meg to Brian, who nodded encouragingly.

Torres sat back in his chair and crossed his arms over his chest. "Okay, trial run. Convince me. But the moment I don't like it, you're out."

"Deal." McCord pulled out a chair, sat down, leaned his laptop bag against the leg, and dug a small notepad out of his back pocket.

The notepad was a familiar sight to Meg. McCord never went anywhere without the small notepad with a pen jammed down the spiral binding. He preferred it to making notes on his phone. Some people got nervous when a phone came out, as they feared being recorded, so McCord swore that low-tech was always the best way to go. He pulled the pen free, flipped open the cover, and leafed through a number of pages. "I know the basics of the case from local reports about the deaths. You'll be looking at motive and you'll have access to information I don't have unless you choose to share it with me and let me run with it for research purposes. So I went for the obvious tack—not motive, but means."

"Meaning the ability to make that shot?" Brian asked.

"Yes. This isn't an amateur, at least not in the strictest sense of the word. It's someone with professional-level skills. One of two things is happening. Either someone with motive is making these shots and taking out the victims, or he's contracted someone with those skills." McCord shrugged, telegraphing his disconnect with the latter. "It's possible it could be a contract killing, but I think chances of that are slim. If you put out a contract on a victim, you're going to get someone who kills with a gun in relatively close quarters. The chance of having serious long-distance skills like that for sale is much smaller. But it's not impossible, so it stays on the table as a less likely option. Either way, no matter what the motive, no matter whether that motive belongs to the killer or the person who hired him, you're looking for someone with impressive skills. So that's who I went after. And if any of the people I've short-listed come up in your lists for direct motive, then all the better."

"How did you find these short-listed people?" Torres asked.

"I started big with USA Archery and worked my way down. If you're going to hone your skills to the level of an actual competition, this is the overarching body. From there, it breaks down into states, which leads us to the Georgia Archery Association, the North Carolina Field Archery Association, and the National Archery Association of Tennessee. They're each essentially an association of local clubs that teach archery to young kids and teens, and run the local competitions. Those competitions go all the way to the state and then the national level. A lot of people are *very* serious about these competitions. It's a source of personal and family pride to medal at them."

"You were looking at kids?" Torres's unease was clear in his tone.

"Not unless they started as kids, aged through the different competition classes, and are now over eighteen. This isn't going to be a twelve-year-old, but I considered anyone who has reached the age of majority."

Torres's shoulders relaxed. "Okay, that seems reasonable."

"I looked into all three state associations simply because while the killings have been in Georgia and Tennessee, all the locations are close enough together that I thought it would be unwise not to include North Carolina."

"There may be a North Carolina connection," Torres said.

"Oh, really? Then I'm glad I included it."

Meg was impressed with McCord's ability to appear completely in the dark when he was, in fact, fully informed. If she didn't know he knew about the possible involvement of the Cherokee, she'd have never guessed it.

"While not all the deaths have occurred in Fannin County," McCord continued, "the majority of them have, so I started here for research at the Fannin County Public Library over on Main Street. They have a complete archive of *The News Observer*, Blue Ridge's local newspaper, all the way back to its conception in 1990. I was searching for any story relating to archery competitions or training. Then I moved on to each individual state group. All the websites have news sections that go back multiple years, and had information on every competition they'd run and all the rankings. That was particularly helpful. But the human touch was still missing. That required a

trip down to Suches and the local office of the Georgia Department of Natural Resources, specifically the Wildlife
Resources Division. And that's where I met Beverley."

Brian leaned around Meg to look at McCord. "Beverley, huh? Sweet-talked her into giving up the goods?"

"Would I do such a thing?" McCord's smirk belied his
words. "Beverley was particularly chatty, especially once
she had my business card in her hand. Which reminds
me." He fished in his laptop bag for a moment and then
pulled out a business card and slid it across the table to
Torres. The classic *Washington Post* masthead was emblazoned across the top, with its slogan "Democracy Dies in
Darkness" below. McCord's full contact information was
listed underneath. "You should have this so you can contact me. Anyway, Beverley knew as well as I did that hunting licenses are public record, so she was happy to save me
the research. She also happens to have a mind like a steel
trap. Not just who had a hunting license, but what kind,
and for how long."

"There's more than one kind of hunting license?" Brian
asked. When Torres chuckled, he shrugged. "City boy."

"Yes, believe it or not, there is," said McCord. "There's
the standard license that covers small game like rabbit,
opossum, or fox. Then there's a big game license that covers turkey, deer, and bear. But with those you also need a
harvest record to document every kill. Unless you're hunting gators and then they have their own harvest record.
Beverley looked up all the information, but a lot of it she
had right off the top of her head, which is impressive because it was a lot of names. Then she started naming off
archery competitors and giving background on them.
Turns out our Beverley is a member of the Fannin County
Archery Club because there isn't one in Union County,
where Suches is located. And from that, I started building
a list. Beverley herself used to compete and win awards,

and one of her kids was really into the sport as a teenager, so she went to a lot of the competitions and got to know the local families and who the major competitors were, including the JOAD kids."

"JOAD?"

"Junior Olympic Archery Development. Kids start in JOAD around age seven, but they're really focused on finding older kids to shuttle into the Olympic system if they're good enough. But if you want to shoot in the Olympics, you have to have serious recurve skills. That's the bow that most looks like what you or I would think of as a classic bow, although that's technically a long bow. But it doesn't have any of the pulleys or cables to shape the bow like a compound bow does, or the locking mechanism of a crossbow."

"We're only looking at a compound or a recurve bow. Not a crossbow. Wrong kind of arrow." Torres picked up his coffee and drained the dregs.

"Then we'll concentrate on just the two. The recurve is the Olympic archery standard because it's so difficult. Recurve bows require increased accuracy and steadiness because of the draw weight and the lack of stability other bows provide. If you're a top recurve shooter, then you have skills you can take to other platforms. But because of the level of skill required, most hunters prefer to use the compound bow or the crossbow."

"I follow you," Meg interjected. "You're suggesting that because it requires the superior technical ability, anyone skilled with the recurve can also shoot a compound bow, but not necessarily the other way around. So we need to know who shoots what."

"Exactly."

Meg turned to Torres. "You know, I'd really like to get my hands on one of these bows. I understand the whole sniper mind-set, but I feel like I'm missing a piece of how he thinks and the skill required because I don't have a handle on his weapon of choice."

"I can arrange that. Let me contact Captain Wilcox. You remember him? The Georgia State Patrol captain who walked us through the first crime scene? He knows his way around archery and if he can't set it up, he can point us in the direction of someone who could."

"That's a great idea."

"I'll call him as soon as we're done here. Maybe I can set something up for later this afternoon or tonight." Torres nailed McCord with a hard stare. "So you've done all this research, and you've talked to Beverley. What's the bottom line?"

"The bottom line is a list." McCord flipped a page in the notebook. "The first part of it is made up of a variety of different competitions over the past ten years to show continuing aptitude with the weapon. Those are mostly young people. The next part consists of individuals Beverley considers to be the top area bowhunters based on harvest records. There are a couple of standouts there, though those are mostly adults. I've narrowed down the list to anyone living in the tri-state area, though I've specifically marked those within a hundred miles of here. I'll copy down the list for you. Got a piece of paper?"

Torres slid a pad of paper across the table to McCord. "Can you organize it by how you found them? Hunting license versus competition, and add in ages and locations if you have them."

"I sure can." For the next five minutes, the room was quiet as McCord made his list into neat columns. When he was done, he passed the pad of paper across the table. "What do you think?"

"I think I see a few names I recognize right off the bat, or at least family names." He picked up a red pen and started circling. "Chuck Gammon. Michael Carter. Jamie

Trammell. Will Cavett. Ike Mynatt. Aaron Kite. Stephen Trammell."

"That's two Trammells," Brian said.

"Mason Cavett makes for two Cavetts," Torres continued. "Hugh Young. Thomas Atwell. Tim Neale." He put down the pen. "And that's just at first glance. I don't even have full names for everyone involved in the businesses affected, so there may be more here. But this is good stuff."

"Thanks," said McCord. "There's more where that came from. It will just take a little more time and elbow grease."

Torres began packing up his papers. "I need to get going. I'm supposed to be in Atlanta at six for a meeting to wrap another case."

"Thanks for the time," Meg said, pushing back her chair to stand. When Torres bent to pick up his briefcase from the floor, she motioned to Brian and McCord to leave and then waited until he looked up again as she paused in the doorway. "Do you still want me to get SAC Beaumont in contact with you as a reference for McCord?"

Torres hesitated, looking down the list on the pad of paper, the circled names standing out in bold red. He shook his head. "I think I've seen enough. I have your word I can trust him?"

"You do. He won't let you down."

"Okay, let him run with it, then. Give him whatever info you feel he needs. But he sits on it. Not one word gets out until I say so."

"I'll make sure he knows that's non-negotiable. Thanks, Sam. You won't regret it. Call me if you get through to Wilcox?"

"I'll try him right now and let you know."

They weren't even at their cars when Meg's phone rang.

"Wilcox will be happy to take you and anyone else you

need to the Fannin County Archery Club tonight. He suggests meeting at seven."

"That works for us."

"Report back to me on it?"

"I will. Thanks for setting this up." She mimed writing something down to McCord and he pulled out his notebook again. "What's the address?" She repeated the address to him for McCord's benefit. "Thanks. I'll let you know how it goes later tonight." She ended the call.

McCord tapped the pad with the end of his pen. "This is the archery club?"

"Yes. I'm a dead shot with a sniper rifle. Let's see if I can translate that skill to a bow and arrow. If I want to get into the head of the person who would use this kind of weapon to kill, this is the way to start."

CHAPTER 14

Syllabary: A writing system that contains one unique symbol corresponding to each spoken syllable in a language. Languages like Cherokee, which use a complete syllabary, enable a speaker who learns the syllabary to be immediately able to both read and write. After adopting their syllabary in the early 1820s, the entire Cherokee Nation achieved 95% literacy within five years, well before the Trail of Tears.

Friday, April 12, 6:55 PM
Fannin County Archery Club
Blue Ridge, Georgia

Meg led the way into the archery club, a long, squat building about ten minutes out of town. She approached a teenage girl behind the front desk. "Hi, I'm looking for Captain Wilcox from the Georgia State Patrol."

"Are you the party from the FBI?" The girl's eyes were huge as she rose slowly out of the chair, her gaze tracking down. "And you brought dogs?" Her words pitched unnaturally high with excitement.

Meg looked down to where Hawk and Lacey patiently stood beside their handlers. Both dogs still wore their work vest with FBI on them in big yellow block letters. "They're our search dogs."

"Cool! Can I pet them?"

"Sure. Hawk, Lacey, sit."

The girl came out from behind the desk and slowly approached the dogs, both hands extended, one toward each dog. Hawk and Lacey had a sniff and then sat patiently under her stroking.

Meg gave her a full minute with the dogs and then asked, "Captain Wilcox?"

The girl straightened and pointed down the hallway. "He's in the range. First door on your left."

"Thank you. Hawk, come."

The group moved down the hallway. Meg pulled open the door and stepped into a long room with bows and other equipment neatly stacked or racked at one end of the room opposite a series of lines painted on the floor, breaking it into individual lanes, each lane ending at a round bull's-eye target at the far end. Dressed in civvies, Wilcox stood beside a rack of bows, studying the equipment.

Meg raised a hand in greeting. "Captain, thank you for meeting us."

Wilcox turned to the group. "I'm off duty. Just Mark will do." He held out his hand to McCord. "We haven't met. Captain Mark Wilcox, Georgia State Patrol."

McCord shook his hand. "Clay McCord, the *Washington Post*."

Wilcox let go immediately, his gaze shooting to Meg. "You brought a reporter?"

"He's okay. He's helping us with research on this case. And he's promised discretion."

Wilcox eyed McCord with undisguised suspicion, as if he'd never met a reporter with that particular trait. "Uh-huh." His eyes locked on Webb next. "And you are?"

Webb extended a hand. "Lieutenant Todd Webb, fire-fighter/paramedic, DC Fire and Emergency Medical Services."

Wilcox still looked slightly confounded, but the lines on his face eased. Clearly, a fellow first responder was familiar ground. He shook Webb's hand and turned back to Meg. "You travel with an interesting group of people."

"You have no idea." Meg studied the long expanse of the range. "Thank you for making time to meet us here tonight. I'm trying to get into this killer's head, but I feel like I'm missing a piece of the puzzle because of the weapon."

Wilcox indicated the Glock in the holster on her hip. "You're obviously familiar with firearms."

"Both Brian and I are. I have additional experience with the Remington 700 during sniper training, but absolutely no archery experience. I'd like to see how the long-distance experience differs. That might give me some insight into how he's planning his kill shots and taking advantage of the terrain, since that's clearly part of his MO. And that might help make the beginning of our searches more efficient."

"Where did you get sniper training?"

"Richmond, Virginia, at the academy. I was Richmond PD K-9 patrol for six years before joining the FBI."

Wilcox nodded his approval. "Good to know. Okay, then, let's show you around a different kind of weapon. But don't get the idea this is more low-tech. Modern compound bows are as complex as a rifle."

"Are you showing me the recurve as well?"

"No, we're going to stick with the compound. That will give you the idea of the skill required, but only more so for the recurve. Basically, all the skill and technique required for an accurate compound shot, it's all exponentially more difficult with a recurve. But the planning for the actual shot is identical. And in a lot of ways, it's not that different from a sniper rifle." He eyed Meg up and down and hesitated, one hand lifted toward the bows. His hand tracked left, then right, before he lifted a bow from the rack.

The body of the bow was a narrow curve that arched out to two flexible outer limbs curving in the opposite direction. An off-center cam and pulley system of wheels on the end of each limb connected them behind the body of the bow through a series of strings and cables to form an undulating letter D.

McCord stepped closer. "That looks pretty high tech."

"Part of the high tech is in the construction itself. This center curving section is called the 'riser.' It includes the grip to hold the bow, the front sight, and the arrow rest. The flexible arms, or limbs, and the cam system at the end of each limb are the key to how the bow works. The recurve doesn't have that, so as you pull back on the bowstring, it gets harder and harder to go each extra inch. Then you have to hold the bowstring steady at that full draw weight as you line up your shot and smoothly release it. Significant strength is required. Mostly men shoot recurve. But with a compound bow, the cam system functions so the majority of the draw weight is at the beginning of the draw. In this way, a sixty-pound draw can be maintained before shooting with only about twenty pounds of draw because of the storage of kinetic energy throughout the bow. This makes it a more manageable weapon for children and women. You look strong, so I'm starting you out with a forty-pound draw. The maximum draw weight women usually master is fifty pounds. I bet you could handle that, but for a first lesson forty pounds is plenty."

"What would be the draw weight for a man?" Webb asked.

"Fifty-five to sixty-five pounds." Wilcox eyed him. "A big, muscular guy like you, though, he could manage seventy pounds. The higher the draw, the more energy stored, the farther your arrow can go."

"What about this killer?" Meg asked. "What would be your draw weight estimate on him?"

"With the distances we're looking at, the lowest draw weight would be fifty pounds. Anything less wouldn't go the distance."

"So fifty to seventy, then." McCord pulled out his notebook. "You don't mind if I make notes?"

Wilcox's eyes narrowed. "What are you planning on doing with those notes?"

"Nothing right now. Not until the FBI clears it. But a story is like an iceberg. You see what's above water, not all the research underneath supporting it that never gets overtly spelled out."

Several seconds of silence went by. Then, "Fine." His lips tight, Wilcox turned to Meg. "A few more features to show you." He tapped on the black bar that projected from the front of the riser and the small black circular piece that jutted out from it to the left. "This will be familiar to you. This is the sight. It's a single pin sight with a small level inside to help with your form as you hold the bow. Now, do you remember at the first location when I told you the shooter would likely be carrying maybe three or four arrows? As an outdoorsman, you want to be streamlined when you're hunting, so some bows come with a built-in quiver. It essentially looks like a rack, perpendicular to the riser, that carries four to six arrows compactly on the side of the bow. If you're hunting and need another arrow in quick succession, it's right there for your release hand to grab and slide onto the arrow rest only an inch away. But remember, an elite hunter only needs one arrow to make a kill." Wilcox looked toward the bull's-eye on the target. "That's the kind of hunter we're looking at here." Wilcox dug in his pocket and pulled out a maroon metal loop with a short tail shaped with finger notches. "To shoot a compound bow, you're going to need a release aid for the bowstring."

Meg studied the metal object that reminded her vaguely of a compact version of brass knuckles. "You don't shoot the bow with your fingers?"

"It can be done, but you'll get a much cleaner shot with a release aid." He held out the gadget for her. "You'll see this particular style has a safety, just like a firearm, to keep from dry firing the bow, possibly before you're ready or have properly aimed at your target. You're right-handed?"

Meg nodded.

"Hold out your right hand." When she did, he showed her how to seat the release aid and use the safety. He extended the bow to Meg. "Now, let's get you shooting."

She took the bow, wrapping her fingers around the grip, and looked back at Brian.

"I have them," Brian said before she could ask. "Lacey, Hawk, come. Let's stand by the wall so the crazy lady doesn't accidentally shoot us."

Meg threw him a dirty look. "You're hilarious."

He bent into a shallow bow and then stepped away with the dogs.

Wilcox led Meg over to the shooting lanes. He pointed down at the circular bull's-eye in concentric circles of black, blue, red, and yellow at the center. "To put it in perspective, that bull's-eye is twenty-five meters away, which is a little over twenty-five yards. Inside, with controlled conditions, so no air currents and on a flat course. The killer is outside, in high-altitude winds, shooting about four times as far over mountain terrain."

Meg shook her head as she stared at the target, imagining the shot from the perspective of the killer. "If it wasn't for the deaths, that would be a pretty impressive feat. Okay, let's see if I can even hit the target."

"You might surprise yourself. You've obviously got a steady hand. Now let's get your stance perfected." He showed her how to stand sideways, straddling the line with her left foot toward the target. Eyeing her position, he gave her left boot a small nudge with his. "Back a bit. Perfect. That opens out your hips and shoulders toward the target." He demonstrated how to hold the bow and watched her mimic his stance. "How's it feel?"

"Comfortable. Not too heavy."

"Good." He stepped closer and showed her where and how to attach the release aid, how to nock an arrow, and how to position her hand for the draw. "Now draw the bowstring back until you hit the mechanical stop."

Meg glanced at Webb. He grinned and gave her an encouraging nod. Closing her fingers more firmly around the release aid, she drew back the bowstring. There was weight behind the bowstring, but it moved smoothly, drawing the two limbs toward the center line of the bow as she pulled. As her hand got close to her face, there was a sudden change in the draw weight, jerking her hand slightly as the off-center cams stopped rotating.

"You felt that jerk and the drop in draw weight?" Wilcox asked.

Meg nodded.

"That's the 'let-off.' That's what lets you take your time to set up a shot, especially on a living, mobile creature like a deer."

"Or a human," McCord said.

"Or a human. You can take your time, make sure your aim is dead on, and then take the shot without the kind of fatigue you'd get with a recurve bow, the kind of fatigue that would make you miss. Now line up the top of the pin in the front site with the center of the target. Gently release the safety. And now comes the hardest part. Maintain your form and aim while you pull back steadily until the back tension releases the bow string."

Meg wanted to wipe her damp palms on her pants, but her hands were full.

"No pressure . . ." McCord murmured.

Without moving, Meg sent him a sideways glare. "You try this for the first time with everyone watching your every move and see how you do." Her eyes narrowed as a plan formed. "Actually, you will try this. You're next, hot-shot." She smiled as his eyes widened with surprise, and turned her gaze to the target.

Meg instinctively fell back on techniques she'd used as a sniper. She steadied her breathing and focused all her attention on the target. She moved her thumb off the safety, exhaled, and at the end of the exhale, drew the bowstring back.

The arrow moved so fast, Meg couldn't differentiate the *snick* of the release with the *thunk* of the arrow striking the target twenty-five meters away. She lowered the bow to her side as she stared down the lane.

"Well done!" Wilcox sounded immensely pleased. "Seven points! For a first try that's very good. Let's try it again. This time, try to keep your draw hand a little more relaxed. When you tensed up, you pulled the hand into a fist and that offset your aim slightly." He handed her another arrow.

She nocked the arrow, drew back the bowstring, aimed, and made her second shot much faster this time.

"Eight points, getting better. Grab a quiver and some arrows and keep going." Wilcox rounded on McCord, who actually took a step backward in response. "The reporter and I are going to have a go at it next."

Webb followed Meg over to the rack. "That was amazing."

She made a show of polishing the back of her fingers on her collarbone. "Not bad, if I do say so myself." She ruined the gesture by laughing and extended the bow to Webb. "Here, hold this while I grab some arrows."

"That is seriously neat." Brian ambled over with the dogs. "You make it look easy."

She selected a quiver, buckled it around her hips, and shifted it to lie against her thigh. "Don't kid yourself, it's not. I fell back on extensive sniper training when it came to actually taking the shot."

"I figured as much. So now you've had a tiny taste of archery, what's your opinion of our killer?"

"I'm very impressed by his skills and planning." She grabbed a fistful of arrows, set them point down in the quiver, and turned to the men. "The advantage with the compound bow is being able to draw back and line up the shot, and then wait if you have to. This killer is selecting locations where the victims will be. He may be in place long before he expects them to be there. Then, when they appear, he can take the time to line up the shot, wait for the perfect moment, and then let the arrow fly. Do you remember how Sheriff Maxwell described the arrow with the mechanical, expanding broadhead? As a three-inch, high-speed drill carving through soft tissue." She pulled an arrow out of the quiver, turning it point up. "We're not talking a small arrowhead like this with a profile in line with the shaft of the arrow. We're talking about what is essentially an arrowhead four or five times as wide composed of razor blades."

"Brutal," Webb said, his eyes fixed on the arrowhead. "There's a layer of cruelty there."

Meg cocked her head in question. "What do you mean?"

He tapped the tip of the arrow. "This works best as a soft tissue weapon, even the more damaging ones, especially when you're considering the distances in question. At twenty yards, that broadhead might break a rib and pass right through, but at farther distances—"

"Like a hundred yards?" Brian interjected.

"Like a hundred yards," Webb continued, "you hit bone and you'll do damage, but I'd bet there's not enough kinetic energy in the arrow to kill. For that you need soft tissue."

"Like this killer is doing," Meg said.

"Right. But even with what you described, depending on what was hit, it could take minutes to bleed out. And it would be excruciating, like being gut shot. There's no mercy in a shot like that."

"Interesting. I didn't think about it that way. I wonder what Rutherford would say about it?"

"You haven't brought him into it yet?"

"It's not my case. But we've hit the three-victim threshold, so maybe it's time to push for it. I'm getting a better feel for our suspect, but he'd be able to clarify things. I'll talk to Torres about it. He may have never worked with the BAU before, so maybe I can smooth the way for him there. It might also help to have someone streamline the connection, in which case Craig can be the intermediary to contact Rutherford and get the ball rolling." She took a step toward the lanes and then stopped. "Did either of you want to try it?"

"It looks like fun, but I'm not stressing this shoulder in any way," Webb said. "Besides, I'm happy to watch you whoop McCord's ass."

"And I'm happy to watch with you," Brian said. "You go ahead. The dogs are fine hanging out with me and I'm more than entertained."

"If you're sure." The *thump* of an arrow striking the target at the far end drew Meg's gaze, and she had to work quickly to wipe the smile off her lips at the combination of McCord's disgruntled expression and his arrow vibrating several inches outside of the outer ring of the target.

"See? I told you. A whooping." Webb's murmur sounded in her ear as he leaned in.

"Behave," she scolded quietly. "Don't destroy the man's ego."

"I won't have to. You're about to do that all by yourself. Go for it." He winked at her.

Meg returned to her lane, stepped into place at the shooting line, nocked her arrow, and attached her release aid with the safety engaged. Then taking a deep breath, she raised the bow to the correct height and drew back. As she lined up the sight with the center of the target, the old stillness came over her as her brain filtered out the voices and sounds around her. It was just her, the weapon, and the target.

Release the safety. Inhale. Exhale. Pull back on the bowstring.

She couldn't keep the satisfied smile off her face when the arrow hit the bull's-eye.

CHAPTER 15

Georgiafornia: A term used by members of anti-immigrant movements to describe Georgia, once a part of the Old South, that is now almost 10% Hispanic and Latino.

Saturday, April 13, 8:08 AM
Trammell Lodge
Blue Ridge, Georgia

Meg got out of Torres's car and turned in a slow circle, taking in the valley around her. Surrounded by natural beauty, the plight of the local residents became crystal clear.

When Meg had called Torres following her lesson with Wilcox the night before to discuss her thoughts on the archer, he'd told her he planned to do interviews the next morning. She'd heard the thread of reluctance in his tone and had offered that she or Brian, or both of them, accompany him. If his Latino background was a disadvantage here in rural Georgia, then maybe they could help balance it out. Torres had accepted her offer. In the end, Brian offered to stay home and work through their standard training exercises with the dogs since they'd missed the previous few days. Besides, he'd reasoned, with her background in the Richmond PD, she'd be a better inter-rogator than him. If a call came through while they were gone, he'd bring the dogs in the SUV and meet her on-site. Meg had agreed, and Torres had picked her up on his way into town.

They started early, wanting to catch the Trammell sons before they were out and about for the day. Now they stood opposite Trammell Lodge. Located on a rise above the Toccoa River, the lodge itself was fashioned from rus-tic timber logs and set deep into the forested hillside, look-ing out over the winding valley below. The sun was up, but the morning was still cool and mist pooled down in the valley, masking the hills in tones of blue-gray.

"This is all going to be underwater after the dam is built." Meg stepped away from the car to move closer to the edge of the hill. She looked north and then followed the river to the south. Down below, she could see houses closer to the river and roads leading into rural communi-ties. "It's all going to be lost." She turned and looked at the lodge and the hill that rose behind it. "Including this property."

"Makes the struggle to stop this dam project a little more real," said Torres.

"Sure does. But even so, murder isn't the way to make that happen."

Together, they entered the lodge, stepping into a foyer of honey-colored pine. A middle-aged woman smiled at them from behind the reservation desk. "Good morning and welcome to Trammell Lodge. Do you have a reservation?"

Torres pulled out his flip case and the woman's smile faltered.

"Special Agent Torres of the FBI. This is my colleague, Meg Jennings. We're looking for Jamie and Stephen Tram-mell."

Color leached from her face. "Those are my sons." The pleasant tone fell away to be replaced by that of a protective mother. "Why do you need to talk to them?"

"It's concerning a case. Where are your sons, Mrs. Trammell?"

She stared at him for a moment and then nodded tersely. "Please go on into the Great Room." She pointed to a doorway. "Make yourself comfortable in front of the fire. I'll bring them in to meet you there."

Five minutes later, Mrs. Trammell joined Meg and Torres where they sat in deep leather armchairs in front of a roaring fire. Three men accompanied her: a middle-aged, redheaded man in khakis and a flannel shirt, and two twentysomething men with their father's red hair, but in a more youthful, brassy tone, and whose nearly identical facial features marked them as brothers.

The two young men looked cautious, whereas the father walked straight to Torres, looked him in the eye, and held out his hand. "Hank Trammell. Mary says you need to speak with our boys."

"I do, sir, yes." Torres stood and shook hands, then flashed his ID and made introductions. The two young men shook hands with him and Meg before taking their own seats together on a sofa with their father. Their mother perched on the arm next to the younger of the two men.

"We're investigating a case and your sons' names have come up during the investigation."

The Trammell brothers exchanged confused glances.

"Agent, we want to cooperate," said Mary, "but I can't imagine how my boys could have anything to do with a criminal investigation."

"Then let's ask some questions and get them taken off the list of persons of interest." Torres turned to the young men. "You're both hunters?"

"Yes, sir." Stephen, the older of the two, looked up at his mother and she smiled encouragingly. "That's part of what we do here. We're mainly a fishing lodge, and Jamie and I, we lead fishing expeditions down at the Toccoa. But occasionally we get asked to take a group out hunting."

"It's not just the boys," interjected Hank. "All four of us are experienced hunters and can lead a party. We're also fully licensed and we make sure all the guests are as well."

"I'm glad to hear that," Torres said. "Jamie, what kind of hunting do you do? Strictly firearms?"

"Mostly, but not always. Any guests I've ever taken out have their own rifles, but me and my buddies, we like to bowhunt sometimes."

"What kind of bow do you use?"

"Compound. I—" He stopped when his father's hand shot out to close over his wrist, his gaze shifting quickly from his father to Torres and back again.

Hank leaned forward to look Torres in the eye. "Hang on a second. This is about those archery murders, isn't it?"

Meg stepped in, hoping a calmer, less authoritative voice would keep the interview on even footing. "Yes, that's the case we're working on. And right now, we're following a wide variety of leads. We're not looking at charging either of your sons at this time."

Hank shook his head in disbelief. "This is ludicrous. Neither of my boys are killers."

"It's the tournaments, isn't it?" Stephen's tone was steady and logical. "It's all our medals. You're looking for who could make that shot. And, yeah . . . we could."

"Stephen!" Mary clamped a hand down over his shoulder.

He looked up at her and smiled. "It's okay, Mom. They already know or they wouldn't be here. They're just doing what they need to. But they're not going to find what they're looking for here, are they, Jamie?"

"No, they're not," Jamie agreed. "But yeah, we could

make that shot. I saw a post on Facebook about it. A hundred yards. With a compound or a recurve?"

"I'm sorry, we can't share that information," Torres said.

"Doesn't matter which," Stephen said, "because we could do it with both. But we didn't. Give us the dates and we'll show you. Mom, can you go get the booking calendar?"

Mary sprang to her feet and rushed out of the room, nervous energy speeding her way.

Both men pulled out their phones and reviewed their schedules with the help of the lodge booking calendar. In the end, the men were able to give alibis for two of the three deaths—out together with a fishing party for one, and at the lodge for the second—but only Stephen could substantiate an alibi for the third killing.

"Do you remember, Dad? You sent me to Chattanooga to meet with that supplier." Jamie distractedly tapped a finger against the back of his phone. "I left first thing and didn't get back until mid-afternoon because of that crash on I-75."

Meg didn't see as much as sense Torres's interest sharpen.

"How do you normally drive to Chattanooga?" he asked.

Torres's tone was so casual, Meg bet Jamie never realized the importance of the question.

"I go there once or twice a month on lodge business. Always take GA-5 to US-74 and from there to I-75 into town. Why?"

US-74. The winding road that followed the Ocoee. Jaime had driven right past Ocoee #2 to get to Chattanooga.

"That route took you close to the site of the murder that occurred that day." Torres refrained from saying "close" was literally under five hundred feet. "It would hardly have been out of your way, and with an archer of your skill, it wouldn't have taken long to do the job."

"But I didn't kill anybody." Horror tipped Jamie's words. "Mom, Dad, I swear I haven't hurt anyone."

Hank's grip tightened. "We know," he said simply.

"Do you have anyone who can vouch for your whereabouts that day?" Torres asked.

Jamie shook his head. "Not while I was in the truck driving back and forth, but I can get the supplier to confirm when I arrived and when I left. But I didn't have any of my bows with me. Why would I need one to pick up supplies?"

"Even if we can confirm your bows were here at the lodge, that doesn't mean you couldn't have another one with you," Torres pressed. "Maybe one your family didn't know about."

"But I didn't. Why would I kill someone I don't know?" Jamie's tone was starting to rise in pitch as his stress level skyrocketed.

"Agent Torres," Hank broke in, "this is nonsense. My boy didn't kill anyone. And he couldn't have done the previous two murders."

"We have to keep all our options open," Torres replied.

"Are you saying we need a lawyer?" Mary asked.

"No, but we will need you to stay in town and remain available for the duration of this investigation. And I need the name and contact information of that supplier."

When they were back in the car, Meg looked at Torres. "Jamie isn't our killer. I absolutely believe him. It's simply a coincidence that he happened to be on the same road that morning, but he wouldn't have had the time to follow the flume in to the dam, make the shot, and then follow it back out."

"I agree, but I needed to make sure. I'll confirm with the supplier, but he seemed genuine to me."

"Good. So where to next?"

"Thomas Atwell of Atwell's Garage and Wrecking. Because of the space needed for the wrecking yard, he has a place here in the valley. He's not an archery champion, but he's high on Beverley's list because he has a high kill count on his harvest records."

They found Atwell on his back on a creeper dolly under a beat-up sedan with only the oil-stained, ragged legs of his coverall and worn, filthy boots sticking out.

"Mr. Atwell?" Torres called.

The man ignored them and kept working, his body jerking rhythmically as if he was wrenching something into place.

"Mr. Atwell?" Torres rapped his knuckles on the quarter panel.

"Busy!" a voice growled.

"Mr. Atwell, I'm Special Agent Torres from the FBI and I need to talk to you."

The body stopped moving, remaining motionless for a few seconds, and then the dolly rolled out. Thomas Atwell was in his midforties with a grizzled beard shot with gray, a heavily lined face streaked with grime, and a scowl. He held a heavy ratchet wrench in his right hand. His gaze shot to the badge Torres held out to him and then settled on Torres's face, his eyes narrowing.

"I don't want to talk to any Fed." He reached up to grab the edge of the car to drag himself back under, but Torres neatly slipped the toe of one shoe behind a wheel, blocking the motion.

"We won't take much of your time, but we need to ask you some questions."

With a muttered curse, Atwell rolled to his feet with surprising coordination. "Make it quick. I got a business to run."

"Do you like to hunt, Mr. Atwell?"

Atwell stared at him, his face a mottled red. "Are you fucking kidding me? You're wasting my time for that?"

"I'm not wasting your time, Mr. Atwell, but I do have a few questions for you."

"And I don't need to hear any questions from a beaner. You're not welcome here. Get the fuck out of my place."

It was subtle, but Meg watched Torres's face go blank at the racial slur. "Sir, this is for a criminal investigation. I know your time is valuable, but I do need to ask about your whereabouts on several occasions."

"You gonna arrest me?"

"Right now, all I'd like is some information."

"Well, you're not going to get it. I'm done Hispandering. Go back to wherever you came from."

"Hey!" Meg wasn't about to stand by and listen to any more. "Mr. Atwell, Special Agent Torres is a law enforcement officer. Show some respect."

"I don't got no respect for his kind." His gaze raked down and then back up her body before taking a step toward her. "But you, honey, I can show you *lots* of respect."

Meg balled a fist, prepared to use it if Atwell laid a grimy hand on her, but Torres already had him by the arm, yanking him back.

Atwell shook him off. "Get your greasy hands off me or I'm pressing charges for assault."

"Come on, Meg," Torres said through gritted teeth, evidently seeing it was a fruitless situation. "We have everything we're going to get here for now. Next time we want to talk to Mr. Atwell, we'll take him into custody first." Torres ushered Meg out of the garage, and only once she was safely out did he follow her.

"Oh yeah? You and what army?" Atwell bellowed from behind them.

Once they were driving away, Meg turned to Torres and

took in his locked jaw and the high color on his cheek-bones. "What a great guy." Sarcasm dripped from her words. "Hates Latinos on sight and thinks women exist exclusively for his sexual pleasure." She shuddered at the thought. "Clearly, he's a lowlife."

"That's an understatement."

"If we want to talk to him again, we may want to send Brian in since we didn't do so well. Where to next?"

"Mason and Will Cavett. Let's hope it goes better than Atwell. I guess it can't go any worse.

Famous last words. But Meg refrained from saying it out loud.

CHAPTER 16

Georgia's Land Lotteries: Seven times between 1805 and 1832, Georgia used a lottery system to raffle off the land taken from the Cherokee and Creek Nations. These lotteries were unique to Georgia; no other state used a lottery system to distribute land, and almost three-quarters of the entire state was distributed under this system. Applicants could only be white males over 18 or 21 (depending on the lottery), orphans, or widows. Lot size varied widely, even in the individual lotteries. The largest lots distributed were 490 acres in the 1805 and the 1820 land lotteries. The smallest were 40-acre gold lots raffled off during the Gold Lottery of 1832.

Saturday, April 13, 10:34 AM
Cavett Family Farms
Blue Ridge, Georgia

"Wow." Meg leaned forward to stare out the windshield of Torres's SUV. "That's the family farm?"

"Has been for nearly two hundred years." Torres brought the SUV to a slow stop in front of a pair of double wrought iron gates. "Though when the Cavetts settled here, it would likely still have been heavily treed. The family had to clear most of this land."

"How much land do they own?" Meg asked.

"Currently, fifty-five acres. But when Jedidiah Cavett won this parcel in the 1832 land lottery, it was one hundred and fourteen acres. Over the years, the family has sold off pieces of it and made a pretty penny doing so. Now they're down to the existing acreage, which is what they need as horse breeders."

"Friesian breeders."

"Isn't that a kind of horse?"

"It is, but a very desirable horse with a high value. The kind of value that keeps a fancy farm like this running."

Meg studied the fields and buildings spread out before them. Past the double gates, the driveway wound up a gentle rise. Both sides of the driveway were flanked by bright white wooden fencing enclosing horse pastures on either side. The left side was hidden behind the tree line that provided privacy from the road, but from their current position, several horses were visible in the opposite pasture. At the top of the driveway, a two-story barn stretched atop the rise, with a row of doors leading directly to a long run of stalls.

"I guess we'll have to buzz in." Torres's words drew Meg away from her examination of the property. He pointed at the small intercom on a curved metal post peeping out of one of the bushes lining the driveway.

"Looks like it. Want me to jump out?"

"No, I'll do it." Torres opened the door, climbed out, and strode over to the intercom. A buzz sounded, followed by about ten seconds of silence. Then a muffled voice came over the intercom. Meg couldn't hear Torres's words, just the timbre of his voice. The gates swung open and he hurried back, jumped in, put the car in drive, and pulled forward into the gap.

"Who did you talk to?"

"Not sure. Female voice, fairly strong accent. She invited us up."

As the gates closed behind them, they wound up the driveway bisecting the pastures.

"I researched the family business," Torres said. "They're well-known and have an excellent reputation as breeders. It sounds like they get top dollar."

"This is an expensive operation, so they'd need to." Through the break in the trees to their left, Meg spotted a second building. "Over there. That must be the house."

"She said to take the left at the fork, so that makes sense."

When the driveway split, Torres turned and followed the curve to the left. From the top of the hill, Meg had a quick glimpse of more pastures past the barn and several equine transport trailers parked behind it. A young man—one of the farm hands?—came out of one of the external stall doors leading a massive black stallion, his mane and tail blowing gracefully in the breeze. Then they disappeared behind the trees lining the edge of the road to the house.

Torres drove toward a house with clearly historic origins, one the family had expanded over decades, or possibly centuries. Built partly of rough-cut pine boards and partly of fieldstone, the house boasted wide picture windows, large stone chimneys, and a steeply pitched roof. The mix of styles might have been jarring on another structure, but here it lent the house the trappings of genteel history.

Torres pulled the car up to the house on the circular driveway and cut the engine. "Let's hope this interview goes better than the last one."

It struck Meg in that moment how young Torres looked. She pegged him in his early thirties, but discomfort, likely born of years of snide comments and little jabs, sketched shadows across his features and melted years off him.

Their knock at the front door was answered almost immediately. The door opened to reveal a tall, slender blond woman in her midforties. Her long, wavy hair spilled over her shoulders and halfway down her back, and she wore a loose, pale-blue chambray shirt over a pair of dark wash skinny jeans. "Good morning." She greeted them with a smile that didn't quite reach her eyes or mute the confusion there. "Please come in, Special Agent . . . I'm so sorry, I didn't catch your name." Her accent was soft and fluid, drawing out her vowels almost to a throaty purr.

"Special Agent Torres. And this is my colleague, Meg Jennings."

She offered a delicate hand. "Savannah Cavett. So nice to meet you. Please come in. Can I offer you sweet tea? Or a soda? Or I could put on some coffee."

"No, thank you, Mrs. Cavett. This isn't a social call. We'd like to speak to your husband and son."

Confusion darkened into alarm. "Mason and Will? Whatever for?"

"We have some questions for them. Are they here, Mrs. Cavett?"

She led the way into a comfortable living room. "They're out at the barn or in the fields, but I'd be happy to call them for you."

"Yes, please, Mrs. Cavett."

"Please make yourself at home. I'll be right back."

After she disappeared through the doorway and down the hall, Meg nudged Torres's arm. "Look at that." She crossed the room to a large, glassed cabinet. Inside was an impressive display of trophy cups, medals, and framed certificates. "Sam, you need to see this."

Torres joined her at the cabinet. "Impressive." He leaned

in to read the names. "These are all for Will. From a range of different competitions. Some national, some state."

Meg bent to look at some of the items displayed on the lower shelves. "The older ones are down here. Smaller competitions. Are those the newer ones?"

"Looks like it. The most recent one is two years ago, but it's a straight run until then. Looks like Will either aged out of the competitions or stopped."

"Or wasn't winning anymore. A few of the ones down here are for Mason. He's won some recent competitions as well. Interesting that his more recent competitions rate a less visible spot in the display."

"Who do you think set this up?"

"My money is on the mother. Clearly, she's very proud of her son, and possibly less proud of her husband."

"Marital issues, do you think?"

"Possibly. We'd better go sit down so we don't look like we're snooping."

Savannah Cavett returned less than a minute later bearing a tray of glasses filled with sweet tea and a plate of homemade ginger snaps sparkling with a topcoat of sugar. "I know you said no to the tea, but they'll be a few minutes coming in, so I brought some refreshments for you, anyway." She offered the tray to Meg first, who took a glass of tea and a cookie, and then to Torres. Meg could practically hear him grinding his teeth, but he accepted a glass and a cookie while they waited.

Savannah proceeded to give a master class on grace under pressure and Southern hospitality as she made small talk with her unexpected guests. But finally, the sound of footsteps was audible in the hallway and then two men filled the doorway. Meg instantly recognized the younger of the two as the farmhand she'd spotted coming out of the barn. Both men wore flannel shirts and blue jeans while they worked with the horses, but they'd removed their boots before entering the house and stood in their socks. There was no mistaking the parentage; Will Cavett looked almost exactly like his father, but with darker hair and smoother skin yet to be weathered by decades of working outdoors.

"I'm Mason Cavett." The elder of the two men spoke as they entered the room. His gaze shifted from Torres to Meg and then to Torres again as the FBI agent extended his flip case. He strode forward, pulled the case from Torres's fingers, and studied it intently before handing it back. "What does the FBI want with us?" His tone was already defensive.

"I wanted to ask you and your son a few questions, Mr. Cavett. Would you and Will take a seat?"

Mason looked for a moment like he might refuse; then he moved past his wife to sit on the sofa beside her. He reached for one of the remaining glasses of tea and half drained it in a series of swallows. Then he stared directly at Torres and waited.

Torres, however, immediately turned to the younger Cavett. "Will, I understand you're well-known in the area as a skilled archer."

Meg read startled surprise in the young man's eyes. "I guess."

"Do you still shoot?"

Mason held up a hand toward his son before he could respond. "Is this relevant?"

"Yes, sir, it is. Will, do you still shoot?"

Will flicked a look at his father as if asking for permission, waiting until the older Cavett nodded sharply. "Yes."

"When was the last time you went out bowhunting?"

Will's eyes went unfocused as he searched his memory. "It's been a while. I bagged some rabbits last February? I think? That's probably the last time I was out. Turkey season opened a few weeks ago, but I haven't had time to go hunting. We're coming up on foaling season."

"What bow do you shoot?"

"Depends on what I'm hunting. The recurve is a challenge, so I sometimes use it for smaller prey like rabbits or opossums. Big game, it's always my compound bow to make sure there's enough force for an effective kill shot."

Without missing a beat, Torres turned to Mason. "I understand you're also a hunter, Mr. Cavett."

"What does this have to do with anything?" Mason demanded.

"I can give you more background, but I'd like you to answer a few questions first. Do you actively hunt, Mr. Cavett?"

"In season, yes."

Meg studied Mason, waiting for any small reaction that might contradict his words. *Careful answer. He's not sure why we're here so he's covering all his bases. Or he's trying to make it look like he is.*

"And you shoot with?"

"Always a compound bow."

"You've won some competitions with that bow."

"I keep my hand in, yeah. A man likes to provide for his family. What we kill, we eat."

"I'm glad to hear that. I'd hate to think the animal was dying simply for sport." Torres turned to Will. "Will, can you tell me where you were on Wednesday morning?"

Will jerked in surprise at Torres's abrupt change in direction. "Wednesday?"

"Yes, in the morning."

"I . . . I—"

"He was with me," Mason interrupted. "Here at the farm."

Not letting him speak for himself.

Torres turned to Savannah. "Can you confirm that, Mrs. Cavett?"

Savannah looked startled as the conversation swung around to her. "Wednesday morning? I met Marnie for breakfast. But they were here when I left around eight and were here when I returned around . . . eleven? But if Mason says they were working with the horses, then that's what they were doing."

"What about Monday morning. And the afternoon of March 29?"

"Let me check my social calendar and get back to you," Mason bit out. "That's enough. Unless you're going to charge either of us with something, we're done here." He stood. "Savannah, please show these two agents out. Will, we need to get back to the horses." He strode out of the living room, his son at his heels.

Will paused only momentarily at the door, glancing into the living room, his face a blank mask. Then he turned and disappeared.

Savannah busied herself loading glasses onto the tray and then stood. "Thank you very much for coming, Special Agents. I'm sorry we couldn't be of more assistance to you."

She led them down the hallway to the front door. Meg looked behind them, but Mason and Will were nowhere in sight.

Time to try a different tack, woman-to-woman.

"You have a lovely home, Mrs. Cavett," Meg said.

"Thank you."

"It seems old. Has it been in the family for long?"

"For generations. The Cavetts have been raising horses here for over a century, though we've been specializing in Friesians for only the past fifty years."

"I heard talk in town about a possible new dam project. That won't affect you here, will it? It sounded like the whole valley would be lost, but surely the government wouldn't drive you off historic family land like this?"

Anger flashed behind Savannah's blue eyes. "They certainly would. But we're fighting it. We have a lawyer and we're taking them to court to stop it. This is my family's land. And it will be Will's."

"Your husband's family land, you mean."

"*Our* family's land. Mason and I are cousins. I was a Cavett before and after marriage."

Meg fought to keep the surprise off her face and compensated by giving a little laugh. "On the bright side, you didn't have to perfect a new signature after the wedding. I'm sorry about your land troubles. That sounds very stressful to have such a significant part of your heritage threatened."

"It surely is. But we're not the only ones affected. There is strength in numbers, and others are joining us in the suit. For us, it's business as usual on the farm because, together, we're going to win. They'll have to find somewhere else to build their dam." She opened the door for them. "Thank you so much for coming. Enjoy the rest of your day."

Meg and Torres stepped out onto the porch and the door closed almost soundlessly behind them. They didn't say a word until they were in the car and rolling down the driveway toward the road.

"Nicely done at the end there," Torres said.

"Thanks. You'd already perfected the bad cop routine, so I thought I'd go for the feminine touch." Meg grimaced. "Though I have to admit I didn't see the first cousins thing coming. That's legal here?"

"It is. You don't see it often, but it does sometimes happen, especially in families where the historic or social connection is particularly strong. It doesn't look like the combined family gene pool has affected their son at all."

"Well, she didn't actually say first cousins, I just assumed it. They may be second cousins or further out."

"If it's relevant, I can find out. You were quiet in there for the questioning. What did you think about the Cavetts?"

"I didn't want to interrupt your rhythm. And, honestly, I don't think he had a problem with you specifically, more likely the badge, but from the Southern belle routine his wife was doing, he might have had a problem with a woman in a position of authority. I thought it was better to let you carry the questioning with Mason. If it had just been Will, I would have jumped in. But I don't like Mason's attitude. He seems to me like a man who would find a way to get what he wants, no matter who is standing in his way."

"I agree. And while Will seemed more circumspect, being raised in that environment with that example, his gut reaction may be similar. Those two are at the top of my list."

"They're each other's alibi without Savannah there to corroborate. So one could be covering for the other."

"Or they could be working together. As I said, at the top of my list."

The gate was open as they approached, so they drove right through it and onto the road. Torres's phone beeped twice as they slowed to a stop. He pulled it out of his pocket, checked his messages, and made a *hmmmmm* sound.

"What?" Meg asked.

"How do you feel about a trip to North Carolina?"

"I hear it's lovely this time of year. But seriously, what's in North Carolina?"

"Qualla Boundary. That was Principal Chief Cobbrey. Their government offices aren't normally open on Saturday, but because I told him I needed to meet with him right away, he's opened the office and will make time for us there today. But we'd have to really move it. It's about two hours' drive time from here and one o'clock is his only availability." He looked up from his phone. "Are you okay to leave your dog for that long?"

"Hawk is fine with Brian. I'll let him know and he'll hold down the fort in our absence."

"Good. Let's head north then, and get the Cherokee perspective on the Copperhill Dam."

CHAPTER 17

Qualla Boundary: A nation-within-a-nation where approximately 8,000 members of the Eastern Band of Cherokee Indians live on a remnant of their once-vast homeland. Not a reservation because the land is held in a federal trust; it can only be sold to other tribal members.

Saturday, April 13, 12:56 PM
US Route 441 South
Qualla Boundary, North Carolina

The Oconaluftee River shot by through Meg's window as they sped down US-441 South.

"We're just about there," Meg said, her gaze flicking from the passing intersections to the map on her phone. "Slow down. It should be the next left. Just past Veteran's Park. There's a parking lot right in front of the Tribal Council House."

They drove past an antiaircraft gun followed by a bronze, life-size statue of a young man in an army uniform. Then Torres turned down a side street and drove straight into the long parking lot directly ahead, pulled into a spot, and killed the engine as he checked the dash clock. "We made good time."

"I thought we'd be late, but you knew how far to push it."

Torres's smile was sheepish. "And luckily we didn't get pulled over."

"Sometimes getting pulled over can be helpful. I've been pulled over for speeding and gotten a lights-and-siren escort to a search scene. Luckily, we didn't need it here."

They got out of the car and crossed the narrow grassy boulevard to the front walk. The Tribal Council House was a long, wood-plank bungalow, fronted by flowerbeds of cheerful spring flowers and a raised porch with welcoming benches. As they climbed the steps, Meg's gaze was drawn to the bright seal at the top of the stairs to the right of the front door. The large circular medallion had a seven-point star in the center surrounded by a wreath of leaves, under which read March 11, 1889. The red band that surrounded the seal declared it the "Seal of the Eastern Band of Cherokee Indians." At the very bottom of the seal were symbols in a script Meg didn't recognize: GWYᎾ DᏰᏢ.

Torres held the door open for Meg and she stepped inside. An older woman sat behind a reception desk inside the door. She looked up at the sound of the door and beamed a smile at the newcomers. "Good afternoon."

"Good afternoon. We have an appointment with Principal Chief Cobbrey. Special Agent Sam Torres and Meg Jennings."

The woman looked down at her appointment book, running her index finger down the day's calendar. "I have you here. Just a moment, please." She picked up the phone, pressed a button, and waited a moment before speaking. "Chief, I have Special Agent Torres and Ms. Jennings here to see you. I will. Thank you." She hung up. "He's ready to meet with you now. Follow this hallway past the council chamber and down toward the end. You'll find his office on the right. His name is on the door."

"Thank you."

Meg followed Torres down the hallway. As promised, the principal chief's office was easily identified. Torres raised his hand and rapped on the door, three quick knocks.

"Come in." The deep voice was muffled by the door.

Torres opened the door and stepped inside.

The principal chief's office, painted in muted tones of gray, was comfortable, but not overdone. An oval conference table and chairs for small meetings stood opposite the door, with a small seating area with a leather sofa and two wing-back chairs to their right. To their left was Cobbrey's desk, with a neatly organized series of documents stacked around his laptop. Nearby, a large curio case filled with a variety of Cherokee art and family and community pictures took up an entire wall.

Principal Chief Cobbrey sat behind his desk. His suit jacket was unbuttoned, as was the top button of his shirt, and a hammered silver medallion hung on a beaded chain around his neck. A man of medium height with a broad frame, Meg placed him in his early sixties from his salt and pepper hair and the deep creases around his dark eyes.

Cobbrey stood and offered his hand across the desk. "Charles Cobbrey."

"Sam Torres." Torres quickly flashed his ID, then shook Cobbrey's hand. "This is Meg Jennings."

They shook and then Cobbrey indicated the two ivory leather chairs in front of his desk. "Please, sit." He settled again in his own chair. "What can I do for the FBI?"

Meg noted the caution in his tone. The Eastern Band of Cherokee Indians was a sovereign nation with its own tribal law enforcement and government, but the FBI still had jurisdiction on their land, just as it would anywhere else in America. But she couldn't blame him. Any people who had been mistreated by the federal government the way Native people had would be naturally wary of further conflict with a government agency.

"I wanted to talk to you about the EBCI interest in the Toccoa valley land in Georgia south of McCaysville. I understand the EBCI has made a claim on that land."

"We have." There was no hesitation now.

"Even though the Tennessee Valley Authority is looking to seize it?"

"They won't be able to do anything until the case has been heard in a court of law."

"But not through your court system," Meg said.

Cobbrey cocked his head to fix her with a sideways stare. "No. If it was, we'd have a fair chance. Instead, it will be through the state system. And when that fails us, and it will, we'll take it to the Supreme Court."

"You think you're going to lose?" Torres asked.

"Chances are slim we'll be successful in Georgia's courts."

"Even though you feel you have a justifiable claim on the land?"

Meg flicked a glance at Torres. Was he pushing just to hear the answers he wanted from Cobbrey's mouth directly, or was he not as solid on his Georgia history as she had assumed?

"It was once ours and was taken away from us by force so white Europeans could claim our resources. We didn't have the strength, the numbers, or the resources to fight back then, but we do now. Our claim to purchase the land is legitimate, as is the current owners' right to sell it. Though many of us see it as buying back our own land. Just like we did the land of Qualla Boundary." His eyes were as hard as his tone.

"But the sale has been suspended by the state at the direction of the TVA."

"For now. We were successful in Tennessee. We can be successful here."

Meg leaned forward in her chair. "Why that land in particular?"

"You mean beside our desire to diversify and to invest in the land, which in itself is a legitimate interest?"

"There must be more to it than that. Why not another parcel of land? What is it about this specific land that would take you all the way to the Supreme Court?"

Cobbrey leaned back in his chair, the fire in his eyes banking slightly at her question. "Because that area has cultural significance to us. There is a memorial for one of our great warriors there. It includes the birthplace of another." His hand rose to toy with the necklace at his throat.

Meg nodded in understanding; now things were starting to make sense. "Thank you for explaining. That gives your desire for that specific land a new perspective."

"Tell me, sir, are any of your members skilled bowhunters?" Torres interjected.

Cobbrey's eyes narrowed on Torres and he was still for a moment, save for his fingers rubbing the hammered silver of the disk as if it were a touchstone. "I feel like we're now actually getting to the reason for your visit. Tell me what that reason is or this discussion is over. I won't have the members of my tribe discussed by federal law enforcement without knowing why. And possibly having one of our tribal lawyers present."

Meg exchanged glances with Torres. It was a classic strategy with these kinds of interviews—try to ask as many questions as you could before letting the subject know specifics about the case, at which point they could then start to craft excuses around those details. But often, at a certain point, you had to give minimal information because no one wanted to be interrogated for no known cause. Meg nodded at Torres in encouragement.

"Because there have been several deaths we feel are related to the land acquisition by the TVA," Torres said. "Or rather, we feel the deaths are related to stopping that land acquisition. The killer uses a compound bow as his weapon of choice."

"You think because the killer hunts with a bow and arrow that an Indian must be responsible?" Outrage colored Cobbrey's words.

"Not at all. So far, no one we've talked to has been Native American." Torres's voice remained cool and collected in face of the snap and fire in Cobbrey's tone. "I'm looking for an elite hunter who has turned his eye to other prey. Some of the members of your tribe are skilled bowhunters. That's the only thing I'm looking for. That and motive, which the EBCI also has."

"You think one of my people would kill to reclaim our land?" Cobbrey cast his eye to a large framed photo of a group of men and women in two rows in a room lined in stripes of pale, blond wood. "Perhaps you think it's one of our council members?"

Meg stared at the photo. The people in the photo covered a range of characteristics—male and female, fair and darker skinned, blond, brunette, black, and gray haired, young and old. Anyone who thought of the Cherokee, or any of the modern tribes, as a stereotype à la the Golden Age of Hollywood didn't have a clue about the diversity of today's tribal populations.

By all appearances, they live together as a diverse population better than their non-tribal neighbors.

"I'm not pointing fingers at anyone in particular at this time. But I'm currently looking at anyone with means and motive, and that includes the members of the EBCI."

"We would also be happy to exclude any members of the EBCI who could not have been responsible." Meg locked gazes with Cobbrey so he could have no doubt about her sincerity. "If you cooperate with us, we'll only look at members who had the particular skill set we need to consider. And if they alibi out, that will be the end of the story. Your assistance will make the entire process go faster. You know Special Agent Torres could come back with all the warrants he needs. But we'd prefer to work with you rather than against you. We'll never be able to truly understand your challenges. But we can try to make the process as easy as possible for you. We have no agenda other than to find the person responsible for three horrific deaths."

"Three."

"Yes, over the past two and a half weeks."

"My people are not responsible. We know better than to use violence to solve our problems. That will only be revisited upon us many times over. We use the court system. A legally binding decision is our only way forward."

"That's how *you* feel. But how do you know that's how your people feel?" Skepticism was thick in Torres's tone.

"Because they are my people." One hand came down hard on Cobbrey's desk. "Can I guarantee the honor of every one of the citizens of our nation? Of course not. That would be naïve. There are over sixteen thousand of us. But we have learned lessons harder than most others. And a few deaths would not stop a government agency. It would be a wasted effort."

"Then help us prove that." Meg looked at the photo of the council members before turning to Cobbrey. "Help us strike you from the list. Then no one else will be able to point the finger at you, either."

For a long moment, Cobbrey simply stared at her, the weight of his decision clear in his eyes. To help the FBI might be seen by some of his people as a betrayal. But it was also the best way to prove their innocence. "All right. What do you need?"

"Hunting records. Archery club memberships. Word of mouth," Meg said. "Let's build a list and try to knock it down. And if there's anyone left standing after that, then help us deal with them fairly. It's all we ask."

His drawn mouth and hard jaw telegraphed both his discomfort with the request and the burden of leadership. But he picked up his phone and dialed a number. "James, come to my office, please. I need your help." He met Meg's eyes across the wide expanse of his desk. "The tribe needs your help."

CHAPTER 18

Werowance: A Powhatan word for a local chief, usually at the village level.

Sunday, April 14, 7:14 PM
Laurel Ridge Vineyards
Blue Ridge, Georgia

The town of Blue Ridge had come out to the town hall in force.

Meg had thought they'd be early when they pulled into the parking lot at 6:15 PM, but it was already over three-quarters full of cars and dirt-splattered pickup trucks—it wasn't just the residents of Blue Ridge in attendance, but also their more rural neighbors from surrounding areas. Two large buses occupied one corner of the lot, and there was heavy foot traffic around the main buildings, the parking lot, and over to the far west side of the lot, where an elevated platform looked out over neat rows of grapevines marching down the west face of the slope. On the far side of the lot, a line of news vans was parked at the edge of the asphalt. Beyond, the ridges and valleys of the Appalachian Mountains rose and fell in shades of emerald, kelly, and hunter green in the early-evening sun.

Now, a quarter hour into the session, the banquet hall overflowed into the foyer beyond the double doors. When more cars continued to pull into the parking lot, the vineyard's social director threw open the glass French doors leading out onto the patio, and more townsfolk crowded in. Blue Ridge Mayor Cassie Taylor had taken the change in stride, having the podium removed from what had been the front of the room and turning the space into a theater-in-the-round. Now she stood, surrounded by packed chairs and a standing room–only audience, a cordless microphone in her hand as she slowly turned in a circle, taking care to include every person in attendance in the discussion. Camera crews were set up against one wall, and the reporters were clustered in one of the impromptu aisles, each holding a microphone and glancing at their own camera crew, perfectly coiffed and ready for a close-up on their killer question.

With Hawk wearing his FBI vest and sitting patiently at her feet, Meg stood toward the back of the banquet hall as Mayor Taylor called Blue Ridge Police Chief Danvers forward and handed him the mic. While Danvers talked about area law enforcement's joint investigation—or at least the information they had all agreed was safe to release—Meg scanned the room.

Torres had handed off his time at the microphone to Danvers because he wanted the case to have a familiar and trusted face. He now stood by the main entranceway, his back to the wall while he constantly scanned the room. Brian stood buried in the crowd spilling onto the patio, just inside one of the French doors, Lacey at his side, but hidden in the crush of bodies. McCord sat in the second row on Meg's side, having eschewed his more obvious notepad for the voice recorder on the phone in the pocket of his shirt. Webb sat toward the rear on the opposite side from McCord. And sprinkled throughout the crowd, Meg spotted many of the faces of the law enforcement officers she'd met that first day.

Like her, they were watching the crowd, not the police chief.

There were familiar civilian faces in the crowd as well. Principal Chief Charles Cobbrey attended with two members of his tribal council. The Trammell and Cavett families were both there. McCord had pointed to a woman who looked to be in her early fifties and mouthed *Beverley*.

Thomas Atwell was conspicuously absent.

The crowd's mood was a combination of fear, resentment, and vigilantism. Danvers, however, was doing an excellent job of explaining the investigation without revealing what the team suspected was the killer's motive. He cleverly handled the media, firmly putting them in their place when they tried to interrupt him with questions after every sentence. Claiming the floor again, uninterrupted, he made it clear the killings were not random, the few specific people who were at risk were being informed, and steps were being taken to safeguard them. The crowd seemed to relax slightly then, the couple in front of Meg reassuring each other in whispers that since the cops hadn't talked to them, they must be safe.

Danvers was stretching the truth, but he did it in order to keep the townsfolk calm. It was true that if the Copperhill Dam was the flashpoint for the suspect, then there were specific targets; however, that number could be quite large and could involve residents from several states and even Washington, DC. Torres had already contacted the CEO of the TVA, who immediately moved to take steps to quietly warn his people, even as Torres was working his way through the list of state politicians who might also be targets. They all knew there was a good chance they'd miss someone, but most of the people in this room were safe because they were never targets in the first place.

Danvers was finishing up. "For the overwhelming majority of you, you are not at risk. However, I understand your desire to protect yourselves just in case, and there are a few things you can do. Be aware of your surroundings. One hundred to one hundred and twenty yards is the range to consider. Anything beyond that, an accurate shot is not possible for this archer with this weapon. Keep in mind the archer is likely wearing camo and will not be visible within leaf cover, but you are safer in town due to its open spaces and lack of an escape route. If you live out of town and can't avoid forested areas, stay in motion. The archer needs to be able to aim at the victim, and a body in motion is a poor target. And keep the terrain and line of sight in mind. If you can't see a location, someone in that location can't see you, either."

A voice from somewhere outside the open French doors bellowed, "Send the son of a bitch my way. Me, Smith, and Wesson will teach him a lesson he won't forget!"

That got chortles and whoops from men around him, but a cool stare from Danvers. "This is not a man to be trifled with. He's not a man to engage with. If you think you know who the archer may be, you will tell law enforcement and we'll follow up on it. This is not a moment for vigilante justice." His stare drilled into the speaker. "You probably wouldn't live long enough to regret the decision, so don't go down that road." Danvers turned his back on the man and continued to address the crowd. "Be aware, be smart, but don't let paranoia rule your life. Now, any questions?"

A flurry of hands shot up with a sudden babble of voices. Holding a microphone, a stylish brunette dressed in a pencil skirt and slingback heels stepped forward from where she stood in the crowded aisle between rows of chairs. Danvers nodded at her.

"Penelope Grand, WXIA News. Chief, as we all know, Atlanta is a hub of illegal drug distribution by the Mexican cartels. Is the methamphetamine trade the flashpoint for the attacks? Or the influx of Chinese opioids?"

"We're certainly considering all possible motives, but we aren't able to share our conclusions at this time. You there, sir. In the second row."

"Who should we be looking out for? Is he young? Old?"

"That isn't information we can share at this time."

"So we should be suspicious of everybody?" Alarm drove the man's tone of voice higher.

"Not at all. This is only one person. You know your neighbors, and the people you do business with in town. You know us. Have faith in the people you know."

"It sounds like you don't know nothin'," a voice bellowed from the back. "We pay your salary. You gotta protect us. Do your goddamned job."

Danvers opened his mouth to speak, but Taylor stepped forward and slipped the mic out of his hand with an apologetic smile. "Wayne, that's not helping. It's a difficult case and it's taking some time, but they're working diligently. In the meantime, we have to do our best to stay watchful, but avoid being paranoid. I understand you're scared, but you have my word on it that all the agencies involved are cooperating and sharing information, and they're doing their level best to solve this as soon as possible."

"But are you sure they're—"

"You have my word, Wayne." Taylor smoothly cut him off. "Now sit down and let someone else ask a question."

There was grumbling from the rear of the room, but the

man sat down. Taylor returned the mic to Danvers and stepped back.

A woman stood up near the cameras. "I read on Facebook that this is a deep state op. How do we know you're not part of it?" A murmur ran through the crowd.

"Ma'am, this case is not a conspiracy theory. None of the law enforcement agencies involved have a vested interest in anything other than apprehending this killer."

Meg noticed the camera crews really zooming in on both Danvers and the questioner. When the town hall hit the news, she had a bad feeling that it wasn't going to be the tale of a careful police investigation that headlined the story, but the threat of a dark conspiracy.

"But big corporations run our government and—"

"Ma'am," Danvers snapped, his temper clearly starting to wear thin, "there is no room for conspiracy theories here."

"That sounds like something a deep state operative would say."

"There is no one like that here, ma'am." Danvers turned his back on the woman. "Yes, you sir."

An older man stood up, but paused, looking over the crowd.

"Sir?" Danvers prompted.

"My neighbor, Larry, he has a bow."

"Just because he has a bow, sir, doesn't mean he's the killer. Lots of people legally bowhunt and don't kill their neighbors."

"But Larry doesn't care about hunting seasons."

"Poaching's not the issue we're dealing with, sir. We're investigating a capital offense, not someone breaking the law under the Georgia Department of Natural Resources."

"But crime is a slippery slope. Once you start down that road—"

"Thank you, sir. I don't hear a question, so I'm going to move on."

The questions went on for a few more minutes, but Danvers had already shared everything he could and the crowd was getting restless with the lack of any new information, so he shut down the questioning.

Taylor stepped forward to close the meeting. "Thank you all for attending tonight and for your questions. We will do our utmost to keep you all apprised of critical information. Chief Danvers and I will stay afterward if you have any remaining questions or personal concerns. And if you have any questions after tonight, please don't hesitate to contact my office, the Blue Ridge Police Department, or the Georgia State Patrol. Stay alert and stay safe. Good night."

The noise level in the room exploded as the crowd stood to leave or chatted with their neighbors.

Time to move.

Turning, Meg saw Torres was already weaving his way through the door on his way to the parking lot to continue watching the crowd. She tightened up on Hawk's leash, forcing him to stay close in the crowd, and stepped forward. "Hawk, come. Excuse us."

They slowly pushed through the throng of townsfolk—*excuse me, pardon me, sorry, if we could just get through*—toward the outside doors. Then they were out in the fresh spring evening, where the temperature dipped dramatically in comparison to the overly warm banquet room of packed bodies. Meg gratefully sucked in a long breath of cool air as a gentle breeze wafted the clean scent of freshly turned earth and new life past her.

In the distance, the sun had set, but the last of the day's glow lit the sky in tones of amber and russet, highlighting wispy clouds sketched across the deepening bowl of sky. The vineyard was located down the west slope of Rocky

Mountain on a long, shallow, fertile stretch of land perfect for the neat rows of vines. This early in the year, the plants were two-foot-tall woody stumps, each with a bright green shock of leaves bursting from the top to wind their way along the supporting guide wires. The vibrant fields were now shrouded in twilight, but still stretched out as far as the eye could see before fading into the shadows.

The vineyard tours were over for the day, and the parking lot was now empty of the tour buses that had taken up large swaths of asphalt earlier. Townsfolk streamed out the double doors in a crescendo of voices as they headed toward their cars. A few paused to chat with friends and neighbors before leaving, but most pulled out right away, traveling toward home and the oncoming workweek. Meg climbed a few steps up a winding concrete staircase that circled the banquet center to curve up the slope toward the upper fields. From here, she could see most of the parking lot and much of the empty surrounding fields.

Fifteen minutes later, the evening light was fading fast, shrouding the fields in gloom. The brightly lit parking lot was mostly empty as stragglers continued to wander out of the banquet facilities. Disappointingly, no one in attendance stood out to Meg in any way; she could only hope one of her colleagues had seen something distinctive. Otherwise, while the session had been useful for the residents of Fannin County, it had not been helpful for the law enforcement team.

The sound of raised voices attracted her attention as a group surrounding Mayor Taylor came out of the building. Meg wasn't close enough to hear the conversation, but angry tones carried clearly in the evening air. Across the parking lot, Torres and Brian stood in opposite corners watching closely. As the group angled toward Meg, she identified Mason and Will Cavett in the pack, and it was Mason's voice that carried over everyone else's. The argument went back and forth between Cavett and Taylor, and while Cavett towered over her, and had bulk and sheer anger on his side, Taylor didn't back down, meeting each strident statement with a calm, measured tone.

Is that about the city's position on the dam, or does it have to do with the legal action mounted against it? Either way, Mason Cavett is not happy about how the mayor is dealing with the situation.

The group stopped behind a Mercedes SUV, but the argument continued. Torres clearly decided enough was enough and started across the parking lot, weaving between cars as he slipped his hand into the breast pocket of his jacket, where he kept his identification. If he was going to break up the escalating argument, he clearly meant to do it as a law enforcement officer.

Everything happened so fast, Meg couldn't tell which sound came first. But through the cacophony of the argument came a scream, several cries of alarm, the shattering of glass, and the explosive, repetitive blast of a car alarm.

"Talon, down!"

Meg dropped low beside Hawk, throwing one arm over his back, her first response being to protect her dog.

There was a moment of silence, then an anguished *"Will!"*

Meg shot up, her position on the steps giving her a clear view of the parking lot. Brian was similarly crouched, only his head showing between cars. He gave her a thumbs-up—*we're okay*—and she returned the gesture. Other townspeople were scattered throughout the parking lot, some crouched low, some simply standing dumbfounded in place, sitting ducks in case of a continuing attack. The group near the Mercedes SUV had scattered, jumping between cars or simply running. Except for Will Cavett, who lay on the ground, and his father, who was crawling toward him. The SUV's rear lights flashed as its alarm continued to shriek. It was then Meg realized its rear window was shattered. But there'd been no sound of a gunshot.

The archer.

Meg sprang to her feet. "Hawk, come!" They jumped off the steps and sprinted across the parking lot. A flash of movement to Meg's left told her Torres was coming in fast from his side of the property.

Meg loosened up on Hawk's leash, giving him room to follow her twisting path around parked cars, and they quickly reached the SUV.

Will lay on the ground, his father on one side and Cassie Taylor on the other. Taylor had her hands wrapped around Will's upper arm, blood seeping through her fingers and staining his sleeve red.

"Someone please call nine-one-one. We need an ambulance." Her voice was impressively calm, a woman used to dealing with crises, especially lately. She looked up at Torres as he arrived, then over at Chief Danvers, who appeared out of nowhere between vehicles. "I must have been next on the list and he missed me. Will was winged instead." She had to raise her voice to be heard over the blasting of the alarm.

Meg and Torres shared a look laden with silent communication. Will Cavett had been hit with his father standing at his side—unless there was another archer working with them, neither of them could be their suspect.

The arrow. Meg circled Will, carefully staying well clear of him, and peered into the SUV through the broken window. Inside the cargo compartment, an arrow was embedded in the back of the rear seats. One quick look told Meg it was the same mechanically expanding head, the same black carbon shaft, the same fletching as before.

The archer was here.

Finally, they had the chance to end this. They were never going to have a better search scenario than this, with two search teams on-site at the time of an attack.

She whipped around, peering over the cars for where the shot originated. But everything outside the glow of the parking lot lights vanished into blackness.

Luckily, the dogs didn't need to see to be able to track a suspect. They just needed to smell him.

"Brian!"

"Right here."

Meg whipped around to find Brian and Lacey beside Torres. She pointed across the parking lot. "We can't get the dogs into the back of the SUV to try to pick up scent from the arrow without it taking too much time, destroying crucial evidence, and letting the shooter get away when we're practically right on top of him, but he's going to leave a fresh trail leading away from there. They'll be able to track it no problem."

"Go." Torres waved them away.

Brian gave her a sharp nod. *Ready.*

Brian, Meg, and the dogs sprinted for the darkness.

CHAPTER 19

Roundabout: A circular intersection where traffic flows in one direction around a central island, and priority is given to vehicles already in the traffic circle.

Sunday, April 14, 8:44 PM
Laurel Ridge Vineyards
Blue Ridge, Georgia

They quickly covered the distance across the parking lot and soon melted into the blackness beyond.

"Damn," Brian muttered. "No go bags." They'd left their packs in their vehicle once it was clear that space would be at a premium inside. "Should we go back?"

"No, minutes here could make the difference in catching the suspect or not." Meg dug into her back pocket. "Use your cell for the flashlight. We'll have to go without the rest." She brought up her flashlight app and illuminated the path in front of them. Within seconds Brian's light joined hers.

They stood at the edge of the parking lot. Beyond them, lit by the cold blue-white light of their cell phones, was the elevated platform. Several steps led up to the wide wooden deck, topped by a sturdy railing. Around it, the ground fell away, sloping downward to the fields below.

Meg turned around and stared toward the parking lot, gauging distance and the angle to the SUV. "This is the right angle, but the height is wrong. The SUV isn't clearly visible from here, and the roofs of the cars on this side would be in the way, even if the suspect is tall. Hawk, come." Lighting the steps, she climbed to the platform and considered this new position. "Brian, come up here. I think this is it."

Brian joined her on the lookout. Across the tops of the vehicles, the crowd of people grouped behind the SUV was clearly visible. In between them, Meg could see right into the SUV. Dropping Hawk's leash, she held up an imaginary bow and drew it back, using her thumb as the sight and trying to connect it to the angle of the arrow lodged inside the cargo compartment. She took one step forward, then a second. "This is it. He was right here. It's a shorter shot than for Hubbert or White. Maybe sixty or seventy yards, max." She crouched down without touching the boards at her feet, not wanting to further contaminate the scents. "Hawk, Lacey, come." She pointed her fingers down toward the wood, stopping an inch above the decking as the dogs came to scent the spot. She looked up to find Brian standing over her. "There was a lot of traffic in this area, so they may pick up different scent trails. If we get separated, stay in touch by cell. If you lose signal, get in touch when you can—"

Hawk whined, drawing her attention. He and Lacey still cast about for scent, but his tail was low and his movements erratic.

"Uh-oh." Brian laid a hand on Lacey's back. "Lacey? Can you find it, girl?"

Meg took a step away and watched them for another few seconds. "We have a problem. They can't isolate the scent."

"How many people were up here?"

"When we drove in? Six or eight. But think about those buses. How many people were on them in total do you think?"

"Maybe forty-five to fifty on each? Assuming they were full."

"Even if they were only half full, that's still forty-five to fifty people who may have been standing on this platform in the last hour. Hawk and Lacey may never be able to isolate a single scent in such a heavily trafficked area. The most recent scent should be the strongest, but they may all be too recent to truly differentiate."

Brian took a single step down. "Then let's try around the platform. If the problem is the massive mix of scents, let's try to find a single track that leads away from the others. After taking the shot, the suspect would have either disappeared into the fields or circled the complex to head farther into the hills. If we find that path, we'll have a shot."

"Makes sense to me. Hawk, come." They clattered down the platform steps. "You go left, I'll go right." She turned away from Brian and Hawk followed her. "Hawk, find."

Hawk cast about for scent, took a few steps in one direction, stopped, changed direction, stopped. *He's not picking up anything definitive.*

A knot of dread coiled in Meg's belly. She flicked a glance toward the crowd seemingly spotlighted in the middle of the parking lot and thought about the downed man lying on the asphalt. *Come on, come on, we're losing time.*

But there was no rushing the dogs. They either caught the scent or they didn't.

Hawk had another false start, trotting five or six steps

before he faltered, stopped, and whined. They tried down toward the fields. *Nothing.* Then farther down the parking lot. *Nothing.* As the minutes ticked by, Meg's tension ratcheted higher and higher as that initial bright hope of catching the suspect slowly slipped through her fingers.

Finally, with a growl of frustration, she was forced to admit defeat. "Hawk, come." The Labrador turned to follow her, his head down and tail drooping. Meg stopped and crouched down, running her hands over his fur. "Good boy, Hawk, good boy. It's not your fault we can't pick up the scent." Hawk gamely wagged his tail and she kissed the top of his head. "Come on. Maybe we got lucky and Brian and Lacey hit on the trail."

But when Meg and Hawk stepped back into the light flooding the parking lot, Brian appeared at the far end. They both stopped dead when they saw each other, and Brian shook his head. Disappointment stabbed like a knife and Meg swallowed a curse, not wanting to further discourage Hawk. Heaving a sigh, she trudged toward Brian.

"Nothing?" she called when they got closer.

"Not a damned thing. My read is that the perp came back through the parking lot and got lost in the chaos of the attack."

"If that's true, then he was here tonight after all, though I didn't see anyone I pegged as suspicious. But there were lots of people. The suspect must have been in street clothes and could have gone into the banquet hall or could have been one of the people who rushed in to help after Will went down. No wonder the dogs couldn't identify the freshest set of tracks because they literally got lost in a huge crowd." She sighed. "Come on, let's go break the bad news."

They started back across the parking lot. An ambulance

was parked near the banquet hall entrance, its rear doors thrown open. Will sat on the rear bumper, his right sleeve cut away and his upper arm wrapped with a white bandage. His mother sat beside him, holding his hand, concern etching worry lines around her mouth and eyes as she watched her son. Mason and Mayor Taylor stood slightly off to one side, now talking in more reasonable tones.

"Things look calmer here now," Brian said.

"You know what they say—nothing defuses an argument quite like attempted murder." Meg pointed to where McCord stood close to the main entrance with Torres. Webb hung back a few feet behind them.

Torres glanced at them as they approached, looked away, and then did a double take back to them as if his brain suddenly registered what he saw. He stared at them in surprise, his hands outstretched in confusion. "You're back already? Alone? What happened?"

"There was no trail to follow."

"What do you mean? You were only minutes behind him. Unless he can levitate, there was a trail to follow."

The weight of Meg's disappointment frayed her temper. "We found where the shot came from. There's a scenic overlook on the far side of the parking lot. It's raised slightly so there was good visibility over the parked cars to where the mayor and her group were standing. In the dark, we couldn't see a figure standing there, but the archer had a brilliantly lit scene below to aim at." Meg tipped her head up toward the LED lights high overhead on equally spaced posts to illuminate the parking area. "Hide in the shadows, make the shot, then disappear."

"So why couldn't you follow him?" Torres's tone was insistent.

Brian grabbed Meg's arm as she was drawing breath to

snarl at him. "I got this." He swung around to Torres. "Meg already said it—there was no trail to follow. It's a scenic overlook. It's had a ton of foot traffic, probably all day. More importantly, the traffic was ongoing until very recently. Did you see those buses parked when we came in tonight?"

"Yes."

"We got here early and were chatting with one of the vineyard staffers as people were filing in. They do a popular Sunday event where groups tour the vineyard, end with a wine tasting, and then get whisked away to a late dinner at one of several local restaurants that serve Laurel Ridge Vineyards wines. The buses were already parked when we got here, and there were groups of people standing on the lookout, enjoying the view over the hills and valleys as the sun was setting in front of them. Then they packed onto the buses and went on their way."

Torres was practically twitching with frustration. "What does that have to do with anything?"

"All those people, standing there within the past hour, possibly the past half hour. Maybe only ten or fifteen minutes before we came out. All that fresh scent."

The twitching stopped as understanding made Torres's jaw drop slightly.

"The shooter added one more scent onto the platform. It was a jumbled mess of scents to the dogs. When a scent is that fresh, and that plentiful, often the dogs can't differentiate the one scent they need to find, especially if it's a scent we aren't carrying to remind them what they're looking for."

Torres held out his hands defensively. "Okay, I get it now." He looked at Meg. "Sorry, I had high hopes on this one."

"Trust me," Meg said, "we did, too. This is beyond disappointing. We did a full search around the platform to cover any direction a single person could have exited, but all the scents combined into one mass exodus toward the parking lot. Once you get close, the scents were pulling the dogs in every direction into the parking lot, but there was no definitive trail to follow. We knew we were out of luck, but kept trying anyway, just in case. But . . . nothing." She looked over at Will. "How's he doing?"

"I've been standing back letting them work on him," Torres said. "Let me go check."

"No need." Webb stepped out of the shadows behind Torres. "It was a pretty deep contusion, but he just caught the edge of the spinning arrowhead blades. They basically carved a half-inch-wide strip of skin and muscle from his arm. There wasn't anything to stitch, so they cleaned it, bandaged it, updated his tetanus shot, and started him on antibiotics because open wounds are prone to infection."

Torres stared at him, dumbfounded. "And you are?"

"Lieutenant Todd Webb. I'm a paramedic with DC Fire and Emergency Medical Services."

"And my partner," Meg clarified. "He's down here to see me when I'm off shift and came with me to the open house tonight."

"And how do you know all that?"

"I went over and chatted up one of the paramedics. Once he saw my ID, he was happy to talk shop. The young man's going to be fine, though he's going to have a pretty impressive scar to show the ladies."

"It's also going to mean he's not going to be able to bowhunt for a while," Meg added. "There's no way he's going to be able to manage the draw weight of a bowstring to aim accurately with an injury like that. If the attacks continue, then we'll know for certain it's not him. In case we need more proof to take him off the suspect list."

"Hard to be the suspect when you're also the target," Brian said. "Unless he hired someone of equally high skill to make that shot to take the heat off him. Which isn't likely, because this isn't a skill you can crowdsource."

"Can't disagree with you there," Meg said. "Sam, we're going to need to revise the suspect list."

"Yeah, I figured that." He ran a hand through his hair. "I feel like we took a gigantic step backward tonight. Not only are we adding a victim to the list, though this one will survive, we had almost all our suspects on-site, and many of them were still here and in plain sight when the shooting occurred."

"You're not wrong about losing ground tonight," Meg said. "I know it's unlikely, but maybe it *is* time to look more seriously at the idea of a contract killer. Even if one wasn't used before, there's no better way to take suspicion off yourself than being in sight when another shooting happens. It's a built-in alibi no one would question."

"Maybe whoever was hired isn't as good a shot, either," Brian suggested. "Maybe that's why the mayor was missed and Will became collateral damage."

"All things we'll have to consider." Torres was silent for a moment as he searched the parking lot, his gaze finally coming to rest on Danvers and several other officers standing in a knot under one of the light posts. "I'm going to go update everyone else. Go home, get some rest, and we'll hit this fresh in the morning." He strode away, covering the parking lot in long strides that spoke of restrained anger.

Meg blew out a long breath. "He's pissed. Not that I blame him. For a few glorious minutes, I thought we'd wrap this tonight, too." Her shoulders drooped. "Pretty discouraging, and not just for Hawk and Lacey."

At the sound of his name, Hawk nudged her hand with

his nose and bumped against her legs, wagging his tail affectionately.

"Let's get them home." Brian ruffled the fur on the back of Lacey's neck. "Then let's get a good night's rest. We need to be ready. I have a bad feeling the clock is ticking and he's not going to wait long to take out the next victim."

CHAPTER 20

Tlanuwa: A giant mythological bird of prey with impenetrable metal feathers.

Tuesday, April 16, 12:32 PM
Lake View Cabins
Blue Ridge, Georgia

Meg and Brian started the day with a light breakfast, followed by a jog up and down mountain roads with the dogs, and then a half hour of agility training and parkour drills using the natural landscape—rocks and tree stumps—as obstacles and balance beams. They returned to the cabin to find Webb and McCord waiting for them with lunch ready to go. Two speedy showers later, they were all sitting down to a meal together.

Meg was settling in with an extra cup of coffee when her cell rang. She glanced at the display—Sam Torres—and then at Webb across the table as she answered the call. "Jennings."

"He got another one."

Meg's head jerked up to find Brian across the room, where he was discussing some intricacy of dog training with McCord. She snapped her fingers twice to get his attention. "Goddammit. If we'd gotten him on Sunday, this one would be alive." She pushed away from the table and stood. "Who and where?" She strode to the front hall closet, opened it, and pulled out first her go bag, then Brian's.

Webb headed for the side door, returning momentarily with her hiking boots.

Meg sat down on the bottom step of the staircase, wedging her phone between her ear and shoulder, and laced on her boots over thick socks pulled over the cuffs of her yoga pants.

"His name was John Greyson and he was killed at his hunting cabin in the Cohutta Mountains."

"Why does that name sound familiar?"

"Because he used to be a congressman in the House of Representatives. He also made headlines recently with his push for Native rights. Greyson himself was Chickasaw."

"Chickasaw, not Cherokee. So no interest in the land involved."

"Not directly, but Greyson was a proponent of Native rights for all tribes, not just his own. His family had a falling out with the Chickasaw leaders in Oklahoma decades ago, and they had enough money saved to leave the reservation and return to their ancestral lands in northwest Georgia. Greyson was the representative for one of those districts. But, given his family's circumstances, and that they were uprooted from the greater tribe in its current location to return to Georgia, he had a deep understanding of what it was to lose your land and want it back. He encouraged the North Carolina Cherokee to reclaim what was once theirs and supported their efforts even though they weren't his constituents."

Meg stood and took the FBI windbreaker Webb held out to her, smiling her thanks as she shrugged into it. One quick glance at Brian showed he and Lacey were ready to go. "Brian and I are ready. Where are we going?" She shouldered her bag, gave Hawk the hand signal for "come," and stepped toward the door.

"The cabin is just east of Crandall. Greyson was getting ready to go hunting when he was shot in his own doorway. His wife was standing only ten feet away inside the house and saw the whole thing. Called for help, but he was already gone."

"The archer was waiting for him to leave and picked Greyson off when he opened his front door."

"That's my take on it. I'll text you the exact location, but it's going to take you over an hour to get there. It's only about twenty-five miles as the crow flies, but twice that on country roads. The cabin is right on the edge of protected lands called the Cohutta Wilderness, so there are only limited roads into that area."

Meg swallowed a curse. They were here in Georgia, and they were still going to lose the killer because they were simply too far away via mountain roads. On top of that, they were literally being sent somewhere so isolated, it was called a "wilderness."

"The sooner we leave, the sooner we get there. Text me the location so I can map our fastest route." She looked up to meet Brian's nod of agreement. "We're on our way."

Tuesday, April 16, 1:54 PM
Off West Cow Pen Road
Murray County, Georgia

They met Murray County Sheriff Jasper at Greyson's cabin.

From West Cow Pen Road, they followed the twin track depressions through weeds and grass up into the hills, finally coasting to a halt behind the sheriff's SUV. As Brian cut the engine, an older, balding man in brown pants, a beige long-sleeved shirt, and a heavy utility belt with his star-shaped badge neatly pinned over his left breast pocket climbed out of the SUV. He stood with his hands on his hips, eying them through the windshield, and worked a wad of gum hard enough to make Meg wonder if he'd recently given up chewing tobacco.

Meg quickly scanned the cabin behind him. It was relatively new, constructed in the style of a rustic log cabin with a tall fieldstone chimney on one side and a wide expanse of front-facing windows. A long, covered porch ran the length of the structure with room for four Adirondack chairs, perfectly angled toward a breathtaking mountain vista. The only thing out of place was the front door that remained open despite the coolness of the mountain air.

They quickly made introductions, and then Jasper led them up the porch steps to where Greyson had been killed. It quickly became clear why the door was propped open.

The body had been removed, but a wide puddle of blood flowed through the open doorway to drip in gruesome trails through the boards of the front porch. The arrow remained where it landed, embedded in the wall to the left of the doorframe.

Sheriff Jasper pointed to the floor just inside the doorway. "Greyson stepped out onto the porch and his wife was almost right behind him. The shot only missed Mrs. Greyson by about a foot, or the killer might have taken them both out." His treacly drawl was thick enough to stand a spoon in.

Standing with Brian and the dogs on the top porch step to stay clear of the gore, Meg turned in place to follow the arrow's flightpath. Situated deep in the forest, the cabin had been built on the top of a rise, the trees in front of the cabin cleared away to reveal the mountain range beyond.

"That was a tricky shot." Meg studied the stand of trees to the north of the cabin. "There's no direct angle from the front that wouldn't expose the shooter to the occupants in the cabin. So the archer had to take cover over there in those trees." She stepped forward, resting her palm against one of the rough-hewn wooden posts supporting the porch roof. "But that meant he had to take the shot from the trees to the doorway, narrowly missing this post."

"It also meant he had to be a lot closer this time," Brian added. "That's only about thirty yards away, maybe less. Which means he risked being spotted." He pointed to the windows stretching across the front of the cabin. "Especially with the victim and his wife on-site. What if she'd gone after him? She didn't need to overtake him, just catch a glimpse of his face. It could have been game over."

"It goes to show how important this crusade is to him. He's willing to risk getting in close to take the shot he needs. This is no game for him." Meg turned to Sheriff Jasper. "Has the arrow been processed?"

"Dusted for prints? Yeah."

"Is there another door to the cabin? I'd like to bring the dogs in to scent the arrow, but I don't want them tracking through the blood."

"There's a back door."

Meg glanced at Brian. "They may not pick up anything through the print powder and the overwhelming smell of blood, but it's worth a shot."

One at a time, they brought the dogs in through the back to scent the arrow, staying well clear of the blood, then backtracked outside again to determine the shooter's position in the trees.

Jasper studied the ground inside the tree line. "The shooter must have spent some time in place, waiting for

the Greysons to come outside, or his movement could
have been spotted when he moved in. If so, there could be
a place where the leaves or ground cover has been disturbed."

"You and your men haven't checked this area out yet?"
Brian asked.

"Only from a distance. When I saw how Greyson had
died, I connected this case to the others and contacted the
local FBI field office. They got me in touch with Special
Agent Torres. He said to keep my guys away from where
the shooter stood until your dogs used it as the start of the
search trail. After that, we could have full access."

"Thanks. On the bright side, that's likely an unused section of the property, so any human scent is going to stand
out for the dogs."

"And the location is going to be close to the outer tree
line. The trees are too thick to move back ten or twenty
feet, especially from this angle and when you have to aim
around the porch post."

"The dogs will tell us that for sure." Brian stepped forward into the trees and gave Lacey a hand signal. "Lacey,
find."

The dogs identified the shooter's location with amazing
speed, both zeroing in on the same area behind a tall
chestnut oak with a wide, sturdy trunk.

Jasper squatted down a few feet away, studying the
crushed ground cover, crumpled leaves, and exposed patches
of dirt with narrowed eyes. "Shooter stood here for a while.
Got restless. Got a little careless even."

"What makes you say that?" Bracing her hands on her
knees, Meg leaned in from the far side of the tree.

"You hunt?" Jasper's gaze cut down to Hawk, who still
sniffed around their identified area.

Meg stifled the expression of horror that nearly slipped by her control. Anyone who knew her knew hunting was about the last activity she'd ever participate in, but for many hunters, a water dog like a black Lab specifically meant duck hunting. "No."

"Hunting in the woods can be a challenge. Lots of obstructions when you're setting up a shot. The shooter was forced to come in relatively close, especially with that porch post blocking part of the doorway. But up close means that even behind a tree with this kind of girth, you'd have to peek out from behind. At first you'd do it carefully." He put actions to words, placing himself out of sight behind an adjacent tree and leaning out slightly to reveal only a sliver of his face. "But after a while, you get a little restless and maybe overconfident and you do this." He stepped out from behind the tree, giving Meg a full-body slice of him from his heavy brown boots to the top of his bald head. "If you're out deer hunting and step out like that, you give the deer a better chance of seeing the larger movement and bounding away. In this case, you run the risk of attracting the attention of anyone in the cabin who might be looking out."

"We're running under the assumption the shooter is wearing camo," Brian said.

"Most likely, but camo doesn't make you invisible. Just helps you blend in." He squatted down again and drew a circle with his index finger around part of the undergrowth. "You see this here? See how some of these softer stems are crushed and broken? Standing out here would have made the shooter partially visible from the cabin. Even in camo."

Meg circled the tree to study the spot, then looked up toward the cabin. "But the shooter would have to step out to take the shot. You'd need more room to shoot an arrow than fire a rifle."

"Right. But imagine you're holding your bow as you stand behind the tree. You'll only have a second to set up your shot, so you've already got an arrow nocked and ready." Jasper mimed holding a bow with a nocked arrow at his side, pointed at the ground. When your target comes in sight, you . . ." He stepped straight out, raised his invisible bow, pulled back, took a second to aim his shot, and released his virtual bowstring. "You don't . . ." He lowered the bow to the starting position, then stepped out, raising the bow, then stepped forward one pace, resettled, then pulled back, aimed, and released.

Meg nodded in understanding. "I follow you. You do the minimum movement because it's faster and doesn't draw as much attention. And stepping out to the right of the tree means more of you can stay behind the tree. Step to the left and all of you is out in the open."

"As long as you shoot right-handed."

"Ninety percent of the population is right-handed, so we have a good chance there." Meg's gaze dropped to the crushed greenery. "Yet the shooter stepped out and around the trunk, where he might have been seen."

"That's my take."

"We think this is an experienced hunter, so wouldn't this be someone who would be used to waiting for his target to wander by?" Brian asked. "Isn't that the whole concept behind a blind?"

"Sure is. But a hunter in a blind is never standing. You sit in some blinds, lie in others. Because standing is tiring, and that makes you fidgety."

"And that's when you get careless and step out where you might be seen," Meg finished. "Got it."

"I'll get in there once the dogs are gone, but I think I see a partial boot print. If so, we'll cast it."

"We'll get out of your way, then." Meg looked at Brian. "Because of the route we had to take to get here, we're too far behind again even though we were in-state at the time of the killing. The shooter will be long gone. We'll do the search, but I doubt we'll find anything useful."

"Won't know until we try," said Brian.

"True enough. Thanks, Sheriff. We'll be in touch." Meg bent and indicated the flattened spot behind the tree and Hawk gave it another cursory sniff. "Hawk, find."

They let the dogs lead them into the trees, the cabin quickly melting into the forest behind them.

Despite the sunshine, only diffuse light trickled through areas of thicker leaf canopy. But the dogs' steps were sure and they trotted forward side by side in total agreement.

The dogs followed no visible path, but pushed through the forest, crunching over dried leaves and climbing over and around mossy boulders. The higher they climbed, the rockier it became, slowing their pace. They took the dogs off their leads, allowing them to leap from boulder to boulder gracefully, leaving their handlers to scramble up after them with significantly less coordination.

"Maybe it's time *we* started doing agility drills," Brian muttered.

"It couldn't hurt." Hooking her fingers over the lip of the rock above her, Meg pulled herself up. "But this makes me think the shooter had to be wearing some sort of pack or sling for the bow. You're not going to manage this climb if you're carrying a bow in one hand. He must be carrying it on his back."

"That makes sense. Also protects the bow from damage when climbing through this rocky terrain."

The dogs led them down again, into thicker tree cover,

but the ground fell away to their right, the trees growing precariously from the rocky ground, some losing their battle with gravity to sag sideways at an angle. Far down below, a break in the foliage revealed the dark, winding bed of a wide river, flowing fast enough that white-water foam was evident more than a hundred feet below.

"What's that down there?" Brian asked.

"If I remember the map correctly, that's the Conasauga River."

"It looks brutal. Let's hope he didn't try to escape that way."

"Doubtful. On our way to the cabin, while you were driving, I was scouting the area on Google Maps. That part of the river has Class IV rapids for white-water rafting. Our shooter doesn't strike me as the insane type who'd try to escape that way, especially after all the rains they apparently had here this spring. The water level looks high and the current fast, the kind of conditions that could sweep you away to drown. I'd bet money on him escaping via dry land because even though he likely knows we have dogs, it would be suicidal to try to ford that river, at least right now."

The path narrowed, forcing the dogs to go one at a time, and Brian dropped back with Lacey. The scent must have been stronger, because Hawk picked up his pace, forcing Meg to break into a jog behind him. But a few minutes later, the path closed in farther as it sunk into a small valley with a track crossing the ridge of a rocky wall rising above them to their right and then falling off to their left. About a hundred feet ahead, the path opened up to a green valley below.

But Hawk's tread was sure, and he was apparently unfazed by the need for careful stepping.

Sometimes it's good to have a low center of gravity.

"Hawk, slow. We're not all as coordinated as you and Lacey."

As if the universe heard her, a loose stone shifted under Meg's boot and she slipped, flailing her arms to keep her balance on the narrow, rocky path, letting out a small cry that brought Hawk up short. "Sorry, buddy." She stopped, catching her breath and her balance, and then turned to check on Brian, still about twenty feet behind her. "Careful up here," she called. Facing forward again, she bent to rub a hand over Hawk's back to reassure him she was fine.

The arrow sang over her back like the crack of a whip, exploding against the rock wall directly beside her.

Meg took only a lightning-fast moment to process the attack before jumping into motion. "Talon, go!"

Hawk bounded forward, leaping down the path. Meg sprinted behind him, careful steps forgotten in the face of a much deadlier danger. A second arrow followed the first, whistling over Hawk's back by mere inches before skittering across the rocks with a metallic whine.

Fury filled her. *What kind of person would target a dog? Her dog?* The answer came with stunning clarity. *The kind of person who would purposely risk themselves waiting at a murder scene for search teams to arrive to pick them off. Especially if the dogs were the intended target. That would make other handlers think twice about joining the next time.*

Because a born hunter wouldn't hesitate to kill, be it human or animal.

They were in big trouble.

They needed to get out of the open, where they were sitting ducks. Ahead, the rocky outcrop on her right crawled away from the path, and blue sky and rolling hills were visible past trees bunched near the path in the distance. *Get into the trees. If he can't see us, he can't shoot us.*

"Talon, run!"

Her heart thumping and breath grating, Meg bent forward and powered after her dog, her eyes locked on the path. Any misstep that would take her down would leave her an easy target for certain death from the gutting of an arrow.

Keep moving.

Another arrow whipped by, this time a few feet behind her. She tossed a quick look to her left, but above her, up the rocky hillside, there was nothing but a blur of boulders and trees.

Taking about three seconds to reload and aim. Rushing it, so his aim is off.

Wilcox's words rang in her head—*An elite hunter only needs one arrow to make a kill. That's the kind of hunter we're looking at here.*

Not so elite now, are you? It's a lot harder when your target refuses to stand still.

Every arrow that missed gave them seconds of escape time, and Meg fully intended to use them. She didn't dare look back, but suspected Brian was safe, wherever he was. If there was just one archer, only one of them was likely the target.

Lucky her.

The path widened ahead as the rocky terrain opened up to reveal a steep slope to the right with the glint of the churning Conasauga River snaking below through scrub and trees. Ahead the path eased downward into the cradle of the forest.

We can make it. Only about sixty feet. We just—

The arrow drilled into the rocky path only a foot in front of her, embedding itself at a steep angle. Meg had only a split second to try to maneuver her foot around it, but she was moving too fast and there was no time to change course. Her left boot hooked on the arrow and she crashed forward into the rock-strewn path, only barely getting her hands up in time to break her fall. Air whooshed from her lungs as the jarring landing nearly knocked the wind out of her. Instantly recognizing the danger of her position, unmoving on the ground, she did the only thing possible and rolled to her right, aiming to take shelter below the edge of the path away from the archer. As she rotated, the pack she wore stopped her sideways motion. Pressing both hands into the dirt, she pushed with all her might, rolling over the bulk of the pack to go over the edge of the path to the hillside beyond.

The force that saved her from an arrow strike now played against her. She reached out to stop her roll, but nothing but mossy rocks, dried leaves, and buried tree roots met her fingertips, not offering any chance for a handhold. Then she was tumbling down a slope steeper than she anticipated, rolling and spinning out of control, her hands outstretched, grasping for any hold. But anything she managed to get a partial grip on ripped painfully out of her hands as inertia carried her downward. Hard rocks buffeted her body, tossing her like a rag doll, and then her only thought was to protect her head rather than stop her slide. Stiff, scrubby branches whipped at her exposed skin, and one ripped across her forehead, slicing like a knife.

She made a Hail Mary grab for another branch as she spun by, this time latching on desperately and trying to swing her body around to dig her boots into the ground downhill to stop her descent. She got her right boot into the dirt, pushing back hard, but it wasn't enough, and her inertia carried her forward into a somersault and then tumbling farther down through the underbrush.

Somewhere in the distance, she heard a dog barking frantically.

Abruptly she went airborne as her body helplessly spun like a top.

Then she was tossed into ice-cold water, the surface closing over her head as the raging current wrapped around her flailing body, dragging her inexorably under.

CHAPTER 21

Strainer: A river hazard caused by an obstruction like a downed tree that constricts the flow of water in multiple places. As the current flows through the strainer it pulls anything on the surface underwater into the strainer.

Tuesday, April 16, 2:47 PM
Cohutta Wilderness
Murray County, Georgia

Meg's knee-jerk reaction to the stunning cold was to gasp in a startled breath, and she only barely caught herself in time to stop icy water from pouring into her lungs. Tumbling through the water, dragged by a current that kept trying to pull her deeper, she kicked out, trying to fight her way back up. A second later, her head broke the surface and she sucked in a huge lungful of air just before water churned over her head and she went under again.

Dragged and buffeted, Meg had the presence of mind to shimmy out of her pack, knowing the added weight would only drag her down or wedge her against obstacles. The bag slithered off, returning freedom of movement and some of her buoyancy. She clawed her way to the surface again, blinking furiously, kicking hard to keep her head above water. Around her, the river seethed like it was just below the boiling point, and flotsam—branches in full leaf and larger tree limbs—stabbed out of the water and then disappeared again under the foam.

Search-and-rescue handlers were trained in wilderness survival because of the amount of time spent outdoors, often in isolated and dangerous locations. Meg knew how to handle a fall into the river, but her training hadn't counted on Class IV rapids as an extra layer of lethal challenge. Rafters and kayakers fell out of their boats all the time, but they had life jackets, helmets, and wet suits to protect them from deadly obstacles and the brutal cold. She had no protective gear whatsoever.

But she knew the rules that could save her life: Never attempt to stand or put a foot down—if it got wedged between rocks, the current would push her facedown into the water and hold her there while she drowned. Assume the defensive swimming position—on her back, leading with her feet so her hiking boots struck any upcoming boulders instead of her head. Try to be aware of how the water is moving and how deep it is. Swim perpendicular to the current to reach the shore and then get the hell out of the water.

Meg scanned the shoreline on one side and then the other, but everything was moving much too fast as she shot down the river.

She sucked in air, trying to keep panic at bay. *You can get out of this. Get to shore. Get where it's shallow. Find the—*

Her mind went blank as the current yanked her under again, and this time she was unprepared and gulped in a mouthful of gritty, frigid water. Frantically struggling to the surface, she desperately coughed water back up.

Move with the current, try to keep above it. Flush drowning is going to be a risk if you get many more dunkings.

Above the sound of the water, a louder roar reached her ears. Trying to rise a little out of the water, Meg stared with horror downstream to where two large boulders broke the surface, white-water foam churning around them as they split the river into channels.

She was going to have to shoot the rapids with no boat, no helmet, and no life jacket.

It was going to be a miracle if she survived the next few minutes.

With difficulty and only limited buoyancy in the choppy water, she struggled to get her body flat on the surface of the river, her boots pointed downstream. Keeping her head up and out of the water, she tried to gauge the best route— was it safer to go between the boulders or around them? She alternately paddled like mad under the surface to keep from sinking and used her hands as rudders to steady her path and steer between the boulders, where she calculated the water was deeper and could protect her from hidden rocks below. Her heart thumped as if some invisible creature was pounding its fist on her chest, and she fought to control her breathing in an effort to slow the rising panic that no matter what she did, she was about to die.

As she got closer to the rapids, the water became choppier and waves broke over her head again and again. Coughing and spluttering, Meg frantically worked to keep herself above water. Craning her head, she checked the distance again.

Twenty feet.

She was close enough now to see some of the branches crashing into the rocks and shattering into splinters on impact.

It's all over if you hit the rocks. You'll shatter like those branches.

Ten feet.

Here we go.

She took a deep breath.

She shot between the boulders, her body lifting from the water for a fraction of a second as the cascade crashed over rocks far below the surface. Then she was back in the water, swept along into an eddy where the water spun, sucking her toward the rocks she'd just cleared. The current pulled her under, tumbling her in a somersault. She fought her way to the surface and launched forward on her stomach, stroking strongly for the water that streamed past the rocks, purposely digging into it with her upstream arm so she got caught in the current and dragged along, popping free of the rapids.

She knew she'd gotten lucky, but that luck might not hold the next time. She needed to find a way out, and she needed to do it now.

Meg whipped her head toward the left bank at the sound of barking, her eyes going wide with disbelief at the sight of Hawk sprinting alongside, trying to keep pace with her. He must have followed her down the hill and then been drawn to the river by the sounds of her struggles.

Now to make sure he stayed out of it. "Talon!" She tried desperately to raise her voice above the roar of the water carrying her downstream. "No, Talon. Stay!"

She had no way of knowing if he heard her. Then there was no time to worry about her dog as the next downstream risk came into view.

A large log broke the surface of the river, snagged on something below the waterline, holding it in place so it lay as a perpendicular block across a large part of the river.

Meg had only seconds to decide how to react. There was no time to try to steer around it, so she could either go over it and risk crashing into it if she couldn't clear the obstacle, or go under and take her chances that she could escape whatever held the log in place.

Going under was possibly a death sentence, as she, too, risked getting caught in the obstruction.

Over it was.

For a fraction of a second she thought about trying to climb on top of the log and staying there, out of the danger of the raging river, but quickly realized the insanity in that plan. If the log rolled, she could get trapped by whatever caught at it from below and it would be game over.

Over and off, then.

Still on her belly facing forward, Meg dug in with an aggressive front crawl, aiming directly for the log, increasing her forward thrust in the water. When she got within ten feet, she stopped swimming, letting her momentum and the current carry her, bracing her hands out in front of her. As she hit the log, she grabbed the top of it, pulling up and levering her torso over it. It was harder than she anticipated; the cold was affecting her coordination, and her muscles were sluggish. Her fingers had trouble grasping the slimy bark, nearly slipping as she pushed her body up. But once she cleared her upper body, she kicked as hard as she could and propelled herself forward, slithering off the log and back into the water on the far side, panting in relief.

She couldn't take much more of this. She needed to get to shore before she drowned.

Flooded from the spring rains, the river was about twenty-five feet wide, and trees rose out of the water instead of along the bank. But if she could get to the side and grab a tree trunk or a branch, she might be able to use it to pull herself out.

Up ahead, several tree branches bent low over the water. Keeping her eye on the branches as she bobbed in the churning water, Meg turned and swam perpendicular to the current, hoping to make enough progress toward the bank that she'd line up with the dangling branches. A strong undertow caught at her, nearly pulling her under and causing her to swallow more water. She tossed her head back to stare up at blue sky, keeping her face above water as she fought to stay afloat and to get her arms clear of the surface.

Closer . . . closer . . .

Meg kicked with all her might, driving her body up five or six precious inches, while swinging her right arm over her head like she was serving a volleyball overhand. The first branch hit her palm with a stinging blow, then whipped away before she could close her fist around it. But she got her fingers around the branch behind it and clamped on, swinging her left hand up to help support her weight in the drag of the river.

She gave herself a moment to hang, coughing and gagging, still three-quarters in the river, her body floating downstream as the current tried to pull her along while she gathered herself.

More frantic barking sounded to her left and she glanced over at the far bank.

Hawk danced at the water's edge, not able to hold still as he desperately calculated how to reach her. He braced himself as if about to leap into the water after her, then shied away, then braced again, his eyes locked on her.

There was no doubt he was preparing to throw himself in the river after her. But if the undercurrent grabbed him, he could drown.

"Hawk, stay." Meg tried to raise her voice further. "Stay, boy. This is way too dangerous for you. I'll—"

The branch broke under her weight combined with the

added drag of the current and she fell backward into the river, her arms slapping the surface over her head as she was sucked under. Hawk's barking cut off as the sound of rushing water filled her ears. She didn't have time to catch a breath, but at least her mouth was closed this time and she clenched her teeth to keep it that way.

Meg clawed her way upward again. Exhaustion was starting to pull at her now, and combined with the temperature of the water, her muscles felt weighted with lead, delaying her reaction time. Her head broke the surface and she pushed her sodden hair out of her eyes to look for her next way out.

Something bumped into her from the side and she jerked, nearly going under. She took a precious second to find out what was in the water with her.

Hawk paddled madly beside her, working hard to keep his head above water, using his body to drive her toward the far bank. He kept himself downstream of her, seemingly sensing the only way out was to swim perpendicular to the current as it carried them along, sweeping them closer to the shoreline.

Part of her had known he wouldn't obey her command to stay, not when she was so clearly in trouble. Dogs were helpers, but search-and-rescue dogs had a drive to save that sometimes couldn't be contained by an order to stop, especially when it was their handler at risk.

Now they needed to save each other because she was terrified this river was too much, even for a natural-born water dog. They needed a plan to get out of the water before the next set of rapids, and they needed it fast. It was one thing to bob along in the brutal, sucking current. It was something else altogether to be slammed full body against the rocks that kayaks and white-water rafts skimmed over. And while she could strategically try to shoot the rapids feetfirst, she wouldn't be able to coach Hawk.

She was lucky to have made it this far with only minor bumps and bruises. But as exhaustion overtook her, staying afloat was becoming a life-or-death struggle. As her reactions slowed, the risk of flush drowning rose exponentially. Time to use the strength she had left, bolstered by her dog, and get to safety.

They floated toward where the river curved to the right, revealing a sight that made Meg's heart rate ratchet up. A maze-like cluster of rocks stabbed out of the river, blocking everything except for a narrow pathway slightly to one side of center. Past the rocks, the river disappeared, dropping out of view.

A drop like that would likely have a back current that would suck one or both of them under until they drowned.

But in a bend in the river, the water at the outside of the curve would be flowing faster than the inside. Time to aim for the inner angle of the bend. Meg pointed to the bank. "Talon! Swim!"

They both pulled hard for the right bank. When Meg's strength started to flag and her strokes faltered, Hawk only swam harder, driving her against the current and toward the bank. Then, suddenly, the rocky shoreline was under her hiking boots and Meg could push up to stand, rising out of water that came only to just above her waist. She slogged forward, gripping the top handle of Hawk's vest with her stiff fingers and pulling him with her until the water was shallow enough that he could stand as well.

Meg staggered out of the river and dropped to her knees, collapsing forward, her cheek against the hard dirt of the exposed bank as she retched up any remaining water she'd swallowed, one arm wrapped around her panting dog. Her lungs worked like bellows, desperately trying to drag in enough air to satisfy her oxygen-starved body. Shaking, she managed to raise herself up a few inches and then collapsed. Hawk wriggled out from under her arm to nudge her with his cold nose, poking at her and whining.

"It's okay, Hawk. I'm okay." Her voice sounded like sandpaper scraped over her vocal cords and she had to stop as a paroxysm of coughing wracked her. "Good boy. My hero."

He licked her cheek, his tongue warm on her frigid skin.

She gave herself a minute to lie there and tried to regulate her breathing, forcing herself to inhale and exhale slowly. Her first few attempts were rocky, her breath hitching in and exploding out, but, gradually, she relaxed her breathing, and her heart rate slowed in response.

This time she got her knees under her and then lurched to her feet. A toppled tree trunk lay ahead and she staggered over and sagged down on it, utterly wrung out from her battle to stay alive in the river. She let her eyes close as her head drooped.

She jerked when a spray of water hit her. "Hawk!"

All four feet braced, the Labrador stopped shaking and looked up at her, practically grinning, his tongue lolling playfully from one side of his mouth.

She couldn't help but smile. "Come here, bud. Let me get that vest off you so you can really dry off." She unbuckled his waterproof vest—it at least remained dry minus the outer cover, which repelled water—and turned her face away as he gave another shake. When he was finished, she buckled his vest on.

Frankly, she was jealous of the fact he was practically waterproof. Between his thick undercoat and its natural oils that repelled water, he was made for an excursion like the one they'd just survived. She was wet, cold, and miserable, while he would be completely dry inside twenty minutes. Meg had the bad feeling she'd remain soggy until they got back to civilization.

Back to civilization . . . that was going to be the trick since she had no idea where they were. Somewhere in the Cohutta Wilderness, but that was about all she knew. And while they were both trained in wilderness skills, they were missing their usual supplies. She'd lost their go bag in the river, so they had no food, water, first-aid supplies, compass, or communication since both her satellite phone and cell phone had been in the bag. Her jacket pockets were now empty, so even Hawk's leash was lost. She ran her hands over both hips, discouragement filling her when nothing but nylon and Lycra met her fingertips. Both holsters—one with bear spray and one with her Glock 19—were gone, lost when she careened down the hill, or as she was tossed through the river. She slid her right hand down her hip to her upper thigh and was rewarded by a rectangular lump.

Relief filled her. She still had the spring-loaded tactical knife she regularly carried in a convenient pocket so she didn't have to hunt through her pack for it when needed. In this case, as her only tool/weapon, the folding knife could be the difference between life and death.

When more wetness trickled down from her temple and over her cheek to drip onto her collar, she pushed it away with the back of her hand. And then stared openmouthed at the blood smeared across her hand.

She ran her fingers over her cheek, which was cold but unblemished, and then up over her forehead. And found an inch and a half gash over her right eyebrow. The slash and sting of something whipping across her face as she rolled down the hill came back to her, and as if on cue, the wound started to throb. She'd been so focused on not dying in the river, she simply hadn't felt the pain. Now that drowning was no longer an issue, the sting of the cut floated to the surface.

Blood continued to trickle down her cheek. Rolling up

the sleeve of her windbreaker, she pulled the cuff of her shirt sleeve over her hand, caught it in a fist, and pressed it against the wound, wincing at the painful pressure.

Hawk nuzzled her left cheek and she opened her eyes to stare up into his familiar face. She ran her free hand over his spiky fur, and his tail thumped against the hard ground.

"Give me a few minutes to get this to stop, then we'll get going."

A few minutes at least got it to slow, even if it didn't stop, and Meg finally gave up. "Come on, I'll deal with it as we go or we'll still be sitting here when the sun goes down." She squinted up at the sun, marking its position moving toward the west as afternoon progressed. Stepping toward the closest tree, she studied the moss growing around the base. It was a myth that moss grew only on the north face of a tree or rock, but it was true it tended to be more plentiful on that side. Meg located an area where the moss grew thicker and higher up the trunk, confirming north to the sun's westward motion.

"Okay, we have our direction." She turned and peered through the heavy trees, but the terrain looked the same in all directions. Closing her eyes, she pictured a map of the area in her head. When she and Brian had pulled off the road on the west side of the river, the river had hugged the outer boundaries of the Cohutta Wilderness, running northwest, eventually crossing a major thoroughfare on the map. Granted, this far out in the middle of nowhere, that major thoroughfare was probably a two-lane road. However, a road meant cars, and cars meant assistance and civilization. They were on the east side of the river, and there was clearly no safe way to ford it, so the best they could do was follow the direction of the river.

But Meg wanted to put some distance between herself

and the water. Water attracted wildlife, and these mountains were full of bears, bobcats, coyotes, and even a few
unconfirmed sightings of cougars, which were likely making their way into the area from Tennessee. Also, if they
got a bit higher, they might be able to find a proper hiking
trail to make their way easier, and might be able to spot a
way out to be able to signal rescuers from a visible location.

Brian.

Meg desperately hoped he'd gotten away when the shooting started. She was nearly certain she'd been the focus of
the archer's arrows, but there was always the chance he'd
been able to reload faster than she calculated and had split
his shots between them, or Brian had become the sole target
after she'd disappeared. If Brian had survived, she knew
without a doubt he'd be frantically looking for her and assuming she was injured and lost, wandering the forest. Or
worse, that she was dead at the bottom of the river.

He'd already be calling in reinforcements, going over
Torres's head and right to Craig. She knew he would, because it's exactly what she would do. The Forensic Canine
Unit had never lost one of their own, but if anyone would
be able to find them, it was the Human Scent Evidence
Team. If she knew Craig—and she did—he'd be calling in
air support. Maybe helicopters, definitely drones. She'd
have to watch and listen for them so she could flag them
down. More than that, when she found rare open areas in
the tree cover, she should try to leave messages indicating
their direction, either by scratching it into larger rocks or
making messages out of smaller ones. The bigger problem for both herself and any searchers was the oncoming
dusk. If she couldn't find her way out in the next few
hours, they'd have to hunker down overnight. As it was,
by the time Brian made contact with Craig, and Craig

mobilized any teams who were free, they'd be arriving at nightfall and wouldn't be able to do in-person searches until morning.

Morning . . . *Todd.*

If she was still stuck in the wilderness when night fell, he'd be desperately worried. And there'd be nothing anyone could do until daybreak. It was simply too dangerous to climb mountains in the dark.

The goal then was to save everyone that worry and to find her way out of the wilderness before they lost the light and had to hole up for the night.

Meg also needed to get moving in an attempt to warm herself. Despite now being out of the water, her teeth chattered and tremors ran through her from cold trapped by her saturated clothing. Time for some brisk exercise to warm and dry herself.

"Hawk, come."

Together, they started up the mountainside. There was no trail to follow, so Meg chose the path of least resistance, circling boulders and snarls of thorny bushes, and using exposed tree roots and branches to help pull herself up. Hawk, seemingly overflowing with energy, bounded along beside her, clearly enjoying a challenging hike where he didn't have to work.

Her wound continued to ooze blood down her cheek, over her jaw, and onto her collar, slowly soaking it, though the trickle gradually slowed.

Twenty minutes later, after the third stumble in as many minutes, Meg came to the conclusion that hiking uphill wasn't warming her fast enough as her teeth continued to chatter and her cold, stiff muscles made her clumsy and uncoordinated.

"Hawk, buddy, I need a minute." Meg stopped, leaning against the rough, ridged bark of an ash tree as she scanned the area around them. At first her gaze passed over a rocky cluster up the hill to her right, but then she snapped back to it. Surrounded only by low, scrubby trees and bushes, it stood in the full sunlight.

Sunbaked rocks were warm rocks, even in April's cool spring weather. Twenty minutes sitting there, maybe laying out some of her clothes to dry out a bit, would be time well spent. When she was warmer, when her brain wasn't short-circuiting with cold, then she'd come up with a plan of attack.

"Hawk, come."

Knowing relief was in sight gave Meg the strength to continue on, to push through when all she wanted to do was curl up into a ball to warm her cold limbs. It took a few minutes, easily twice as long as it normally would to cover the distance, but then the rock structure loomed large before them. Laying her hand on one of the boulders, she almost moaned in pleasure as the toasty warmth sank into her chilled skin, making her fingertips prickle.

"Twenty minutes, Hawk. I'll be all right after that. Lie down in the sun and you'll be dry in no time."

Hawk happily lay down in the sun on top of a long, flat outcrop of rock, letting out a gusty sigh. Meg took a few minutes to collect a dozen or so medium-size rocks and fashion them into an arrow beside Hawk, indicating their direction in case a drone passed overhead.

That task done, Meg unzipped and peeled away her soaking FBI windbreaker, then stripped off her waffle-weave Henley, leaving her in a thin, long-sleeved athletic pullover. She draped both garments over sun-warmed granite—grimacing at the wide patch of blood at the neck-line of her Henley—and then selected a large, flat ledge, slightly inset from the other rocks around it so she was protected from the wind in the lee of the formation. Hooking her fingers in her hair elastic, she yanked it out, freeing her long hair from its ponytail. Gathering it at the base of her skull, she squeezed out the excess water and then spread her hair over her shoulders to dry.

Sitting down, she bent to unlace her boots, struggling at first over the water-logged laces with stiff, clumsy fingers. But one at a time, she unlaced each boot and poured any remaining water out onto the ground with a soft *splat* before setting it in the sun to dry. She pulled off her socks, wrung them out with both hands, and lay them beside her. Wiggling her pruned toes, she leaned against the sunbaked granite at her back with a long sigh of satisfaction. She closed her eyes and basked in the reflected heat warming her chilled skin.

Her eyes flashed open and her head snapped up at the low rumble of Hawk's growl. Hawk stood, front feet braced, his head low, his lips pulled back over his teeth as he released another rumble of warning. But what alarmed Meg the most was the fact that his gaze was focused on a spot about two feet to her left.

She slowly turned her head and then stifled the gasp of surprise that threatened to squeak through her clenched teeth.

A rattlesnake lay three feet away, coiled on the warm rock and poised to strike.

CHAPTER 22

Uhstahli: Once there was a giant Inchworm that lived in Cherokee country high on a hill above a village. From below, the Cherokee couldn't see the Inchworm standing on top of the rocks, but when the men were out hunting, the Inchworm would lean forward and grab a woman from the village.

Tuesday, April 16, 3:31 PM
Cohutta Wilderness
Murray County, Georgia

Meg froze as she quickly assessed the situation. She couldn't say for certain, but she was sure the snake wasn't there when she sat down. She was cold and dull-witted, but she wasn't that out of it. More than likely, the snake had been searching for warmth and had come up through the rocks to sun itself on the low ledge. She'd let her guard down, but its movements had attracted Hawk's ever-vigilant attention.

The broad, flat head and heavy tan body ending in a black tail with black Vs marching point down toward the tail told her it was a timber rattlesnake. It lay partially coiled, but had to be easily four or five feet in length. Most alarmingly, while the front half of its body was protectively coiled into itself, ready to strike, her anti-venom was in her go bag at the bottom of the Conasauga River. Up here, with no medical or veterinary assistance, a snakebite could mean a painful death for either herself or Hawk.

And dogs didn't like snakes. Not that she did, either, but she wasn't going to take a run at it.

Hawk stood about five feet away, but was poised to jump into the fray, and Meg had no doubt he could do it in a single leap. He growled again and the snake responded with a warning shake of its rattle.

"Talon, leave it. Back. Stay." Meg kept her voice low, but her tone of voice was pure command.

Hawk reluctantly broke from his aggressive pose and took a step back.

"Stay," she reinforced, but then had to turn to the snake. Hawk was now far enough away that she could safely deal with her own risk.

She knew what to do if she and Hawk encountered a rattlesnake while out on a search—don't startle it, back away quietly, and stay out of attack range. Two out of three of those options were already lost to her. Hawk had already startled it and if the attack perimeter was typically about half of a snake's body length, she was already in range. And she knew how fast a rattler could strike.

She'd never see it coming. She'd just feel the stab of its fangs.

She inched away from the snake, not taking her eyes off it, almost mesmerized by the periodic flick of its jet-black tongue as it scented the air. Scented her blood?

Slowly. Sloooowly. Another foot and you'll be clear.

Too slowly. The rattlesnake pulled in tighter and added a hiss to the rattle.

She was running out of room on the rock, so she slid one bare foot to press against the side while she planted the other one out about a foot. She could ease off the rock, but the snake was losing patience.

One . . . two . . . three!

She pushed off with both her braced foot and her hands to launch herself off the ledge, propelling herself forward, wincing when loose stones pushed into her bare soles as she stumbled away. Out of the corner of her eye she saw a flash of movement and knew she'd missed the strike by a fraction of a second as the snake struck where she'd sat on the rock. Luckily, it didn't calculate to follow her as she bolted, and it missed her completely.

Reaching Hawk, she grabbed the handle of his vest just in case and turned to look back. Having missed its target and been denied a warm spot to bask in peace, the snake was slithering away between the rocks, going back into hiding.

Letting out a rough laugh, Meg sank down beside her dog. "What do you think? Do we have the worst luck in the world today or what?"

Hawk simply gazed at her, unblinking.

"On second thought, don't answer that. We're not out of the woods yet. Literally."

Meg waited a full five minutes, then, when the snake didn't reappear, she darted over to the rocks, snatching her socks, boots, shirt, and jacket, and retreated once again. Bracing her back against a tree trunk, she pulled her wet, clammy socks and boots on and then fought her way into her Henley and jacket. At least for now, the material held the ghost of warmth, but she suspected that wouldn't last long.

"Let's keep moving. The faster we cover ground, the faster we'll get out of here." She marked the sun again and they headed as close to northwest as the terrain allowed.

When Meg found a sturdy branch along the way, she picked it up and tested it as a walking stick. Liking the heft of it, she gave it a test swing, nodding in approval of its dual use as a club. Pulling out her folding knife, she pressed the button on the handle and the blade sprang free. She made quick work of one end of the stick, slicing it into a point to dig into the dirt for extra support. Secondarily, it could also be used as a weapon if they came upon another bear when they didn't have bear spray.

It was slow, painful going. One of the most important rules for search-and-rescue was to keep your feet dry, something not possible in her case. Inside of an hour, Meg was reminded why when painful blisters developed and eventually popped, causing her to lean more heavily on her walking stick and limp with each step, further slowing their progress. The lack of a defined trail made traversing the terrain a challenge and required pushing through the underbrush and climbing up and down rock formations. When the terrain and tree cover allowed for it, she left another arrow marking their path.

They were pushing through thick forest when Meg heard it—the high-pitched whine she still sometimes heard in her nightmares. *A drone.* But this drone wouldn't be carrying a bomb; it would be carrying a live video camera. Meg looked up to see nothing but pine branches and foliage overhead.

"Hawk, come! We have to get out in the open!"

They ran. Meg ignored the pain lancing through her feet as they scrambled over the rough terrain, looking for a break in the trees. They needed somewhere they could be visible from above. If she could signal the drone, the operator on the other end watching the video screen would be able to identify their position and send help directly to them.

Up ahead, sunlight hit granite as the trees gave way to a rocky patch. But the whine of the drone was already starting to fade slightly.

"Hawk, this way! Faster!"

They ran for the clearing, bursting out into sunlight. Meg could see the drone as a dark object hanging in the sky, slightly ahead of them. Throwing her arms over her head, she waved madly, jumping up and down. "Here! We're over here! Come back this way!"

But the drone carried on, moving farther away, slowly getting smaller and smaller as the sound of its motors died away, the operator considering that area already searched.

Discouraged, Meg cursed and sank down onto a boulder. Hawk nuzzled close to her, pushing his nose against her throat and exhaling down her shirt. "Hawk, down. Down, boy." But his affection tugged a small smile from her. "I'm sorry, buddy, we tried. Looks like it's still just us." She looked up in the sky. "But maybe they've seen one of the arrows and they'll do another pass. We'll have to listen for it." She pushed to her feet. "Come on, Hawk. Let's keep going."

Away from the river, as dehydration reared its ugly head after their sprint, Meg questioned the sense in staying away from an important water source, until scrabbling in the underbrush made her call quietly for Hawk to stop. A minute later, an enormous wild boar meandered out of the brush, its nose to the ground as it snuffled for acorns or small rodents.

"Hawk, stay." Meg kept her voice quiet and dropped one hand down to rest lightly on his back.

But while his eyes stayed locked on the boar, Hawk didn't show any interest in it beyond simple curiosity, making Meg grateful for both his temperament and training that discouraged aggression unless it was in self-defense. Or, in an emergency, in defense of her. The image of Hawk, teeth bared, leaping at Daniel Mannew to clamp his teeth around his wrist filled her mind.

They waited while the boar rooted around for a minute

before lumbering off downslope, in the direction of the river.

Better to be thirsty than forced to mess with those tusks.

But as they continued their journey and as the sun coasted toward the horizon, hunger and thirst became a real issue. Hunger was a gnawing ache in her belly, but the headache starting to pound had more to do with exertion and her cotton-dry mouth than the slice over her eyebrow. Hawk had to be feeling it as well, though, as always, he pushed on willingly. As her energy level dropped, Meg had to consider that after a day of exceptional exertion to save her own life, followed by hours of difficult hiking, they weren't going to make it to civilization before dark. Perhaps it was time to look for a place to shelter overnight. If she could rest and dry her boots and socks, with renewed energy, they could be warm, dry, and fed by lunchtime tomorrow.

And in the meantime, while they were avoiding the river, she'd watch for unexpected water she knew could pop up in the mountains from small springs or flowing down folds in the rock.

Heavy clouds closed in, blocking the sun and making both time and direction more challenging as the light level dropped. *Keep going until it's too dangerous to continue unless you find shelter first.*

They pushed on.

The path of least resistance had led them from the taller reaches of this edge of the wilderness and down toward the valley. Meg carefully watched their altitude, still cautious of the wildlife watering at the river, not that they could see the river from where they were so deep in the forest. All she could see in every direction were rocks and trees, with occasional peeks at the leaden sky through the canopy above. But she knew they weren't alone in these woods. She'd seen bear scat, and on two occasions had spotted deer foraging for food, one doe round with her on-coming fawn.

But then there came a more foreboding sound when a yip, following by a high-pitched, extended howl shivered through the trees.

Meg froze, her gaze darting from side to side. "Hawk, stop."

He halted and looked up at her, but her attention was drawn back to the forest around them. Another howl cut through the forest, then another. And another.

Coyotes. And more than one.

It was impossible to tell where the sound was coming from up here in the hills, where sound ricocheted off rock and flowed through the valley between peaks.

Hawk stood on alert at her side, his ears perked as his gaze traveled the forest while he scented the air.

The sound came again, this time clearly from their left. And closer.

It was answered by a bark from behind them.

Had the smell of the blood soaked into her shirt attracted them?

Coyotes could travel in both family and hunting packs. If this was a hunting pack looking for its next meal, they could be at risk. A single coyote wouldn't be an issue; she could haze one coyote—yell, stomp her feet, throw rocks—and scare it off. But there was strength in numbers, and where a single coyote couldn't take down anything larger than a small dog or a cat, a pack of coyotes could band together to take down larger prey, like a deer.

They were fiercely territorial animals. In this case, they would see Hawk as competition, and as such, they would want to exert their control over the area. She knew that control in their eyes would involve eliminating the competition. They could have the area; she and Hawk would be happy to leave it.

Goal number one then was to avoid the coyotes. Just in case, she transferred her walking stick to her left hand and dug her knife out of her pocket, freeing the blade. She had no interest in hurting a wild animal, but she'd be damned if she'd let one of them hurt her dog. They'd have to look for a meal elsewhere.

"Hawk, come."

Ignoring the stabs of pain from her battered feet, Meg picked up the pace. At this point, exhaustion was a constant drag on her, but she would not allow herself to be a vulnerability to the team.

She scanned the area around them. Below led to the river and at least one of the coyotes. It sounded like there was at least one behind them. Ahead, the forest continued, undulating over the mountain slope before dropping from view. About thirty feet to the right, a rocky outcrop marched in large, jagged steps farther up the slope. While it would be a climb for her and a challenging parkour exercise for a well-trained dog like Hawk, she hoped it would be a harder and potentially impossible scramble for the smaller coyotes. They needed to put some space between themselves and the pack, and that would be the best way to do it given the local terrain.

Another howl. This time, when Meg whirled around, she caught a shadow of movement in the trees.

Closing in. Time to move quickly.

"Hawk, come." She jogged toward the rock face, Hawk right on her heels.

They were almost there when the first coyote stepped out of the trees, its teeth bared and its pale-yellow eyes fixed on Hawk as a low growl rumbled from its throat.

Cursing the lack of ten extra seconds, Meg stepped in front of Hawk, turning the walking stick around so it was point out toward the coyote. The animal was easily fifteen feet away and not within reach, but Meg wasn't about to let it get near her dog. "Go on!" she yelled, stomping her boots and waving her right arm. "Get lost! You're not welcome here!" Putting her thumb and pinkie in her mouth, she blasted out a sharp, high-pitched whistle.

The coyote took a single step back, startled, but then its gaze flicked past Meg, who quickly followed the tell and stepped sideways to keep her back to the rocks, Hawk behind her. Two more coyotes stood at the edge of the trees, and a few feet over, another stood in the lengthening shadows.

Four. Not good.

The coyotes started to move in, spreading out to trap them.

"Talon, up." Meg risked a quick glance behind her. Hawk stood quietly, but his hackles were raised and his lips drawn back to expose his teeth. "Talon." She could feel his reluctance as he finally looked at her. "Up." She pointed at the rock formation with the point of her knife. "Up, now." He hesitated for a moment, and she was about to command him again when he turned away, gathered himself, and leaped to the first level. He nearly slipped on the narrow ledge, but caught himself.

One of the coyotes lunged in, growling and snapping, watching the focal point of his aggression leap partly out of reach.

"Back off!" Meg swept the walking stick sideways, catching the coyote in the chest, making it stumble back several feet. The two coyotes to her right paced back and forth across from her, their heads down and their eyes locked on her, noses tipped up to scent the air the same way Hawk would. *Definitely smelling my blood-soaked shirt.*

She didn't dare look at her dog. Keeping her eyes fixed on them, she turned her head slightly so Hawk couldn't miss her words. "Talon, up!" There was a brief pause and then she heard more scrabbling and the sound of him landing above. He was now out of reach.

Now it was her turn. But how to manage it with four coyotes closing in on what smelled to them like a wounded animal?

Step one—get them to move back.

With a bellow, she stepped out toward them, shifting her grip on the walking stick to the end and swinging it in a wide arc. The coyotes jumped back a few feet, startled by the noise and staying clear of the pointed end of the stick.

Not far enough.

She repeated the action, swinging the stick back and forth a few times until they stopped moving. She'd lost the initial scare factor.

Meg knew running from a coyote was inviting attack, but a technique meant to be used on one coyote wouldn't work for a pack. And there was no way to scale those rocks without turning her back on them and having both hands free, which meant the knife had to go away. Keeping her eyes locked on the animals, she braced the back of the blade against her thigh, snapped it into the handle, and then slid it into her pocket. Then she turned and sprinted for the rock wall, tipping the stick against the rocks as she took a running leap for the next level, adrenaline giving her the rush of energy her exhausted body needed. She grasped the overhang and pulled herself up, finding a toe-hold with her booted foot to boost her the rest of the way. Just as she was pulling up her back foot, teeth grasped her heel and she jerked her boot free.

She looked down into four sets of feral yellow eyes. "Sorry, boys. Better luck next time."

She grabbed the end of the walking stick and drew it up to lean it against the higher rocks and then scrambled with more speed than grace up to the next level, pulling her walking stick after her. She found Hawk standing at the edge, looking down at the coyotes as they leaped against the rocks, barking and whining.

Meg ran her hand down his back. "Good boy, Hawk. Now, let's go the rest of the way."

The barking intensified as they climbed and jumped higher, finally standing at the top of the formation beside a tree growing at the very edge of the upper level, its roots breaking from the rocky soil to hang over the edge like gnarled fingers. Meg gave them one last look as she straightened at the top, and then called her dog and turned away.

The light level was dropping and Meg wanted to put as much distance as possible between herself and the coyotes in case they found a way up or around. Finally, she conceded it was simply too dangerous to continue in the dark, and they needed to find shelter before one of them walked off a cliff.

They settled into a copse of trees, scurrying under the lower branches of a white cedar to collapse onto a layer of dead leaves that cushioned them from the hard dirt and rock below. Meg set her back against the tree and called Hawk to sit between her spread thighs. Wrapping her arms around him, she sighed with relief at his warmth. She shivered in the cool night, the dampness of her clothing drawing any remaining heat from her skin. She desperately wished for a fire, but with no emergency matches or even a flint, it would be an exercise in futility.

Exhaustion crawled through her, dragging at her with inexorable fingers, but she didn't dare close her eyes. She knew Hawk was the best early warning system possible, but she wouldn't depend on him to protect them both while she slept. They would remain awake together. She pulled the walking stick closer to her left side, the point facing outward, and then pulled her knife from her pocket, holding it in her right hand, with her thumb on the button to open the blade, if needed.

If anything hunted them tonight, they'd go down fighting. And with vigilance, they'd survive until morning.

They'd get out in the morning. They'd find help and she'd make sure Brian was okay. She'd get out of her wet clothes and would finally be warm.

She needed to stay awake until then, which turned out to be harder than anticipated. She found herself occasionally nodding off and then snapping her head upright, trying to focus on something—anything—in the dark. But the clouds blocked the moon and stars, and they were alone in the utter blackness.

But were they really? What was out there that could see her, when she couldn't see it?

Suppressing a shiver, she huddled closer to Hawk, drawing strength from his even breathing and relaxed posture. For now, they were safe.

When it started to rain hard enough that water drizzled through the branches, Meg cupped her hands, collecting the drops until there was enough for first Hawk and then herself to drink. Their thirst slaked, she huddled closer to her dog, curving her body over his in an attempt to keep him dry, while she waited in the dark, miserable and cold, for the sun to rise.

CHAPTER 23

Nunnehi: The name Nunnehi means "traveler" or "one who goes about." In Cherokee legend, the Nunnehi show themselves to humans they like, and intercede on their behalf.

Wednesday, April 17, 8:43 AM
Cohutta Wilderness
Murray County, Georgia

As she hobbled over the next rise, Meg caught a blur of color below them—a flash of red, followed by a glimpse of black and white.

Meg froze, almost unable to believe her eyes. "Hawk, stop." She blinked a few times and looked again. She was so tired, she couldn't be sure she wasn't hallucinating. But no, there it was again. And when she blinked, it didn't disappear.

Lauren.

Meg waved both bands over her head and tried to yell Lauren's name, but the sound came out raspy and not nearly loud enough. "Hawk, it's Lauren and Rocco down there. They've come to find us. Speak!"

Hawk barked and Meg waved her arms again.

And from down below came the answering bark.

Rocco.

They'd been found.

Meg nearly dropped to her knees in relief, but forced herself to put one unsteady foot in front of the other. She could rest once they were safe, but they still had a long way to go.

She and Hawk kept up their slow, steady pace. In contrast, Lauren and Rocco were on the run, climbing over rocks and then jogging uphill. As they came closer, Meg cracked a smile, and then winced when her dry lip split. "Fancy meeting you here."

"Oh, thank God we found you. We've been out of our minds." Lauren threw her arms around Meg and squeezed.

Pain ricocheted through Meg and she let out a small cry.

Lauren let go immediately. "Are you hurt? Where?"

"I think it might be safer to ask where it doesn't hurt. But it's nothing serious. Bumps and bruises, mostly from an unexpected trip down the river. I wasn't doing too badly yesterday, but then I stiffened up when I stopped moving overnight." She pressed two fingers gingerly to her eyebrow. "This bled like crazy but finally stopped."

Lauren touched her jaw with gentle fingers, turning her head. "I can see that. There's blood all over your cheek."

"I couldn't see to clean it off. I must have misplaced my cosmetics mirror," Meg joked. "But it did get us into a touch of trouble with a pack of coyotes who could smell it. How's Brian?"

"He's fine. When you two got split up yesterday, you were the only target. He and Lacey got away without a scratch."

"Thank God." Meg looked down when Rocco pressed against her legs. "Hi, Rocco buddy. Am I ever glad to see you." She looked up and met Lauren's eyes. "Who's out searching?"

"Everyone. Brian and Lacey, Scott and Theo, McCord

and Webb, several local law enforcement teams. Craig is here coordinating."

"I figured he'd send Brian out after me, or maybe send one additional team to help out, not mobilize the whole unit."

"He couldn't have stopped us. It was officially mobilize us and come with, or watch us walk out the door without him. Craig wouldn't have considered any other option. When Brian called us yesterday afternoon and told us about the attack and that you'd disappeared and weren't answering your sat phone, we scrambled. Caught the next flight to Atlanta out of Reagan, but by the time we arrived it was too dark, so we had to wait until first light to get out here. Webb and McCord found your go bag at the river's edge almost right away. And we knew there was no way you left it there."

"When we got shot at, I dove out of the way of an arrow and ended up falling down a steep slope."

"Not just 'an arrow.' Try 'four arrows.' Which are now being analyzed by the crime-scene techs. Okay, so you ducked all those arrows and went down the hill. What happened then?"

"I ended up in the Conasauga River at the bottom of the ridge. I had to ditch the bag to keep from drowning." Meg tried to shrug, but her stiff shoulders didn't cooperate and it came out as a one-sided lurch. "As a result, I lost all our supplies, our water and food, communications, and the GPS, so I had no idea where we were. However, Hawk knew where I was and came after me. He jumped into the rapids as I was beginning to really struggle, and helped me get to the side."

Lauren squatted down and ran her hands over Hawk's dirty fur. "Of course he did, you big hero." She kissed the top of his head and stood. "I'm going to let the others know you're okay and to call off the search, including air support." She pulled her satellite phone out of her bag and dialed. "Craig, it's Lauren. I have them both. Yes, they're okay. Banged up, exhausted, and probably in need of food, water, and a doctor, but no serious injuries. Yes, please let them all know and bring them in. We're on our way. If we need assistance, I'll let you know." She hung up and tucked the phone away. "Are you okay to keep going? You look like you're about to fall down. And you're limping."

"I hurt everywhere, I'm so tired I could sleep for a week, and there are blisters on my blisters, but we'll keep going."

"Good. But first . . ." Lauren slipped off her bag, set it on the ground, and rooted through it. She pulled out a bottle of water and handed it to Meg. "Drink this."

"But Hawk—"

"Is next. Leave him to me."

Meg unscrewed the bottle with shaking hands and then drank more than half in a continuous series of swallows, soothing her parched throat. By the time she looked down, Lauren had a pair of collapsible bowls set up, one with water, where Hawk lapped thirstily, and one with high-energy food. She stood and pushed two energy bars into Meg's hand. "Energy bars are all I have, but they'll do for a start. Eat those, finish the water, take a minute. I know they're all dying to see you for themselves, but you'll do better on the hike back if you have some energy. It's easily an hour."

Meg sat down on a nearby rocky shelf, unwrapped a bar, took a bite, and chewed thoughtfully. "You know, I'm really not fond of these, but they've never tasted better than right now."

"When was the last time you ate?"

"Lunch yesterday. Then I lost everything." She jerked upright as a thought occurred to her. "We need to call

Craig again. When I went down the hill, I lost my service weapon. We need to recover it."

"We will. The place is swarming with search teams. But I'll give Craig the heads-up. Where do you think you lost it? On the hill?"

"That would be my best guess. The grip probably got caught on something as I was rolling and it got yanked out. Or maybe it came off with the holster. Either way, I know exactly where we were at that point." She described the location to Lauren, who called Craig to pass on the information.

Lauren gave her a few minutes to eat the bars and wash them down with a second bottle of water. By that point, Hawk was also fed and watered and was standing with Rocco. "You ready to head back?"

Meg pushed to her feet. "Absolutely. We've been in this wilderness long enough."

It took them over an hour to hike to a parking lot near the river with the help of the GPS in Lauren's satellite phone. Finally, they came down a well-traveled path that angled toward the road. Leaving the trail, they broke from the trees into a parking lot full of cars.

It was a scene Meg was familiar with: Craig running the op from the hood of his car, a phone at his ear or radio in hand and a map spread out to track the locations of the teams. Teams coming in from their searches and packing up to move out. Extra personnel standing nearby, ready to assist anyone who needed help.

It was a scene she'd worked hundreds of times. But for the first time, it was for her. People had flown in from out of state to find her, and local law enforcement had turned out in force. She knew she should feel mortified, but was simply too exhausted to drum up the emotion.

"Meg!"

Her head snapped up at the sound of her name to find Webb sprinting across the parking lot toward her.

"Looks like someone is happy to see you." Lauren angled out of Webb's way so he had a straight path to Meg. "I'm going to go check in with Craig. Rocco, come."

Reaching her, Webb pulled Meg into his arms, lifting her right off her feet, her walking stick dropping from her hand to fall to the ground with a clatter. "Your shoulder . . ." she whispered.

"Is fine. My God, I've been frantic all night long, scared to death you ran into trouble out there." He put her down and stepped back, taking in the cut over her eye, the streaks of blood down one side of her face, and the crusty neckline of her shirt. Gently cupping her cheeks in his hands, he angled her head down to examine her wound. "You did run into trouble out there. What happened?"

"We were shot at. Trying to avoid being gutted by an arrow, I dove off the path and rolled down a steep hill. Something slashed at me on the way. I think it was a tree branch. At the bottom of the hill, I got tossed into the Conasauga River, and then had to fight to keep from drowning while I shot the rapids without a boat. And before you ask, there's no concussion. I didn't hit my head. But the gash was a problem, because I got blood all over me and then that's what I smelled like."

"Predators."

"Yes, the worst of which was a pack of hungry coyotes who were looking to defend their territory from an interloper." She looked down affectionately at Hawk. "We managed to get away from them, but it got a little too close for comfort for a while there."

"I'm beyond glad you were successful. The wound needs a really good cleaning, which is going to hurt like hell, and then I can close it for you."

"Stitches or that awesome glue you used the last time?"

"Glue. It's better for facial injuries and decreases the chance of scarring." He frowned and turned her head slightly sideways. "You might scar, though. Maybe you'd prefer a trip to the ER and a plastic surgeon to do the job right." He tipped her face up to him.

"You'll do the job right. After all, you're the one stuck staring at this face a lot of the time."

"Any other injuries I can't see? When you came down the path you looked a little unsteady. I could read the exhaustion, but is there more than that?"

"I'm generally banged up, but otherwise okay. I got lucky. When I went down that hill, I could have hit a tree or a rock and broken my head open or cracked my spine. I'm bruised, and I have some smaller contusions and blisters from hell, but the head wound is the worst of it. When we get back to the cabin you can help me clean up and do a full check. But by tomorrow I'm going to look like . . . what was it you called it? An Arizona sunset?"

"Yes."

"That's it. I feel like I'm bruised everywhere." She closed her eyes and let herself sag against him. "I'm so tired. I didn't dare let myself rest last night. I dozed off for a few seconds, but that was it." She raised her head when running footsteps announced McCord's arrival.

"Meg! You're okay?" McCord rubbed a palm over her shoulder. "We were worried about you and Hawk. Hawk, buddy. How are you? High five!"

Hawk, who had been sitting beside Meg, lifted one paw and slapped it against McCord's extended palm.

McCord ruffled his ears. "You're filthy, my man, but you look good." He straightened. "Did you tell her?"

"Not yet." Webb's response was almost a growl.

Meg stiffened and pushed away from Webb, but he kept

ahold of her shoulders. "Tell me what?" Her gaze shot from Webb's frown of displeasure to McCord's anxious eyes.

"I was waiting to make sure she didn't need medical attention first. And she does."

Meg tried to pull out of Webb's hands and toward McCord, but Webb held her fast. That in itself made her stomach dip. "What don't I know?" she insisted, knowing practical Webb would never sugarcoat the situation.

"Lacey's been hurt."

Fear sluiced through her like ice water. "*What?* How badly?"

"Bad."

In a flash, she was back in that dark alley in Richmond, Virginia, crouched in the pouring rain, her dead K-9 in her arms, his blood smeared all over her hands and uniform. The memory of that agony rolled over her like a wave, her breath catching and her vision going grainy. "Where is he? Brian!" She pulled one shoulder free, but Webb managed to grab her again.

He pulled her in closer and got right in front of her. "Meg, take a breath and listen to me."

He waited until she met his eyes, and she knew he could see her terror for Lacey mixed into memories of Deuce's death.

"They're not here," he continued. "When Brian carried Lacey out—"

A moan escaped her. Carrying a dog out meant the injuries were critical. And carrying a full-size German shepherd out of the deep wilderness would have been a challenge even for someone in Brian's top condition. But he'd done it in an effort to save his partner's life.

"Craig called in air rescue to take Brian and Lacey to the nearest emergency vet. It was going to take too long otherwise to get out of here by the mountain roads. Craig got in touch with a clinic in Chatsworth so they'll be ready for them when they arrive. They've got surgical facilities and a couple of vets standing by. They know it's a law enforcement canine coming in. Brian and Lacey should be arriving shortly and they'll do everything they can."

Meg's knees threatened to buckle and only Webb's support kept her upright. This horrifying news on top of the strain of simply surviving the previous eighteen hours nearly knocked her flat. Webb seemed to sense that and walked her backward, toward the edge of the parking lot, then lowered her down to sit on the trunk of a fallen tree at the boundary of the forest.

Across the parking lot, Craig and Lauren jogged toward them.

"What happened?" Meg whispered.

Webb crouched down in front of her so they were eye-to-eye and took her hands in his. "It was a cougar attack. They're extremely rare in this area, but they've been spotted in Tennessee, so it was only a matter of time before they drifted south. They were on their way back after Lauren found you, when they crossed the cougar's path. It went for Brian first, but then Lacey got in there and the real scrap started. She drove the cat away in the end, but she was critically injured. By the time Brian finally got her out, she'd lost a lot of blood. Meg, you need to be prepared that this might not end well. Brian's going to need you." His eyes dropped to where she normally wore the pendant, but it was absent as she didn't wear it on searches for fear of losing the irreplaceable totem. "You're the only one of us who really knows what he's going through."

"I need to go to him." She looked at Craig, who ran up to stand behind Webb. "Craig, I need to go to Brian. He shouldn't be there alone."

"Agreed. Webb, can you and McCord take her?"

"Yes. Meg needs treatment, but I'll see if I can beg some supplies from the clinic."

"Otherwise she checks out?"

"So far, but I'll keep an eye on her."

"Uncle Sam is paying for all this, so tell them to add her supplies to my bill," Craig said. He gave Meg's shoulder a squeeze. "I'm glad to see you, but I'll catch up with you later. We're waiting for Scott and Theo to get back, and then the three of us and the dogs will be right behind you."

"I'm driving." McCord pulled out his phone and called up his map app. "Where are we going?" Craig gave him the address and McCord typed it in. "Got it. Let's go."

Webb pulled Meg to her feet. "There are dry clothes, shoes, and a couple of towels in the SUV. You can change as we go."

She yanked her hands free and used nervous energy born of pure fear to sprint with the men and Hawk across the parking lot toward McCord's SUV.

CHAPTER 24

Totem: An object or symbol believed to have special significance to a family, clan, or society.

Wednesday, April 17, 10:22 AM
Dalton Veterinary Services
Chatsworth, Georgia

McCord stopped the SUV right in front of the door of the clinic. "Go. We'll bring Hawk."

Meg gave him a sharp nod. "Hawk, stay." Then she was through the door and running up the front walk.

After changing into dry clothes, she'd spent the entire trip trying not to back-seat drive as McCord skillfully managed the narrow, winding mountain roads. She wanted him to open it up to sixty on roads that could handle a maximum of twenty miles per hour, many so treacherous as to require convex mirrors around their hairpin curves. Once they had to stop short of a turn as an eighteen-wheeler maneuvered around the curve using both lanes of the two-lane highway. The driver had cut it so close, he'd been only a hairbreadth from brushing against the rock wall. Luckily, he'd made it through and they'd been able to continue on. McCord had pushed the speed as much as he could, but they all recognized that dying on the way there wouldn't help Brian at all.

But now—*finally*—they were there.

She jerked open the door to find a cheerful, bright reception room with a young woman in scrubs sitting behind a tall desk. But Meg's eyes were only for Brian, sitting by himself at the far end of the room, his head in his hands.

"Brian!"

His head snapped up, his gaze fixing on her, eyes full of pain she felt like a blow to the gut. She'd felt that pain herself and it had nearly killed her.

Yet sliding in behind the pain was relief at seeing her in one piece. "You're okay."

"I'm okay." She dropped to her knees in front of Brian and gathered him in. For a moment he was limp and motionless, and then his arms clamped around her fiercely, almost too tight for her to draw breath as he pressed his face against her throat. He simply held on as tremors quaked through his body.

"She tried to protect me." His voice was only the thread of a hoarse whisper. "The cougar came out of nowhere and went for me, got in a few swipes, and she jumped in between us. It went for her throat. She fought it off, got in a few bites of her own, and in the end drove it away." His breath caught. "And then she collapsed. Her breathing . . . it was so . . . shallow." And he broke.

Out of the corner of her eyes, Meg saw the door open and Webb, McCord, and Hawk enter. She thrust one hand out toward them, palm out and fingers spread—*Stop!*—and then turned her attention back to Brian as he shook in her arms. He was struggling to control himself, and she could feel his measured inhalations as he tried to keep himself from hyperventilating.

He pulled away and rubbed his hands over his face.

That's when Meg saw what she'd missed in her rush to get to him—the torn and blood-soaked material over his upper right arm and right side. With a gasp, she pulled back to run her gaze over the rest of him. "You're hurt."

She tried to gently tug his right arm forward so she could see it better, but he pulled it from her grasp. "It's not that bad."

"It looks bad. You need to let Todd examine you."

"Later." He let out a shaky breath. "I need to pull it together. Can't fall apart."

Meg clamped both hands over his. "Listen to me, Brian. Nobody knows what you're going through better than me. That's your partner in there. I know you're married to Ryan, but in many ways, Lacey is your other half. She's your heart dog. Of course you're terrified and upset. But you brought her in alive, and she's full of grit and spirit. She's going to fight to get back to you. And we're going to hold on and wait for her."

He nodded silently as his breathing steadied and his trembling slowed. He noticed Webb and McCord still standing by the door and he slumped, his head dropping as his face flushed. "They're going to think I'm overreacting."

"Never." When Brian looked up sharply, she continued. "They know what these dogs are to us. What we are to them. They're here to stand vigil with you. To support you. And Craig, Lauren, and Scott are incoming." She pushed off the floor to take the chair next to him. "We're all with you, every step of the way."

Brian tipped his head sideways to rest against her shoulder. "Thanks," he whispered.

Meg leaned her head against his and threaded her fingers through his, holding on tight. "Always." She looked at the men and gave them a nod to come closer. "Hawk, come."

Hawk trotted over, but instead of going to Meg, he went to Brian, sitting between his spread knees and resting his chin on Brian's thigh.

Brian dropped his free hand to Hawk's shoulder to stroke. "How do they know?"

"I don't know, but they always do."

Hawk didn't move over the next hour, simply comforting with his presence. Webb got up, talked to the receptionist, flashed her his ID, and then went into the back rooms with her. He returned five minutes later with gloves, disinfectant, bandages, and a tube of Vetbond. He dealt with Meg first as Brian watched and held her hand, occasionally wincing as her grip became overtight while Webb cleaned her face and throat, and then sealed and bandaged the wound over her eye. Then Webb insisted on checking out Brian, working around Hawk, muttering over the wide spread of the claw tracks on his side and upper arm. Luckily both sets of scratches were relatively shallow and were easily cleaned and dressed. Then Webb retreated a few seats away to sit beside McCord, as if sensing that Meg and Brian needed a little space.

Shortly after, they were joined by Lauren, Scott, their dogs, and Craig. For a roomful of people, it was deathly quiet, with only rarely muted whispers. A few times Meg noticed McCord texting and figured he was keeping Cara up to speed with developments.

Surely news had to come soon. How long could the surgery take? That would depend on the wounds, of course. But, as Meg reminded Brian, the longer they sat with no word, the longer Lacey held on.

The outside door to the clinic opened and a slender blond man stepped in, pulling off a pair of sunglasses. Meg stared, blinked, stared again, and half rose out of her chair. "Ryan?"

Beside her, Brian jerked in surprise and inhaled sharply.

Then he was out of his chair. His husband met him half-way across the room, pulling him into a tight hug, holding on to him, one hand cupped behind his head, the other splayed wide over Brian's back, rocking him from side to side.

Meg collapsed into her chair and turned to stare at Webb and McCord. "How did he . . ." Her voice trailed off as she caught McCord's eyes locked on the men, a satisfied smile curving his lips. "That's who you've been texting."

McCord nodded. "I knew Brian would need him, and I had Ryan's number in my contacts from the Stevenson case. I called him from the trail parking lot as soon as I knew where they were taking Lacey because that impacted travel plans. Ryan dropped everything and ran for the airport. By the time he got there, I had a flight arranged for him. And then a car at Chattanooga."

"That's amazing. It didn't occur to me to do that."

"You're too close to this. It hits too close to home for multiple reasons. I'm on the outside looking in and could be detached enough to help Ryan. I've been in contact with him via text since he landed. Then it was a forty-five-minute drive here."

Meg stood, circled Webb to McCord, and bent to press a kiss to his cheek. "You're a good guy, McCord. Cara would be proud of you."

"So she said when I told her." He looked at the two men, one devastated, the other shoring him up. "No one outside of another handler is going to understand what he's going through more than Ryan. And God forbid the worst happens, he'll need both you and Ryan to get through it."

"That's not going to happen. I—" Meg shot upright as the door to the clinic opened and a young woman in scrubs stepped through. "Mr. Foster?"

Brian stepped away from Ryan and spun around. He couldn't say anything; he just stood there bracing himself for the worst.

Meg moved forward so Brian stood between herself and Ryan. "This is Mr. Foster," she said. "How's Lacey?"

"She came through the surgery well."

Brian almost went to his knees. Only Ryan and Meg, each grabbing an arm, held him steady.

"She's not out of the woods yet, but she's young and strong. The next twenty-four hours are critical, but I'm extremely optimistic."

"Can I see her?"

"Sure. She's in recovery, but she's starting to come out of the anesthetic and she'd be steadier in strange surroundings if you were with her. Come on back."

Ryan looked at Meg, who stepped away and nodded to him. Hand in hand, the men disappeared into the back rooms.

Meg dropped into the chair beside Webb, tipped her head against the wall, and closed her eyes.

He leaned in and brushed a thumb over her cheek. "You're exhausted. I should get you out of here."

"No, not yet. Soon, but not yet. I need to know Brian will be okay. I mean, Ryan is here, but . . ."

"But you've lived through what he's going through and worse. You understand it at a visceral level."

"Yeah." She turned her head sideways to find him close. "You don't think this is too much hullabaloo over an animal?"

"These aren't just animals. In many ways they're the other half of you." His brown eyes were deadly serious; there was no mistaking his sincerity.

She gave him a half smile. "And here I thought you were supposed to be my other half."

"What you and I have is different from your love for

Hawk. But that love is just as deep and just as important. You expect to lose Hawk someday; he has a life expectancy that's only a fraction of yours. But it's a different thing to have that life taken early. Worse, to have it taken tragically. That's a wound you don't easily recover from, as you know all too well." He clasped her hand in both of his. "And I know this day has to have floated some terrible memories too close to the surface for you. So while you're watching over Brian, I'm going to watch over you. When you're satisfied you can leave him, I'm going to take you back to the cabin, check out any other injuries you might have, and put you to bed for some long overdue sleep. Later, you can tell me all about what happened yesterday on that mountain."

"That sounds good to me. I'm so tired right now I'm not sure my brain is firing on all cylinders. I'd probably leave something out of the story, like how Hawk got me out of the river." She raised their clasped hands and rested her cheek on them. "Thank you for taking care of me. And of Brian."

"You're welcome. It made me wish I'd brought my med pack, but I wasn't supposed to be working on this trip. Luckily, the clinic was happy to supply me once the vet checked out my credentials." His gaze flicked up to the bandage covering her eyebrow. "How's the laceration?"

"Sore, but not that bad. In a day or two I won't even notice it."

"Unless you end up with a scar. I did my best to make it precise. It will heal well; I just don't know how invisible it will be in the end."

"Well, if I end up with a scar, then I'll look like a sexy adventuress." She tried to match her teasing tone with a ghost of a smile, but knew she was too tired and drained to pull it off.

"A sexy adventuress with some serious wear and tear."

Meg covered a yawn behind her hand. "Exactly." She laid her head on his shoulder. "You mind?"

"Not at all."

"I'm going to close my eyes for a minute or two."

"You've been awake for over thirty hours of pure physical and emotional stress. You're going to doze off, but I promise to wake you when Brian comes back to let us know how Lacey is doing."

"I won't doze off. I'm just going to rest my eyes. They're kind of burning at this point."

"I bet they are." Webb shifted, slipping his arm around her and tucking her more securely against his shoulder. "I've got you. Go ahead and . . . uh . . . rest your eyes."

"Thanks." Meg closed her eyes, let out a long breath of stress and tension, and dropped straight into sleep.

CHAPTER 25

Trail Trees: Hardwood trees deliberately bent to grow horizontally several feet above the ground. The bend makes the tree visible at greater distances, even in snow. Such trees were used by North American indigenous peoples to mark game trails and trade routes.

Wednesday, April 17, 4:18 PM
Lake View Cabins
Blue Ridge, Georgia

Meg came down the staircase a little unsteadily, holding tight to the railing and still feeling half asleep after her nap.

When she had gradually resurfaced from sleep to multiple voices downstairs, she'd thrown off the covers and swung her legs over the side. She'd instantly regretted the action—her stiff, battered muscles protested any movement whatsoever, and she had to sit still for a moment before attempting to stand.

She stopped halfway down the stairs, peering into the living room at the unexpected crowd of people, when she had expected only Webb and McCord.

Torres and Craig sat on the couch, facing an open file

folder on the coffee table with lists and photos spread across it. McCord took the armchair, while Webb sat on the raised stone fireplace hearth near a cheerfully snapping blaze. Lauren and Scott had pulled dining room chairs close to the agent and their SAC as they discussed the case.

Meg took another few steps down, and the motion attracted Webb's attention. As soon as he saw her, he was on his feet, coming to where she stopped on the bottom step.

His eyes searched her face with concern. "I thought you'd sleep longer, but you were only down for a few hours. That won't make up for last night."

"I could have slept more, but I don't want to sleep so long I can't sleep tonight." She scanned the room. "Where's Hawk? When I went to sleep, he was on the bed with me, but he was gone when I woke up."

Webb pointed toward the couch. "He's behind the couch, stretched out with Theo and Rocco by the fire."

Meg rubbed her hands up and down her arms. "A fire sounds nice, actually."

"After how cold you were, I bet it does. Come on over. You want coffee?"

"I'd love some." She stepped onto the floor and winced.

He slipped an arm around her waist and let her lean on him as they made their way slowly toward the fireplace. "Sore?"

"Oh yeah. That's going to last for a few days."

"From the bruising you have, I'm sure it will. Tell you what—before bed tonight, have a long soak in the whirlpool tub, and when you get out, I'll give you a massage. That will relax you enough to sleep well."

"Deal. As long as you won't hurt your shoulder doing it."

"Actually, it would sort of be exercise for it without being too strenuous. And you love a massage, so it's good all around."

"This time I could really use one. I have to be ready to get right back on the horse when the next call goes out."

"We'll get you there. But for now, come join us. Torres has been bringing Craig, Lauren, and Scott up to speed."

"With McCord sitting right there?"

"I think he noticed that Craig accepted McCord's presence with no fuss, so he did, too."

"McCord can chalk up another conquest."

"They're practically notches in his bedpost at this point."

Meg was smiling as she lowered herself down to the hearth and turned to hold her hands toward the flames dancing behind the fireplace screen. She couldn't keep a sigh of pleasure from slipping free. "That's nice. I'm not nearly as cold as I was, but it still feels good."

"I'll grab us both coffees. Be right back."

A few minutes later, Webb handed her a steaming mug and then settled beside her on the hearth in time to tune in to the case discussion as Torres finished walking Craig, Lauren, and Scott through the current suspect list. Hawk wandered over to settle at her feet. Meg ran her hand over his clean coat—when they got home, Lauren had washed Hawk—and then turned her attention to the conversation, when Webb spoke up.

"I know I'm not supposed to be here, and I'm not supposed to have an opinion, but if you don't mind some outside thoughts, it looks to me like you're pigeonholing the suspects."

Displeasure flickered over Torres's face at being second-guessed. "What do you mean?"

"The list of suspects you have. I know a lot of them came from recent shooting competitions, but you seem to be angling toward young males. Is there a reason for that? I didn't hear anything that would skew the selection that way, but maybe I missed something."

"I . . . uh . . ." Torres stopped, his brows drawn together as if he hadn't realized the pattern. "The largest limiting factor is the actual method of death. It's not like shooting a gun. It's a physical method that requires a great deal of skill."

"I totally agree with the skill aspect. But I watched Meg learn how to shoot in a fifteen-minute lesson. Now, grant you, she wasn't an expert after one lesson and she's in really good shape, but she managed to convincingly nail the target."

"Todd has a point," Meg said. "Maybe we're not finding someone who fits because we're looking at this through too narrow a lens. It doesn't necessarily need to be someone who can bench-press two-fifty."

"And as you showed, it doesn't have to be a man. I'm just suggesting if you're reviewing your lists to see what you missed, maybe open up the options a little wider. Consider both genders and a range of ages."

"It certainly can't hurt. And—" Meg stopped at the sound of the front door opening. Ryan came through into the front hall, followed by Brian, who shut the door behind them. Both men looked exhausted, but Brian's earlier expression of abject misery had eased.

Brian looked over at the group, his eyebrows raised in surprise, and raised a hand in greeting.

Craig got to his feet. "How's Lacey?"

Brian murmured a quiet word to Ryan and they moved into the living room. "She's holding her own. They're going to keep her sedated for the rest of the day and for the night so she doesn't move around too much. The next forty-eight hours are critical, but the doc is very optimistic. They told us to head home and we can come back tomorrow morning. If anything changes, they'll call us." He tried to smile, but it wobbled before falling away.

"They're not sure what the lasting effects will be. There's a lot of soft tissue damage to her torso and neck and her front legs from fending off the attack. We'll have to see if she's . . ." He swallowed hard. "If she's able to be active like she was before."

Meg could hear the unspoken message behind his words loud and clear. *We'll see if she can do search-and-rescue. We'll see if we're still a part of this team.*

Meg pushed off the hearth to stand, swayed for a moment as she got her balance, and walked stiffly over to Brian. She stepped into him for a hug, and his arms looped around her in response. "She's strong," she murmured in his ear. "And she's a fighter. Don't count her out. She'll need time to recover, but you'll be back with us before you know it."

Brian pulled away just far enough to rest his forehead against hers. "I don't know what I'd do without you guys."

"Good thing you aren't going to have to find out. Come and grab a seat by the fire. We're discussing the case and we need your insight."

If Brian suspected she was simply trying to distract him, it didn't show in his eyes. "Let me get Ryan settled in my room. He simply walked out of work today, so he needs to go catch up on a few things on my laptop."

Working as an archivist at the Smithsonian in DC, Ryan was responsible for some of the museum's larger collections. It spoke to his priorities that he'd simply walk away from his work when Brian needed him.

"Sure, come back when you can." She sat down on the hearth as Brian and Ryan headed for the stairs. "Sorry, where were we?"

"We were talking about possible suspects." Torres's words were nearly a flat monotone.

"Right. I think Todd's suggestion has merit. You didn't come up with the list on your own, we all contributed. Maybe we were all looking through the same narrow scope. Time to think in broader terms."

Craig's phone beeped from where it lay on the table, alerting him to an incoming message. "Sorry." He pulled out his phone and checked the message. "It's Rutherford. He says he's ready to deliver the profile."

"Does he want to send it to us?" Meg asked. "Or would he be willing to Skype in? That way we can actually discuss it."

"Let me ask him." Craig texted a reply and then sat back. "He doesn't know about yesterday's attack unless someone else has told him. We were in a rush to leave town yesterday, and with the BAU at Quantico, it never occurred to me to fill him in. I wonder if it'll change his profile?"

"Only one way to find out," Lauren said.

Craig's phone alerted again. "He sent his Skype ID so we can contact him, and then he'll follow it up with his usual electronic copy."

"We can use my laptop," Meg said, bracing to rise to her feet.

Webb pressed her down with a hand to her shoulder. "I'll get it. You stay put." He strode across the room and then took the stairs two at a time.

Lauren met Meg's eyes across the table. "It looks like he's recovered."

"They'll keep him off active duty until his shoulder is fully healed, but it's really coming along. I bet he'll be back to light duty in less than a week and active duty the week after that. Which will be good, because I know the inactivity is killing him."

Brian came down the stairs, looking up after Webb. "Where's Todd going? He seemed in a rush."

"He's saving my battered body a trip up the stairs." She patted the hearth beside her. "We're going to get the profile from Rutherford."

Brian sat down next to her and leaned in close. "Thanks for including me," he murmured.

"We wouldn't have you anywhere else."

His gaze flicked to her forehead. "How's the cut healing?"

"It pulls a bit whenever I move my eyebrow, but otherwise it's not too bad." She took a deep breath, needing to put into words the feelings swirling inside her for the past few hours, manifesting into a muddle of bad dreams while she'd slept. "I was really lucky I didn't break my neck or crack my head open during the fall or in the river, but I think I sucked up all our collective luck." She grabbed his hand and held on. "Brian, I'm so sorry. If I'd been able to stay on my feet . . . If I'd been more alert—"

"Stop. You aren't responsible for what happened to Lacey. We were in the wrong place at the wrong time."

"But if I hadn't tumbled down that hill, I wouldn't have gotten separated from you, and Craig wouldn't have had to launch the search teams—"

"If you hadn't tumbled down the hill, you'd be dead now from the arrow that would have hit home while you lay on that path. Then I'd be without you and I'm not going to contemplate that. No, the only person responsible for Lacey is this killer. Without him, we wouldn't be here, and we certainly wouldn't have been out there. So I don't want to hear another word on the subject. You got me?"

Blinking back tears from a combination of exhaustion, stress, and relief, Meg let out a short, jagged laugh. "Loud and clear."

Footsteps on the stairs heralded Webb's return, Meg's laptop under his arm. "Here you go." His gaze stayed fixed on her face for an extra second or two, but if he noticed the bit of extra moisture in her eyes, he didn't comment on it.

"Thanks." She opened her laptop, booted up, and logged in. Within a minute, the familiar tones of a Skype call rang through the speakers. Then a new window opened and Rutherford smiled back at her. He was in his office at Quantico and, as usual, was nattily dressed in a dark suit, crisp white shirt, and an emerald-green tie. "SSA Rutherford. Thank you for your flexibility."

"Ms. Jennings. I'm happy to be able to accommodate the team."

Meg turned the laptop toward Craig and Torres. "I'll pass you over to SAC Beaumont and Special Agent Torres."

"Beaumont. Special Agent, good to meet you."

"Good to meet you, too." Torres shot a quick glance at Craig, who gave him a go-ahead nod. "SAC Beaumont tells us you have the profile ready to go."

"I do."

"We wanted to update you on the latest development." His gaze flicked to Meg. "Actually, I'm going to let Meg do that, since she was directly involved." He spun the laptop around to Meg.

"We had another attack yesterday," Meg began. She laid out all the details from Greyson's murder, to tracking the suspect, to the surprise attack in the wilderness, and ending with a *Reader's Digest* version of her escape and rescue from the wilderness. "Does any of that change your profile?"

Rutherford sat back in his chair, one hand stroking his chin as he studied something on his computer monitor located below the webcam. Then he shook his head. "No, it adds a layer. It clarifies some things about the shooter. And it definitely speaks to her current mind-set."

"*Her?*" Meg's gaze shot to Webb, who had pulled back to stay out of range of the webcam. He returned the look with a shrug and raised eyebrows.

"Yes, I think your archer is a woman."

Torres turned the laptop toward himself and Craig. "That suggestion was raised a few minutes ago here, but I don't see it."

"Classic confirmation bias," Rutherford replied. "Your life experiences tell you to see a certain thing, so you more readily absorb information that confirms those beliefs. It's a common pitfall." He smiled, a bright flash of teeth in his black face. "But that's why you have me."

"Then we've gone astray on this case." Torres's tone carried a hint of self-recrimination. "Why do you think that?"

"Let me lay it all out for you. Is everyone there up to speed on all the case details, or do you want me to go over it all?"

"No, we just did a review. We can move right to your analysis."

"Excellent. Then let's start with the differences between male and female serial killers. Only twenty years ago, one of the BAU's own profilers pronounced that there were no female serial killers, but we know much better now. In fact, about one in six serial killers is a woman. But they tend to be overlooked because of the classic female persona as the nurturer and the caregiver. Hard to believe someone like that would commit such heinous crimes, but without a doubt, they do."

"By people who don't fulfill that role?"

"Not at all. By women who do, just not for that victim at that time. Many women kill their own spouses or their children, individuals for whom they once held that role but don't any longer."

"But there isn't a caregiver of either sex that ties these victims together," Torres protested.

Meg met Craig's gaze, seeing her own thoughts reflected there. *He's convinced it has to be a man. So much so, he's rejecting the profile before it's delivered.*

"Rutherford," Craig interrupted, "are you suggesting that the caregiving aspect of this case is related to motive? It's why she's killing?"

"That's it exactly. Let me give you a little evolutionary psychology so you can understand some of the differences between male and female serial killers. You likely all know about early humans and the concept of hunting and gathering. Before the rise of agriculture, that's how the human race survived, and there tended to be a pretty clear dividing line between the sexes—the males went out hunting to bring home meat for the family group, and the females stayed closer to home, raised the children, and gathered nuts, berries, and root vegetables to supplement the meat, or replace it entirely if the hunt was unsuccessful. But you can see traces of those characteristics in modern serial killers. Men hunt for sexual partners—overwhelmingly, the reason for killing is tied to sexual satisfaction. Whereas women only rarely kill for sexual satisfaction. More often than not, they kill for financial gain, where they gather resources to support their young. That's what I see in this case."

"You agree the dam project is the impetus?" Meg asked.

"I would have agreed up to ten minutes ago, but then you told me about Congressman Greyson's murder. That changes things, but only slightly, and it does, in fact, solidify the motive—the protection of the family home and lands. There isn't just one threat; there are two—the dam project and what the current occupants of the valley could view as encroachment by the Eastern Band of Cherokee

Indians, who are attempting to stake their claim to land that was once native territory before their removal."

"Irony, clean-up on aisle four," McCord murmured too quietly for Rutherford to hear, but earning a flash of a grin from Meg.

"If you look at these killings," Rutherford continued, "you can see where a female suspect checks the most boxes. Women tend to be the most pragmatic killers, and often their motives revolve around larger stakes than personal lust or revenge, unless it's revenge against someone who has harmed one of their own. They also tend to be 'clean' killers, with poison being their preferred weapon. But in this case, while the deaths are violent, they are at a distance, so there is no mess to her personally or emotionally since she doesn't have to experience the agony of the victim up close. She doesn't need to be there to watch life drain away, she just needs to make sure the job gets done."

"That is pragmatic," Craig said.

"And she has the skills to accomplish her goal. But what's interesting is yesterday we saw the first chink in her armor."

"Why would you say that?" Meg asked. "If you ask me, the shooter was pretty efficient."

"In the initial kill, yes. But then look at what came after. She waited around for the search teams she knew would come because you'd made local news and you attended the town hall where Mr. Cavett was wounded. But when it came time to take Ms. Jennings, Mr. Foster, or the dogs out of the equation, she failed. Now why is that?"

"You don't think it's because we were on the move and too difficult to hit with any accuracy?" Brian asked.

"I don't," Rutherford countered. "I think the fact that such a talented archer missed repeatedly showed her reluctance to shoot at all. She was torn. She felt she had to eliminate the threat to herself, but where she felt justified killing for her family, she didn't for herself."

"The mother figure always putting herself last," said Lauren. "It's classic. It's exactly the way my mother would reason out the situation. Meg and Brian weren't directly threatening her home and family. She waited all that time, but when push came to shove, she was second-guessing herself."

"And that showed in her faulty aim when she was shooting at Meg," Brian finished.

"That's my read on it," Rutherford said. "Her uncertainty these killings were justified manifested in an unsuccessful attack. The others were all clean."

"An elite hunter only needs one arrow to make a kill. That's the kind of hunter we're looking at here," Meg murmured.

Rutherford leaned into his monitor, his brow crumpled in confusion. "Sorry? I didn't catch that."

"I was repeating what Captain Wilcox of the Georgia State Patrol told me when I asked him how many arrows the shooter would be carrying. He said an elite hunter would only need one arrow to make a kill. But she missed with four." Meg turned to Brian. "I wasn't sure if she was shooting at both of us or just me."

"Just you." Brian's gaze swung to Craig. "I couldn't actually see her in the forest. The arrows came out of the trees every few seconds. The first one would have hit you, but you bent over to say something to Hawk and it sailed over your back. And then after that, you were moving and she never had a chance."

"I disagree," Rutherford interjected. "This is a hunter who's used to dealing with unpredictable animals. They don't stand around waiting to die. She knows how to hit a moving target. And yet she consistently failed."

Scott tucked his overlong legs under the chair and leaned forward so his voice would carry to the microphone. "What's your take on how fast these killings are happening?"

"Ah, yes, that angle. You all know how many killers have a cooling-off period. That period can be days, weeks, or sometimes years as the killer is battling his urge to kill, before finally giving in. But that's not what's happening here. These killings strike me as being coldly calculating. This suspect isn't battling an urge to kill. She has it planned out and she's striking as opportunity, likely both for the victim and her own schedule, permits."

"Her own schedule." Scott propped his elbows on his knees, staring thoughtfully at the laptop monitor. "Because she has a family who may have no idea she's doing this."

"I suspect they are totally unaware. They'd either try to stop her from any more murders, or if they agree with why she's killing in the first place, they might actually try to help."

"If they had the skill," Brian said.

"If they did, they could help by being backup if the shot missed. If they didn't, they could help by drawing out the victim or in any other number of ways. But these murders consistently only seem to have one killer."

"And the dogs are certainly not disagreeing on a single track leading away from the kill sites." Meg dropped a hand onto Hawk's head, stroking her fingers over his silky fur. "If they'd disagreed on the scent trail, or found a secondary fresh trail, they would have let us know. No, there's only been one shooter out there."

"The bigger question is why have five deaths happened in the past three weeks?" Rutherford posited. "What's the rush? It's like she's racing a ticking clock. Special Agent Torres, is there something that's forcing her hand right now when it comes to either the dam project or the application by the Cherokee to claim that land?"

"Not the EBCI claim." Torres flicked through a couple of pages in the pile, pulled one out, and then scanned through it. "But tomorrow they're doing the official announcement of the dam project."

Meg and Craig exchanged startled glances. "Why didn't we know about this before now?" Meg asked. "That's exactly the kind of situation that would draw out this suspect. Where is it, and who's going to be there?"

Torres's lips tightened at the edge in Meg's tone. "You didn't hear about it because I only found out about it today and there were a few other things going on." He stared directly at Meg and Brian.

Brian bristled beside her, so Meg laid her hand on his knee and squeezed. *I've got this.* "Do you have any details about it?"

"Some, but I've already asked for more and I hope to hear back from the TVA this afternoon. It's at the Fontana Dam, and at least one TVA bigwig will be there." He held up a hand to forestall Meg's next question. "The identity of the bigwig is part of what I'm waiting for."

"This is exactly the kind of event at which this suspect would want to make a splash." Rutherford's voice brought everyone's attention back to the laptop. "I'm unfamiliar with that particular dam. Is it in Georgia?"

"North Carolina." Torres met Meg's eyes. "About an hour out of Qualla Boundary. We drove past the exit on US-74 on our way there. It's supposed to begin at four o'clock, so we'd better plan on being there."

"We'd better plan on a lot more than that," Craig said. "This could be our chance to wrap up this case, so we need to work out a strategy. But we're getting off track." Craig glanced sideways at Torres's closed expression.

"Rutherford, help us narrow it down. Can you give us your specific profile of this killer?"

"I'll e-mail you my detailed report, but here is what you need to narrow or redefine your lists." Rutherford glanced down at his desk and what was likely his notes. "You're looking for a female in her early thirties to midforties, of middle or upper class, with a postsecondary education. She's fit, and an experienced hiker and hunter. She's married, or has been, possibly multiple times, and if she's religious—and since it's the South, I'm betting she is—you have a nearly one hundred percent chance she's Christian. Last point, but you knew this already, there are land and offspring in the mix. She's not doing this for herself."

Meg waited two beats for Torres to say something, but he seemed lost in his own discouraged thoughts. She grabbed the laptop and angled it toward her. "Thank you. That gives us something substantial to go on."

"I'll e-mail you the details right now. Let me know if you need anything else or if you get more information to add to the profile. As always, I'll revise as necessary. Good hunting and safe travels home." Leaning in, Rutherford cut the connection.

Meg closed the laptop lid and then shifted her gaze to Craig, who stared unblinkingly at Torres.

"Something wrong?" Craig asked.

Torres gathered himself to say something and then stopped before trying again. "Was my read on this case so far off?" He looked up, scanning the face of the FBI team members. "Do you trust this profile?"

"Yes." The answer came in unison from Craig, Meg, Brian, Scott, and Lauren.

Torres sat back abruptly with a little jerk. "So yes . . . my read was off."

"Yours. Mine. Brian's," Meg said. "None of us picked

up on the fact it might be a woman. We've only been looking at men."

"To be fair," McCord interjected, "remember Beverley's
list? They were all men, too."

"That's true. But Rutherford is right about the confirmation bias and not just for Sam. Right from the beginning of the case we've all been describing the shooter as
'he.' But just because five out of six serial killers are male,
doesn't mean the sixth is as well."

"Don't beat yourself up, Torres," Craig said. "This is
why we have Rutherford and the BAU. They have skills
and knowledge we don't. But he can't investigate like you
can or search like my teams. When you put us all together,
we get the job done. So where are we moving forward?"

"We're back to the drawing board." Torres looked
down glumly at the papers spread across the table. "Which
means all this is useless."

Meg turned to Torres. "Remember the research list we
gave Chief Cobbrey when he said he'd help us. 'Hunting
records. Archery club memberships. Word of mouth.' We
need to go back to basics. But this time we have a leg up
because we already know some of the people involved."

"Who are you thinking of?" Webb asked.

"There are a few women we already know are hunters.
Mary Trammell, for instance. Her own husband pointed
out that she hunts."

McCord leaned forward, started to speak, then hesitated. At Meg's raised eyebrows, he said, "I hate to bring it
up because she's been so helpful, but Beverley at the Department of Natural Resources is also an archer."

"I think I'd put her lower down the list. I have trouble
seeing what her motive might be. Just being an archer isn't
enough. Mary Trammell is going to lose her home and
business all at once, and both likely would have gone to

her sons unless the dam project is stopped. That gives a powerful motive that's directly in line with the profile Rutherford just delivered. She also fits for age and marital status, and likely for religion."

"We don't know if she hunts with a bow or a gun," Torres said.

"Very true. That's the kind of information we need to find out. All I'm saying is we're not exactly right back at the starting line. This time we understand the players and what they're fighting for."

"And this time you've got us as well." Craig tapped on the stack of papers. "Let's go back to the lists, discuss the townsfolk you've met up to now, talk about who else to include. And then start interviewing and collecting alibis again. The answer is here; we just need to find it." He looked up, his gaze traveling to touch each team member. "Let's get to work."

CHAPTER 26

Hunting Blind: A device used by hunters to reduce the chance of being detected.

Thursday, April 18, 7:37 AM
Lake View Cabins
Blue Ridge, Georgia

The first text came through from Craig shortly after Meg got out of the shower.

Torres asked me to go with him to do interviews based on the revised suspect list. We're heading out now.

She quickly typed in her response: **Good. I think he could use your expertise. Heads-up—some of the local residents have a problem with Latinos and may be reticent to talk to him.**

Thanks. More when there is more.

Meg went downstairs with Webb to find a kitchen full of dogs and handlers in addition to Ryan and McCord. Scott, Lauren, and Craig had spent the night in a nearby cottage, and Scott and Lauren had returned at Brian and Meg's urging for meals and to await news. They ate together and then Meg walked Brian and Ryan out to Ryan's rental car and waved them off as they headed for Chats-

worth to see Lacey. Then she headed inside and spent a
half hour working her body through careful stretching and
yoga to ease some of her soreness.

By shortly after eleven, Meg was impatiently awaiting
more information.

"You keep checking your watch," Scott commented.
"Craig is trying to move this along as fast as possible."

"I know." Meg forced herself to take a deep breath and
try to blow out some of her stress with it. "But the announcement starts at four o'clock. If they don't nail down
a suspect this morning, it's going to take us almost two
hours to drive there, and we need to be there an hour
early, if not more, to get the lay of the land and to set up to
intercept the shooter. Craig knows that."

"I don't think Craig expected to be out pounding the
pavement this morning." Lauren poured herself another
cup of coffee. "He hasn't handled a case like this for a long
time, but I think Torres needs a little help at this point."

"And he doesn't want it to be you or Brian," McCord
said from behind his laptop, where he sat at the kitchen
table.

"What do you mean?" Meg asked.

McCord studied her over the top of his glasses. "He felt
backed into a corner last night."

"What? How?" Meg looked from McCord to Webb,
who shrugged. "You think so, too?"

"I think he felt out of place. He's not wet behind the
ears, but he seems to still be learning some of the ropes in
a location where sometimes his skills aren't wanted simply
because of the color of his skin. And then there's all of
you, a cohesive unit with your own language and unspoken shortcuts, stepping in to analyze his case."

"And bringing in the BAU," McCord continued. "You

guys talked to Rutherford like it's just another case to work together—"

"It *is* another case to work together."

"For you, but not for Torres. You suggested Rutherford to Torres and pushed for his contribution." When Meg opened her mouth to argue, McCord steamrolled over her. "It was the right call, and Rutherford's contribution will likely break this case open, but all it did was highlight the fact that Torres's short list of suspects was too narrow."

"And then when you found out about today's announcement, you kind of jumped down his throat," Lauren added. "You didn't mean to, and it was one hundred percent because you'd had a hell of a day and were short on sleep, but he might have read it as a personal dig."

"Damn." Meg sagged back against the counter. "That's not what I meant to imply at all."

"Of course you didn't," Webb said, "and we wouldn't have taken it the way I think he did, but he doesn't know you like we do. That's probably why he asked Craig for his opinion in the case. Not only because he's an investigator and not a handler, but also because he's experienced. It sounds like he's second-guessing himself and doesn't feel confident the right doors will open to him personally."

"And possibly because Craig has a fresh perspective, not colored by what Torres thinks may have been errors on his part in this case," Scott added.

Meg cast her eyes up at the ceiling and shook her head. "If Brian was here, he'd agree with me that we don't have any complaints about how the case was handled. We're equally to blame for not expanding the list."

"Something maybe to mention to Torres at some point then, because I'm not sure he sees it that way."

"Yeah, I'll be sure to." Meg's phone rang and she pulled it out of her back pocket, checking the name on the display: Sam Torres. "And now might be a good time." She accepted the call. "Jennings."

"It's Sam. We have a problem. Is everyone there?"

"Except for Brian, who went to see Lacey, we're all here in the kitchen. What's going on?"

"Can you put the call on speaker so we only need to go over this once?"

"Sure." She switched the call over to speaker, laid the phone on the table, and motioned everyone to step closer. "Okay, we're all here. What do you think is the problem?"

"Beaumont and I have been interviewing new suspects all morning. We started with Mary Trammell. And let me tell you, her husband wasn't happy to have us there, questioning his wife after I'd already been there to question his sons. Beaumont had to step in. But she does bowhunt."

"Is she a suspect, then?"

"No, she alibis out for every shooting. She works the front desk at the lodge, so she's always in sight of her family or staff. There was no way she could have gotten away to do it. So then we moved on to McCord's contact at the Wildlife Resources Division at the Georgia Department of Natural Resources. We didn't tell her we were looking specifically at her, so she was very helpful."

Meg glanced at McCord, who worried a pen back and forth between his fingers, appearing slightly stressed that Beverley-the-peach might be a suspect and he'd missed all the signs.

"She realized she'd made an error in the original list," Torres said. "The way McCord asked the question about the hunting records, she thought you were only looking for men."

McCord dropped the pen as if it suddenly burned his fingers. The peach had thrown him under the bus.

Torres was still talking. "The high kill harvest records

actually had a few other names on it. Two of them are women. The first is Marlene Sanford. She and her husband are farmers west of Blue Ridge Lake. We found Mrs. Sanford on the family farm this morning. When questioned about her whereabouts, she told us she was home on the farm at the time of the first killing. But she left for a visit at her mother's in Ohio on April seventh and didn't come home until yesterday, which puts her out of state for the last three attacks. She gave us a number of names to substantiate that."

"Not Mrs. Sanford, then. Who is the second woman?"

"Here's where things get interesting. It's Savannah Cavett."

Meg's head snapped up to stare at McCord. "Mason's wife and Will's mother?"

"That's her. Her harvest record is nearly as impressive as her husband's. But she doesn't have the lists of trophies behind her name, which was our main thrust early on. According to Beverley, she's an A1 archer."

"We had no idea. No one mentioned that she hunted. You saw the cabinet with all the awards. It was just for the men. She even comes across as someone too fastidious to get her hands dirty killing wildlife."

"Needless to say, we wanted to know more, so we went to talk to Mrs. Cavett."

Meg exchanged glances with Lauren. "I hear a 'but' coming."

"There's a 'but' all right. She wasn't home. Left first thing in the morning for a spontaneous shopping day in Atlanta. Won't be home until tonight. And she's not answering her cell phone."

"That looks suspicious on the surface, but when we went to talk to her, didn't she alibi out for the time in question? She said . . . didn't she have a lunch date?"

"Breakfast. With someone named Marnie. Mason Cavett was angry I was questioning his wife, and he gave me her contact information to prove me wrong. The only problem is that Marnie turns out to be Marnie Turnberry, the owner of the local bookstore in town. And on the morning in question, she wasn't out having breakfast; she was doing inventory with several staff members. She wasn't initially very forthcoming when we questioned her about why Savannah would use her as an alibi, but we finally got it out of her after pressuring her with the charge of obstruction of justice for impeding a federal agent in the lawful discharge of his duties. Apparently, Savannah called her later that same day, desperate and begging for help. She needed someone to say she'd been with her that morning. Marnie and Savannah go way back to being childhood friends, so Marnie agreed she'd tell Mason if he asked that Savannah was with her."

"Mason? This is a murder investigation; why would her husband be asking?"

"That's just what Savannah told Marnie. She said she needed cover in case her husband asked because she'd been off with another man at that time and didn't want her family to find out."

McCord let out a low whistle.

Meg braced both hands on the table and leaned in. "So Savannah got cover for a potential murder by convincing a girlfriend to cover for an affair she wasn't having?"

"Looks like it."

"That's interesting. Sam, do you remember the trophy case in the Cavett living room? All those older awards for the son in the place of honor at eye level and the husband's more recent awards down below. We wondered if their marriage was struggling. Maybe we weren't far off. It certainly sounds like the affair cover-up was a convincing story for the friend. And actually, it was pretty smart thinking." Meg looked up at Lauren, who was nodding her agreement.

"You think so?" Torres said. "It didn't work for her."

"Only because you pressured Marnie with jail time. Otherwise, girlfriends will go to the wall for you in ways a male partner might not." She glanced at Webb and threw him an apologetic shrug in response to his raised eyebrow and pointed look. "If it had been Savannah's husband asking, Marnie never would have told him the truth. And I bet Savannah was counting on the spotlight never falling on her. She comes across as a delicate Southern belle. Lets her husband and son have all the accolades and all the glory. I wonder how much of that is because she has an overbearing, competitive husband who isn't pleased to have a wife with skills that might overshadow his own?"

"That could be part of it. She could also be using our own unconscious prejudice against us so we saw exactly what she wanted us to see. But under the lady of the manor routine, she may be the one in control. What we do know is Mason can't alibi her for any of the other attacks."

Meg pulled out a chair and sat down. "What about the town hall attack? We know she was there for that. But . . ."

"What?"

Meg took a second to bring back the scene from where she'd stood on the staircase. "You were right there when the shooting happened. So was McCord. And Todd. Mason and Will were standing with the mayor, but Savannah was nowhere to be seen." She turned to McCord and then Webb. "Did either of you see her?"

"Afterward," Webb said, "when she was sitting with her son at the rear of the ambulance. That was the first time I saw her."

McCord sat back in his chair and crossed his arms over his chest. "Same here. I didn't see her when the shooting happened. But you're implying she went after the mayor with her husband and son standing right there? Isn't that risky?"

"It would be," Meg replied. "But if she's really that good, she may have thought she'd be able to make that shot. But then she missed."

"What if . . ." Webb stopped, frowned, and then stepped forward to rest his hand on the back of Meg's chair and leaned in. "Agent Torres, Beverley said Savannah was good?"

"Very," Torres said. "Less kills than many overall, but more per actual hunting trip. She just didn't get out as much."

Meg turned to look up at Webb, who was staring at the phone, his brows drawn together in concentration. "Where are you going with this?"

"That attack happened when her son and husband were both under investigation. Rutherford described female serial killers as going to great lengths to protect and gather resources for their children. What if that attack wasn't about the mayor at all? What if Mrs. Cavett was actually trying to take her son off the suspect list by making him a victim?"

Meg stared at him openmouthed as she worked through the scenario in a new light.

"That would be incredibly risky," Lauren interjected. "She could have killed either her husband or son."

"Or another innocent bystander," Scott said.

"I really wish Brian was here. He was standing with me on the platform where she took that shot. First of all, it wasn't as far away as some of the shots. Maybe only about fifty yards. And while the shooter was standing in darkness, the parking lot was brightly lit. She could stand there, unseen, line up the shot, and take it when she was absolutely ready. If she meant to wing Will, that's exactly what she did. She made him the victim and cleared him of all suspicion at the same time."

"If that's true, then she really *is* that good," Torres said.

"Note that she moved to clear Will and not Mason, another nail in the marital strife coffin. Also, think about what she was wearing that night. All black, except for a bright red and silver scarf she could have taken off, wound up, and stuck in a pocket when she wanted to blend into the background."

"But what did she do with the bow?" McCord asked. "When we saw her later, she didn't have one with her."

In her mind, Meg went back to the platform, raised on sturdy posts as the hill sloped down into the vineyard fields below it.

The fields.

"She tossed it. The fields below the platform are full of rows of grapevines. The bow I shot at the archery range maybe weighed six or seven pounds max." Meg looked at McCord for confirmation of the weight he'd held and he nodded. "She could have grabbed one end of the bow and flung it out over the fields, and it could have spun out twenty or thirty feet down the hill. Put the scarf on again, head into the parking lot, and launch into the shocked, panicked mother act. There was so much chaos at the time, she could have melted into the crowd and no one would have noticed because no one was looking for the shooter to come *into* the crowd. Only move away from it. But that would also explain why there was no defined trail leading away from the platform, just one more that joined the mass of trails leading into the parking lot by the tour participants."

"And if the platform was raised off the hillside, she could have come earlier in the day or the day before and hidden the bow underneath it for access later," Scott suggested. "And then returned at first light the following day to retrieve it from the fields."

"It all makes sense," Meg said. She paused for a moment, giving her brain time to make connections. "You know, there are a few other things that make sense if you think Savannah is the culprit."

"Like what?" asked Torres.

"First off, the fancy arrows. Custom made, with specialized materials, shipped in from out of the area. The Cavetts would be able to afford materials like that. She may not even have ordered them, maybe Mason or Will did and she just helped herself. And remember her sphere of influence. Sam, do you remember what we thought about Mason? That he was someone who would make sure he got what he wanted, no matter who stood in his way."

"I remember."

"She may have adopted some of that attitude and taken things into her own hands. You know she was protective of the land. Her family's land. They're not going to sell voluntarily, so if the land gets taken from them, what are the chances they'll be fairly paid market value for it?"

"Pretty small I would bet."

"That's another layer then. I do have one question, though."

"What's that?"

"I understand the locations for many of the deaths. Family homes or hunting cabins. Favorite places to hunt. You live in this area, that's not hard to find out, especially for people who have been in the area and part of the hunting community for decades. But the death at Ocoee Dam

#2. How could Savannah possibly have known Gord White would be there that day?"

"That one's actually easy," Torres replied. "When it comes to a scheduled repair, especially if they are going to have to divert water from the flume, it's carried in the papers, on local TV, and on the TVA website because it affects energy production. My guess is the repair was carried on the local media and Savannah knew someone would be coming out to the flume, just not who. It may be that White wasn't the target. The target was simply whoever came out from the construction company."

"If that's true, then it's really a case of wrong place, wrong time for Mr. White. Okay, this is all lining up. You said Savannah is in the wind now?"

"Yes," said Torres. "We have to assume she's on her way to the Fontana Dam."

"Then we need to get up there, too. And fast. We're losing time."

There was a pause at the other end of the line, then, "Craig here. I have that covered. There's a helipad just outside Blue Ridge on US Highway 76. The Georgia State Patrol are sending a helicopter at noon to carry the five of us and the dogs to the dam. We'll save at least an hour that way. We'll have time to get the lay of the land, hopefully before she gets there or at least before she comes onto the site. I have the TVA police, and both the Graham and Swain County Sheriff's Offices in the loop as the dam is officially in both counties. Everyone is on board to assist. We're on our way to the helipad now. See you there." He ended the call.

"Time for us to go." Meg pinned McCord with a flat stare. "You can't come with us, but I know wild horses won't keep you away." She turned to Webb. "Probably both of you, so the same instructions apply. Stay back, and stay out of the way. It's a public place and will likely be crawling with media, onlookers, protesters, hikers, and run-of-the-mill tourists. Stay alert and stay clear of that announcement. If it really is Savannah, she's not going to be anywhere near it, but I don't want anyone getting caught by a stray shot. I'd never hear the end of it from Cara."

She turned to her dog. "Hawk, come." She ran her hand over his head when he stood at her knee. "Let's finish this once and for all."

CHAPTER 27

Eminent Domain: The right of a government to seize private property for public use. After the creation of the Great Smoky Mountains National Park in 1934, Fontana village became a copper mining town; but just after December 7, 1941, the federal government ordered that mining interests on Eagle Creek in western North Carolina be terminated immediately. With that order came notice that the Tennessee Valley Authority was on its way to Graham County. A legislative act had already authorized the construction of a gigantic hydroelectric power dam on the Little Tennessee River. The location of this project, one of the largest engineering feats in history, was to be on land already acquired from the Aluminum Company of America (Alcoa). Construction of the new dam—to be named "Fontana"—began on January 1, 1942.

Thursday, April 18, 1:44 PM
Fontana Dam
Graham and Swain Counties, North Carolina

"This is amazing," Scott said from where he leaned over the edge of the dam. "Come and take a look."

Meg, Lauren, Scott, and their three dogs stood on top of the dam, on the concrete path that spanned the structure and carried a throughway of the Appalachian Trail. A shiver ran down Meg's spine at the thought of what was on the other side of the solid concrete barrier wall where Scott perched. "You know I don't like heights. Why would I willingly look over the edge?"

"Because when's the next time you're going to be this close to a structure like this?"

"I'll bite." Lauren came to stand next to Scott and bent forward to look straight down. Her hands tightened on the railing that topped the barrier wall, her knuckles standing out in stark white with the force of her grip. "You're right. It's impressive."

"That's what I'm saying."

Meg rolled her eyes and let out a long-suffering breath. Then, clamping on tight to the waist-high metal railing, Meg cautiously leaned slightly out to peer down the river side of the dam. The steeply angled concrete stretched down—way, way down, over forty stories down—all the way to the multilevel powerhouse at the bottom next to a parking lot that appeared to be full of toy cars. Nearby, neat rows of switches and transformers carried the electricity generated in the powerhouse to the lines that distributed it all over the state. Staring down the wide expanse of concrete to the river below made Meg dizzy, so she straightened and turned her back on the terrifying drop to stare out at the peaceful blue waters of Fontana lake on the opposite side of the dam. "You know, that is one pretty lake."

Laughing, Scott swiveled to face the lake, taking in the smooth surface and undulating shoreline edged with thick forest. "Sure is." Movement drew his attention to their right. "Here comes Craig." He raised his hand in greeting. "Do you know what's going on?" he called.

Craig, dressed in casual clothes—a rare occurrence—waited until he was closer so he didn't have to shout. "Yes.

Come on back toward the Visitor Center so you can see how this is going to go. It will be easier if you actually see the setup."

They followed him along the top of the dam, and the tightness left Meg's chest as the sides of the river gorge rose to meet the edge of the dam and she didn't feel like she was poised hundreds of feet above a killing drop. Taking the deep breath she'd been unable to draw for the last fifteen minutes, she scanned the area around them.

The glassed-in Visitor Center was a long building with a circular section at the end nearest the dam. Stairs climbed that curve, leading to a round platform on the roof where visitors could look out over the breadth of the dam. A crowd of people buzzed over it, setting up a low platform in front of the dam and electronic equipment to capture the announcement. A circular driveway wound in front of the Visitor Center, and past it, a long, U-shaped parking lot stretched parallel to the river.

Craig stopped at the top of a flight of steps that led down to the parking lot area. Beyond the steps, two enormous chutes tunneled steeply into the ground, mirroring the angle of the dam. More than thirty feet across each, they opened toward the lake, separated from the body of water by heavy steel gates.

After her mini-lesson at Ocoee Dam #2 and the flume, Meg recognized these as the dam spillway, but the sheer scope was mind-boggling. She peered over the edge, but the tunnel simply melted into darkness stories below. She took a step backward from the spillway tunnel, happy to put several feet between herself and that unending drop into nothingness.

"The media announcement will take place up there on the dam overlook." Craig pointed to the hum of activity on the roof of the Visitor Center. "They're supposed to start at four o'clock and expect both local and national media to attend. Honestly, it sounds like it's going to be a crush."

Lauren turned away from the center to face Craig with an expression of doubt. "And knowing what we do, or at least what we suspect, they think proceeding with the announcement is a good idea? Shouldn't they consider canceling it? Torres has shared everything we know with all levels of law enforcement?"

"He has, including the TVA police. Needless to say, they let the TVA administration know, especially the guy who is supposed to be making the announcement."

"Who's that?" Scott asked.

"Kenneth Buckner, the Senior Vice President of Resources and Operations Support. He's the guy spearheading the Copperhill Dam project. Torres and I talked to him, but he wouldn't cancel."

"Does he have a death wish?" Meg asked.

"No, but he's really sick of protesters and bureaucracy. He just wants to get this project off the ground. Also, he knew Gord White, the third victim, personally. As far as he's concerned, if he can do something to help catch the person who killed White, he's all in. But we did manage to convince him to at least take reasonable precautions. We're going to put him in body armor under his suit. Every attempt made has been a torso shot, so we're going to protect against that. The other thing we're going to do is have a lot of officers in plain clothes all over the facility. She's not going to be able to get close enough to take an accurate shot. But we're going to let her get close enough to try."

"What about all those reporters?"

"We're going to keep them well back. Anyone who is going to be close is going to be Buckner's 'staff.'" Craig put air quotes around the word with both hands. "We don't dare put Torres out there because if the suspect is Savannah, and she's observing through binoculars, she might recognize him, so Torres will have to stay inside the Visitor Center. You guys will be out there"—with both index fingers, Craig covered the ground on the far side of the parking lot—"and I'll be in the parking lot. You'll be looking in toward the Visitor Center watching for her. I'll be looking out, doing the same. And then there will be sheriff's deputies stationed in the woods at the edge of the only road leading into and out of the complex. If she makes a move, we'll all be after her in seconds. Let's go and get a better lay of the land." He continued down the stairs and then stopped on the third step from the bottom, leaning over to look down the spillway shaft. "By the way, I've been told they'll open these gates just before the announcement."

"Isn't this kind of a bad time to lower the reservoir level?" Meg asked.

"Apparently when they open the gates it makes for a hell of a show. And they want to give the media a show."

Scott squinted at him. "A show?"

"One of the TVA guys in there told me this dam is too tall to have spillway gates at the top to run down the outside of the dam because it would destroy the dam foundation over time. These tunnels were drilled through the mountain rock when they were building the dam to keep the water moving, so after the dam was complete, they made them the spillway. But because of the height, the water reaches ninety-five miles per hour by the time it's at the bottom, which would erode the foundation there as well. To counteract that, they built a concrete ramp at the bottom that shoots the water one hundred and fifty feet into the air so it lands four hundred feet downstream. It supposedly looks pretty impressive—like a giant explosion of water. They want to have that going during the media visit."

"It's the TVA's version of fireworks."

"Essentially. When you see it, don't worry that something's gone wrong; that part is scheduled." He led the teams across the walkway, around the edge of the circular driveway, and then up the stairs curving around the building and to the top level. Law enforcement personnel, many still in uniform, gathered on the overlook as technicians bustled around, taping down cables and arranging a podium and microphone. Craig walked to the area behind the platform. "Let's analyze where she can and can't take the shot from so we can figure out where to place the teams."

Meg gazed out across the expanse of the river valley. "Not from the far side. That's hundreds of yards. She'd be in range on this side, but the ground drops away here toward the river four hundred feet below, and that angle wouldn't work for a shot. And I can't see her shooting from the top of the dam. She could get in range, but she'd be totally exposed."

"I agree. We'll place people there to dissuade her, just in case. That takes care of north and west, leaving us with south and east." He squeezed out from behind the platform and moved to the opposite edge of the overlook trailing handlers and dogs. "There's a lot of treed sections in this direction, but it would be possible to shoot from the far side of the parking lot, just south of Fontana Dam Road, all the way to nearly the south end of the lot. More significant is that hill." He pointed to the land that rose to the east of the parking lot, topping the asphalt by easily one hundred feet. "She goes up there, she's shooting down at us. It's pushing the distance, but not by much."

"It pushes it less than the south end of the parking lot. I don't think she's going to shoot from down there."

"I agree, that's much less likely. Here's what we'll do. Scott, you and Theo cover the entrance to the parking lot.

Stay back in the trees a few feet so you aren't too notice-able, but make sure you have line of sight on the announcement. You don't have to hear it, but you need to know if she takes the shot. Lauren, I want you and Rocco up that hill. Try to line up with the end of the Visitor Center; that will put you only about a third of the way down from the road, but that's likely where she'd take the shot from. Meg, you and Hawk should position yourself down a little farther toward the south end of the parking lot, about halfway up the hill. That way you can respond to an alert from either above or below your position."

"Where are you going to be?" Lauren asked.

"Right there." Craig pointed at the narrow green space that ran the length of the parking lot between the two sides of the U. "As I said, you watch the Visitor Center, and I'll watch the hillside. For a change we're going to be close enough geographically that I asked the Graham County Sheriff's Office to loan us earpieces and throat mics. I want full communication, and that's going to be the easi-est way and is mostly hands free. If anyone sees her, report in and we'll all go for her. If you end up out of range of the close communications system, switch over to your sat phones. And if it's not Savannah Cavett, or on the small chance Rutherford is wrong and it's a guy, we nail who-ever the perp is. Male, female, young, old." Craig turned to look at the podium. "We draw the line here."

Thursday, April 18, 4:05 PM
Fontana Dam
Graham and Swain Counties, North Carolina

They were in place.

The TVA crew was running a little late, but the Human Scent Evidence Team was in position, as were law enforce-ment personnel. Meg spotted faces she'd seen earlier on the overlook now strolling the grounds and the top of the dam in jeans, flannels, and jackets, rather than uniforms and utility belts. But she was certain that under the flannels and jackets, every officer was armed and ready for action.

Only confirmed media personnel were allowed onto the overlook, but a rowdy group of fifty or sixty protesters gathered on the grass approximately twenty feet from the circular wing, chanting and waving placards, held back by a line of TVA police. It was a good thing Buckner had a sound system, or no one would hear a word he said. Hikers following the Appalachian Trail drifted in and out of the "Fontana Hilton's" Visitor Center with its free public bathrooms and showers, and tourists wandered along the top of the dam, staring openmouthed at the river far below. Craig was visible on the green, casually seated on a long bench between a pair of saplings. He appeared at ease, but Meg knew he was constantly scanning the hillside, road, and parking lot, watching for any sign of movement.

The spillway was opened about fifteen minutes before, first with the mechanical rumble of the steel floodgates as they lifted, and then with a whoosh of water as it rushed down the twin spillway tunnels. Four or five seconds later, a roar quaked from below as water burst from the spillway to shoot down the river. From where Meg was standing, she could see a fine mist rising, even at this height, downstream from the dam.

Meg stood partway up the ridge that rose over the dam complex, well hidden in the trees, but watching through the small pair of binoculars she always carried in her go bag. From where she stood, she could see the quiet direction working behind the chaos to keep the media well separated from the platform, and the general public separated from the overlook all together. Past the overlook, near the stairs by the spillway, Webb and McCord leaned against the railing, watching from a distance. She satisfied herself they were well clear of any potential arrow, and then swung the viewfinder to the podium just in time to see Buckner step onto the platform.

Here we go.

She bent and unhooked Hawk's leash from his collar—all the dogs were working incognito without their FBI vests—and then ran a hand down his back. "Ready, boy?" She kept her voice low.

He gazed up at her with bright eyes, his tail wagging madly. He was ready.

Let's see where this goes. I bet she's going to strike sooner rather than later.

There was a short buzz of static in her earpiece, and then Craig spoke. "Okay, teams, this is it. Stay sharp."

Being sharp certainly wasn't a problem. Meg had been in position for almost an hour, and both she and Hawk had been raring to go the whole time. But there'd been no sign of the shooter and not a whisper of sound that wasn't part of the natural landscape.

She's a hunter with a high kill count. She knows how to move quietly through the woods.

A low drone came from across the parking lot. Buckner was speaking, and while his words were indistinct, the tone of them carried through the air. In response, shouts came from the protesters, trying to simultaneously drown out the announcement and to attract media attention to highlight their objections.

There was a flash of reflected sunlight as one of the cameramen turned to aim his camera down at the screaming mass of people below.

Glass exploded just below the concrete lip of the roof, the crash of shattered glass ricocheting through the valley and off miles of concrete. Shouts of anger turned to screams of terror as protesters reacted to the noise and ran or dove for cover. Up on the platform, multiple people jumped on top of Buckner to force him down to the ground, as the frenzied mass of media members scattered out of the way of a second shot.

"I see her!" Craig was on his feet in the parking lot, pointing at a location higher than Meg, but not far from her location. "All teams! The suspect is near the top of the ridge. Meg, she's about forty feet above you."

Meg froze for a moment, concentrating on the sounds around her. And then the sound of running feet and breaking branches filtered through the trees. "We are in pursuit. Hawk, come! Find her!" She took off uphill, but instead of going straight up, she cut toward the south on a diagonal. There was no way this woman, who made it a habit to disappear into the woods to make her escape, would make a run for the only road heading into the dam complex. No, she'd go south, running parallel to the road as it followed the curve of the river. She'd make her way to wherever she left her car and then disappear on the back roads of Graham County.

Not if Meg could help it.

They didn't try to hide their footfalls, but raced after their suspect at full speed, darting around trees, pushing through underbrush, and leaping over rocks.

And then she saw it, a flash of vague movement in the trees. The kind of vague movement that someone wearing camo to blend in might produce.

They had her.

Meg hit the button for her mic. "I've got her. She's heading south, no, southwest. She's going downhill. She may be heading for the river."

"Copy that," came Craig's voice. He was breathing hard, so Meg knew he was on the move as well. "All teams, move to intercept."

But the Southern belle wasn't going down without a fight. Meg poured on the speed, Hawk matching her pace, occasionally moving away to avoid an obstacle, but winding his way back to her. Her sore muscles screaming in protest, Meg gritted her teeth and bore down. She was not going to lose Savannah because her body betrayed her.

Ahead, the runner became clearer. Blond hair, either short or tied back beneath a green and brown cap. Camouflage pants and jacket. A camouflage pack on her back with the bow strapped to the outside. But Meg couldn't see the shooter's face.

They were closing in on the fleeing figure. *Time to test the theory.* "Savannah!" Meg yelled.

The figure jerked around to look back.

Gotcha.

"I have positive ID," she told the team. "It's Savannah Cavett."

"Stay with her," Lauren said. "We're right behind you."

"She's definitely heading for the river."

They had to be more careful here as the slope pitched downward, and Meg slipped more than once on the slick moss that grew in patches on the forest floor.

As they closed in on the river, the roar of water grew louder and louder, and soon Meg could see the plume of water shooting into the air between the trees. Another minute and they cut through the last of the forest to find themselves on the edge of the river above an angled slope of fieldstone leading down into the water. Water from the spillway shot up in the air in front of them. It angled toward the center of the river, but a fine mist surrounded them, settling a moist sheen on her already sweaty skin.

Savannah was about thirty feet ahead, sprinting down the edge of the forest, and Meg tore after her, Hawk hot on her heels.

Savannah took the time to glance behind her, taking in the woman and dog racing after her, gaining as she paused at the river's edge.

Her eyes grew wide and alarm flickered over her face, followed by desperation.

Then she turned to sprint along the bank, dropped her backpack onto the riverbank, and leaped into the geysering water to disappear completely into the spray.

CHAPTER 28

The Road to Nowhere: North Carolina Highway 288 was buried under the waters of Fontana Lake after Swain County, North Carolina, decided to give up land claims to the federal government for the creation of the Great Smoky Mountains National Park in 1934 and eventual construction of the Fontana Dam. The National Park Service promised to reroute the highway along part of the lake through the park but didn't fulfill that promise. Construction on six miles of the road was actually completed in the early 1970s but then stopped due to environmental issues. In 2010, the project was officially put to rest, and Swain County accepted a $52 million payout from the federal government not to complete the road.

Thursday, April 18, 4:16 PM
Fontana Dam
Graham and Swain Counties, North Carolina

A vision of Brett Stevenson—the perpetrator of last fall's urbex murders—as he floated fifty feet below her in the Delaware River impaled on the remains of a pier support pile flashed before Meg's eyes.

Fury filled her. *I am* not *losing another one. She killed four men, then tried to kill me and Hawk. She can damned well stand trial for it.*

She hit the talk button. "We're at the river. Savannah just jumped in. I'm going in after her." She pulled out her earpiece so she couldn't hear Craig's expected protest. Then she unsnapped the chest strap on her pack and dropped it on the ground behind her, followed by her jacket. Pulling off her throat mic and battery pack, she tossed the equipment on her jacket. One look at Hawk and the gleam of bright determination in his eyes cemented the decision for her. "Let's go, Hawk. Find her!"

Meg sprinted for the spot where Savannah had disappeared, and clambered down over the rocks. Spray hit her cheeks with stinging force, and she turned her back to it. Gathering herself, she pushed off in a shallow dive, aiming toward the center of the river, where the depth was greatest. The water was an icy shock, but with the sun-warmed top layer of the lake mixed into the river, not as bad as the Conasauga.

When she surfaced, the world was lost in a cloud of white spray and foam, but the jostle of her dog beside her told her Hawk had followed her.

She's trying to lose herself in the spray, trying to escape under cover. Follow her downstream.

"Hawk, come!" She bellowed the words, not sure if her dog would hear her, but knowing if any of her was above water, even in this deluge, he'd follow her. She struck out in a strong front crawl, gliding along with the current and the push of the spray, quickly realizing Savannah's strategy was smart. She couldn't see or hear anything in the spray, even this far downstream from the dam. If Savannah could gain significant distance from them in the middle of the river, it might give her enough of a lead to get away.

They'd know who their suspect was, but would they ever catch her?

Meg swam onward through the plume of water, searching, but constantly glancing at Hawk, who stayed close. If it were her, she'd aim for the opposite bank, hoping to lose any pursuers under cover of the spillway runoff. Basing her sense of direction on the pull of the river, Meg cut across to the far side.

Swimming was a challenge, simply due to the sheer inundation of water from all directions. Breathing without inadvertently inhaling the heavy mist was nearly impossible, and Meg took to trying to suck in air through clenched teeth and nearly closed lips, seriously limiting her oxygen intake, but keeping fluid out of her lungs.

She wondered how strong a swimmer Savannah was and how she'd manage the difficult conditions.

It was Hawk who sensed her first. Swimming beside Meg, he suddenly shot forward, a dark blur in a slightly thinning cloud. It was only then that Meg could hear cries for help over the roar. She kicked hard, propelling herself forward, staying just behind Hawk as he frantically tried to both move forward and stay afloat.

They found Savannah, desperately trying to keep her head above water as her arms flailed over her head where it tipped backward. Spray poured in her open mouth, choking her, as the heavy camouflage hunting gear weighed her down.

Meg instantly recognized the danger of the situation. It was all too easy for a panicked swimmer to pull down a rescuer, putting them both at significant risk of drowning. And there was no rescue equipment or a life jacket at hand. A quick review of the situation told Meg her only way to save Savannah was to swim up behind her, get both arms under her and looped over her shoulders so she couldn't be grabbed, and kick her way to the shore. She

also knew that plan would only work if Savannah cooper-
ated.

No choice but to try.

She had to swim around Hawk, but Meg came up behind Savannah just as she went under momentarily and
then came up spluttering.

Meg got her arms looped under Savannah's armpits and
then back over her shoulders. "Savannah, stay calm." She
had to yell over the roar of the water. "I can get us out of
here, but you have to help me."

The other woman struggled and Meg's grip started to
slip. With a shriek, Savannah heaved in her arms, jerking
her right arm free to reach behind her and dig her fingers
into Meg's hair, dragging her beneath the surface with her
as she sank. Meg instantly let go, her only thought to get
free before Savannah drowned them both. She grabbed Savannah's wrist with both hands, digging her fingers into
the nerves and tendons on the soft underside, and squeezed.
Savannah's fingers went limp, and Meg yanked her head
back as the hold released and pushed herself away.

Meg gratefully popped up to the surface, sucking in air
and searching for any sign of Savannah or Hawk, who
she'd lost completely in the spray. When no one surfaced,
she cursed and took a deep breath before going under.

She went under, again and again, hands spread wide,
searching for Savannah, but she couldn't feel anything or
see an inch in the murky depths of bubbles. When she surfaced, even this far from the spillway as they floated
downstream with the spray clearing, she couldn't see
Hawk, either. That struck more than a little bit of panic
into her heart.

"Hawk! Hawk, speak!"

Nothing came back but the roar of water.

She needed to get out to see if Savannah and Hawk were
downstream out of the worst of the mist. She kicked off,

heading to the bank, the mist clearing as the water level dropped.

Lauren stood on the bank, thirty feet downstream from Craig as they both stared hard at the river, searching for any sign of movement. Meg waved an arm over her head. "I'm here!" She pulled again for the shore. "Can you see them? Hawk or Savannah?"

"Nothing," Lauren called. "I don't see Rocco, either. He dove in, too. He must have been able to hear you out there."

Lauren jogged over as Meg got her feet under her and stepped onto the bank, turning around to stare into the river as water sluiced off her.

Webb and McCord ran out of the trees upriver and sprinted toward them.

"Where's Hawk?" Craig bellowed as he got closer.

"I don't know!" Meg yelled back. "We got separated. Rocco is out there somewhere, too." She turned to Lauren, who ran along the edge of the bank farther downstream. "Anything?"

"No, but if that plume of spray goes on for four hundred feet, they could be anywhere in there."

"I'm going back in." Meg stepped toward the river, but then stopped as a dark form caught her eye as it materialized out of the cloud of white.

Hawk came out of the mist, swimming slowly and bobbing uncharacteristically. Alarm spurted through Meg— *Has he hurt himself?*—but a second later, she realized he was towing something. Not something. Someone. Savannah. He had her wrist in his mouth and was swimming to shore, pulling her along behind him as she lay on her back. Then Rocco came into view, the cuff of her camo jacket in his teeth as he pulled at her other side.

"They have Savannah!"

Meg ran into the water, Craig and Lauren right behind

her as she waded out to meet Hawk partway. He was laboring hard, his breath blowing harshly through his teeth as he struggled to keep them both moving.

"Good boy, Hawk. We have her. Let go." Meg grabbed one of Savannah's arms, and Craig took hold of the other, partially lifting her out of the water. "Let go, Hawk."

On the far side, Lauren gave the same direction to Rocco.

Hawk seemed almost reluctant, as if he considered the job unfinished, but he obeyed the command and let go of Savannah's wrist. Without the added weight, he quickly swam the rest of the way to shore and then clambered out, bracing all four feet to give an enthusiastic shake as water droplets flew in all directions. Rocco trotted out of the water after him, also stopping long enough to shake himself dry.

They dragged Savannah onto dry land and then laid her in the long grass at the edge of the forest, rolling her onto her side as she coughed and gasped.

Meg turned to look for Webb, but he was already closing fast. "Can you check her?"

"Give me some room." He dropped to his knees and bent over her.

Craig activated the talk button for his microphone. "Torres, do you copy?"

With her equipment upstream with her bag, Meg could only follow Craig's side of the conversation.

"We have Savannah Cavett. We just pulled her out of the river. I have a paramedic down here, but I want an ambulance and I want her checked out at the hospital before we take her into custody. We do this by the book." He nodded at whatever Torres said. "Good. Buckner is okay? What about the protesters? There was a lot of glass flying around . . . Glad to hear it. Okay, we're bringing her up. Beaumont out." Craig turned to Webb. "She checks out?"

Webb stood. "Yes. I agree she should be thoroughly

checked out at the ER before you take her in, but she's clear to move."

"Good. Help me get her up." Together Webb and Craig got Savannah on her feet; then Craig pulled out a pair of cuffs from his jacket pocket. "Savannah Cavett, you're under arrest on four counts of first-degree murder, one count of attempted murder of a federal law enforcement officer, one count of attempted murder, and one count of aggravated assault." He cuffed her. "You have the right to remain silent." Craig continued on with the Miranda warning as he started walking her up the beach.

Scott and Theo broke out of the trees and jogged over to meet them.

Lauren shook her head. "You know, Theo is a hell of a scent dog, better than Hawk and Rocco, maybe better than both of them put together. But try to light a fire under that bloodhound when he's not in the mood and get him to move at top speed in a crisis? Good luck." She looked down at the dogs that ambled around their feet. "Now you two heroes, you each deserve a special treat for that act of bravery."

"They were incredible," McCord said. "Just wait until the story for this case publishes. I have the perfect picture for it."

Meg stared at him. "You stopped to take pictures?"

"A video, but yeah. You guys had it in hand. You didn't need me. So I filmed the rescue." He pulled out his cell phone and waved it at Meg. "Don't leave home without it. There's going to be a great frame of Hawk and Rocco dragging the suspect in to shore."

Rolling her eyes and laughing, Meg knelt down to stroke a hand over her dog. "Hear that, Hawk?" His ears perked up at his name. "You're going to make the front page! That's my boy." Worn-out, she let her head rest for a moment against him and he turned to bump his nose against her affectionately.

"Meg."

She raised her head at the sound of Webb's voice, to find him standing over her, holding his hand out to her.

"Come on, let's get you dried off. Again. You know, if you want to do this much swimming in the great outdoors, we should pack you a bathing suit."

She snorted a laugh, slapped her hand into his, and let him pull her to her feet. "But that would take all the challenge out of it, wouldn't it? Thanks. Honestly, I've had it with bodies of water after this case. Unless it's a nice warm bath. But cold rivers are off my list for a while." She looked over to where Craig and Scott were marching Savannah toward the hill. "Come on, we have one more job left to do."

"What's that?"

"Hand Savannah over to Torres. This is his case; he needs to make the official arrest."

"But didn't Craig just..." Webb trailed off. "Ah... Torres doesn't need to know that. Trying to give him some of his own back?"

"Maybe. He worked hard on this case, and he deserves the win." She smiled as she looked over the river, where two dogs had pulled victory from the jaws of defeat. "We're going to make sure he gets it."

CHAPTER 29

Black Bear Totem: People having the black bear totem have a great deal of confidence in who they are and where they are going in life. They have patience and excel in waiting for the right moment to complete their visions.

Wednesday, April 24, 7:14 PM
Cookes Park
Washington, DC

"Keep your eyes closed," Webb said, pulling his truck over to the side of the road.

"How long are we going to keep this up?" Meg asked.

"Not much longer." McCord opened his door. "Hang on, we're coming around to get you."

Meg leaned toward Cara, who sat in the back with her, also with her eyes closed. "Have you peeked yet?" she asked.

"No. Maybe it's time we—"

"Here you go." Webb's voice sounded to her left as the door opened. "Give me your hands and I'll help you out."

Meg held out her hands. Webb took them in his and tugged her toward him.

"You realize we look ridiculous," she said.

"Reach out your foot for the running board. A little farther. Yes, that's it. And no one is here to see you, so don't worry. Besides, we're just about there."

When she stood on the running board, he let go of her hands, grasped her around the waist and lifted her down. Once she had her balance, Webb wrapped an arm around her waist and walked her around the rear of the truck.

"One step up, and you're there. That's it." He turned her to face away from the truck. "Are you both ready?"

"Sure," said Cara.

"As we'll ever be, considering we don't know what's going on," Meg said.

"Okay, then, you can look," McCord said.

Meg opened her eyes.

They stood on the sidewalk in front of a redbrick, two-story federal-style duplex. The front of the structure was covered with mullioned windows topped by decorative white pediments and flanked by long black shutters. Two identical heavy black doors were deep set into stark white casements between heavy wrought iron lanterns. A short wrought iron fence separated the structure from the sidewalk.

McCord held out his arms like a showman. "Ta da!"

The women looked at each other in confusion and then at the men.

"I don't understand," said Cara. "What are we looking at?"

"Our potential new place," McCord said.

"Places," corrected Webb. "It's a duplex." He turned to Meg. "You said you needed something in town. Something with space for Hawk. Something close to Cara." He grinned. "Is one connecting wall close enough?"

They both turned to look at Cara, who stood wide-eyed with her jaw slack. "I still don't think I understand. I'm not looking for anything yet."

"And now you don't have to." McCord moved to stand

in front of her, blocking her view of the duplex. "Move in with me, if you'll take me and my completely crazy dog. And if you like it, we can live right here."

"And we'll take the other side," Webb said. "It's relatively close to the Hoover Building, my firehouse, and the *Washington Post.* You'll be next door to each other. What do you both think?"

It took Meg a moment to speak she was so stunned. "I'm . . . I'm a little speechless."

"I'm not." Cara threw her arms around McCord's neck and gave him a smacking kiss. "I love it. And yes, I'll move in with you and your crazy dog." Her body went motionless; then she pulled away from McCord. "Wait, my brain just kicked in. I'm getting excited and I don't know if we can afford it. What's the asking price?"

Webb rattled off a figure. "That's the cost of each side in separate sales. Think it's doable?"

"We'd be selling the Arlington house and splitting the proceeds, so yes. Can we see inside?"

"We can." Webb pulled a key on a gold fob out of his pocket and dangled it. "Only this one, though." He pointed at the door directly in front of them. "The other side's still being finished. But they'll be identical units. It's totally unfurnished, so you won't have to picture your stuff in there around someone else's." He tossed the key to McCord, who deftly caught it. "Have at it. We'll be right behind you."

McCord grabbed Cara's hand and they slipped through the gate, ran up the front walk like a couple of kids, opened the door, and disappeared inside.

Webb contemplated Meg and her silence. "You say you're speechless. Is that good or bad?"

She turned to face him, reading his anxiety in the furrow between his brows. She smiled and the furrow eased. "All good." She looked back at the duplex. "You found a place that works for every one of my requirements. And it's even in a gorgeous classical style."

"I thought that might be icing on the cake for you and your love of classic architecture."

"How did you ever find it?"

"Kirk, one of the guys on shift B, buys and flips homes to earn some extra money. He bought this one and was fixing it up. He knew I was looking for a place and told me about it. Told me I could have a look at it before he put it up for sale. I was certainly considering it. Then he told me it was a duplex, and I got *very* serious about it."

"All those other places. I kept turning them down and you just kept looking."

"Given enough time, I was confident I'd find the right place. Want to see inside?"

"You better believe it. But first . . ." She pushed up on tiptoe and kissed him, letting it linger. "Thank you. I put you through the wringer on this and you hung in and found the perfect solution."

He smiled, the gold flecks in his eyes catching the last of the evening sun. "Don't say that until you see inside."

"It's already perfect. If something inside doesn't work, we can fix it." She took his hand. "Come on, we can't let them have all the fun."

They stepped into a small entrance hall that opened out into a living room on their right and then continued into an open kitchen and family living space. High ceilings were framed by crown molding and oak hardwood floors gleamed. Up a flight of stairs edged with a heavy wooden banister and covered with a charcoal runner, they could hear McCord making plans about how to set up the master bedroom and Cara oohing over the clawfoot bathtub.

Following the hallway past the staircase, Meg entered the kitchen, taking in the white cabinets that gave the space an open and airy feel, and contrasted the jet-black granite countertops. She ran one hand over the counter, the granite cool and satiny under her fingertips. "What year was this place built?"

"Just past the turn of the century. But Kirk basically gutted both sides and had them refitted professionally. New wiring, new plumbing, new walls, new floors." He turned in a slow circle, taking in the mostly empty space. "But he kept the spirit of the original structure. Kept the high ceilings and refinished the molding himself. Used a lot of the same materials to give it a historic feel." He walked over to a fireplace framed by white wood with a heavy mantel and a stone hearth. "I was thinking this would be great for cool winter nights. And right here." He stepped back a few paces, and drew an invisible square on the floor. "This would be the perfect spot for your ugly-as-sin recliner."

"Love me, love my recliner."

Walking to her, he slipped his arms around her and pulled her in. "I do love you. Even if you come with that God-awful recliner."

"You must love me. I put you through hell to find this place. I love it. And I love you."

"I know it's not the biggest place in town—" Webb cut off at Meg's laugh. "What?"

"If it was the biggest place in town, we wouldn't be able to afford it, even collectively. We don't need big. How many bedrooms and bathrooms upstairs?"

"A master with en suite, two more bedrooms, and another full bath. You can go up and look."

"I will. But first . . ." She slipped from his arms and took his hand, pulling him along with her to the sliding door at the back of the family room. Unlocking it, she slid it open. The sun was setting behind the house, washing the backyard in the soft glow photographers called the "golden hour." They stepped out into cool spring air and onto a small flagstone patio, surrounded by a healthy new lawn. "It's even got a great yard. But . . ."

"What are you thinking?"

Meg was about to speak when footfalls behind them had her turning around to find Cara and McCord standing in the open doorway.

"This is great, too." McCord stepped out into the patio. "Webb, your buddy does amazing work."

"It wasn't all him, but he knew to hire the right people. The place is impeccable." Webb swung back to Meg. "You were about to say?"

"I assume the two backyards are the same?"

"As far as I know."

"Obviously everyone would need to weigh in on this, but what about removing the dividing fence between the two yards?"

Cara clapped her hands together in enthusiasm. "I love it. That way the dogs will have a shared space. And though Hawk's here by himself, he won't really be alone. And the dogs can safely come and go as much as they like from either place."

"Exactly."

"It works for me," Webb said. "McCord?"

"Me too. Gives my insane energy machine more space to tear around." He elbowed Webb's arm. "And that way Cara and I don't always have to mow it. You guys could do half."

"Always looking on the bright side, aren't you?"

"You bet. So . . . what do you all think? Do you need to mull it over?"

"I love it," Meg said decisively. "I want it."

"Don't be hasty," Webb cautioned. "You haven't seen the whole house. This is a big decision. I told Kirk I'd get back to him tonight, but I can ask him for a few more days. Not much more than that, though, because if it's not going to be a private sale, he wants to get it up with a Realtor pronto."

"Cara's seen the whole house." Meg turned to her sister. "Your take?"

"It's amazing. It's perfect. More than that, I can see us in the space. All of us in our own space."

"That's all I need. McCord?"

"Hell, yes. We're in."

"There's your answer. Call him tonight. We want it."

Webb's grin was a combination of relief, satisfaction, and anticipation. "You got it."

Meg's phone beeped from her back pocket. She pulled it out and glanced at the message, relief washing over her like a wave.

"Who's that?" Cara asked.

"It's Brian. They're home with Lacey now and they just got back from an appointment with their own vet. He's very happy with Lacey's progress. He says she's going to need physiotherapy, but he doesn't see any reason why she can't come back to the team given some recovery time."

"That's a relief," said McCord.

"You have no idea."

They spent the next twenty minutes strolling around the house, making plans and virtually placing furniture. Leaving Cara and the men in the kitchen discussing paint colors, Meg wandered upstairs, slowly moving through the rooms, imagining how she and Webb would fill them.

Webb found her standing in the master bedroom, gazing out the window, her lower lip caught between her teeth. "Hey."

Meg turned to find him standing in the doorway, feeling slightly uncertain as he studied her.

"I turned around and you were gone." He crossed the room to her and tipped her chin up with one finger so he could see into her eyes. "You look pensive. If you're not sure about the house . . ."

"No, I'm sure about that. It's just . . ."

When she paused for too long, he prodded her. "Just what?"

"It just made me look at where I am. Where we are."

"I think we're somewhere solid."

"I agree." She looked down the hallway, toward the two other bedrooms. "But looking at that empty space . . ."

"Ah."

She could see the understanding in his eyes, knew she didn't have to say more. But she owed him that. "We've talked occasionally about kids. I know you want them."

"And you do, too. But us moving into this place isn't supposed to put any pressure on you." When she turned her face away from him, he pulled her in, forcing her to either look up at him or spend the entire conversation staring at his throat. "I'm serious about that. I understand what you do, and how important that is to you. More than that, I understand that the dangers of your job and being pregnant are the kind of combination that could take you off the team."

"I'm thirty-three. I can't wait forever if we're really going to do this."

"I'm not suggesting you do. But I am saying it doesn't have to be this year. Or the next, or the one after that. I know part of what weighs on you is Hawk. How many more work years does he have in him?"

"He's four. Maybe another four or five years at most? It's not like he's a drug sniffer at the airport. His job is physical and he's in top shape, but it's hard for older dogs. At a certain point, they can become a detriment to the search. I'll never put him in that position."

"So then maybe we wait. Wait while he's still in his

prime and you're loving being out there with him. Okay, maybe not *out there*, you guys did that in spades in this case, but out on a case with him. And maybe as he ages, you find a different type of work for him, and that's when you can step back from the dangerous work yourself and start looking at options. There are no hard and fast rules, Meg. We set our own schedule and we do it our way."

She stared up at him for a moment, studying him, looking for any sign that he was placating her, and finding nothing. "You'd be okay with that?"

"Of course. What you're weighing, it's the same thing for the women at the firehouse. The guys, their wives get pregnant and they take some time off around the time of the birth, but that's about it. The women don't have that option. There's a life inside them that could be developmentally damaged by the toxins in the smoke, or by the mother's raised body temperature if she spends too long in the seat of the fire. Every call is an extra risk for them as a result. Some move to light duty to keep them off active calls as soon as they know. Some stay active until they get bigger and the pregnancy becomes a risk to them or other team members. But they don't have the option of just taking a few weeks off simply because of the physical nature of the job. It's the same with you, and in some ways worse. There's no office component to your job where you can sit and put your feet up through a pregnancy. You have a tough, physical, occasionally dangerous profession. It would be better not to bring a child along for that ride. It's not forever. It's just for now and for however long you need it to be. And we can revisit those plans at any time." He looked over her head to scan the bedroom. "In the meantime, I think committing to live together, to buying this house together, are all the plans we need for now." Mc-Cord's booming laugh rang from down below, earning an eye roll from Webb. "Getting used to living next to Mc-

Cord will be challenge enough. Let's not drag an innocent child into it. That would be mean."

That pulled a chuckle from her. "You know, you put up with an awful lot from me. Trying for months to find a place for us, making concessions for my dog, adjusting your timelines for our future."

He gave her a cocky smile. "What can I say? I'm a prince. Now, what do you say we go join those crazy kids downstairs?"

"That sounds like a great plan." Linking fingers with him, she led him toward the stairs. "You know, Hawk is going to love this place. Lots of space inside, that big combined backyard, and there are two parks within only a few blocks. He's going to be happy here."

"We're all going to be happy here. It took a little while to find it, but this place is definitely worth the wait. And I can't wait to see McCord out front shoveling the sidewalk. I'll trade cutting the grass for that any day. Just imagine him out there in a blizzard, shivering with a shovel, and Cody bouncing around, knocking down snowdrifts as fast as he can build them. I can't wait to see that."

Laughing, they walked downstairs and into their new future.

Acknowledgments

This may be the fifth book in the FBI K-9s series, but every book has different research needs, and I was once again lucky to receive assistance from some extremely knowledgeable and helpful individuals.

This book would not have existed without Shane Vandevalk. From his initial story suggestion of a compound bowhunter with a penchant for disappearing into the woods after taking a life, to his assistance with hunting and wilderness scenarios, and finally to title brainstorming sessions resulting in one of his titles being selected for the novel, Shane, you've been invaluable! Many thanks for your continuing contributions.

Captain Lisa Giblin was once again my window into the world of firefighters. With her assistance, I was able to craft a realistic life-and-death scenario leading to the accident that would put Webb on leave for a short period of time, but not end his career or his life. She also ensured all my firefighting language and details were correct during that pivotal scene. In a little taste of real life, Meg listening in on Webb's active scene was taken directly from Lisa's life as a firefighter where her husband, Chief Dave Giblin, would follow her active scenes when she was on duty.

Isaac Cowan of Bass Pro Shops in Niagara-on-the-Lake was kind enough to share his expertise when I was looking for detailed information on bowhunting. He provided all the information I needed on archery equipment and technique, as well as hunting strategy. He was a great sport and didn't even flinch when I said, "I'm an author and I need to pretend to kill someone with a compound bow." He just jumped in with both feet. Thank you, Isaac!

Scott Fiedler, part of the TVA's Public Relations Department, was kind enough to put me in touch with Scott Walker PE PG, a TVA Dam Safety Engineer, when I was delving into research on Ocoee Dam #2 and the historic Ocoee Flume. Scott Walker kindly answered all my questions and provided extensive documentation on the construction and operation of the flume and its downstream powerhouse. Scott and Scott, please excuse any literary license taken with this amazing piece of local history.

Thanks as always to our critique team—Lisa Giblin, Jenny Lindstrom, Jessica Newton, Rick Newton, and Sharon Taylor—who graciously found time to squeeze multiple reads into a short time period already full with work lives and family crises, and who nevertheless provided insightful and thoughtful ways to strengthen the novel. Your efforts are always very much appreciated!

My agent, Nicole Resciniti, is always only a text, e-mail, or phone call away, and is ever ready to answer any question or provide any assistance I need. I'm so glad you're by my side.

Grateful thanks to my editor, Esi Sogah at Kensington, for her astute guidance from the beginning of this project through all its various stages. Once again, it's been a pleasure working with you in this next adventure in the series!